Weeping Widow's Heirloom

K. A. Moore

Published by K. A. Moore, 2025.

This is a work of fiction. Names, characters, businesses, places, events, locales, and incidents are either the products of the author's imagination or used in a fictitious manner. Any resemblance to actual persons, living or dead, or actual events is purely coincidental.

Book cover Shutterstock photo

Book cover design KA Moore

Editing by Ginny and Judith at Bookhelpline

ISBN 9781957223094 (ebook)

ISBN 9781957223162 (paperback)

Also by K. A. Moore

Relics Series

Relics

The Key

The Chosen

Standalone

Watching Her Sleep

Sentinel

Weeping Widow's Heirloom

Dedication

For my mom, who gave me a quick one-sentence idea for a book and told me to run with it. This is for you, Mom. I hope you enjoy it.

One

Rain dampened the cracked, thirsty soil, soaking into the cold, dank ground. Small rivers tracked over the dirt where the drops collected too fast to be absorbed, forming an eroding moat before meeting the grass. Soon the weather would shift, and it would be snow falling instead of the chilly late August. That was one thing about living near the mountains. Fall slipped into winter faster than in the city.

The casket was lowered to its final resting place a week ago, and Shelby Samuel missed it. She swiped at the tears on her cheeks. Uncle Rupert's unexpected death stunned her; he had always been so strong and healthy.

It didn't make sense that her parents hadn't told her so she could attend the funeral. They said they didn't want to interrupt her lifelong dream of attending an antiques expo and traveling the country. Did she love the old works of art people shared with the world? Absolutely, but not more than her uncle.

Shelby's heart ached; her time with him ended. She thought she still had years left. She smiled at the memory of running around his antique store, Rupert's Relics, as a child. Her mother's baby brother, her junior by eight years, doted on her when she visited during the summers while her parents took their annual trip to Egypt to visit family.

Shelby had no cousins to turn to for help with this heart-aching burden. Uncle Rupert never married or had children of his own, leaving her as the only child on either side of her parents' families. Late in life, in their mid-forties, doctors insisted her mother defied the laws of medicine bearing a child when most couples started accepting the fact they would be childless. Shelby, a tiny bundle of joy, burst onto the scene, the miracle baby they dreamed of, but as they aged, figured was out of their reach. Now retired in their seventies, they still adored their only child.

Her mother told Shelby the coroner's office informed her it was a massive coronary. They said he was gone before his body crumpled to the docks behind the store. Nothing could have been done, even if he were inside a hospital at the time his heart stopped. She was glad he didn't suffer and now walked in Heaven, but it still stung he wasn't in her life. She knew she would see him again.

Rupert's Relics, nestled in the town of Red Peaks, a quaint countryside retreat, drew her in, even as a child. Everyone knew everybody else, including extended families who visited. Red Peaks delivered a tremendous small-town atmosphere with a larger city near enough to travel to in less than thirty minutes for those who craved contact with a bustling civilization packed with shopping centers. The small church she attended as a child happened to be the only one nearby unless someone wanted to drive for almost an hour.

The town backed up to hills that appeared to bleed in the fall when the shifting sun glinted off the red shale rock at the right angle for a couple of hours at dusk, giving the illusion that they dripped blood from the peaks erupting from the pines dusting the lower elevations.

The raindrops increased in size, her bangs clung to her forehead, and her tears mixed with nature's. She hadn't had the opportunity to grieve yet; she'd been too busy packing all her earthly possessions and arranging her move to Red Peaks. The company she worked for was sympathetic to her inability to give a full two weeks' notice when she quit and offered to sublease her apartment to her replacement when they hired someone.

Her mother informed her of the small service for Uncle Rupert's friends in the community and store employees. It happened during her parents' annual trip to Egypt to visit her mother's elderly parents, who were unable to travel anymore, so no one in the family attended. Shelby didn't understand why her mom kept it from her.

Her mother was distraught that they could not take the trip, but they became trapped when a dust storm swept through Egypt, shutting down the airports. Her mom wanted to be there to say goodbye to her brother but had to wait until travel opened up to catch the earliest flight out.

Another deluge of rain swept through just when she thought it would let up. Glancing around, two more mounds of fresh dirt awaited headstones. One further up the hill and the other directly across from her uncle's resting place. A shiver quaked up her spine, not due to the weather. A man dressed in dark clothing stood outside a black truck across the way. She couldn't get a glimpse to see if he was someone Rupert knew. He raised his hand but didn't approach. Shelby waved in answer to his friendly acknowledgment.

The responsibility for Rupert's Relics rested squarely on her. The will had yet to be read, but her mom asked her to take over the store. They would sign over any part her uncle left to them, so she would be the sole owner. Rupert's Relics was a cutesy store that dabbled in all types of antiques, from great pieces of furniture to Depression glass and oil lamps. If it originated from the 1970s or earlier, they considered it vintage and displayed it for purchase.

Shelby sighed as she swiped at her cheeks again before walking away from his grave. Her black pantsuit soaked through and clung to her skin. She was alone except for the man watching her earlier. All she thought about was laying her head down to prepare for the anticipation of the expedited ownership of her uncle's shop.

Rupert's Relics was one of her favorite places. She had only fond memories of spending time with her uncle every summer. Once old enough, she learned to ring up sales and deliveries. She always knew she would end up in Red Peaks to help with the store and buy it from her uncle one day. Her heart ached at his absence.

Uncle Rupert planned for as much. That was why she worked so hard for her business degrees: so she could run the quaint shop without needing to hire additional people for the logistical side. She never entertained any other future than this one. Just not the way it fell into her lap.

Her uncle Rupert's apartment above the antique store would be her home until she cleared out the house he owned. She previously slept there during her visits and smiled at the memory of feeling like such a grown-up when he allowed her to stay there alone in her late teens. Her uncle remained on the couch when she was younger before he bought the cozy stone cottage later in life. Cozy? She snorted at herself. The house fit the bill of a mansion.

She'd move once she emptied the house, relieving it of its hoarder's situation. Uncle Rupert amassed more antiques in his cottage than in the store. He could never make up his mind on what he wanted to keep or part with. It sat in the middle of twelve acres, the closest neighbor on the other side of a hedgerow, while the rear of the property ran flush with a forest. Her uncle appreciated the serene nature that surrounded the structure.

She sagged into the driver's seat after draping a towel over it, which she'd removed from the back hatch. She dared to glance up the hill one last time before pulling onto the road out of the cemetery. A headache bloomed behind her left eyebrow. She massaged it with her left thumb.

Movement out of the corner of her eye captured her attention. The man slid behind the wheel of a black truck with tinted windows. Another hasty wave, which she returned, her only communication with him so far—the perks of small-town life. Everyone greeted you, even if they didn't know you. He seemed familiar, but she couldn't place where she knew him from.

Another fresh mound of dirt fascinated her as she continued to the exit. What was up with the fresh graves? The historic county cemetery heralded four newly dug gravesites. Her breath hitched and caught in her throat. She angled her car toward the exit, and two more drenched mounds appeared as the rain increased, hammering against her windshield with relentless anger blurring her view. It drowned out the singer crooning to music through her speakers.

Lightning crackled, sending bolts of static electricity across the sky through the dark, swirling clouds, changing shape and growing before her eyes. The expanse overhead darkened to an eerie gray-green. Thunder followed, making her jump. Another streak of shocking white light blinded her as it arched down and hit the tree at the graveyard's entrance. She slammed on her brakes, both feet pressing the pedal as hard as possible.

Splinters and bark flew everywhere as the trunk toppled onto the hood of her car, bringing it to a jarring stop and popping the back wheels off the ground. The metal roof above her caved in, almost touching her head, shattering the windshield. The seat belt imprisoned her as the airbag deployed a split second before her head snapped forward, bouncing off the chemical-laced fabric, burning her eyes and nasal passages. Her knees hit the dashboard with an agonizing crunch; her car, not equipped with the newer under-the-dash airbags, offered no shield to her lower extremities.

Everything faded away.

Two

She was startled by a knocking on the passenger window. "Shelby."

She wanted to raise her head but was dizzy, and her heavy arms refused to budge.

"Shelby, unlock the doors." Frantic knocking sounded to her right.

She blinked several times when she lifted her head. The interior of her car came into focus. She tried to use her left hand again, but it collapsed to her side. The view out of the fragmented windshield lacked a pretty scenery. The front of her car vanished while steam crept and crawled along the hood from under what was left of the front end. A branch larger in circumference than her thigh buckled into the roof over her. Luckily, it hit there and did not land entirely where she sat.

"Shelby."

She rubbed her hand across her forehead through a sticky wetness, her palm coated in red. She'd already had a headache brewing while at her uncle's final resting place, but now it screamed behind her skull. She closed her eyes again and reclined back, batting the airbag out of her way.

"Shelby, come on, unlock the door. I have an ambulance on the way for you, but I need you to open the door." The mysterious baritone called from her right, making bumps erupt along her arms.

As she glanced over, she noticed concern etching itself onto the man's features on the other side of the passenger window, increasing the intense vibe in his dark blue eyes.

"I don't know if you remember me, but my name is Dean. I work with your uncle. I mean *worked* with him."

It clicked. He was the man she bumped into for five minutes in passing during a visit less than a year ago. Clean-shaven then, now he sported a well-groomed, closely trimmed full beard and mustache.

"Dean?" Shelby shook her head, clearing her thoughts—bad idea. The pulsing behind her eyes increased.

"I'm right here, but you need to let me in." Worry furrowed his brow.

Her numb fingers groped for the doorknob. It did nothing.

"Shel, hit the unlock button. You can't use the door on your side. The limb damaged the frame, so it won't open."

She shut her eyelids.

"Hey!" Dean's voice boomed as he slammed his open palm against the window.

She jumped, fumbling with the controls on the door panel before finding the unlock button. The cool storm air made her shiver as it rushed through the passenger side and over her still-wet clothes. His fingers hit another button before he opened the back door and climbed in behind her.

His warm hands gripped her on either side of her neck, holding her head straight. She tried to turn and see what he was doing, but he stopped her.

"Don't move if you can help it." His calm voice broke through the fog in her brain.

"Dean? You knew my uncle..." Something warm and sticky dripped into her eye.

"Yes, I did. He was a great man."

"Don't go."

"I'm not leaving you." Sirens cut through the last of her muddy thoughts. "Don't move while I unclip your seatbelt so they can help you."

His right hand moved for a split second, and the pressure on her ribs eased.

She tried to turn her head, but he held it immobile.

"My legs hurt."

"I'm sure they do. Let's wait for the paramedics to arrive before we try to move you out of the car, okay? They'll have all of the equipment to do it safely."

"Um, sure. I'm bleeding." Her breathing increased in intensity; tightness banded around her ribs. She looked at the mangled mess of the front of her car, then at her hand. "Oh my gosh! I could have died!"

"Slow your breathing, Shel; I don't want you passing out on me. The adrenaline dump will be over in a minute. Can you stay with me?" The deep timber of his voice soothed the building panic as her body started to shake.

"What's wrong with me?" The trembling vibrated through her limbs.

"This is normal. Just relax with me, and it will be over soon." The rich depth of his voice lulled her into a calmness.

She liked how he shortened her name. No one had ever done that before as far as she could remember. She tried to breathe like he told her to. "My chest hurts."

"It's because you're hyperventilating. I want you to hold your next breath for a couple of seconds. You're breathing too fast." Dean lowered his tone even further and spoke calmly.

"It hurts, Dean." She rubbed her fist against her sternum.

"Try not to move, Shel."

Her lungs stuttered as a sharp pain shot through her thigh when she tried to move her legs. She cried out and gripped his wrists as she took another shuddering breath, but the aching made her exhale before she wanted to.

"Don't move your legs."

She curled her hands into her pants.

"That's it. Slow breath in...let it out gradually. You're doing great."

An ambulance stopped on the other side of the tree. The flashing strobes bounced up and over the limbs and leaves, reflecting off the drops of water and casting prisms of color in all directions. Someone ran up behind her vehicle, startling her.

"Shh, it's okay. It's the caretakers of the property," Dean assured her.

"I'm fine. I'm okay." She didn't know who she tried to reassure more with her statement, Dean or herself.

She shuttered her eyes.

"No, you stay awake, Shel. Come on, open those beautiful greens for me." Dean tightened his hands, supporting her neck.

She opened her eyes wide when she realized she smelled gas.

The paramedics made it over and around the base of the trunk to the car's passenger side, where they joined them.

"Sir, were you in the car with her?" One paramedic took in Dean, who was sitting behind her, stabilizing her neck.

"No."

"Ma'am, what do you say we get you out of this mangled mess of a car?"

"Sounds great, but I can't move my legs, so you'll have to help me. I think they're pinned."

"Do you have sensations in your legs?" An edge in Dean's voice caused her to tense.

"Yes, the pain is a hint they're still attached; I just can't move them." She started to turn her head, forgetting he restrained her.

His lips neared her ear. "Try not to move your head."

"Sorry."

A second paramedic approached with a C-collar and fitted it around her neck, freeing up Dean. The firefighters directed him from the vehicle and instructed him to stand several feet away. She missed his warmth.

A firefighter joined them with an apparatus. "Ma'am, this will take a few minutes to free your legs, then we'll slip a backboard under you and angle you out of the car. Try not to move. We'll do all the heavy lifting and moving that needs to be done. Relax while we get you out of here. Okay?"

"Heavy lifting? Guess I shouldn't have eaten the second half of my bagel this morning." She tried to joke to block the panic that welled in her.

Several of the men chuckled. "Are you ready?"

"Sorry, yes, let's go for it." She closed her eyes.

"Shel, keep your eyes on me, okay?" Dean stood by the front wheel, looking at her through the side window. The firefighter glared at him before looking down to work out how to extricate her from her car.

She tried to nod but remembered about the neck brace a second before her chin hit the plastic. It was amazing how often someone motioned with their head; she was unable to stop the natural movements people used in their everyday lives.

The equipment they operated to raise the dash was quieter than she imagined it would be. At one point, they draped a thick blanket over her, obstructing her line of sight; claustrophobia reared its evil ugly head.

She tried to breathe through the panic of not seeing Dean, unsure why he gave her such comfort.

The firefighter in the backseat held her hand. "You're doing great. We're right here. I want you to tell me if anything changes on your legs or if you have any sharp pains anywhere else as we work to free you. You need to update us of any changes because that could be the difference of life or death or even walking again."

Shelby squeezed his hand when the apparatus got louder as it crunched through the dash. "Okay."

Before she knew it, they tilted the seat back after removing the blanket and arranged the hard plastic molded board under her. Sliding her out of the car, the two men easily positioned her on the gurney. She hissed through the throbbing with every pulse in her thighs that increased as it rushed through her uncompressed blood vessels. It felt the same as adhering a band-aid to your finger and then feeling the pulse with each pounding of the heartbeat. Only twenty times worse. Tears leaked out and dripped into her hair. Dean appeared at her side seconds after they started strapping her down. He wrapped her fingers around her wallet that he placed next to her.

"I'll follow the ambulance if that's okay with you." He appeared unsure of what to do next.

"Don't ruin your day sitting at the hospital waiting for me. I'll be fine."

He started to turn from her before she blurted, "Dean, thanks for being here today. I'll officially meet you on Monday as your boss when I'm not pinned under a giant elm."

"Anytime, and it was an oak."

"What?"

"If you have such a crazy story to tell, go with the more impressive tree. Oaks are larger and heavier than elms, which are softwoods. It's a more thrilling detail than a pathetic little elm." He gave her a chin lift.

Shelby laughed, then groaned as her upper body twinged.

The paramedic interrupted. "Sir, we need to go."

"I'll see you at work." He jogged to his truck, already on his phone.

The gurney bumped along the ground as they lumbered around the large, fractured obstacle and over to the ambulance. Shelby cringed as her headache roared to the front with all the jostling. A chainsaw ripped through the air as two police cruisers moved out of the way of the ambulance. She barely saw them as they slammed the doors, hampering her line of sight.

Finally able to breathe, she clasped her hands together, indecisive about what to do with them. Her knuckles turned white as one of the paramedics climbed in the side door, sat above her head, and started talking into a headset while he cleaned the muck from her forehead and pressed down on a gauze pad. Seconds later, the large diesel engine rumbled louder as they turned the colossal rig around and headed to the county hospital several miles from Red Peaks.

The paramedic in the back forbade her to fall asleep, but the bright bulbs aggravated her headache. He apologized, declining to give her anything until the doctors saw her to make sure it didn't mask a more serious injury.

The doctor at the emergency ward greeted the ambulance at the bay. The paramedics spouted off her vitals and the details of the crash with extrication. They wished her luck and passed her off.

After the scans, x-rays, and an exam revealed negative life-threatening injuries, they gave her something for her headache and sent her on her way.

Now, how did she get home? Shelby rubbed at her temples while waiting for a cab to pick her up. The doctors had used the word lucky to describe surviving her ordeal. She knew it was a miracle. Her deeply bruised legs, thankfully, didn't have any breaks. They told her to take it easy over the next couple of days and to come back if the pain increased.

The television in the corner caught her attention. The volume was off, but the closed-captioning flashing across the bottom of the screen made her cringe. Several deaths of elderly victims who lived alone had been attributed to the work of possibly one man. Each of the fatal encounters involved a widow or widower; police were requesting families to check often on loved ones, especially if they fit in that category.

Shelby lightly ran her hand up and down her thighs as the show flipped to a commercial. She couldn't imagine walking up and down stairs if she'd had to rely on crutches or wear a cast. The doctor suggested over-the-counter meds if she experienced any discomfort after today's near miss but to expect the stiff, sore muscles to be worse the next day. She thanked God for protecting her. She believed God's divine will was the only reason she didn't join Uncle Rupert.

She toyed with calling her friend Skye but wasn't sure of her schedule. She ran a local beauty salon in town. It was usually reserved for several weeks out if you needed an appointment. She wouldn't feel right if she had to cancel with clients to be her chauffeur. Skye was her closest friend in Red Peaks. They went everywhere together during the summer holidays.

Shelby hadn't thought through how to get home when she dismissed Dean's offer to follow her to the hospital.

Three

Dean waved at the tow truck driver as he strapped down Shelby's sedan. The car was on the way to the closest dealership awaiting to take receipt and get the ball rolling for the insurance company. Seeing her grief as she'd wept over Rupert's final resting place tore something in him.

Blessed with her mother's olive skin and green eyes, she was gracefully beautiful. He knew he would tower over Shelby's five-foot-two height by almost a foot. Shelby was only twenty-nine years old, and Dean knew Rupert hadn't planned on this change in her life for another decade or more. But with his loss, she was now stepping into his shoes to run Rupert's Relics.

She'd held her head high as she walked away but the moment the lightning struck the oak his whole future flashed before him. His gut roiled that she was almost taken out of his life so soon after moving to Red Peaks. He would keep his distance until he took care of a few items she had no business being a part of. She wasn't aware of the effect she had on him.

He didn't want her to be alone while visiting the cemetery, so he kept an eye on her while she grieved. In the few minutes he saw her when she visited, he was hooked and drawn into those beautiful copper-flecked green orbs.

Rupert gave him a hard time when he witnessed Dean's reaction at seeing her for the first time. Dean wasn't in Red Peaks for anything of the sort.

He sent off a message to Justin Nance, his co-worker, letting him know about the accident. Justin responded that he would meet him at the store.

He was tempted to go to the hospital for an update on her condition, but he didn't want to overstep the bounds she set that he not follow her. Oh, he was well aware that she did it so he wasn't tied up for an unknown amount of time waiting for test results. She released him from any further obligations surrounding today's events. He wasn't sure how to react to that. It had been a long time since someone put him above their own comfort.

Four

Shelby's cab pulled up to the curb. She slumped in the back and gave the shop address as their destination. The fee would cut a nice little chunk out of her checking account, but it couldn't be avoided.

Shelby didn't want to pay for a new car right away. Uncle Rupert's love of everything vintage extended to his automobile. The 1970s-style truck painted army green was in serious need of snow tires to even get around. Uncle Rupert had complained that the power steering was going out, and it was hard to muscle around corners, and that was if it started at all with the faulty alternator. Hopefully, the truck could chug through its sputtering existence until insurance paid the claim.

She didn't have to be a genius to know there was no salvaging the wreck. She hated shopping for vehicles; the astounding cost and then losing so much value after driving off the lot irked her. More interested in making a buck, they usually tried to slip in other costs, such as extended warranties, which should be offered at no cost, in her opinion, as a courtesy of buying the cars they sold. You'd think the quality of the vehicle spoke for itself, or they wouldn't have to sell an overinflated warranty.

She rested her eyes and let the sound of the road under the tires lull her to sleep as she rode forty minutes to her destination.

"Ma'am." The driver's low voice tried not to scare her in his whispered attempt to call out to her, but she jumped anyway.

"Oh, I'm so sorry. I didn't mean to fall asleep." She fumbled with her card and handed it to the driver for the fare. She added a nice tip and scooted out of the vehicle as fast as her sore limbs let her. Thankfully, Dean had the foresight to know she needed her identification, insurance cards, and debit card when he slipped her wallet to her earlier.

The cab driver waved as he turned around in the parking lot and headed toward the highway. A man, not Dean, bolted out the door to Rupert's store as she approached. The man wasn't overly tall; she would guess under six foot. He had a leaner physique than Dean. He also boasted blue eyes, quite a few shades lighter. They almost appeared a silver gray. His close-cropped hair stubbled all over his head.

"Shelby! Oh, darlin', are you okay?" He took her by the elbow as Dean held the door for them to enter.

"I'm sorry, but who are you?" She angled her head to look at the stranger.

"Justin, I work with Dean." He smiled, his eyes twinkling.

"What are you guys doing here? You know you don't have to work today. The store doesn't reopen until Monday. I want to review my uncle's accounts this weekend to jumpstart where we stand." She grimaced as she took the first step up the staircase but turned as Dean spoke.

"We've kept everything going until you got here. I believe your mother contacted us to get a read on the situation and see if it benefited you to keep Rupert's open, waiting for your arrival. We offered to stay, and she agreed it would honor Rupert by not closing. I'm sorry about your uncle. He was a great man." Dean's perusal made goosebumps flare over her.

She recognized Dean now that she didn't look at him through a haze of pain. An imposing guy, around six foot two inches and over two hundred pounds, with the most amazing dark blue eyes. His brown locks fell slightly longer on top, but the short-sheared sides made his eyes pop.

She was unsure of the working dynamic between the two employees at the store. Did they work well together and did they hold professional attitudes when dealing with each other? She couldn't stand workplace drama.

She hadn't had the pleasure of meeting Justin Nance yet. The newer hire her uncle had spoken about was shorter than Dean, but only by a couple of inches. Even though she could tell he followed an intense workout regime due to the defined muscles shadowed under his form-fitted shirt, he was not as bulky as Dean.

Her uncle's stature lacked height as she did, so she wondered how he found two massive men to hire. Both were enormous compared to her; they towered over her short stature, and she weighed only one hundred and ten pounds. She had no doubt they could toss her in one of the antique trunks at the store if they wanted to. She shivered, not sure where that thought came from.

Shelby sucked in a breath, trying to keep the waterworks at bay. She hadn't had any luck with that since hearing of her uncle's death. Her grief overwhelmed her when she least expected it. She was in town only a couple of days and already carless, hurt, could have died, and she wasn't sure if she could take much more.

"You're injured. Why wouldn't we be here to check on you?" Justin turned her head with a gentle grip on her chin. "Those black eyes look great, by the way. I think you can begin a new trend. Forget the smokey eye rage. The raccoon mask is a hit." He winked.

"Wow, nice." She couldn't help the chuckle that escaped.

She hadn't looked in a mirror yet. A hot, scalding shower or a long soak in the tub sounded perfect. "I'll be back down after I clean up."

"Take your time," Dean grumbled.

Peering up the stairs that loomed before her, she wondered if there were always so many to climb. Surely not. Putting one foot in front of the other, she ascended toward the privacy of her room. Her shoulders ached; her legs were on fire. She wanted to curl up under the covers and not move for the next week. Unfortunately, that was not an option. She had a store to oversee to ensure it stayed open for anyone who wanted to browse their merchandise. Since the day Uncle Rupert opened the doors, they never closed, except on Sundays, so she wanted to honor his name by keeping to that schedule.

She stopped at the fourth stair. "I appreciate you guys coming in today. It means a lot that you stopped by, but please go home. I'll be fine. I'll see you on Monday."

"Sure thing." Justin bounded out the door, gone in a flash.

Dean studied her but didn't say anything.

"Honest. I'm gonna crash for the next two days, okay, poor choice of words. I'll rejoin the land of the living on Monday." Shelby turned.

A soft touch at her elbow had her stopping in her tracks. "Did you need anything before I head out? Someone to harass you by text message, a call every couple of hours, or anything? Oh, I had the car towed to the dealership in the next county."

She gazed into the darkest blue eyes she'd ever seen. The small movement of her head made her dizzy, and she swayed but only for a second before Dean made sure she was steady. "No, thanks. I stocked up on food when I came into town this morning. Doc said I don't have a concussion, so I can sleep straight through with no concerns."

He gave a single nod and switched on the security system before exiting through the front door, locking it behind him.

The steam from the shower did wonders, but she knew the injuries on her legs would take a while to heal. She almost cried when she saw the damage to her face in the mirror. However, it could have been worse. The faint bruising would only darken in the coming days before it started to fade. Luckily, the laceration skirted her hairline, diminishing her fear of a visible scar. Pulling on yoga pants and a bulky warm sweater, she shut out the world and crawled into bed. Moisture dampened her pillowcase as she thought about her uncle before she tumbled into dreamland.

Five

Shelby shrieked the next morning when she glimpsed her eyes in the mirror. The bruising appeared darker than when she went to bed last night. How was she ever going to cover up the deep purple marks? She pressed on the puffy skin watching it spring back.

Thankfully, her headache remained a dull annoyance instead of throbbing with every pulse of her veins like before. Four pills later, she crept down the stairs at a snail's pace. The doctor told her to increase the generic meds instead of springing for a full-blown controlled substance prescription. She hadn't wanted the hassle of having the driver stop to fill a script and then take her home, so she'd opted for the upped dosage of generic meds.

The bagel, slathered in cream cheese, skated on the slick, purple-flowered plate she balanced on her coffee cup as she traversed the stairs. Not steady enough on her feet to forego the railing, she tipped the cup enough to center the plate without sloshing the scalding liquid.

Shelby groaned as she took in her uncle's office. Stacks of papers cluttered every surface. Uncle Rupert, the master of organized chaos. This would take her hours to sort through.

Breakfast would fuel her and encourage her to dive in. Shelby sighed and selected the first slip of paper on the metal industrial desk's smooth surface. The antiques that traveled through this store, and he had this atrocious thing in his office? She sighed when pages tumbled off the chair, scattering across the tiles in a morbidly jumbled mess.

Her phone jingled, and checking the screen told her it was her mom.

"Hey, sweetie, how did your trip to Red Peaks go?"

"Well, a freak streak of lightning catapulted a tree onto my car." When her mother shrieked, she quickly added. "Calm down, I am fine, no broken bones or anything. My car is toast."

"Oh, we can give you one of ours," her mom offered.

"That isn't necessary. Uncle Rupert's truck is still in the parking lot. I'll putter around in that until insurance finishes their investigation." Shelby pulled up the website for filing a claim and filled out the online questionnaire. She included the name of where her car was stored and the contact number she had to search for.

"That old rust bucket? Is it even safe?"

"If it was for Uncle Rupert, then I think I can handle that tank." Shelby hit submit and marked that off as completed.

"If you're sure. There is something your father and I wanted to talk to you about." Her mom hesitated.

Shelby's gut churned. "What's that?"

"We are buying a house and extending our trip. But only if you don't need us to come out. You will always be the first priority in our lives. Buying a house out here has been a dream of ours. I'm not sure how much longer my family will be around. Losing Rupert made me consider making the most of our time left with my elderly relatives." Shelby could hear stress in her mother's voice, which wasn't usual.

"Mom, you and Dad have to do what's best for you. I'll have to update my passport and come visit as soon as all this crazy calms down." Shelby stared at the piles of receipts littered on the top of the desk.

"Crazy? What crazy? We can be there in a couple of days." There was something off about her mom.

"I'm talking about the accident and the store being wholly my responsibility. It's just a lot to take in. I don't doubt that I can handle it, but it's an incredible life change." Shelby finally admitted out loud her stress at being handed Rupert's Relics.

Her mom didn't say anything for a minute. "Shelby, you are the brightest and most determined person I know. If you put your heart into something, you have always succeeded, just like I know you will this time. What have we always said?"

"Put it in God's hands and let go of trying to control everything." Shelby laughed. Her mother always knew what to say to make her feel better.

"That's my girl. Oh, it looks like your dad is trying to get my attention. He said to tell you hi and that we got the booking on an eight-day cruise down the Nile, which we wanted to do this time. Our phones won't work since we didn't buy a SIM card when we got here, but we will get one later since we hope to live here parttime and split our time between here and you."

"Have fun. I'll talk to you when you get back. I love you and Dad." Shelby laughed when her dad yelled in the background that he loved her, too.

Shelby amazed herself by how much she had accomplished, only interrupting her progress with bathroom breaks and ordering lunch to be delivered. She scared the poor food delivery driver and had to promise that her badly bruised face wasn't from a violent attack to keep him from calling the police.

She sorted everything into useful stacks ready to file. Her uncle, who utilized the equivalent of a DOS prompt technology, missed his chance to jump into a practical application age or at least let his toes dare to dangle off the edge.

The cloud would be perfect for file access and backup options. But what if a fire destroyed the store? All his records and tax receipts would be toast, literally and figuratively. Shelby brought up a search engine and perused scanners to digitally convert files and read documents to sort them as she wanted them stored.

The one she liked the most, with the best rating and options, floated in the mid-price range, so she put in the order. She was glad to see an estimated delivery date in the next few days or so. Sliding the stacks onto the credenza, she cleared off every surface in the room. The chairs she would leave; she liked the pattern and how they added to the ambiance of the decor.

The tacky desk had to go. She would keep an eye open for one worth moving in since she would only replace it if something fell into her lap instead of forking over money she wasn't ready to part with.

Shelby organized the drawers next and emptied the files she separated from the many she already skimmed over. She discovered the employee files behind a false back. Dean's name glowed an orange highlighted color, and in large print, block letters stated "permanent worker" on the folder.

Odd.

Justin didn't have much, just his years of experience, and he started working for Uncle Rupert a few weeks after Dean.

He usually ran background checks for bonding purposes when dealing with expensive stock. Still, she couldn't find any trace he followed that routine with Justin, and it wasn't like she could ask Uncle Rupert why. She wasn't sure if Justin would know why his file lacked sufficient background checks or if Uncle Rupert shared the sort of extensive actions he took when hiring.

Dean's file was quite a bit larger. Bonding paperwork, background, DMV photo, a very lengthy resume, with very few job switches, the usual things her uncle determined would make a trustworthy member of his staff.

She slid them back into the drawer, locked it with the key from the center organizer, and palmed the small, toothed chunk of metal. She would keep those files inaccessible. It wasn't like they wanted to read over each other's notes, but she believed in privacy, and if they wanted the other to know their history, that was up to them to share.

Proud of what she accomplished, Shelby was shocked to see it was later than she usually ate. She had another day before they opened. In the morning, she would inventory what they carried and would familiarize herself with the items for sale in the showroom. She wanted to sit down with Dean and Justin to hear their opinions of the inner workings and see if they had any suggestions to improve them.

Church was out of the question with her injuries. She never did like attention, so she chose to stay home and watch the sermon from the local pastor online the next morning.

She settled in for a night of mindless reading of the suspense thriller she bought to entertain herself during the downtimes in her hotel room while at the antique expo.

After double-checking the security app, she turned off the lights as she went upstairs.

The lumpy futon was surprisingly comfortable. After changing into flannel sleepwear, Shelby put on her green-and-yellow striped fuzzy socks. Wiggling her toes, she glided to the kitchen and brewed chamomile tea.

Carried away in the plot and character drama, she escaped into a world of adventures and rescues. Masculine men who saved women in distress, who then turned around and saved their men. There were always happy endings, unlike in real life.

When Shelby's eyes drooped, she tucked the book under the edge of the bed and floated into a fitful slumber.

Six

"I can't believe you saw a tree flatten her car." Justin's voice drifted from the front as Shelby descended the stairs on Monday morning.

Dean relaxed against the wall. His ankles were crossed in the same manner as his arms were over his chest. "Unquestionably the craziest thing I've ever seen. I thought it crushed it like a tin can until I climbed over the trunk and saw the damage."

"Still wild." Justin hesitated as she joined them.

"Should have seen it from my viewpoint. Almost had to change my pants." Shelby strolled to the front door and reversed the sign to announce them open. The chuckle from Justin made her smirk, but Dean's grunt bothered her. What happened to the sweet guy who held her head steady and shortened her name?

Why did he have a problem with her making a joke about it? It happened to her, not him. So what if the front of her car was squashed beneath the weight of the sixty-foot oak? It could have been so much worse. If she thought about what happened, almost being pulverized, she would lose it and not be able to function. The slight tremor in her hand as she turned around traveled up her arm.

Dean's dark blue eyes scrutinized her, and he glowered at her hand. She fixed her stare on the front display window. Strolling to the counter, she asked Justin for a duster and went about cleaning. Dean disappeared to the back. He oversaw the online transactions and shipping of the items they sold over the internet. Looking at the ledger flaunted it as a lucrative part of the money coming in. Who knew people bought an antique, sight unseen, and had it shipped to them across the country?

Justin came up behind her, lightly slung his arm around her, and pulled her back for a gentle hug. "I'm glad you're no worse for wear, Shelby. You were lucky."

She patted his forearm wrapped around her. "I know. I was there front and center, remember?" A shiver worked down her spine. "God looked out for me."

"It's over and done with; come here." He turned her and pulled her into his strong arms.

She was startled when he kissed the top of her head. The next second, he released her, gripped his own duster, and cleaned the higher ledges she couldn't reach without the small ladder they kept in the utility closet. She shook herself from the endearing kiss, catching her unaware, and continued to swipe the duster over the knickknacks and delicate displays, not sure what to say or how to take his action. She hadn't been around someone so touchy-feely before so she chose to ignore it for the moment.

Some of her favorite collections weren't the pieces of furniture but the elegant glass. They brought back memories of her dad's family. His mom collected every piece of pink Depression glass she got her hands on. Her collection impressed Shelby. Now, her father's property after her grandmother's death a couple of years ago. Her grandfather resided in a care facility due to dementia plaguing his fading mind. He'd forgotten Shelby years before, and it broke her heart when her father faced the same fate as her, and his dad no longer recognized his own son.

She rubbed at her temples as she took a break. Cleaning became a simple task when she had help and didn't have to continuously climb up and down from the small stool they used to sweep all the dust on the higher shelves away. Several small collections of dishes adorned one of the corners—sets she had never seen before. She swore they weren't there when she wandered through the store over the weekend.

"Justin, do you know where these came from?" A priceless tea set in a rare print in excellent condition sat off-center on the ledge. She had only seen pictures online.

"Which ones?" He peered over her shoulder, the warmth from his chest close to her back. She was uncomfortable with this, not knowing her uncle's employees. Well, they were hers now. The familiar ache settled over her, and she rubbed her hand against her chest.

He touched her shoulders and, if possible, moved even closer. "Oh, those. Found 'em in an estate sale and got a *killer* deal on them." He shrugged and walked off.

Shelby wasn't yet sure how to address his propensity for physical displays of friendship and obliterating personal boundaries.

Auctioneers know the value of sets this pristine and usually don't let them go for a low price. "Wait, what estate sale? Uncle Rupert didn't have anything on his calendar." Her uncle kept impeccable records in and around the surrounding counties, to keep the supply high. Nothing in his notes on his desk calendar mentioned current auctions.

"Some small town two counties over. I scour auctions online and am part of a chat group that shares the ones not widely advertised. I go in, sneak a peek, and jump-start the bidding. So far, it's succeeded in keeping the auctions in my favor. A leap in the bid makes people think you have more money than you do, so they don't try to outbid a high starting offer."

Shelby hefted herself onto the stool by the register. Tenderness running through her thigh reminded her of what she suffered a few days earlier. "Brilliant."

"Aww shucks." His smile made his dimples pop. Shelby didn't remember him having dimples when she encountered him on Friday. Her heart galloped. He should smile more.

"I discover many of my pieces that way, but old, long-forgotten barns are also treasure troves for the random pieces families have ignored over the years."

"Barns are horrible places. The heat and humidity alone warp and destroy wood and veneer if left for too long." She had seen it happen more than once when she went with her uncle to estates when the family wanted to donate heirlooms to his store when they had no one to leave the exquisite pieces to.

"You're telling me, but sometimes they have them wrapped tight enough to keep out the elements, and you find treasures. Look at the armoire at the back of the display room."

"The Frothingham? It's flawless! You found that in a barn?" She gestured to it. "Right there? No way it sat in a barn for any length of time!"

"Honest, old man Kramer asked me to take it off his hands so he didn't have to worry about moving it when his daughter put him in a home as he explained it." Justin softly brushed his shoulder into hers as he joined her.

"You know the man from whom you got it?" He spoke of him like a family friend.

"Naw, just someone I ran into in the grocery aisle and struck up a conversation about collectibles. He lives in the next county. Not sure why he shopped at that particular store; it's not even near his house." Justin shrugged and leaned his prominently veined muscular forearms on the glass-encased counter, staring out the front windows. "Think we'll be busy today?"

He jumped up and darted out the doors, not waiting for her answer. Shelby peered through the glass. He squatted in front of a small girl whose large crocodile tears perched precariously on her cheeks while other streaks of wetness dampened her skin. The mother was trying to soothe her daughter when Shelby saw a splattered chocolatey ice cream cone in a massive splotch on the gravel lot.

Justin held up his finger and jumped in his truck. He tore down the road. Shelby headed to the doors as the mother took a small cloth and wiped away the girl's sadness. A few minutes later, his truck pulled in. He held another cone in his hand for the little girl.

The mother almost hugged him when her daughter's smile brightened her face. Then he bounded back into the store as if nothing had happened.

"So, boss lady, we gonna be busy today?" Justin picked up his phone, reading the screen.

"It's always hit or miss on Mondays. But who knows if any gawkers will want to brag they came here after my uncle's death, to see if I have what it takes to operate Rupert's the same as my uncle did. I don't get people so intrigued with death; it's disgusting. I wanted to close the store the week after the funeral, but Rupert's Relics has never closed. It felt wrong not to have this place open for him." She tried to avert her eyes from checking out her employee's muscles when she spotted a hideous bruise on his left arm.

"Justin!" Shelby lifted his hand, turning it over to inspect the discoloration better. It blurred into a hard-to-see, imprecise shape.

Justin twisted his arm, showing her the edges. "That's nothing. I fight a piece of furniture at some point or another daily. No biggie. I think you take the cake on injuries, though." He lifted his chin at her legs, peeking out from under her skirt, which started to develop varying shades of purple on her thighs, a kaleidoscope of colors. She concealed most of the raccoon mask discoloration with a bit of concealer and powder. She would have to keep giving it a touch-up as the day went on.

She chuckled. "I didn't do it to myself, though, unlike you. A large honking tree decided to throw itself at the mercy of my car as opposed to you getting in the ring with a dresser. The oak won, by the way, if you couldn't tell. I always wanted a compact."

The rumble of his laugh launched goosebumps down her arms.

"We're happy to have you. At least I am. Be careful around Dean. I don't have a good feeling about him." Justin patted her hand.

Shelby didn't know what to think about Justin's comment, so she started to change the subject when a man entered the store whom she hadn't had a chance to seek out.

"Sam, it's good to see you." Shelby darted around the counter and embraced him.

"I wanted to stop by and let you know I'm sorry about Rupert. If you need anything, you can come down to the hardware store, and I'll get you set up with whatever you need. Rupert kept an account with us and paid it at the end of every month. I am extending you the same courtesy we gave him." He bopped her on the end of her nose. He had done that since she was a little girl.

"Thanks, Sam. Tell your lovely wife hello." Shelby knew Sam, one of Uncle Rupert's dearest friends, would help in any way he could.

The bell jingled throughout the store as the door opened again. A man in a posh dark blue business suit sauntered in. "I'm looking for a Shelby Samuel."

"Yes?" She strolled over as Dean stood next to Justin, and Sam showed himself out.

"Nice to make your acquaintance; I represent Rupert Reda in disseminating his last will and testament." He pulled a legal-sized bulging manila envelope from his briefcase and handed it to her. "His will states all his earthy possessions and store he bequeaths to his niece, a one Shelby Samuel. In the envelope, you will find his will attesting to his requests and a letter he wrote concerning his effects and wishes.

Normally, I would wait for a formal reading, but his only living family, your mother, already gave her permission for everything to be given to you and doesn't contest its contents. She is aware of what his will states and signed off on this being the official dissemination of his estate. I am sorry for your loss. Is there anything you'd like to ask?"

She rapidly blinked and shook her head. Her mother said they would come back to town for the reading. She expected her to be here when she dealt not only with her grief but also with how to tackle her life after finding out her uncle's wishes.

"If you should have any questions later, there is a number and address where you can reach me. Your uncle was an amazing man, just so you know. In the short time I knew him, he made an impression on me and the staff in my office." He bowed his head and made his way outside.

She swallowed hard, her voice a broken whisper. "Excuse me."

None of the men said anything.

Behind the office door, she plopped into the chair behind the desk. Her hands shook as she bent up the brass clasp, eased back the flap on the envelope, and dumped the papers out. The lawyer's cover letter stated what would be in the subsequent pages. As promised, his work address and phone number were printed under the signature.

The legal documents would have given her heart palpitations if she had to listen to them presented to her and her parents. This may be for the best. She rapidly blinked, and true to his word, the lawyer laid out everything in exact detail. Shelby, the sole beneficiary of the store, the apartment upstairs, and his cottage house. She took a moment to grasp the finality of his words. The store had never overwhelmed her, but now, sitting as the owner and one responsible for every legal facet of the day-to-day operations, payroll, and employees, it hit home and buried her in dread. Uncle Rupert was supposed to show her every facet. And only when she was comfortable would he pass it on to her.

What if she couldn't make it work? What if she lost everything?

This was a mistake; she craved more time to prepare. She was supposed to roam the world for a few years after finishing her college degrees early. Travel to other antique venues and stores to see how to take Rupert's to a whole new level. She swiped at the tears that distorted the words. Before she talked herself out of it, she overturned the last page in the packet—her uncle's letter to her.

My darling Shelby,

If you are reading this, then my time has come to an end in this world. I am sorry I'm not there to help you take over our store. Yes, "our" store; you are the heart and soul behind it. I knew the first time you spent the summer with me and your excitement over a miniature thimble to an enormous armoire you were my legacy. I built it to what it is today with you in mind taking over and us running it together before I retired and saw the world. But if you're reading this, my time came long before I meant for it. God is in control, so I know it's according to His timing. I'm sorry I'm not there to hold your hand through this. My only regret is the pain you are experiencing because of me.

I have great employees in Dean and Justin. Please keep them on board until you know them better and make a final determination to let them stay on staff. I am confident you will see what I see in them. Until then, if you can help an old man out by keeping a promise I made to them and let them work there with you.

Tell your mom how blessed I was to have her as my sister. She gave me the greatest gift I could ever hope for. That is you, my dearest niece. You were the light in my world when you came to live with me in the summers. I didn't know what I missed until I held you the first time, and you curled your tiny hand around my finger, squeezing with more strength than any infant should have. We had a connection I doubt I would have had if I'd had children of my own. You imbued my life with so much love I didn't have to look to someone else to have a family of my own.

Please don't think I missed out because I never needed anyone except you. So, it is with a heavy heart, that I leave you now when you aren't prepared for what is in store for you. Keep your eyes and mind open and rely on no one. Not all things are as they seem. The smallest sayings could have the biggest meanings. Focus on what you hear. You will understand soon enough, but I can't say more than what I already have, or I fear it will put you in mortal danger.

Love with all my heart, your uncle Rupert.

A sob broke the silence.

The letter rocked her to her core. Danger? What was her uncle talking about? He dealt in antiques. What could be so deadly about them? Tears streamed down her face, falling without permission. The ink smeared as she wiped her hand across the page, ruining her uncle's words. A hiccupped sob choked out. She tried to stop them, but it was no use. She wanted her uncle to explain his puzzling letter, which held more mysteries than answers.

She scrubbed her hands over her face and rinsed her warmed skin in the basin in the bathroom, getting herself under control before heading to the front of the store. There was nothing to do for her red-rimmed, puffy eyes. Thank heavens for a waterproof coverup.

The day flew by with very few customers, so she continued cleaning and dusting all the items. Dean even helped with the back wall. He didn't say much and contributed to the conversation only when asked a direct question. His shyness knocked her off-kilter. She wasn't used to men being shy. He started in her direction on more than one occasion when she rubbed at her temples before Justin got to her first and offered her a drink or something for a headache.

Dean slunk off to the back of the building, inventorying the furnishings stored off the main floor without saying a word. She wasn't sure how he moved around so silently. Something about him she couldn't quite decipher. Not sure if it was a bad feeling or a good one. She watched him to see if she could figure it out. Letting them work for her killed two birds with one stone: honoring her uncle's wishes and not having to look for replacements right away.

At closing, she appreciated neither man interrogating her during the day about what the lawyer had given her. She didn't bring it up. "Okay, see you guys."

She nodded at both as Justin headed out. Dean retreated to the warehouse for his coat, and Justin pulled out of the parking lot. Dean placed his hand gently on her shoulder.

"Are you all right?" He leaned in.

"Just sad. I miss him so much." Shelby pressed her lips together.

"You can come to me if you have any questions. I only have this place's best interest at heart." Dean's words hit home. "I'll address any worries no matter how outlandish they may be."

What did he consider outlandish? She rebuffed some of the topics she assigned to that category.

Shelby shook her head. "Okay."

"Lock up." Then he was gone.

She flicked the switch and punched in the code to the alarm.

For some reason, the store took on a malevolent aura as she passed by the immaculate shelves to the hallway and the staircase.

She stopped to grab the will and her uncle's letter—what she could read of it after bawling over the document. She didn't want them left in the office. Years ago, her uncle mounted a safe in a wall compartment in the apartment. At the same time, he had one installed in the floor in the office, so she would leave everything in there.

A small salad was all she could tolerate, food-wise. She curled up on the sofa under the plush thick blanket her uncle bought the last time she visited, when she'd mentioned how chilled she got after her uncle forgot to turn on the vents before her arrival.

"Oh, Uncle Rupert, what do you mean with all the cloak and dagger nonsense in your letter? How dangerous can Red Peaks possibly be?" She scratched her head, trying to think of anything from the past when her uncle worried about living or working here.

Nothing came to mind.

Creaking on the stairs froze her where she sat. Another rasp emanated past the landing, and she bolted off the sofa. She whirled around, looking for anything to use as a weapon. Not even a baseball bat sat next to the door. She pulled the cast iron skillet off the back burner and tiptoed over.

A nail rubbing on a board announced someone on the other side of the door. She knew that sound well. It acted as an early warning when her uncle arrived in the mornings with breakfast.

She prioritized fitting a peephole to spy on anyone on the other side as a priority.

The knob turned but stopped due to the bolt she'd twisted when she entered. Shelby backed up and weighed her options. It wasn't as if no one knew she lived above the shop; small-town gossip ran rampant about everyone's business. The brass-plated doorknob jiggled again.

"I'm calling the police!" she yelled.

Pounding footfalls disappeared as they ran. Loud chirping made her yelp.

Her phone rang. "Hello."

"Hi, this is the Mayday Security Company. We have an activation at your location." The woman on the other line informed her as if she couldn't hear the shrills in the background.

"Yes, someone's in my store. I think they ran away." Shelby punched in the code to silence the flashing panel inside the apartment door.

"My colleague is calling the police department; I'm going to stay on the phone with you until they arrive."

"Shouldn't I call 911 and tell them?" Shelby would prefer to speak directly to a dispatcher.

"Not necessary; we can relay everything." The woman's condescending voice mocked her.

"I'm calling the police directly." Shelby hung up even as she continued to protest.

Shelby told the dispatcher what happened, and she confirmed their computers denoted a call for service. They had two deputies en route: one twenty minutes out and the other on the other side of the county. She informed Shelby she would have them step it up because Shelby had said she heard someone in the store on the other side of her door. That was vital information Mayday hadn't disclosed to the dispatcher. So much for police having accurate info before they arrived.

Pound, pound, pound.

Shelby yelped.

That was not the deputy.

Seven

"Shelby, it's me," Dean spoke loud enough for her to hear him through the door.

"What are you doing here?" Shelby's voice was muffled.

"I get notifications on my phone when there is a trigger. The company also called me when you disconnected from them, and they couldn't get you back on the line. They were concerned for your welfare."

Shelby tugged open the door. "You're a contact on the account?" Her fingers tightened around the handle of the frying pan.

"I should have told you that Rupert added me since I live closer than his cottage. He thought it would help with response time."

She released the air in her lungs in a whoosh. Her white-knuckled grip around the handle loosened, sending a rush of pink color through her fingers.

His left eyebrow arched at the pan hanging in her grip.

"Oh, sorry, I didn't see anything else to do damage with, so I grabbed this." She chuckled as she nudged it to the back burner of the stove.

Dean indicated for her to shadow him. Her legs shook, making her steps wobbly. He forced himself not to step forward to steady her. "That works in a pinch. Tell me what happened. The front door was unlocked when I drove up, but I didn't see anyone."

Scraping against the concrete floor in the back had her spinning toward the double doors. Dean clasped her wrist and moved her behind him, walking backward, shuffling them toward the front door.

"If someone who isn't me comes out here, you run."

"I'm not leaving you." Shelby huffed, clawing at the back of his shirt.

He twisted his neck to take her in. "We are not having this argument. You run when I say. I can't go in there and concentrate if I have to worry about your safety. It will only distract me and get me hurt or worse. Then there will be no one between them and you." Dean cupped her cheek.

She nodded, her eyes wide. Dean saw the moment she conceded he was right.

Dean inched forward. Shelby tugged his arm. "What if the person in there has a gun? I want to wait for the police."

He inched his mouth to her ear. "I'll be back. I want to see if someone is here."

"No." Shelby's panic was palpable.

"We aren't safe otherwise." He clutched both her hands and pressed them to her, then held up his hand and backed away.

He retreated as he sought to discover the reason for their heightened unease. When he flipped the switch, the fluorescents flickered and then brightened. He listened before going further. Scrutinizing the rows and seeing the bolt in place on the back door, he headed to the front.

Dean marched back through and scanned the area before he saw her with her back to the wall, halfway concealed. He pulled her to him. "I think they're gone. Tell me what you heard."

"I settled on the couch to watch television and clear my head. A lot happened in the last few days, causing me to toss and turn. I heard someone on the bottom stair. You know how the board rubs against the nail when so much weight is distributed on the right side?"

When he nodded, she continued; he was relieved she didn't act like an out-of-control woman exaggerating the details to get attention.

"Well, then, I heard another stair groan under the pressure of someone's weight, and I selected my weapon of choice. I heard them by my door. The next thing I know, they tried to turn the knob, but I locked it as soon as I went inside out of habit from living in the city." Shelby shivered.

"I'm here; nothing's going to happen." Dean signaled for her to go on. "Did they say anything?"

She shook her head. "No, but then I got mad and yelled I'd call the police. I heard them run away, and the sensor tripped. I got a call from the company saying they saw a trip on the beam, and when I told them someone was in the store, they said they called the police and to stay on the line, and they would relay everything. I thought it would delay info getting to the deputies responding, so I hung up, as she adamantly told me not to, and called the police directly. The police dispatcher confirmed that the alarm company hadn't informed them that I heard someone, so I was glad I called because they expedited the officer's response from that bit of information. Then you knocked on the door and gave me a coronary, by the way."

"I returned to town after an evening with a friend and received the call. I was down the street." Dean looked at the flashing red and blue strobes hitting the front windows.

"Put your hands above your head and leave them there!" a voice yelled.

Shelby and Dean did as instructed.

"I'm the owner and the one who called, and this is my uncle's employee! My employee," Shelby announced loud enough for the deputy to hear, then, under her breath, said, "Ugh, I never thought I'd be saying that anytime soon."

Dean chuckled but never took his eyes off the open door.

The officer swept his gun into the room and surveyed the scene. "Miss Samuel?"

Shelby waved with her arms still in the air. "I live upstairs, and someone tried to open my door."

"You can put your hands down." The deputy keyed the mic on his shoulder and declared the additional responding unit to downgrade.

Dean sat on the stool by the register.

The deputy asked Shelby to repeat the story again, and as he wrote it down, a second deputy stalked through the front door. He was massive, and he ducked to enter. Dean would not want to go up against him in a dark alley, a lighted alley, or anywhere else.

"You clear the building?" He asked the deputy, who was talking to Shelby.

"Not yet."

"Got it." He looked at Dean. "Want to show me where everything took place? Then, if you can turn on the lights to the warehouse without entering the room, I'll make sure there isn't someone still inside."

Dean nodded and took off as Shelby continued her murmured conversation with the lawman. The first deputy failed to clear the building first, creating a safety issue if someone was still there. He showed the second officer the stockroom, and he worked to check every nook and cranny for anyone lurking in the room.

***

Shelby was curious if she should continue living there if she had to bear with people breaking into the store and trying to get into her room.

It was indisputably a good idea to make a couple of rooms livable at the cottage before waiting and moving all at once. Surely, her uncle didn't keep the entire structure in hoarder conditions, and if she could stay there sooner rather than later, it would be for the best. Yes, the cottage was out in the middle of an undeveloped terrain, but the house had thick, sturdy, solid wood doors. The windows had two locks each. She was lost in her thoughts and missed the officer's query.

The officer touched her elbow. "I know this is a little scary, but they usually don't return after breaking in the first time. In my years on the force, I have never seen someone come back a second time. You should be fine staying here. Make sure you lock up in the future so this doesn't happen again."

Shelby bristled at his comment, insinuating her at fault as to how they got in. But why wouldn't the sensor trigger when they entered? Unless they knew the code.

"Nothing found in the back, and it's sealed up tight, so it's not the point of entry." The second officer made his way to the front. "Need anything else?"

"No, you're good to go. I'll see you out there." The first officer clipped the cover on his notebook and tucked it back into the front pocket of his black uniform shirt under his gleaming badge.

"Thanks for coming out. When will a copy of the report be ready?" Shelby wanted to know how the deputy intended to write it up.

"Well, I didn't take a report because nothing was taken, and you probably left the front door unlocked. It happens. Someone was probably curious about the store; it spooked them when you yelled out about calling the police. And the harsh winds creating the smallest movement, activated the door sensor, but here is our call for service number if you have anything further." He scribbled on the back of a business card and left it on his way out.

"I *did* lock the door." Shelby slammed her palm over the card, bending the edge as she picked it up and stormed to her office.

Why didn't they believe her?

"You going to be okay for the rest of the night?" Dean relaxed his right shoulder against the doorframe. He still wore his jeans and red long-sleeved henley-style shirt from work that morning.

"Yeah, sure, great." She tried to walk past him when he gently wrapped his fingers around her bicep.

"It's okay if you aren't, you know. Nobody is going to think less of you. It's not a bad thing to lean on friends." He let his hand drop when she nodded.

"It's been a long day; go home."

"Shel, come bolt the door and do the alarm so I know it's secured before I leave." He tilted his head toward the front door.

"You mean like I did when you left and told me to?" Shelby mumbled to herself, not intending for Dean to comment.

He stopped and took her in. "You did?"

"Yep. Go home. I'm tired, and I'll probably fall asleep before I can lug myself up to bed."

"I can take the couch if it will make you more comfortable." Dean hesitated, partially outside.

"No, thank you." She offered him a tired smile. Also, she liked the futon better than the twin bed.

He let the latch fall in place while she punched in the code on the blinking screen. She got the green light, showing it active. He checked his phone before he gave her a thumbs-up and trotted to his car.

Shelby turned and braced herself for the all-consuming fear of someone waiting to jump out and grab her, but it never came.

Weird.

She trudged up the rickety staircase and secured the door behind her. Then, on a whim, she wedged a small table chair under the knob.

Once she removed antiques from her uncle's house, she'd move in and enjoy the serenity of the woods. Even with the massive square footage difference between the two and all the ways someone could break in, she still preferred to be out there than in here.

Still wired from the break-in, she pulled out her tablet and perused news articles. She shivered as she read about a murder in the next county over. She remembered the broadcast while waiting for a taxi at the hospital. Were some of those mounds in the cemetery related to this?

When the clock clicked over to ten, she called her mom because it would be eight in the morning over there. She kept the drama of the day to a minimum as she recounted the hassle of the break-in. Sometimes, her mom could make her feel like a little kid whose parents were prepared to rush out and protect her. She downplayed how scared she was to prove to herself she would handle what life threw her way. After talking for an hour and a half, she disconnected, feeling better just hearing her parents chattering back and forth on the phone. That was what her dad considered a three-way call, yelling in the background to join the conversation. Their cruise left in two days, so they would be out of touch.

She smiled at herself before climbing into bed. She never felt herself fall asleep as the clock ticked over to one in the morning.

Eight

"Watch out!" The desk tilted almost off the back of the tailgate.

Dean darted to the left and braced the legs of the antique roll-top, shipping out on this morning's truck, with his massive hands. His biceps flexed against the tight T-shirt he wore.

Her mouth hung open, awe-struck by the rippled corded muscles along his back flexing under his shirt. How much did he have to work out to obtain his physique? It should have taken more than two men to keep the desk from crashing and splintering into a mess on the concrete floor of the loading bay.

"Nice save." She patted him on the shoulder, and he slightly flinched and skirted to her left out of reach.

"Just doin' my job." Dean disappeared around the side of the truck to deliver the bill of lading to the driver where the cargo was bound.

She wasn't sure what it was about him that alluded he hid a deep, dark part of himself. She'd never met someone so standoffish as Dean. Some days gave her whiplash. When Justin was absent, he bared a calm and almost sweet side. As soon as Justin walked in, he became distant and made himself scarce.

Numerous times over the last two weeks, she caught him watching her as she learned the ropes of their duties with the store and the computer programs Dean downloaded for efficiency. Justin, on the other hand, flirted but not overtly so. Whenever she looked up from a corner of the store where she cleaned, rearranged, or organized new products, he'd flash one of his signature dimpled grins and make her knees go weak. Shelby promised herself to never get personally involved with an employee. She started repeating the mantra daily. Of course, she'd never been a boss, so their working relationship was in its infancy. Everyone had quirks, and they were discovering each other's. She hoped he wouldn't push the topic and ask her out again, but it tempted her when he shamelessly flirted in the quirky way he did.

The door to the back of the dock swung open and rattled against the wall behind it, reverberating along the rigid metal frame. Justin stood there, a darkness in his eyes, as he faced Dean. She shivered as she wondered what had happened. Sweat dotted his brow while his nostrils flared. His lips pressed into a thin white line, emphasizing the fine wrinkles around his mouth. A storm brewed on his face, something she imagined glimpsing in a nightmare.

He straightened to his full height of five feet eleven inches, his muscular, solid-framed mass tensed. Justin wasn't a slouch in maintaining his form, but his pale blue eyes and dimples caused most of the women customers to swoon. She didn't doubt the younger women came in to catch a glimpse of him. He was polite but never inappropriately interested in anything beyond business transactions. His flirtations included those who straddled the fence about buying an antique; he sweet-talked any woman into purchasing it. Shelby often saw women slip their number to him before leaving with merchandise.

Maybe she would have fallen for him in another lifetime, but she would only have a professional relationship with him. If she could only convince herself to keep those promises, she told herself. "Justin, is everything all right?"

He stormed up to her, making her take a step back. Dean darted to her side and pressed his hand against Justin's chest.

Justin glared at the truck behind her as it pulled away from the building before lowering his voice. "Some feds in the front want to speak with you. Something about stolen antiques?"

"Feds? What could they want with Rupert's Relics?" She put her hand on his forearm.

He towered over her slight build but backed off when Dean pushed. "Not sure, babe, but they don't look like they are messing around. They didn't even crack a smile with a few jokes about men in suits." His eyebrows hit his hairline.

"You didn't! Oh please, oh please, oh please, tell me you didn't try to crack jokes with them? Justin!" What was he thinking? She pressed the heels of her palms against her eyes.

His chuckle cut out when Dean raised an eyebrow and stormed in the direction of the hall leading to the front of the store.

"Did they say what they wanted?" Dean's low, rumbling voice permeated the room.

"Nope." Justin popped the "p" and glared at Dean.

Dean spun around, and his hands landed on his hips. "Did you ask, or are you just eager to send someone else to handle them?"

"Not my rodeo, not my problem. I merely work here."

Shelby's mouth gaped at Justin's words. That didn't sound like the man she had gotten to know over the last couple of weeks. He never sounded so selfish and arrogant.

"Excuse me." Dean's long strides took him to the front.

Justin smirked and hooked his arm through hers. "He is too easy to rile up. They asked about some of the pieces. Something about relatives saying elderly family members were conned. I informed them to talk to you. I figured we could approach them together. I'd never leave you in the lurch."

She shivered as he ran his knuckles down her arm over the thin blouse she wore. It distracted her briefly before she realized what he told her. The feds were scrutinizing her antiques. Why? His hand on her lower back, pushing her toward the store, transported her back to the here and now.

"They have nothing to go on. I have all the signed documents from the auctions or owners of every piece I've ever brought in." Justin continued to press her forward, the heat from his hand warming her skin.

"That's right. We don't accept any pieces without written documentation designating their origins and permission to release the ownership." She breathed easier. Justin had a point: They verified everything. His detailed acquisitions were the best she'd ever seen.

Uncle Rupert had a run-in with a customer of a sibling who sold him a piece the other family member felt should be left with relatives rather than sold for profit. It caused such an upheaval and garnered threats to sue him until the original customer said they approved the sale. Afterward, he adopted the motto: no acquisition without a contract, transferring the ownership of said items to the store, which withheld one hundred percent right to do with the piece as he saw fit. A policy she kept in place.

It kept people from going back on their word. It safeguarded the store's liability from other families, upset that items weren't distributed to distant relatives, and monies split evenly throughout the remaining household, especially on the more expensive pieces. The sad fact was that more and more people opted to sell relics or antiques and part with their history for the dollar signs attached to those items. She would have kept everything in her family for generations if she had her say. The stories and memories of living in a house with those antiques made them worth more than any amount someone would pay for them.

As a little girl, she stayed away from the consignment side because her uncle said if she scuffed or damaged anything, he would have to pay for them and lose money on the reduced price in the final sale. After a customer said an heirloom sported a scratch not there before he displayed it, Rupert shut her rantings down with pictures of the day she handed it off, showing the offending graze before being relocated to Rupert's Relics and her signature declaring its condition. Not long after, he rebuffed carrying anything on consignment, no matter how much someone pleaded with him.

"I promise, spending not even five minutes with you, they'll know you would never commit a crime. I'll be by your side through the whole thing. We'll get through this together. I'm acquainted with how different law enforcement agencies work. I have inside knowledge of ordinances and laws." When she furrowed her brow, he held up his hand. "I can't explain why right now. You're going to have to believe me."

Shelby nodded, and he stopped her, catching her elbow with his warm, calloused hands.

Justin's breath whispered over her earlobe. "Don't give them more than they ask for. Be short and to the point in your answers so they won't think you are holding anything back. Also, don't embellish your responses; it will look like you are nervous. The same with rambling. Try to keep that under control. When they smell blood in the water, they will go in for the kill, thinking you're withholding something."

Her heart lurched at his nearness. Dean stood off to the side, talking to one of the men in the front of her store.

"Ma'am." The taller one fixed on her, making her shiver.

Their boring, low-end black suits, thin ties, and dull black shoes gave away their jobs. She always chuckled when movies portrayed federal agents in boring attire exactly as these two wore, showing the world they couldn't suppress their station of being agents.

"How can I help you, gentlemen?" Shelby tried to keep her voice steady.

The man in front of her opened a leather wallet, showing a shield with an eagle perched on top and the words Federal Bureau of Investigations stamped in the rigid gold-plated metal and identification with his picture. "Special Agent Heath Irving and that is Special Agent Matt Jackson. We have some issues regarding an ongoing inquiry. Is there someplace we can talk in private?"

Justin squeezed her hand, catching the agent's eye.

"Um, yes, my office is this way." Shelby wondered if her trembling knees would give out as they walked the short distance to her private office.

Her hands trembled as she gathered stacks of papers from the seats of the two chairs and dumped them on the floor in the corner of the room. "Excuse the mess. I'm still reclaiming my sense of balance and have been in town for about two weeks. I had this organized before I started purging the old files from the new. Please have a seat."

The man who conversed with Dean closed the door behind him, leaned against it, and crossed his arms. "Have you heard of the murders in and around the region?"

"Murders? I thought you wanted to pinpoint certain questionable antiques?" Her stomach lurched, and butterflies more than fluttered. They took up MMA fighting stances, ready to throw down. Her belly, the ring gearing up for a beating. She swallowed down the bile burning the back of her throat. How did that involve her store? Shelby clenched her hands in her lap under the edge of her desk as her eyes darted between the two.

"The surge in elderly deaths connected with missing antiques and collectibles has led us to this location. Your store has seen a rise in supply and demand, which coincides with this. Relatives approached our offices, bringing to our attention physical validations documenting indentations in carpets and vacant spaces in the residence after discovering their loved ones' deaths. Images of family functions depicted those antiques filling those voids. It ties the missing pieces to the posts on your website." His brown, intense eyes bore into her, making her flinch.

"Do you realize I have only been here for a couple of weeks?" Shelby's knee bounced.

"Doesn't mean you aren't involved." Agent Irving's face had to be made of stone. There were no twitches, smirks, or any sign of life behind his dark eyes.

"I have nothing to do with those deaths! Every piece I sell here has documentation to back its authentic purchase or donation status. I keep meticulous records, as my uncle did well before his death. I can have all those documents ready immediately if you tell me what to copy. I'm more than happy to help in this matter." Shelby spit out her thoughts, bouncing her leg at the idea of someone tying her store to the deaths of the elderly.

Her memory of the day of her accident flitted back to several upheaved piles of earth. Were those due to the killer? Landmarks of his handiwork?

"We appreciate any cooperation you can give us. We'll need to schedule a formal interview regarding your purchasing, if you outsource any of your collectibles, and what stock you have now. I'll have to photograph all locations you stockpile inventory to match against our records." Agent Irving, who flashed her his badge, hadn't moved a muscle since he joined her in the office.

"Am I a suspect? Do I need a lawyer for the interview?" Fear clouded her thoughts. She wiped the sweat from her palms down her black slacks, trying to keep the motion minimal, not wanting them to think the movement insinuated her guilt.

"Why do you need a lawyer? Is there something you're hiding?" Agent Jackson pushed off the door, so he stood over her.

How cute. They tried an intimidation tactic, but they didn't realize she had been so much shorter than everyone her entire life; tall people didn't bother or scare her. They were in for a rude awakening if they thought this little bad cop routine would work on her. Spending her life in jail because of the power they wielded was another matter. She was nervous over the inquiry, of course, but having nothing to do with those deaths settled something profound in her. She had the forms to prove every purchase in her shop and every sale. The outcome of their audit of her records would prove it, but the fact he tried to use his size to scare her would never work.

She rose to her feet and handed her business card to each of them. "Gentlemen, if you'll email me what files you need on the items in question, I can help settle any doubt you have about myself or my business. In the meantime, please let me know when you would like to schedule an interview, and I'll have my lawyer coordinate our schedules. Otherwise, if you are done, I bid you good day." She inched around the agents and opened her door, standing to the side, letting them know she declared the meeting concluded.

They each took out a business card of their own and laid it on her desk. "We'll be in touch. There are a few case inconsistencies we are ironing out and will send you a broken-down list. Also, we are working out of the police department. When you finish compiling the data you can bring it by there."

Agent Jackson extracted a slim silver camera and raised an eyebrow.

"All of our stock is in the back. Help yourselves. I have nothing to hide." Shelby raised her own brow in exaggeration to his.

The agent's mouth twitched.

Justin propped himself up by the cash register, drumming his fingers along the surface with his right hand while resting his chin on his left.

Dean had yet to leave the spot he'd been in when the agents went to Shelby's office. His dark blue eyes cut through her like he saw inside her, unnerving her, to say the least. Not one for idle chitchat, he watched everything, his dark blue orbs carrying the conversations he didn't speak out loud. He rarely spoke face-to-face with the customers on the showroom floor.

"They need full admittance." She gave him a small smile, and he returned it with a chin lift before sauntering to the back. Not sure why having him acknowledge her felt like a win, but it did. His quirks weren't enough to discourage her from giving up on him just yet.

Dean held his hand up to the agent and hurried to her. "Having a lawyer present isn't a bad idea. You can decline their demands until representation counsels you of your rights and if they need a warrant to search the premises."

"Why would she need a lawyer? She doesn't have anything to hide. It will only make her suspicious in their eyes. What are you trying to do, Dean?" Justin murmured, his voice pitched low.

"I'm looking out for her." Dean didn't break eye contact as he tilted his head to the side.

Justin hissed, "Are you trying to ruin her and shut this place down? What would her uncle say? He would give them unfettered access if they asked because that was the type of upstanding citizen he was."

"Justin is right. Please show them around." Shelby put her fists on her hips, not one to back down to a challenge.

Dean took a second, then turned and moved to Agent Jackson. She didn't know what to think of what he said. Would it be better to consult with an attorney? The one who handled her uncle's business seemed trustworthy; if he didn't manage criminal cases, he probably knew a lawyer to endorse. Was Dean right? Did she need to bring this to her parents' attention and get their opinion? If they wanted to come to town, would they be caught up in the mayhem? Could it put them in danger? She didn't want to be the cause of her parents caught up in the web of a killer.

Her uncle's letter warned of danger. Dean seemed to have the store's best interest and hers at heart. Next time, she would take his advice. He seemed to be calm and composed, not someone to jump to conclusions.

Nine

Shelby tallied the receipts for the day and stuffed the deposit into a bag before locking it in the safe in the floor. Her head popped up when the agents' voices followed Dean to the front door.

The bell tinkled its delicate chime with the opening and then closing of the door behind the agents as they left. Dean didn't wait before he disappeared, muttering something under his breath about not trusting the authorities. Justin smirked.

"So, what did they want? I didn't want you to negotiate uncharted waters with them yourself, but they would have strong-armed me out of the office if I barged in." Justin gave her a one-arm hug, slightly tugging her to his side. "No matter what, I'll be here. Let me know what they want, and I'll go through my files on my end and make sure they match what Rupert has so we cover the store. That way, they won't be able to take it from you."

"They not only want to audit our records but informed me some of our antiques might be connected to deaths of elderly in and around the vicinity." Shelby shook her head. "That doesn't make sense."

Justin cringed; this wouldn't be good for the store's reputation or Shelby's uncle's, but if something tied to someone's death, he would do what he could to help. He didn't want her to be railroaded.

"Come on, it's time to close. Let's go grab some food." Justin switched the sign hanging on the door and turned to her.

"Justin, I'm not sure I'm up for dinner. I also don't want to give you the wrong idea about us." She fiddled with the strap on her bag.

He'd flirted more than once, mentioning his attraction. If he were honest with himself, some of his remarks might not have been appropriate for a subordinate and supervisor relationship. They weren't overdramatic, but a small giggle or compliment back led him to believe her feelings were mutual.

Justin held up his hands. "Whoa, nothing like that. Grub between a co-worker and boss. I respect you more than to try and push something you don't want. If we develop a friendship and nothing more, I'd consider it as one of the best blessings in my life. Counting you as a friend is more than anyone would be lucky to have."

"You know, I'd like that. I'll see if Dean wants to go with us." She pivoted on her heels before Justin said anything and disappeared through the swinging door to the back.

Justin dodged to the door and propped it open to watch their interaction.

Dean turned, his phone up to his ear. "I have to go."

"Sorry, I didn't mean to interrupt." Shelby inched back.

"No, it's not anything important. What can I do for you, Shelby?" Dean's dark blue eyes studied Shelby.

Several seconds passed. Something in his face told Justin he hid more than the facts on the other end of the line. What was he concealing? Justin realized he always seemed to be ending a conversation with someone on the phone every time he entered the same room. Shelby huffed.

"Shelby, is there something wrong?" His gaze narrowed as he took a step toward her.

She stepped back, stopping his forward motion. "No, um..." She waved to the front of the store. "Justin wanted to grab dinner, and I wondered if you wanted to join us." She took another step in reverse. A few more and Justin would have to dart back to the counter so he wouldn't be caught eavesdropping.

"Tempting, but I have new pieces from Justin to catalog and publish to sell."

"I saw a couple of them unloaded. They're in great shape. I can't believe he said he found them in another barn under a couple of tarps." She joined Dean at the new four-poster bed frame. "You would think there would be some warping and heat damage from being in a hot, humid environment for who knows how many years."

He ran his hand over the curvature of the bed posts. "I agree, these are exquisite."

"I'm tempted to use these in the master bedroom at the cottage." Shelby got a dreamy look on her face.

A smile Justin didn't like spread across Dean's face.

"So anyway, are you saying no?"

His smile disappeared. "Sorry, maybe some other time?"

"Yeah, sure. Don't put the bed frame or dresser on the site yet. I'm serious about purchasing them." She turned and strolled from the docks.

Justin kicked back with his feet up, waiting for her when she returned. "Dean going to join us?" It took everything in him to act surprised when she answered.

"Nope, he's working on the pieces you procured today. They are very nice, by the way." She snatched her purse from her office as she met him at the front door, using her key to latch it behind them.

Shelby smiled at Justin when he mentioned going to the local diner down the street and meeting him there. He didn't want to push her to ride with him; it could make it into something more than two co-workers going out for a bite after work.

He heard the music cranked up on a country song on the radio of her uncle's truck. She pulled onto the street, yanking on the wheel hand over hand to turn the stubborn steering wheel, and headed toward the diner behind him.

A dark shadow distracted him as he glanced back at Rupert's Relics. It quickly disappeared around the back. It matched Dean's height, or did the lights and angle distort the dimensions, making it appear taller than it was? Why would he be watching Shelby and Justin leave?

Shelby's silhouette bounced on the seat of Uncle Rupert's truck, the bumpy, rough suspension not as smooth as his newer truck. The insurance company had already totaled her car and was reassessing her claim when Justin showed her what she could get for a used one from online ads, adding a couple of thousand to her claim check.

Shelby slammed on the brakes as she used both hands at the same time to turn the wheel, her bumper almost kissing the car in the first space by the door. When she got out,

Shelby swung her leg back to kick the fender but apparently thought better of it before joining him.

Justin didn't rush to her. He didn't want to embarrass her with his concern that she almost crunched into another car.

Justin hooted across from Shelby as she told him about a time she wedged herself in a wardrobe. Her uncle heard her calling his name, but every time he got close, a customer came in and interrupted the search. He imagined Rupert rushing from furniture to furniture in a frenzied bid to find his niece.

"Did he panic? I can almost see him getting frantic with how much he obviously adored you. Having you there in the store but unable to find you. What happened?" Justin bent forward as his shoulders shook.

"After a couple of hours, I fell asleep, so I stopped calling out for him. He did panic, as you implied, and called the fire department after flipping the sign to closed so no one would interrupt his search. They had to use one of their thermal imaging devices on the antiques to search for a heat signature to tell which one I was in. He was mortified he had to call them, but when they told him how hot I was and partially dehydrated, he was relieved," Shelby reminisced.

Shelby's retelling of the story made him feel he was there, picturing the scene she described with such clarity, making it a great adventure.

She almost doubled over as she held her abdomen. He wished he had a place he grew up that held memories near and dear to his heart. She explained her parents would drop her off, promising to return in a month. Later in her teens, she figured out they called her uncle and confirmed everything was going all right, then extended their trip abroad. She never perceived it as any sort of abandonment by them. It only made her adventurous summers more exciting. She had such a great caring family who never let her doubt she meant the world to them. She said she had no doubt they would return immediately if she wanted them to. Justin's heart pulled at the childhood every kid dreamed of.

"How did your parents take it when they heard?"

"They took it pretty well and said Rupert did the right thing calling the fire department and they planned to bring me back next year. He was so scared they wouldn't let me stay with him anymore."

"You sound like you have great memories of your time with Rupert." Justin glanced over to see her eyes twinkling with something he couldn't quite identify, but it made his heart tick a little faster. She was a very beautiful woman. He wondered why she didn't have a boyfriend.

"I did. He loved me so much. It was like having a second father. Don't get me wrong, my dad is the best; I may be a little biased. But to have a second father figure was amazing. Every Sunday was a time to spend with our Savior, at the small church at the edge of town, and I cherished those moments more than any others spent with my uncle. I count myself blessed to have such a great family. There isn't a lot of us. My mother's family all live out of the country so they go visit often. Some summers, I tagged along, but others, especially when I got older, I stayed in Red Peaks and helped in the store."

"Sounds like a great childhood." His eyes drifted as a memory distracted him. "Where is your mother's family from?"

"Egypt. They travel there every summer and sometimes around the holidays. It's getting harder for them since they had me later in life, but they debated retiring there."

"Would they leave you, or would you go with them?" Justin emptied his glass and winked for the waitress to refill it.

"I'll stay here. I love my family, but this country is my home, and I love Red Peaks. I always knew I would end up here when I finished school, and it would be my forever home." Shelby smiled.

His plans evolved as he stared at Shelby. She called to him on a spiritual level, and his deep gut reaction stirred something he had never experienced before.

They swapped childhood stories and he was surprised as several people said hi as they passed, welcoming Shelby home to Red Peaks. She knew more people than he realized. Someone named Skye had a small child on her hip and gave Shelby a hug and then joined her husband at a booth in the back.

A guy at the counter yelled for them to turn the television up. It was a new edition for when Moe's was overcrowded during a sporting event; the overflow came to the diner.

"Today, we have learned that a federal agency is in the area working in conjunction with local authorities. They are refusing to make a statement, but inside sources hint at a possible serial killer targeting the elderly. With eleven mysterious deaths on their hands, local police are scrambling to get a handle on a possible suspect. While the federal agency has informed us they will make a statement soon, they are asking everyone to be vigilant and lock their doors. If you don't know someone, call the police and don't let them in. Suspicious activity is to be reported immediately. Again, take every precaution as the serial killer's number of victims will only grow as his reign of terror continues."

You could hear a mouse squeak all the way outside in the alley by the dumpster, it was so quiet. No one said anything and a couple of elderly folks paid their bill and rushed from the diner. Justin covered Shelby's trembling hand in silent support as she sat unmoving, knowing she was thinking about Rupert's Relics being at the center of the federal probe into the crimes.

A woman stopped by the table. "Oh Shelby, just look at you, deary. You grew into such a pretty woman. Rupert will be missed. I told Sam you should come over to dinner one day so we can catch up."

Justin remembered Shelby talking to a Sam in the store that first day.

"Sure thing. Let me get situated first, then I'll let you know." Shelby smiled.

***

Shelby returned Justin's quick hug as he left and made her way back to Skye and her family. Justin was great and easy to talk to. Even her ex-boyfriend couldn't hold a candle to Justin. It had been a long time since she hung out with someone where the conversation flowed with no awkward pauses.

Skye stood up as she approached. "Bout time I get to see your ugly mug."

Shelby cracked up as she hugged her friend. "Says the woman who should wear a bag over her head."

They had given each other a hard time since the first moment they met as teenagers. A boy was taunting and bullying Skye and called her ugly when Shelby jumped in, throwing her soda on him, telling him he should wear a bag over his head. He ran away crying. Of course, Uncle Rupert had scolded her for calling names and said there were better ways to handle it.

A week later, when he went on a grocery run, he came back and said how he had to stand up for an elderly male trying to cross the road, and the kid was making fun of how slow he moved. Rupert laid into the youth, telling him to find a better use of his time, then had a talk with his mom, who worked at the library. The kid never made fun of anyone again.

Now, every time Skye and Shelby saw each other, they greeted each other with the comments that initiated their best friend status decades earlier.

"You settling in okay?" Skye fed her son a french fry.

"Yes. I'll head out to the cottage soon and see what kind of mausoleum my uncle created out there. I'll give you the first shot at anything you guys may be interested in."

"Thanks, but with another one on the way, we are putting off buying anything for ourselves and concentrating on the next little nugget." Skye ran her hand over her still-flat belly.

"Congratulations!" Shelby slung her arm around Skye's shoulders.

"So, who was your hot date?" Skye winked at her.

"Not a date. Just an employee." Shelby felt the heat rise in her face.

"Riiight." Skye cackled when her husband snorted.

They talked for a few more minutes before Shelby excused herself and told Skye to stop by Rupert's someday and that she would see her a church. Shelby kissed Skye's son's head before leaving. She yearned to meet that someone and have a family of her own. All in God's timing.

"I heard Rupert was tangled up in the whole ugly trouble. That he was using his store for the killer to offload the merchandise and they were working together to make money. Isn't that what all people kill for nowadays? Money?" A brunette loudly whispered as Shelby started past their table.

Her friend shushed her as Shelby neared. The brunette gasped. "That is poor form for her to come here. Bet she took over for Rupert. I heard she's planning on buying a flashy new car. I find it curious she can afford something like that."

Shelby rapidly blinked while she rushed from the diner.

Ten

The hinges creaked and groaned a long, continuous tune as the maroon front door swung open, giving most horror movie sound effects a run for their money. Dust motes danced in the sunlight, streaming in, bombarding the dark and chasing away the shadows.

Shelby should have made a trip to her uncle's cottage sooner, but the unreliability of her uncle's truck and the possibility of it stranding her twenty minutes from the shop kept her from venturing farther than town.

She couldn't wait any longer to make the purchase, as her uncle's truck was a death trap. She hated to drive it even when it worked well enough to start. She would park it back in the space behind the store where her uncle left it the day he died.

Shelby shook her head and smiled as she remembered the sales rep's excited boasting about the roomy cargo area of her new tank of a sport utility. The salesman told her it was one of the best safety-rated vehicles on the road. She almost asked him how it rated against trees splintered by lightning but stopped herself before uttering the words.

She was in a holding pattern until the FBI emailed her their list of demands involving Rupert's Relics. So she thought a trip to the house a week after having dinner with Justin would help distract her overactive imagination about the case.

The musty smell made her insides churn. She yanked open curtains and lifted window sashes to air out the place.

Temperatures forecasted to reach the mid-fifties today, so with the work she planned, it wouldn't freeze her out completely. Once she started sweating, it would be amazing. It was one of the many reasons she preferred living so close to the mountains. She saw God in every aspect of nature and loved his creations, from the varying plant life to the tiniest of animals and birds in differing varieties.

One of the first things she would replace was the sun-faded threadbare curtains. The original color at the uppermost section, where the curtain rod fed through the gathered seams, was ten shades darker than the green fabric where the sun bleached out the material. She cringed at the early seventies style with elevated jacquard flower and leaf patterns throughout.

Taking in the room, she had imagined clutter strung from one end to the other, given how much Uncle Rupert said he stored in the house. As she made her way to the back, she opened all the windows to try and muster a cross breeze to help air out the stuffy odor from being closed up the last few weeks.

The cottage would not be what someone would describe as quaint. Enormous monstrosity—was one descriptor a friend of her uncle's had given it. As you entered the foyer, a large, great room with vaulted ceilings sat directly in front of you. To the left sat the master bedroom with a walk-in closet and bathroom outfitted with matching his-and-her vanities facing each other in the middle of the room and a clawfoot tub beyond those. Two double doors opened from the great room to a covered patio with a lanai layout and a built-in stone fireplace. Next came the dining room across from the kitchen, which sat to the right of the foyer.

She knew a basement existed under her but had yet to venture there in all the years her uncle owned the place. He told her he used it for storage, and he didn't want to take the gamble of one of his towering stacks of junk falling on her and squishing her beneath its weight.

As she traveled farther back in the hallway, where the light didn't shine, she had to feel her way down, to expose more rooms. The shades were closed in each of them, offering a soft glow around the shape of the windows but nothing more.

The further she got, the more crowded it became. There were three doors on one side and two on the other. She had the luxury of a bedroom with an en-suite private bathroom and an enclosed patio beside a grilling station.

A third held a bed. Previously a bunk bed, crudely sawed off with uneven posts, showing the unstained wood on the tops. And by the blankets mussed around, her uncle had probably slept there instead of in the master bedroom on the opposite end of the house. There sat three desks, including one rolltop and a huge colonial kneehole bowfront desk with simple, sharp lines. She would love to have the latter in her office instead of the industrial metal one there now. She could ask Dean and Justin to bring it over one day. Or at least have Dean contact their shipping company for the short delivery trip.

One small, slender door with narrow built-in shelves hinted at a linen closet, while the other led to a restroom, the bedroom with the mangled bunk bed, a fourth bedroom, and last but not least, a study with bookshelves lining three of the walls. Taking in the small bedrooms next to each other, Shelby wondered if she should turn the bathroom into a walk-in closet instead of the slim design of the one with pocket doors since a washroom lay across the way. The laundry room rounded out the accommodations on this side with a mudroom leading to the three-stall garage.

Shelby perused the bookshelf blocking the wall at the end. It was littered with great classics in leather bindings she always wanted to read but never took the time to. Once she had her life back on track, she'd start from her most anticipated to her least and work her way through them.

When she turned toward the kitchen, her shoe snagged on a nail, and she fell when she tried to untangle the sole from the rusty protrusion. She put her hands back, catching the edge of a bookcase to lessen her tumble, when a click sounded.

She kept herself mostly upright but noticed a gap between the shelves and the wall when she shuffled away from the bookcase. Bracing her feet shoulder-width apart, she pulled one of the ledges. A slight movement spurned wild ideas into all sorts of bizarre scenarios.

Her heart raced. What had Uncle Rupert done to the house? She pulled again, and it moved even further away from the wall. She jogged out to her car and returned with the penlight from the glovebox she kept there for emergencies. The beam of light exposed a three-inch gap. A covered compartment?

She gripped the light between her teeth and pulled back again, straining her physical limits. Her feet stumbled when the bookcase swung free of the wall, taking a small door with it and opening it into another chamber—so much bigger than her flashlight illuminated.

Shelby wiped her sweaty hands on the torn junk jeans she wore and felt around the wall inside for a light switch, hoping a spider hadn't woven a web over it. A yelp of glee escaped as light bathed the section. She gasped. Rows of antiques—not just by the entry, overflowed the space. What had her uncle been up to?

Her whistle echoed in the room as she stooped into a house of wonders. Dressers, beds, curio cabinets, and more crammed into this tiny room put the warehouse behind the store to shame. She ran her hand over several pieces. There was no dust to leave demarcations in as she swiped across moving blankets held in place with bungee cords. The legs of the furniture garishly peeked out from the bottom. He took better care of these relics than the rest of the cottage.

The large moving blankets obscured the differently sized shapes, so she wasn't sure how to proceed. Did Dean or Justin know about this? When she visited last, her uncle described Dean as a friend. Did he confide in him? Why wouldn't he mention this in the letter? Would any of them be on the FBI's list?

A stack of stunning quilts draped over a dresser. Hand-stitched intricate designs made the vibrant fabric colors even more breathtaking. Shelby would keep them to use around the house. A thud made her jump. She quickly secured the secret entrance and made her way to the front.

Edges of the curtains flapped from side to side. A book lay on the floor with the cover creased halfway under as the crinkling of the pages slapped back and forth below the only light in the front room. A metal, intricately carved floor lamp with a stained-glass shade in a fruit and leaf pattern, was plugged in by an armchair. Was that what made the noise? Had the book dislodged from the arm of the chair by the breeze? Shelby shook her head and didn't hear anything else, so she started what she came out to do: clean the house. She initially ordered a mattress with the store's address, but luckily, the back-ordered status meant the ability to modify the shipping to the cottage.

Justin would get a kick out of the riches she found, but then her breath hitched at the thought of sharing with anyone. She wanted to keep it hush-hush for a while longer. Were these connected to the investigation? Something nagged her in the back of her mind to not tell Dean or Justin. It wasn't as if she maliciously kept anything to herself, but what if it put her uncle in a bad light with the FBI? She couldn't risk one of them letting it slip before she was mentally prepared to face doubts about her uncle's integrity.

Rupert's faith and testament as a Christian to live a life for Jesus wouldn't deter someone from believing the worst in him.

She didn't distrust Justin and Dean, but until she knew them better, she'd keep this little morsel to herself. It reminded her of being a kid, ready for a great adventure.

Several hours later, the living room looked homey again. She decided to move all the bulky items she wasn't a fan of to the dining room; they would make a great sale for the store. Then, everything would be in the same place when the shippers came to pick it up, with no hesitation about what went or what stayed. The living room looked so much roomier with half the stuff removed.

One big difference between her and her uncle was related to their favorite styles and decor. Uncle Rupert preferred classic, overstated, lavish designs, while she preferred nice, clean lines and simple elegance. Shelby brushed her hands on her jeans, amused at the amount of dirt she wore on her clothes. She shook her head and walked the perimeter, double-checking all the windows and pulling the curtains in place. She didn't need someone traipsing around, peeping in, and spotting an item that tempted them to steal.

She pulled the door behind her, and a little niggle in her memory popped as she took in the wilted flowerbed and reminded her, her uncle hid a spare key at one point. Her days were nonstop since coming to Red Peaks. She vetoed leaving it out for someone to come and help themselves to what her uncle owned.

She lifted three different flowerpots and found nothing. Kicking at the rocks decorating the front flower beds, she whimpered when she got a little enthusiastic with one. Her toe throbbed as she hopped around in a circle, biting her tongue. Her ankle rolled as she lost her footing and knocked loose a rock. It fell into two pieces, exposing the immaculate inside to the mud and elements.

"Uncle Rupert, what did you do with the spare?" Shelby rubbed her hands under the spigot after dropping the mud-encrusted rock to clean off most of the dirt before climbing behind the wheel to go back to the apartment.

She made a mental note as she drove to replace all the locks before she'd spent the night there. The image of a silhouette of a man standing over her bed while she slept sent shivers through her. Did the person who broke into Rupert's come out here and take the key? She hadn't noticed anything to suggest someone had torn through the house. Even with all the hoarded pieces, nothing looked out of place or missing. She had no way of knowing if her uncle had more unaccounted-for items.

Sitting in front of the TV, she finished toweling her hair dry and slumped back, letting her damp hair rest on the back of the sofa. She needed to sleep, but she was too wired. Why did Uncle Rupert bury so many treasures in a secluded room? Was the room already there when he moved in? Or was it added on after the fact? His letter didn't tip her off to what he'd done. What was the significance of separating those from everything in the store and cottage?

She couldn't wait for her mother to call. Shelby sent a text asking to speak with her since they were back from their eight-day sea excursion down the Nile a week ago. Did Uncle Rupert confide in his only sibling about the inner workings of Red Peaks' crisis? Delving into the underbelly of a ruthless serial killer? She hadn't told her about the FBI wanting to investigate the store. What would her mother think? She'd been in town less than a month and already embroiled in problems that would make most attention seekers balk. Ha, problems. What a ridiculously inappropriate word for the mess she found herself in. Talk about an understatement.

Would she change her mind about her ability in Shelby to take on the store alone? The thought of them stepping in dimmed her excitement about sharing her find. With her parents having her later in life, they sometimes forgot she was an adult and wanted to still coddle her.

No, it would be better if she kept everything to herself.

When she received the list from the feds, she would compare it to everything in the room. This also created another issue. What if these were what they sought? Would it implicate her uncle in crimes she knew he had nothing to do with? Did she take the risk and sully his name?

She rejected the idea of being the one to tear apart everything he worked so hard to achieve. She would conduct her own reconnaissance and then hire a lawyer if her case was serious enough to shut down the store.

Uncle Rupert wasn't considered elderly, but what if his death wasn't a health emergency? Was he a victim of the serial killer? Shelby couldn't breathe. Her hands started to shake. There would be more than one research she would be running. How hard would it be to obtain a copy of the death certificate and autopsy report? They reported all the victims perished by strangulation, and Uncle Rupert died of a heart attack. It gave her a little comfort he hadn't fallen prey to a psychotic hunter.

Hiring a lawyer seemed like the best option for handling all the red tape. Either way, nothing would stop her from discovering the truth on her own or with the agents' help.

Eleven

"Come on, gorgeous, let's go out tonight. We never officially celebrated you moving to town. It's already been a month. It'll be fun. The meal before doesn't count. Yo Dean, come join us tonight to make it officially her welcoming feast." Justin practically jumped around in front of her.

Dean stepped through the doorway from the loading dock. He had just arrived after being gone all afternoon, overseeing a few small deliveries personally. He didn't know how someone had so much pent-up energy at the end of a long day.

Shelby pinched her nose. "Oh, alright. A small celebration would be great, but nothing crazy. I don't usually drink if I'll be driving, nor do I like big crowds."

"Dean, you in?" Justin slid his arms into his coat and then held out Shelby's for her to do the same.

"I can make it work." He narrowed his eyes at Shelby.

He had distanced himself since the cemetery incident. It would have been better if it had never happened, but there was nothing he could do about it now. He couldn't take the chance she died. Rupert's needed to be open or it would ruin his plans. He wished she hadn't seen that side of him. At least not yet. He saw her confusion every time he was terse or walked away. There was so much going on that he didn't want to drag her into it. Labeled as unapproachable was better than her left twisted in the danger that lurked in the town.

When he started working with Rupert, he heard amazing stories about her. After a short time working side by side, the older man had wormed his way into Dean's heart. He didn't like her getting chummy with Justin. It put a kink in his plans if he had to navigate through some newfound relationship goo-goo eyes between the two.

Admitting Rupert got to him only made his tasks harder. He wasn't used to making true friends and moved around a lot, so he preferred to keep all acquaintances superficial to avoid attitudes when he moved on to the next great adventure with little to no warning.

Dean had become a pro at keeping people at arm's length but couldn't deny he wanted to know Rupert's niece better. Shelby was like a breath of fresh air. He would move on soon enough, keeping his fences up and ready to leave town as soon as he finished. He hoped it was before there was permanent damage to Rupert's Relics reputation, or Shelby would lose everything.

Justin's enthusiasm was contagious. Shelby easily latched on to it and let it influence her when Justin wanted to do something. For example, tonight, Dean would rather address a detrimental situation discreetly without witnesses than go out and be awkward when he had to carry part of the conversation.

Dean shouldn't expose them to his social ineptitude. He put on a mask because he was a master at projecting a façade to shroud his true nature. Some had called him a master manipulator. It had kept him alive when his life depended on it.

Justin held the door for them and took care of the deadbolt behind him.

"One car or separately?" Justin slung his arm over Shelby's shoulders.

She slowly untangled herself. "Separate cars in case one of us has to duck out early."

"Got it. Let's go to Moe's; they have happy hour." Justin didn't wait for the other two to agree and pulled out of the parking lot, leaving them standing in the dust kicked up by the tires.

Shelby blushed and met Dean's gaze. "I guess Moe's. Can I follow you? I'm not sure where it is."

Dean nodded and waited for her to pull up behind him before he turned left and led her to the restaurant-slash-bar. He regretted saying he would join them but didn't want to make himself stand out more than he already did. Staying under the radar and blending into the background saved his life on more than one occasion.

With her uncle out of the way, he didn't have to worry about what he was up to at the store and moved around more freely, staying out of sight in the back. If he played his cards right, he would be long gone before she figured out his true identity.

Continuing his distance when his attraction only grew stronger every day made him lose his mind.

***

Shelby was shocked when Dean joined them. He seemed not quite shy or standoffish but more like an intense introvert.

He'd never been rude to her but didn't go out of his way to talk to her or Justin.

Shelby scanned the parking lot, looking for a space. She could see Justin's car in the front spot, and she snorted. "Of course."

Dean motioned to her that the lot was full. He pulled down an alley but pointed to a street a block over with a parallel parking spot between two cars. This would test her new car's ability to park itself. She held her breath as the wheel spun freely from her hands. She cringed as the beeps alerting her to the danger of an obstacle went to a solid tone. Her bumper never kissed the other car, and soon, she stood outside looking at the perfectly parked vehicle.

"Shelby!" a woman screamed across the street.

Dean lingered at the entrance of Moe's.

"Skye?" Shelby hadn't found time to have lunch with Skye since her son came down with the flu and passed it on to her.

She jogged across the road to Shelby and almost knocked her over. "Seriously, we need to have lunch soon."

"Says the woman who was puking her guts up last week."

"I know, and now I'm on my way home to the hubby and kid." Skye glanced at Dean.

"My employees are taking me out to welcome me to town, so I need to go, too. I'll text you, and we can coordinate times around your son's after-school activities." Shelby gave her a quick hug.

"Oh, employees? Like that guy you were with at the diner?" Skye teased.

"Don't start." Shelby cringed and hoped neither Dean nor Justin heard her.

She hadn't even stepped inside, and already she wasn't a fan of the crowded, popular hangout. The scents were rich with hearty-smelling food. Her mouth watered as they took their seats and decided what to order.

"Did Dean tell you about the time a lady all but threw herself at him, and he had to excuse himself from the floor, declaring a shipment that was due to be picked up so he had a reason to detangle himself from her vampire-red claws?" Justin told story after story since they sat.

Most of them entailed embarrassing Dean. She felt terrible for him.

"Rupert would have skinned us alive if either one of us dated her. One of his policies was no one dates customers." Dean tipped his water glass toward Justin. "Not my type anyway."

"Not your type? Are you not a warm-blooded American? She was prime pickings for the small town we live in." Justin drained the last of his beer, slammed his glass on the table, and beckoned for another one from the cute waitress who had been waiting on them all night.

She would earn herself a good tip with how much Justin had her running in every which direction. Shelby didn't comment on his drinking since it was supposed to be a special occasion in her honor. He was an adult, and it was his life to live. He pushed her to try one of the red wines he stated would pair perfectly with her meal. He had been right. It was a delicious, sweet wine, but she didn't finish the still half-filled goblet in front of her.

"So, Shelby. Do you have a boyfriend back home who will be moving here?" Justin braced his arms on the table, giving her all his attention.

"I don't..."

Justin wiggled his finger back and forth. "Nope."

"Nope?" Shelby looked to Dean for guidance. He only shrugged.

"You are not our boss. Once we are out of the office, you become a friend. And friends talk about personal aspects of their lives. Therefore, I deem this a conversation amongst friends hanging out after work. So, spill."

"No boyfriend for a few years. I finished my last class for my degree early and had a full-time job, so I didn't date someone I couldn't devote my time to. It's not fair to ask someone to put me first but not be able to do the same for them. When you're in a relationship, that person should be a priority, and if you can't devote the best of yourself to someone, then it's not only a waste of your time but also theirs." Shelby hadn't meant to word vomit, but when Dean gave a slight nod, her embarrassment diminished that her mouth ran away from her.

"Speaking of dating, either of you seeing someone?"

"Naw, it's nothing like the reason you said. It's just around here; there aren't many to choose from." Justin tipped back and winked at her.

Three people gathered near their table as they waited for the waitress to clean the booth they wanted to sit at. "Did you see the news? The killer struck again today. Said they are no closer to identifying him than they were last month. Isn't that the owner of that store they say is involved?"

No one said anything for a few moments. They absorbed the information the killer took another life. They moved off to their seats when the waitress got their attention when they stared at Shelby. She wasn't sure why they couldn't catch them. She thought the FBI should have a clue by now. They were all together today working, so hopefully, that would ease the agent's minds that Rupert's Relics was involved. Wait, Dean was gone for most of the afternoon. But wouldn't the delivery slips he put on her desk confirm where he'd been?

"Dean, what about you?" Shelby wondered if Mr. Tall, Dark, and Mysterious had a Miss he was interested in. Why did her heart clench at that thought when, two seconds ago, his alibi for the last murder was on her mind?

"I don't have the time to tie myself down to someone." He glanced at his watch. "I have to go. There's a shipment going out in the morning I have to be up and at the store for. Are you guys good to get home?"

Shelby glanced at her wine glass. The burgundy liquid settled in the lower half, and then she looked at Justin's plethora of beer mugs.

"I live down the street, so I'll walk back in the morning to pick up my car. Jack always lets me leave it if I need to. It's all good, brother." Justin smirked when he smiled at the waitress yet again.

Dean frowned. "You sure you're good?"

Shelby half smiled when the waitress flirted with Justin, diverting his attention. "Yes."

"See you two later." Dean gave a two-finger salute, then stalked out into the night.

"The man is an enigma." Justin shook his head.

Shelby positioned her elbows on the table and her chin on her folded hands. "What do you mean?"

"I've been with the store for over six months. Dean's phone has been attached to his ear so much lately; all he does is stand by the docks and yammer on about who knows what. Watching the trucks come and go as if it were his personal belongings in them. I know he probably has some tail somewhere, yet I never see him with anyone. Tonight, he said he didn't date or have a significant other. Then who does that man talk to? We all know no grown man talks to his mommy for hours on end. And where was he this afternoon while we were working, when the killer attacked again?" Justin slanted away while the waitress cleared their plates and empty dishes.

"Maybe he doesn't mix business with pleasure. A lot of people at my last job never discussed their significant others at the office. I think it's good practice. It doesn't blur the lines and make uncomfortable moments where you work." Shelby wanted to know more about her employees but to keep her mindset that she was the boss. She was definitely not entertaining the thought one of her employees may be a suspect.

Justin harrumphed and then tipped back on two legs of the chair. "So, how are you liking Red Peaks so far? Kinda small town for a city gal."

She laughed. "You forget I spent almost every summer here growing up. I love it, and a small town is perfect for me. Uncle Rupert would always make it an adventure when I visited. He would tell me about far-off places each piece came from with crazy tails of pirates, princesses, and scoundrels. Oh, I figured out he made them up after I reached a certain age, but it never got old hearing them. Those are my favorite memories I have with him."

"No kidding? That's kind of cool, actually." Justin stared out the window briefly before dropping his chair back onto all four legs. "So, Princess Shelby, would you care to join me one night, just the two of us?"

"I'm still on shaky ground with the drastic change my life took over the last month," Shelby rushed out.

"I hear ya. Rupert was a friend in the short time I knew him, and I hope he knows I would help his niece in any way I can." Justin twined his fingers with hers and gave her a quick squeeze before releasing her.

"Justin, I'm not sure if it's a good idea to date someone I work with. It can lead to wounded emotions and heartache. I don't want to be the cause or the recipient while I'm still adjusting to my uncle being gone and getting my legs under me by taking over Rupert's Relics." Shelby's voice was strained.

"You're thinking too hard. Friendships or something more isn't supposed to be this much work." Justin swung their hands left and right, shaking the tension out of her arm.

"Then there's the FBI. If I throw anything else into the mix, I don't think I could keep my head above water, so to speak. I feel like I'm drowning." Her fingernails dug into the palm of her other hand.

"Between you and me, I have some *experience*, so to speak, and an inside track in dealing with police, authorities, and the courts. The open case is nothing you need to stress about. It will all work out; trust me. I expect a call if you need anything. I don't care if it's carrying in supplies. Don't feel like you have to take everything on by yourself."

Shelby squeezed his hand. It felt good to have someone in her corner. "I appreciate that. I'm not the best at asking for help."

"Is anyone?" Justin tossed the napkin draped over his leg on the table. "Let's get out of here. I'm gonna go crash so I can be at work on time. I hear my new boss is a stickler." He joked as he slung his arm around her.

They had taken care of the tab several minutes earlier, before Dean left.

"Wow, she sounds like a horrible boss expecting employees to be responsible adults and take their jobs seriously to earn their paycheck." Shelby cracked up when Justin clutched at his heart and acted like he stumbled to the side, wiping non-existent tears from his face.

"See ya, boss lady. Princess Shelby, when you have your head above water and not just bobbing against the current, I'll be here. You're worth the wait." Justin bowed and winked at her as he sauntered down the road. She walked around the corner, pausing by a dark alley with a flickering light bulb affixed above a steel door, on her way to her car.

She was rooted in place, unable to get her legs to obey her. No man had ever said such sweet words that stole her breath.

She hadn't realized how late it was, and the broken streetlights at the corner where she parked obscured her car and everything around it.

A whispered swish of fabric caused her to speed up her stride. She wished Justin had offered to escort her to her ride. It would have been the perfect opportunity to test her reliance on others.

A cat meowed somewhere behind the building before a second one joined in. The yowling drowned out everything else. Shelby quickened her steps. A tin can rolled along the gutter, adding to the symphony playing its lonely tune. Not another soul was in sight.

Shelby fumbled with the fob before remembering she didn't need to press the unlock button; it would sense her closeness and open independently. She wasn't accustomed to all the new computerized options on her vehicle. She climbed in and held down the engine ignition button until it roared to life, giving her a sense of security.

A tall silhouette slunk behind the corner of the restaurant they'd left. The person's manner of carrying themselves was familiar, but she couldn't quite place who it reminded her of. She shook her head and reversed to angle out of the parallel parking spot she'd had difficulty finding when she arrived.

The galloping rhythm of her heart slowed the farther she got from town. Rupert's Relics loomed in the distance. She never understood why her uncle chose a location on the outskirts to open his store. An address on the main drag would have pulled in tourists who visited the small touristy town during the peak seasons. As she unlocked the door and stumbled inside, she rearmed the security app as a dark truck slowed out front.

Shelby took cover behind a post, blocking the driver's view of her. They drove slow enough to be considered parked. The headlights blinked out, leaving on the yellow-tinted parking bulbs. They cast a haunting glow to the surroundings. Low-hanging branches swayed and reached from their massive trunks, gripping nothing before the wind blew them in the other direction.

A couple of agonizing minutes ticked by before the headlights illuminated the road again, and the engine roared as they charged around the curve and out of sight.

Her imagination ran wild with scenarios of spooky figures chasing her, with elongated arms reaching out to snag her clothes and hair. It was precisely why she hated scary movies. She turned on every light to chase away the boogeyman. Morning would come soon enough, and with it, the bright sun would lure her into a false safety, hiding the frightening illusions.

Twelve

Shelby dodged around her car as she dropped off a package at the post office for a customer who purchased a glass doorknob that needed to ship out the next morning. The bins were around the back, but the gate was halfway closed, so she had to get out to slip it in the drop box. She couldn't pass up on a piece of pie to go from the diner. It had been a month since they ate at Moe's, and she would rather cook at home than spend money on frequently eating out.

A cute elderly man, whom she recognized as Mr. Stein, Uncle Rupert's neighbor out at the cottage, waved as he walked into the library. She turned to head to her vehicle.

Dean? Shelby would recognize him anywhere. He was not tiny, so blending in with his height was impossible—at least not in Red Peaks. He darted his head in several directions before he slunk down an alley. She dropped the piece of pie on the driver's seat and locked the car.

Her feet clomped on the historic brick-paved street as she tried to keep her shoes quiet. She thought he had gone home after he left work, but he lurked around downtown. Shelby had been late getting back, but Justin offered to stay while Dean left an hour early for a personal reason while she waited for a late delivery at the post office.

Dean spoke with a man wearing a dark shirt over light-colored jeans. The two of them exchanged several unknown items. She progressed forward, staying in the shadows. They spoke in hushed tones, and she couldn't make out their words, only the hum of their low voices. Chills broke out up and down her arms when the conversation turned heated. The night shaded the sharp contours of the other man's face, giving him a menacing vibe. The profile of the sharp crook of his nose seemed too large for his face.

Shelby inched forward, skirting around the next trash can, almost losing her footing. She stumbled to the brick façade of the building she stood next to. Holding her breath, she blinked her eyes to see if they detected her failure at being stealthy. Her hands shook with adrenaline as she took three more steps forward.

"She's a trusting person," Dean hissed.

"Yeah, but it's only a matter of time; you're taking too many risks! With the body found today, how long will it be before she looks at you?" the other man snarled.

Dean fisted his hands at his side. "I refuse to leave; this is where I can do the most damage. We have too much at stake to stop now. I will not give up, especially since we are so close. Neither one has a clue. If you try to replace me, it will demolish everything I've accomplished."

She inched forward, scarcely concealed by the next doorway, which jutted from the wall. Her shoe collided with a brown glass bottle, sending it skittering from the dark shadows, ringing out in the tranquil night. Shelby gasped and ducked down, balancing on the balls of her feet behind a rotten, smelly trash container.

Stomping feet led to her hiding spot. She squinted. Dean wrapped his fingers around her bicep as she lost her footing backpedaling after he pulled her to a standing position.

"Shelby, I can see you!" Dean's red face was inches from hers. The engorged vein in his temple pulsed.

He yanked her toward the main street, steadying her at the same time. "Are you following me?"

She tried to wrench her arm free and put her left hand against his chest, pushing against him. "What? No!"

"How much did you hear?" Dean's harsh whisper was hardly audible as he looked around.

If only she had heard something more, she wouldn't be so confused about his anger. Or the unease slithering down her at the fact he hid a terrible mystery and the conversation about another body, which hadn't made the news.

He caged her against the brick building behind her as someone passed on the street. He put his elbows on either side of her head, blocking the person's view of her, and lowered his voice. "How much, Shelby? Did anyone see you come back here?"

The gentle way he protected her head from the brick was in direct contrast to the venom she saw in his eyes before he marched her away from his meeting.

"Nothing!" Her voice wobbled.

"Don't lie to me! I need to know so I can do damage control." He studied her, breathing heavily. He swept a stray hair from her forehead.

His shortness of breath wasn't from being out of shape because she'd seen the size of the antiques he was able to move. So, was it from an adrenaline rush? He lowered his eyelids and touched his forehead against hers. His lips scarcely grazed hers. She wasn't even sure it happened.

"Come on." Dean stopped them inside the alley's shadows, not stepping into the light and into her freedom.

Shelby yanked back on her arm, freeing it from his grip. "Let me go!"

His dark blue eyes pierced hers for several seconds. Shelby couldn't look away and squirmed under his penetrating gaze. "Leave this alone; there are some things I can't tell you. Don't tell anyone what you saw or heard. I can't protect you if you poke around in things you have no business in. Shel, I'd never forgive myself if something happened to you."

The pleading in his voice was something she wasn't prepared for. She nodded and would have stumbled if he hadn't clutched her elbow.

By the time she looked back, he was gone. Her eyes filled as she blinked to clear them. What happened? He had always been subdued and somewhat unsociable at work, but this was beyond his normal brooding behavior. Was he immersed in something dangerous? Who was the guy? His pleading to have her be discreet sank in. This better not turn around and bite her later on.

She absently rubbed her upper arm and grimaced when her fingers brushed the bruised tissue. She rolled her eyes and hiked back to her car.

Thirteen

The following day, Shelby ran a few errands, still unable to erase the anger in Dean's grip and words. What did he mean, do the most damage? Ominous and somewhat distressing. Yet he kissed her. He was the most confusing person she had ever met. The news announced the body he spoke of. It was found an hour before Dean left, clearing him in her mind of doing the deed.

She headed to the shop after grabbing what she needed at the hardware and craft store, waving at Skye as she raised the blinds on the front windows of her salon.

Justin waited as she opened the hatch of her small SUV to help her with her purchases. She wanted a special memorial sale in honor of her uncle on what would have been his next birthday. She went into town to pick up decorations and new sale signs to upgrade his old paper cards. He thought they were so hip back in the day, being printed on cream-colored paper from the first printer he bought when his business was doing well.

She found brown watercolor paper and old-fashioned brass cardholders to complement the ledges housing their smaller items.

"Hey!" Justin tore the bags from her hands. "What happened?"

Shelby tried to pry his fingers from her arm, which he gently held. He rotated it in several different directions to inspect the finger-shaped red marks that were already starting to bruise. "Nothing."

"Don't tell me nothing!" Justin scolded.

The back door to the shop opened, and she heard Dean rummaging nearby. Justin already didn't like him, so there was no way she could tell him. She didn't go out of her way to protect Dean, but she gave her word she would keep quiet about it. No one was getting hurt by staying silent, so she would honor her promise for now.

Dean leaned against the doorframe and watched Justin holding her arm. "What's up?"

"Look what someone did to her! You can see finger and thumb-shaped bruises! They weren't there yesterday. So, it happened between when we left and now. I demand to know who did this to her!" Justin glowered.

Dean shoved off and approached, his eyes widening. Did guilt mar his features? She cringed and tried to jerk her arm away when his fingers grazed the bruises.

She knew his muttered "sorry" was for more than a repentant utterance; it was heartfelt.

"It's okay. I'll heal."

"I want to know who did this!" Justin ranted.

"Justin, stop; it was an accident. It won't happen again. I bruise easily, so they probably didn't realize how a normal grip would do something like this." She never looked away from Dean. She wanted him to know she knew he didn't mean to bruise her. It didn't mean she trusted him. The meeting was odd, but people were allowed their privacy.

"You know who did it?" Justin fumed. "Dean and I can go have a chat with the person. Teach them this isn't how you treat women. Boyfriends should treat their girlfriends as if they were the most precious gift."

Shelby shivered as Justin's fingers lightly grazed up and down her arm. Her heart warmed at the concern and anger he portrayed for her. She twined their fingers together. "Justin, no boyfriend to speak of, remember, so leave it. If a man in my life did something like this, there would only be a second chance once, depending on the circumstances. Otherwise, he would be punted to the curb with an assault charge on his name."

With that, she turned, laced her fingers through the loops of the shopping bags, and strolled to the office, her head a chaotic mess. Justin seemed genuine about how much he cared for her. The attentiveness he showered her with made her feel special.

Shelby spotted a coffee from the shop in town. She smiled when she saw the smiley face drawn on the side and Justin's name. She shook her head and emptied the contents of her shopping bags on the desk after shoving her organizers to the side. She forced away all thoughts of the two men she worked with and got busy organizing the labels, excited about how great they would look.

A few hours later, she realized she hadn't heard a peep from Dean or Justin. It was just as well since she was distracted by her project. Standing back, she surveyed the new signage and quickly loaded them up in the bags to carry them to the front of the store.

She swapped the old for the new, and it took several long moments before everything was exchanged. A smile quirked up at the corner of her mouth. Every display now had an attractive watercolor paper sign in light tans to brown hues, giving it a classic look. She burned the edges, before putting them in the holders, so it added to the vintage style. She was always praised for her artistic calligraphy penmanship. She didn't know where she got the talent for scriptwriting, but she picked up a pen one day and, with a little practice, detailed such beautiful letters that people believed she printed them on a machine.

Shelby stood back and surveyed her work, a bright smile on her face. They turned out better than she expected.

"Wow, those look great." Justin approached her, glaring at the bruised skin before he flung his arm around her.

"They do, don't they?" Dean didn't join the two of them, but when the back door latched, she assumed he left.

"Shelby, I wish you would tell me who did this to you. You should file a police report for assault. If you let them get away with it, they will only think they can continue to harm people. I hate that you were hurt," Justin said, goading her.

Shelby dipped under his arm and turned on him. "Justin, it was nothing. I didn't even feel it. If I thought the person did it intentionally, I would be the first one to notify the police. Trust me, in all honesty, I'm not concerned. Go home."

"Shelby, I won't leave it alone; I hate the idea of someone hurting you. I like you and want to protect you. Is it wrong to want to take care of someone who means a lot to me?" Justin followed her to the office.

Shelby breathed, "I like you too. I'm not ready to take it further. Oh, thank you for my drink earlier."

"You're welcome, babe." His hands landed on her hips as he lay his chin against her shoulder. She cleared her desk from the paper debris from her earlier crafty escapade and shuffled through the paperwork she hadn't filed yet. "Come on, give us a shot."

"Can I think about it?" Shelby knew she would always wonder if she didn't try.

Justin's hands disappeared. "Really?"

She spun around. "Give me some time."

He mock-pouted, making her laugh. He tucked a piece of hair behind her ear and let his hand linger on her face.

"Go home. I'm done for the day, so I'm closing the shop."

Justin snapped his heels together and gave a sloppy salute. He ducked his head and kissed her cheek before hurrying out of the store.

Shelby chuckled as she watched him jog to his black truck with oversized tires and leave the parking lot. A few minutes spent in her office would make a world of difference.

Fourteen

Shelby looked tired. He still wanted to know who bruised her, but she was tight-lipped about the whole ordeal. A sickly yellowish-green tint left a faint shadow of what it had been since the event four days before. If he got her out somewhere and plied her with a couple of drinks and slowly broached the subject, she might let something slip.

"Yo, Shelby." He tapped his knuckles against the wood doorframe of her office.

"Yeah, what did you need?" She didn't look up from her monitor.

"Want to grab something tonight? You've been working too hard."

She slowly raised her head. "Justin, I'm not sure it would be a good idea."

"Are you saying *friends* never eat or hang out?" Justin plopped into the chair across from her.

"Well, they do, but..."

"Good. Since we're *friends* building a new relationship, I think we should have dinner every so often."

"I have a lot of work to do. Uncle Rupert wasn't the best filer. This place is a zoo, and the new scanner came in, and I wanted to get everything uploaded to the cloud so I can store these paper files in the basement." Shelby was cute when she rambled.

Justin held up his hands. "Say no more. I know what to do."

He darted out of her office before she asked what he was up to. He ordered a pizza. Friends ate pizza together all the time. It was probably the easiest food delivery, confirming his intent to keep them in the friend zone. Her promise to think about them moving to the next level bolstered his confidence.

Shelby muttered as she wrestled with the plugs, trying to hook up her new contraption to scan the documents.

"Need a sledgehammer to demonstrate who's boss?" Justin grinned when she squealed and jerked around, making herself almost trip over the cords that were now in a jumbled mess around her.

She turned red and shook the plugs in his face. "Justin, don't make me hurt you. Don't sneak up on me!"

He was unsure if it was because she was embarrassed for squeaking like a mouse or because she was mad. He hoped it wasn't the latter.

"I come bearing gifts." He held the cardboard box on the palm of his hand as if he were a waiter with a tray of food.

She smiled as she ditched the last cord in her hand. "My hero! I'm starved."

"Figured food at work makes it a business meal where we discuss the riveting balance of paperwork versus the spark option." Justin dropped the box on the filing cabinet by the door and pulled paper plates and napkins from behind his back.

"Spark?" Shelby perked up and wrinkled her nose.

"Yes, it's quite ingenious. You establish which files are irrelevant and put them in a pile. You keep adding to the waste until everything is cleaned off your desk. Then you add the spark factor." Justin smirked as she leaned in, enraptured by his description.

"What is this spark you mentioned twice now?"

"Like from a match and make a large bonfire out of the headache sitting in front of you." Justin howled as she threatened to throw a stapler at him.

"We are not burning anything! There are sodas in the fridge behind you," Shelby pointed over his shoulder.

"No way, you got a fridge? Rupert never had one. I'm moving in."

Shelby snickered as she took a large bite. The cheese strung from the piece of pizza to her mouth, and she had to use two fingers to tear it off to keep it from stringing further. With a full mouth, she mumbled, and her eyes almost rolled into the back of her head. "Thiff is soooo good."

Justin puffed his chest. "Glad I fed you. You're scary when you haven't eaten in a while."

"I am not!"

"Yeah, okay," Justin glimpsed Dean's shadow before he appeared in the doorway.

He only lifted a brow to Justin.

"You want a slice? And please back me up on this; she's a bear when she hasn't eaten in a while." Justin inhaled half of the next piece of pizza in a single bite, burning his tongue with the scalding hot cheese. He panted, blowing out his breaths, putting out the fire in his mouth.

"I plead the fifth, but I'll snag a slice." Dean helped himself before nodding and bidding them goodnight on his way out.

"Do you need any help?" Justin pointed to the new equipment Shelby eyed as she skimmed a large, unfolded, color-printed, easy-to-use setup guide, flipping it over and over in her hands.

"Do you know anything about scanners? I need to hook it up so I can transmit everything to the cloud. Then I can organize these pages as we go, put them in bankers' boxes, shove them into the basement, and clean out this pigsty."

"I do, actually. I'm pretty handy with electronics. I had to download my friend's entire hard drive once when they accidentally restored it to the factory setting instead of resetting it. The whole mess almost gave them a coronary before I told them I'd helped set up the cloud so it would be straightforward to reload everything."

Shelby's shoulders drooped. "That is such a relief. I'll pay you overtime if you want to stay tonight and at least help me get started. Then, I can save documents between helping customers throughout the day. I can arrange several boxes and organize as I go."

"How do you want to structure it so I know how to create the online folders?" Justin tossed his crust in the trash.

"I reckon by acquisition date, and then by the manufacturer." Shelby glanced around at the stacks of files and the numerous filing cabinets.

"Sounds easy enough. We can label a folder for the unknowns without markings if we are unable to pinpoint who the craftsman is. But most of them should have some hint." This would give him more time to spend with Shelby.

Justin made his way around her cord pile, unplugging one to switch it around to the correct port. Once everything was in place, he held up his hand and wiggled his fingers.

"Does your brother, who you mentioned when we cleaned the store on my first day, at least live around here?" Shelby handed him the manual when he asked for it.

"Doest my ears deceive me? Are you asking me something personal?" Justin clutched his heart.

Shelby bellowed a full-blown laugh. "I'm sorry, you're right. We're at work, and I shouldn't ask a personal question." She mimed zipping her lips.

"I'm messing with you. No. Our parents died when we were still small boys, and my grandparents raised us." He looped the last cord around, hooking it into a cord organizer screwed into the base of the monitor, and gave a short nod.

"So what did you mean when you said you have experience with law enforcement?" Shelby moved a stack of forms to the right on her desk.

"I can't really get into the details due to open investigations, but I know their procedures and how they operate." Justin tightened the last cable.

"What can I expect next?" Justin caught the uncertainty in her voice.

"Give them the files on everything they ask, and then they will let you know if they need further documentation. If they find anything off, that is when you need to worry. Make sure you are forthcoming with everything you know."

"But I really don't know anything. It's no different than someone coming in on the end credits scrolling across the screen wondering what happened." Shelby huffed.

"Relax. They will see that and figure out you aren't up to your eyeballs in the muck of this world. Now scooch it, chick." He wiggled his fingers for her to move and occupied her chair once she got up. The quick guide made for an easy installation. They discussed how to outline the folders, and before they knew it, several boxes held scanned pages.

Soon the clock ticked past midnight.

"Oh my gosh. It's so late." Shelby started shoving Justin out of her office. "I can't believe how late it is. I'm so sorry. You don't have to come in later if you don't want to. Your next paycheck will reflect the overtime you put in today."

Justin covered her mouth with his hand. "Take a breath. You're going to pass out. I never knew a human who talked so fast. Sheesh, woman, give a man a chance to organize his thoughts." Justin tucked a bit of hair behind her ear.

"So you said, 'human.' Do you mean you know animals who speak fast?" She quirked her lips.

"I'm going home." He chuckled as she shooed him out the door. He waved as he pulled out of the lot.

Today had been a good day. She was opening up more and relaxed with his joking and flirting. Now, he had to persuade her to agree to a date. He would give her the time she wanted, but some things he couldn't tell her about himself yet. His nerves flared to life about how she'd take the facts of his deception. He didn't think it was too terrible, but not everyone understood why he never settled down.

She was the reason he wanted to stick around. Usually, his job took him from place to place, looking for the next significant pursuit or takedown. He may have found it in her. Only now to convince the other half of himself, the closed-off, wary-of-trusting-anyone's side because of his past. Complications grew with the prolonged delay, but if the last two months interacting with each other hinted at the issues they skirted, it would keep him on his toes. Justin rubbed his hand against his sternum. The stirrings inside when she was around told him everything he needed to know. Time to settle down. Shelby was the path to the bright future blooming in him.

His phone chimed with a message as he pulled behind his cabin. Reading over the text, he felt lighter. Setting the next stage of his plan in motion turned out to be easier than he thought. Shelby was his, even if she didn't know it yet. The need to preserve his identity to remain anonymous would be behind him soon enough.

Justin pulled out leftover jerk chicken and rice. The pizza earlier filled him up, but hours passed since then. The microwave dinged as he changed clothes. Not bothering to re-plate the dish, he ate standing in the kitchen. The stone tile floor chilled his bare feet.

He emptied the container into the sink, promising himself to take care of it later. Exhaustion pulled at him. It was a new day to show Shelby he was someone to entrust with her heart.

Fifteen

Shelby crossed her legs, which she stuffed into thick flannel pajamas, and sat with her back against the pillows after pulling out her laptop. Her hair was wrapped in a towel after the extra-long, extra-hot shower she splurged on when she got upstairs.

She couldn't get the black truck out of her head, so it was useless sleeping if she didn't want to have nightmares. She had seen it more times than she wanted to admit, including tonight, sitting down the turnoff on the side road across from the store when Justin left. It was time to stop denying it was following her. Staying far enough away, she never got a description of the driver. She figured the feds would have their secret spy people tagging along. A serial killer roamed the countryside, so she couldn't fault them for using all of their skills to capture him.

Since she moved to town, she hadn't checked the website page for Rupert's Relics. It was one of the first chores she wanted to complete. It was undoubtedly outdated and would need a complete overhaul, and she wanted to post about her uncle's death. Here she was two months later, keying up the website.

Shelby blinked twice before believing the sight before her. The website was good—no, actually, it was phenomenal. It had all-new, updated stock. Did Justin oversee that part also? He was well-equipped and tech-savvy when converting the files to digital. She clicked on administrators and found her and Dean's names as people with permission to change the page.

Dean?

She admitted to herself the layout impressed her. She clicked on several of the pieces, their postings current. She couldn't wrap her head around the quality of work she saw. Why on earth did he work for pennies compared to what designing websites for others, including large companies, paid? Dean, an elusive technological wizard, showcased pieces to appear as priceless works of art. Under Uncle Rupert's picture was a small, very well-written obituary. She swiped at a stray, errant tear, wanting to thank him for the kind words.

She opened a second browser and searched through antique collector groups to compare other websites to hers. Several had her chuckling as she attempted to navigate through their pages. Many, infantile in design, in an attempt to make them look professional, used every free template available, but only achieved cluttered confusion.

Hmm, she was interested in the next one to pop up. Vintage Stagecoach Rustling. The page loaded, and several pieces took her breath away. Whoever owned the site definitely ran an A-game. Stories accompanied each antique, no matter how small. Some were great and quickly pulled her into the history told through the owner's words.

The memories and emotional value attached to these items made them priceless to relatives, and she was jealous of their connection to large families who had passed them down through generations. Her breath hitched as she clicked on the next page. The armoire and dresser looked familiar.

Selecting the name generated the neighboring county and owners' information, including origin and provenance.

Her heart galloped, pressing at her ribs, when she toggled back to her website and scrolled through previously sold relics. The same two items appeared on the collector's segment on the third page.

With the history and love easily confessed with these antiques, there was no way they would have parted with them. She scrambled off her bed only to look at the clock and realize it was after one. She left her office not more than an hour ago. It was too late to verify the slips, so she would admit defeat in solving this mystery right away. She giggled at the thought of being spotted in her duck pajamas by one of the guys if they came in early. Her mother bought them as a joke, and Shelby wore them proudly.

Shelby saved the pages to her favorites and decided it was time she brushed off her investigator's hat until the next day and did a little digging to solve what her heart insisted had to be a mistake. Or was her uncle a part of the murders? Did he have an accomplice? If he did, did that person kill her uncle like so many of the owners of these precious heirlooms?

She immediately scrubbed it from her mind. Her uncle would no sooner cause harm to another person, much less murder these widows to take their precious memories tied to their property to make a buck.

She huffed at herself for even thinking along those lines, wordlessly asking for her uncle's forgiveness, then slithered under the covers and settled in for the night. She would gather as many facts as possible and take them to the authorities. The news mentioned a serial killer but didn't say killers. So, her uncle was not connected since the spree continued after his death. Justin brought in the antiques and Dean shipped them. Her uncle wasn't involved but what about his employees?

Agent Irving's card, with his personal cell number written on the back, taunted her from her wallet. She would call him when she had tangible evidence to help their case. She didn't want to take what she had and only slow them down if she was wrong, sending them on a wild goose chase. Or worse, they'd peg her uncle with the misinformation and terminate the investigation, letting the real killer slip through their grasp and move on to continue his horrific crimes.

There was only one question floating around in her head: would the killer catch her before she caught them? It would be a race to see who would be left standing when it was all said and done.

Not tired, she wrote down every piece she remembered at the cottage to make it simple to examine the acquisitions.

She wanted to toss around a few ideas, but the only person she wanted to talk to was Justin, and she was curious whether it was a good idea. What did he mean he had the inside track on police procedure? The inquisition was her responsibility, not his. Granted, he was interested in taking their working relationship in a personal direction. He was an obvious flirt and pleaded with her to go out with him, but she still couldn't expose him to the fallout if the FBI case took a turn for the worse.

She wanted him to be able to find a job somewhere else if Rupert's was shut down. A tear leaked out at disappointing her uncle.

***

An undercover agent skirted the trees on the other side of Rupert's. The light clicked off in the apartment above the store. He wanted to run up and tell her she had no situational awareness. He followed her from the diner and she had no clue.

He yanked out his phone and hit a number he was quickly becoming familiar with and sent off a text.

Undercover: Shelby is coming into her own in the store. She is a natural at running the business.

Rana Samuel: Of course she is. What do you think she had been doing all the years over the summer months? How is she mentally dealing with everything? If anything happens to her, I don't think you understand the damage me and her father will do to your agency.

Undercover: Mentally, she is struggling. My team came in and informed her about the case.

Rana Samuel: Oh, does that mean we can come back and be with her through the investigation? Because I will tell you again I don't agree with how you are putting our baby girl in danger.

Undercover: No, they informed her there was a case but nothing more. We need her in the dark about all of this. You were right; she isn't able to keep her feelings hidden. She broadcasts them in everything she does. For her safety and your own, we sent you the stipend so you would stay in Egypt longer. I personally promise I am taking her security seriously. This is the best course of action so he doesn't disappear. I received permission to tell you he is leaving no traceable evidence. No DNA, no fingerprints, no witnesses. The FBI can't arrest on a hunch. We need Rupert's open to stall him from moving on. You even informed us that Shelby wouldn't stay away from Red Peaks once she found out about Rupert, or if he didn't respond to her texts or calls. They spoke every week. Our linguist could have fooled her with a little bit acting as Rupert, but the rumor mill of Red Peaks would get back to her.

Rana Samuel: You better make her your priority, since we already know how well that worked out for Rupert.

Undercover: I understand. You have my solemn vow I'll step in front of any bullet someone aims her way.

Rana Samuel: We will stand down for now, but don't get our baby killed. We wouldn't survive it.

The undercover agent jogged to his truck, ready to call it a night. He needed sleep because tomorrow would be a repeat of today. Keeping Shelby out of a killer's crosshairs.

Sixteen

Shelby was appalled by the lengthy list of items the FBI had finally emailed her requesting assistance with for their audit. The printer whirred, the rollers spinning as it warmed up to print the spreadsheet. It would take her months to find all the documentation.

Page after page printed, finishing with a total of twenty sheets she shuffled together. Was there anything not listed? How could so many pieces be implicated? The simple answer was they had the wrong intel.

Wait.

It was better than she initially believed. Along with every piece, they had required documentation, including the purchase order for acquired pieces, any fees written off for tax purposes, by whom they were bought, and the bill of lading from the shipping company that delivered them.

Why did the government have to have a page and a half of instructions on submitting the appropriate paperwork for their side? It was a big waste of time and resources. She wanted to teach them a thing or two about efficiency and organizational skills.

Shelby pulled out a drawer full of highlighters, opted for the most worn one, and highlighted the names of the pieces in question. Her uncle had a bad habit of seeing a sale on office supplies and ordering an overabundance, even if ten unused items sat on the shelf in the closet. His motto: "Well, they never go bad."

Working through the oldest and most worn pens, pencils, and other such items, would allow them to use the overstock so they saved the newest for last.

The spreadsheet touted a mix of neon colors. She marked the specific items in yellow with the matching documents in pink, leaving blue for completion and ready to be handed in. If she stuck to a method, she could have it done in no time.

The FBI gave her a month to prepare the files. Glancing at the desk calendar, she didn't see a problem with hitting the deadline before Thanksgiving. She emailed back to confirm she received their request and would begin working on it immediately.

Dean stuck his head in and knocked on the doorjamb. "Got a minute?"

"Sure." Shelby put the pages in a file folder and secured it in the desk's drawer.

Dean motioned for her to tag along to the stock room. "I know you wanted to take a second look at these to furnish the cabin. Are you still considering them?"

Shelby took in the beautiful bed again. A smile pulled up at the corner of her mouth. "You know what? You only live once, right? I want them. This would go great in my room with the antique quilts I found in...um...a closet. Did I tell you about those?"

"No, you didn't." His hand stopped caressing the headboard.

She almost gave away that there was a hidden room before she remembered how little she knew of either of her employees. She would keep that little gem to herself for a bit.

"Shelby?"

"Oh, sorry. Yeah, one bedroom had a stack of gorgeous handmade quilts in it. They would look great on this."

"Rupert didn't strike me as a collector of hand-stitched works." Dean narrowed his eyes.

"I didn't think so either, but I found a stack in the house, so he must have been." Shelby ran her hand over the ornate posts.

She didn't remember seeing a bed on the agent's list. Finally, one thing went her way, which meant she could move and set up the cottage. She decided if there was a piece in question, she should leave it untouched for now with the confirmed disputed items. Glancing over at the trunk, she smiled at a dresser and an armoire from a similar era. These exquisite pieces would be her first purchase for the cottage.

"Please write up a slip, and I'll transfer the funds into the store's account this afternoon. I'll split the commission between the two of you." Shelby turned back toward her office when Dean's light touch on her shoulder halted her.

"Justin brought the pieces in. I won't take part of his commission away when I didn't do anything to help sell them." He nodded.

He sat on a bench under a picnic table and started filling out the bill of sale. His makeshift workstation was surrounded by packing materials. Bubble wrap, packing paper, packing tape, moving blankets, and so much more. She hadn't ventured to this side when she browsed the inventory.

"Is this thing your desk?" Shelby sat in the rickety metal folding chair on the side.

"I don't need much to work out here. It does its job." Dean pointed with his pen to the side at the old, broken table, where stacks of paper trays littered the entire surface while he utilized the other end.

"Yikes." Shelby laughed. "Anything would be an upgrade compared to this."

Dean gave her one of his rare heart-melting smiles before he went back to work.

She didn't interrupt him anymore and took the pages from him when he finished. The price matched the total cost they had on the tags if sold to a paying customer. Her admiration went up when he didn't try to cut into the store's profit margins to look good for his boss.

The frustration of what happened in the alley between them simmered under the surface, and she hoped it wouldn't lead to a tense work atmosphere.

He never brought it up since that night, and neither did she.

Dean guided her by the elbow toward the hallway. "Shelby, I've needed to say something to you for a while and have been a coward for not saying it before. I'm so sorry I bruised you when you saw me. I never meant to grab you hard. I wanted to steer you out of the alley for your own protection."

Could he read minds?

Shelby situated her hand over his. "Thank you. I didn't know what to think, and to be honest, I thought about letting you go. Can I ask why you got so mad at me for seeing you talking to that man?"

"I'm sorry, but no, I can't give you an answer right now. There are things in my life I don't talk about to others. I'd never forgive myself if you were dragged into my mess. Promise me you won't say anything to anyone about it. At least for a while. I'll explain when and if I can."

Shelby didn't want to promise, but then, of course, there was no one to tell except Justin, so she only nodded. "For now."

"Okay." He gazed his dark, penetrating blues at her as if looking for something. A tingle trembled through her core before he blinked and stepped away. "I've got a shipment."

"Thank you, Dean." Shelby waved the pages in the air.

"Sure, I fill those out all the time. Doesn't take but a second." He headed toward the dock as a large truck pulled up.

"No, for observing the original price and not lowering it."

"I remember someone demanding to be treated as if she was a paying customer when she purchased something." He pursed his lips turning them into a thin white line, then turned to a pallet jack, pushing it toward the driver, who hopped out of the cab.

Shelby shook her head and smiled at Justin, who was helping a customer guiding her by a hand on her upper back and pointing to an item, as she passed on the way to her office. The woman giggled as Justin spoke low, making it appear as if they shared an intimate moment.

She grabbed her purse and headed out to meet Skye at the diner. They finally had openings in both their schedules, and she couldn't wait to catch up with her friend.

"I'll be back," Shelby called out as she passed Justin and the woman, who hung on to his every word.

Skye already settled in a booth and waved to her when she walked in.

"I'm starved," Skye announced as the waitress strolled up with a pen stuck in the bun on top of her head.

"The special is chicken fried steak and mashed potatoes and gravy, along with green beans."

The waitress didn't finish as they both blurted they wanted the special.

The woman laughed and walked away, returning with two glasses of water and telling them that their meal would be out shortly.

"So, tell me what it's like working with two hot men? How do you concentrate?" Skye rapidly blinked her eyes.

"Stop it; they are my employees." Shelby took a sip. "Although Justin has made it obvious he wants to ask me out for a date."

"So, why not?"

"Skye, would you date a hair stylist that worked for you?" Shelby remembered when Skye had a crush on one of her employees before he left and moved to a larger city.

"I'm married." Her defensive stance wasn't going to win her any Emmys.

"Uh huh, sure. Like before Seth left and you hadn't met your husband yet?"

Skye almost spit out a mouth full of water. "Hey, no fair, that was before I met my hubby."

"Whatever."

After their food was delivered, Shelby and Skye caught up on what had happened with Shelby since she came into town.

Skye heard the rumors surrounding the tree falling on Shelby's car in the cemetery and the break-ins but wanted to hear the truth from her best friend. Shelby filled her in on the actual events that occurred.

Skye leaned forward. "Rumor has it that Rupert worked with the killer and told him where to find the next victims. Then the killer turned on him so he could keep all the money to himself."

"Uncle Rupert would never!" Shelby raised her voice.

Skye held up her hand. "Sweetie, I know that. Rupert had to be the kindest man I know. I'm just letting you know the gossip that is circulating in my beauty shop. I'm not saying they are right, but you have to remember that I own the salon where all those old biddies congregate. I have front-row seats when they act as if it's their civic duty to proclaim it a public service message to inform people for their own safety. It disgusts me, but if I reprimanded them, I would lose half my clientele."

"I know, I know. It still makes me mad that people chose to follow along instead of following their hearts about someone they knew for decades." Shelby looked at the clock above the counter. "Oh, shoot. I have to get back."

They quickly paid and hugged, promising to do it again soon.

Seventeen

Shelby couldn't believe she overslept. After tossing and turning the first several hours, she lay in bed, deprived of the rest she needed to tackle the day. Her first chore after coffee was to look up the invoices from the items she jotted down from memory that she saw in the cottage.

Her boots slid on the slush Dean shoveled from the parking lot as she ran toward the building. He stopped and rested his arms on the handle of the shovel, quirking an eyebrow at her before giving her an impressed nod as she made it to the door while he continued to clean up nature's mess.

Shelby deserved coffee from the shop down the street if her day was already off to such a wonderful beginning. The sludge Justin made was so strong she'd have to triple her caloric intake by adding enough sugar and creamer to make it palatable. The outing into town and back took longer than she wanted since a storm dumped five inches of fluffy white flakes.

Justin was nowhere in sight when she stomped her boots on the front mat to shake off the excess snow before she headed to her office. She sat her coffee cup down, the delicious cinnamon-vanilla aroma escaping around the stirrer in the vent. A Red Peaks snow globe sat on her desk. She shook it and watched the glitter swirl around the dome. It had to be from Justin.

Usually, she didn't close her office door, but today, it was necessary if she rifled through purchases and did some digging. She tapped her fingernails on the wrist rest in front of the keyboard as she waited for the computer to boot up. Customers browsed nonstop, and Dean had his hands full with online orders. Christmas, still several weeks away, brought out holiday wish lists and shoppers eager for rare gifts no one could top.

The screen background, a picture of her with Uncle Rupert when she was young, popped up. Now, she was in business. She pulled up the website and owner's name from the article that the news listed as one of the victims.

A search revealed those same pieces sold two months ago and shipped out a few days after processing. The name and address on the purchase order matched where the shipping company delivered them, but the names on the original documents didn't match the FBI's.

She pulled a small notebook from her purse and was logging everything when there was a knock on her door, and Dean's head poked through. She tried to click out of the screens, but the delivery confirmation page was still up when he strolled in.

"Is anything wrong?" His eyes were glued to the screen. He stood in a wide-open stance, spine stiff.

"No, not at all." Shelby stowed the notebook in a small inside pocket of her jacket when she finally had the shipping screen minimized, only to see the vintage stagecoach website open behind it.

"What page is that? Those look like some of the items I filled orders on." Dean peered over her shoulder.

She ought to rearrange her office so the monitor didn't face the door. "Oh, it's a website I browsed last week."

Dean frowned when she clicked out of it. "I have an excellent memory of our orders and any background if you need it. Is this a concern with my job performance? Is there something I need to know about?"

"You know, maybe, but not right now. Not about your job skills. I mean, those are fantastic. I might have some things I want to run by you, but not yet. Anyway, I was meaning to talk to you about Rupert's Relics website. I see Uncle Rupert made you an administrator."

"He was definitely not tech savvy, so he figured it would be easier if I handled setting it up and filling the online orders. You should have seen him when I tried to teach him how to attach a picture and description so they linked to each other with one click; it was sad." Dean smiled.

Shelby almost choked on a sip of coffee and held up her hand while she got her coughing under control. "Try showing him how to stream movie apps on a television. It took me almost fifty phone calls between the two of us to teach him not to delete an app or buy everything he clicked on."

"I know it's not the same for me as it is for you, but I miss Rupert. He was great." Dean flipped the snow globe around, sending the snow into a rampant swirl.

"It means a lot you two got along, and he had you in his life before ..." Shelby sniffled before shaking her head.

"You're going to get through this. We haven't exchanged numbers, and I wanted you to know if you needed anything to call me, like the night someone tried to break in. We should have done this the first week you were here." Dean wiggled his fingers for her to give him her phone as he set the decoration on the desk.

She unlocked it and handed it to him when Justin requested her help with a sale. She nudged around Dean and walked briskly to the front.

"Oh, you sold the Haviland china set." Shelby saw the giddy look of the elderly woman who handed over her credit card.

"Sure did. Can you help wrap them so they don't break before this lady gets them home?" Justin gave her a carton he grabbed from the back.

"Absolutely. This is a lovely set." Shelby made small talk while she wrapped each delicate item.

"These are the same pattern my grandmother had when I was a little girl. I had to have it as soon as I saw it. Gosh, these bring back memories. Of course, back then, they delighted in using these as regular everyday dishes because hardly anyone owned a separate set they didn't use except on rare occasions." She teetered back and forth on her cane, not steady on her feet.

"Do you have someone to help unload these at your home?" Shelby cringed as she took another unsteady step.

Her smile told her she did before she even answered. "My young grandson is staying with me this winter to help me out after my hip surgery."

"It's great he's able to be there for you." Shelby put in the last teacup and nodded to Justin.

The bell jangled and Shelby saw two of gossip-central's ladies walk in. She wanted to groan as Justin carried the box out to the woman's car.

"Shh, there she is," the one with thick blue eyeliner stated.

The other lady, wearing bright pink sweatpants with the word "hot" across the rear that was a size too small, mock whispered, "Heard Rupert was working with the cartels shipping drugs out of the furniture the killer gave him."

"Come on, ladies, I'm sure you can come up with something more original than that." Shelby scoffed. "Or do you have the inside track on how a cartel operates?"

"Well, I never!" The blue eyeliner woman spun and stormed past Justin, who held the door for them both.

"What did they want?" He joined her.

"Nothing good." Shelby headed to her office.

Her phone sat on her desk, but Dean was nowhere to be found. She unlocked the device and smiled when she saw his text to confirm he had the correct number.

Shelby shucked off the snow boots she hadn't changed out of after her coffee excursion and put her hands on her hips, surveying her options for rearranging as she slipped on the ballet flats she kept under her desk. Her uncle had the desk facing the wall since it took up so much room. Turning it to face the perpendicular wall next to the door would keep her monitor from prying eyes if someone walked in on her.

The moving company hefted over the antique she found in the cabin the week before. However, until she emptied this monstrosity, it could wait.

The corner closet was surprisingly empty except for toner and office supplies. She quickly removed the contents from the desk and piled them in the closet out of the way. Next, she turned off and unhooked the computer, monitor, scanner, and other equipment and piled them up on the credenza behind the desk.

She didn't want to be that boss who always hid away behind her door and the guys contemplating her withholding business from them. She wanted to have an open-door policy.

The metal desk was heavier than she thought it would be; it didn't move a centimeter when she gripped the edge and tugged. She shifted between it and the wall and had room to brace one of her feet behind her and shove off. She barely moved one side away from the wall when Justin popped his head in.

"What are you doing? You're going to strain a muscle!" Justin held up his palm and then yelled, "Yo Dean, need your help moving something."

Stomping boots sounded. "No need to yell. What is it?"

"Shelby is trying to move her desk by herself. I swear it probably weighs more than she does." Justin placed his hands under one side while Dean lifted the other.

"Where are we moving this to?" Dean dipped his head.

"The docks, can you use this out there? I had the one on the east wall of the warehouse moved from the cabin to replace this."

Dean and Justin tilted the large desk, angled the legs around first, and maneuvered it without damaging the walls. Extremely proficient, as if they had done this thousands of times before.

"This is a better desk than what I have out there," Dean grunted as they moved through the showroom.

They quickly and efficiently moved the new one into her office faster than she thought they would.

Shelby directed them where she wanted it, and they also arranged the rest of the smaller items, including two matching wing-backed chairs, so they sat in front of her desk instead of one next to it and the other by the door.

"This looks better." Justin clapped her on the shoulder and then left.

Dean stood, taking in the room for several minutes. His eyes bore into her as she sat down and positioned the monitor to see it more easily. She was on the fence about asking him for a favor. An overwhelming urge to confide in him scared her. Was it God telling her it was time to stop fighting the battle alone?

"Do you have a minute?" She redirected him before he hid in the storeroom.

"Sure." He nodded at the door, asking if she wanted it closed.

Shelby shook her head. "How are we doing on stock? I was thinking about having some of the pieces I moved to the dining room listed for sale. I need to move out enough so I won't feel smothered." Shelby averted her eyes.

She angled the monitor to face away from the door at the corner of the desk. Dean lifted an eyebrow as he hid a grin when she shifted it farther away from her. An optometrist would probably scold her for not setting an appointment earlier before she was playing trombone with a computer screen.

"We should be able to accommodate several items. There's a sizable shipment going out. Some rich guy on the

East Coast bought several of the colonial pieces stored for a year. The truck is scheduled to arrive around eight, so I'll be here early to ensure everything goes smoothly," Dean informed her.

"Great. I'll call them today and schedule it." She half smiled.

"When are you available? I'll see what they have open." Dean rammed his hands into his pockets.

"You don't need to; you're not my assistant."

"I know who to assign to move the larger pieces, and they're used to dealing with me, so it's no bother." Dean shrugged.

Shelby let him manage the particulars of getting everything set up. "Any day after work will be fine for me."

Dean made the call before he got a few steps from her door. His footsteps plodded up and down the hall, unable to stand still, while he arranged the details with his contact.

Shelby would confide in Dean about something she hadn't told anyone yet. It may turn around and bite her, but she wanted to put her mind at ease. If he kept her confidence, he was someone to depend on. If not, it wouldn't be detrimental if he blabbed.

"Can I trust you with something?" Shelby met his eyes.

Dean sat. "Absolutely."

"I haven't told anyone else about this." She picked at a hangnail that had been bothering her all morning.

"Is it something involving the FBI?"

Would Dean refuse to help her if he thought she kept vital facts from the agents?

"Yes, no, I'm not sure yet."

Dean nestled into the thick cushions of the wingback chair and crossed his ankle over his left knee. "You can trust me with anything, Shelby. We can figure this out together. Your uncle would want you to know you can come to me. No matter what it is. I know your uncle has been gone for two months, and determining who to trust takes time, but I'm here all the same."

She stared at him for several seconds, deciding to do what Justin suggested and rely on someone. A knot in her stomach clenched because she asked Dean instead of Justin, but she thrust it away. For an unknown reason, she wanted to trust the man in front of her. Shelby would focus on her reaction later. She wasn't only choosing Dean due to her uncle's faith in him, but something deeper pulled her to this man. She would see if he lived up to her expectations.

"I went to clean and air out the house when I noticed a bookcase with some rare and old books. I tore my shoe on a nail sticking up, and with how klutzy I can be, I caught my balance on a shelf." She chuckled.

She craned her neck to peek down the hallway, causing Dean's eyebrow to lift a fraction. "It exposed a back panel when the shelves pulled away from the wall. When I opened it, there was a door I'd never seen before. The upper section had been overlapped with drywall."

"Oh, exciting. It's a shrouded panel, like in a spy movie. Something your uncle would have installed." The timber of his voice plummeted an octave as a hint of laughter tickled the edges of his words.

"Yes, it is! I found an entire hidden room once I got past the first obstruction. I think it was a fifth bedroom at one time. I can't wait to investigate what else is back there. We haven't had an opportunity to talk for me to ask if you knew anything about it." She felt like a schoolgirl discovering an ancient burial site with wonders waiting to be uncovered. "Did you know my uncle well?"

The fact he mentioned secret entrances and rooms being something her uncle would have built hinted he knew him better than she thought. And if her uncle let him know his wild, adventurous imagination, then he saw something in Dean to make him rely on Dean so profoundly. If Rupert was comfortable alluding to his secrets, it would be good enough for her—for now.

She always enjoyed mysteries and cryptic stories behind the antiques her uncle displayed. During her visits, she would ask nonstop questions, as a little girl unable to reach the cash register without a pink step stool he spray-painted. She put every sticker she had in her collection on it. She wondered what ever happened to it.

"I'd love to go through it with you." A smile graced his face, transforming him from the brooding, distant person she knew him to be into a heart-stopping man.

Had she been wrong about him this whole time? She wanted to believe there was more to him than the persona he put out there. The distant man of mystery hiding things no one wanted to see in the light of day.

"Great, we can determine when would work best and go from there." Shelby grinned.

"Since you have my number, shoot me a text." Dean stood and stopped at the end of the hall to talk to Justin about something she couldn't quite hear.

She wiped her hands down her legs to eliminate the sweat. Who knew she would be so nervous sharing this with Dean? He seemed to take in stride the fact that her uncle's propensity for adventure had led her to trust someone she was still unsure how to act around.

Shelby strung cables across the back of her newly acquired magnificent desk before ordering a cord organizer to adhere under the lip to keep them out of the way. She'd tried to salvage the old one, but it snapped in two when she tried to remove it.

She arranged the drawers so they held everything pertinent, clearing the tops off, including the credenza and four-drawer lateral filing cabinet. The stained wood grain matched perfectly.

A vintage tea set under a glass-top display was stolen from the showroom to create a serving display on the sideboard. Next, a Victrola completed the serene look she was going for. She would pick up a few plants on her next trip to town.

Standing in the doorway, she smiled. It was a beautiful office. As you walked in, the filing cabinet and sideboard, now sporting the tea set, stood against the far wall behind the desk. The desk faced two chairs, while the Victrola nestled in the corner on the same wall the door opened up to. The angled screen provided privacy and negated the worry about someone seeing something they shouldn't.

The space now gave off a tranquil vibe. Even the Red Peaks mountains encased in a glass dome had a home on the corner of her desk.

"Okay, this has to be one of the coolest office setups I've ever seen. I thought we would never sell the old phonograph." Justin peered over her head. "Like the snow globe."

"I love those things. I have a cheap kiddie plastic collection of those upstairs."

Justin winked at her.

"I'll write up a bill of sale and transfer the money out of my checking account and into the store's." Shelby sat behind her desk.

"Why? You technically own everything here."

"I'll always record my personal purchases from the business for tax purposes at year-end." Most people wouldn't think of those things, but the government will stick it to you in an audit if they catch it.

Justin took in the office again before he left, saying over his shoulder, "Good honest woman right there, folks."

Shelby giggled; he was such a character.

Eighteen

Justin sat back when the waitress cleared their dishes and gave him his new drink. He'd talked Shelby into going out for a bite to eat.

Shelby didn't know any in-depth details about Justin and wanted to learn more about the man who intrigued her. "What about you? Any family besides your brother you told me about?"

"Nah. Dad's a mean drunk, and Mom left us with him to save herself instead of taking us with her."

Shelby had no words for the shocking info Justin spilled, which contradicted what he said previously in her office. He acted nonchalant at the abuse he suffered from a parent. A parent should cherish each of their children, putting them ahead of their own needs. Had he made peace with it years ago and moved on? "Justin, I thought you said they died?"

"Oh gorgeous, don't give me sad eyes. I didn't want the pitying look you are throwing my way, knowing the level of depravity I grew up with. Some families are so much worse out there. I survived it and cut him out of my life a long time ago. And, I was nervous with my new boss and didn't want to admit the background where I come from." Justin slanted his drink as if saluting, then swallowed half in one gulp. "Think Dean has as messed up a childhood as I do with how he doesn't join in much when we are around the store? Who knows what skeletons he has in his closet."

"I'm not comfortable discussing Dean like we're gossiping." Justin wasn't wrong with Dean's aloof actions at work. But Shelby would not get into a discussion with one employee about another. It was impolite and not professional since she was their supervisor. It was paramount not to show favoritism and disrespect one in front of another. She hated seeing it in other jobs she had and promised herself she would never do it to someone else.

Justin frowned as if she insulted him personally. Maybe dinner with an employee trying to be a friend was a bad idea. "Shelby, I didn't mean to upset you, but there is something about him that rubs me wrong. I'm not sure I trust him, especially around you. You mean so much to me, and I want to protect you, is all."

Why did Justin feel the need to protect her from Dean? If her uncle was a pro at judging people's intent, as her childhood boyfriends attested to, then why would he trust his secrets with Dean? Although the alley did nothing to endear Dean to Shelby, the guilt in him when he saw the damage he did with his grip couldn't be ignored, or the heartfelt apology in the warehouse.

Shelby pulled her left leg up, resting her foot against the inside of her right thigh, and changed the subject. "What brings you to this place in the middle of Red Peaks? Are you from around here?"

"I've always abhorred large cities. Mindless people rushing around, never friendly with their neighbors. People live next to someone for years without learning their first name. They are suspicious of everyone, so you don't make lasting friendships. I love the small-town vibe and did a lot of research before deciding on this quaint little retreat." Justin's eyebrows danced as he smiled.

Shelby couldn't help but laugh as he perfectly described her similar thoughts. Yes, you had your little gossipmongers. Usually, they were the women sitting in a hair salon, heads under dryers, who had been in town for ages and knew everyone. The flip side was that everyone came together when a tragedy struck.

"You said you had a brother before. Are you close?" Shelby never knew what it was like to have a sibling since she had nothing to compare it to—Skye was her closest friend.

"Sort of. I mean, we each have our own lives and are busy, so we don't get together like we should, but hey, that's life and being an adult. I always tortured him as a kid, so I think he still holds a grudge for some of the pranks I pulled."

Justin didn't strike her as someone who would intentionally be mean. "This I have to hear. What kind of pranks?" Shelby didn't know if he was someone who would try something at work.

"The typical frogs in the bed, pouring hot water on him while he slept, so he thought he wet the bed. The usual boys being boys."

Shelby gasped. "You're horrible."

He winked and then snatched the bill lying on the table. "Totally kidding. I never pulled those jokes on him; he pulled them on me because I was younger and always wanted to be his shadow."

"Oh no, we are splitting this." She reached for the receipt. "Justin, this isn't a date. We are each paying for our own meal."

"Or a *friend* is offering to pay and will let you pick up the next one." Justin crossed his eyes, causing her to chuckle like he intended his funny face to do.

"Okay, friend. I'll be right back." Shelby made her way down the side of the bench seats and to the bathroom in the back.

After washing her hands, she started out the door when it swung open, and barely missed slamming into her as she hopped out of the way. Several teens giggled about the yummylicious guy by the register. Their word, not hers. Shelby smiled; they gabbed about Justin. He defined the definition of yummy.

"My lady?" He made a bowing motion as she moved past him to walk out.

He smiled at her and stopped as he headed in the opposite direction from where she parked. "See ya, boss." He gave her a salute and strolled to his car.

"Are you okay?" Shelby knew she wouldn't be with the number of drinks he had.

"I'm going a few blocks away. You know what, it's a beautiful night for a walk. Then I can enjoy the morning to retrieve my car before work." Justin winked, and she flushed with heat.

Justin surprised her tonight with his fun, quirky sense of humor. He always had a smile or a laugh for something either one of them said. She couldn't lie to herself. She was drawn to him. His mesmerizing light blue eyes appeared almost silver-gray didn't hurt. He exercised a lot because his muscle definition pushed at the threads giving the impression of tailor-made clothes hugging his body. She shook her head and backed onto the street, running down the town's central hub of activity.

Despite the nagging thoughts in the back of her mind about Justin's opinion of Dean, she had a good time. It was nice reminiscing about younger times at her uncle's.

Her phone pinged with a message. She pulled into the parking lot to read it.

Justin: Had a great time. Next time you pick, but no raw food, blah, gross. Night, m'lady.

Shelby chuckled as she replied, *Deal.*

The door to Rupert's opened, and she looked down at her keys she didn't use to unlock it. The bell's jingle still reverberated off the walls of the showroom, announcing her arrival.

Her phone still sat in her palm. Justin was closest.

Shelby: Hey, you busy?

Justin: Nope, what's up?

Shelby: Wondering if you forgot to fasten the door?

Shelby crossed her fingers, hoping it was an oversight.

Her phone rang, causing her to jump.

"Shelby, I didn't, but you did. Don't go in. I'm five minutes away."

"I'll be in my car."

He disconnected, and she hurried to press the button to let her into her vehicle. Then she shook her head, still unused to the sensor detecting when she approached.

Almost five minutes had passed when she saw headlights illuminate the dark road with too few streetlamps. Justin hopped out of his car, originally left at the restaurant, and jogged to her. He must live near where they enjoyed pot roast with potatoes and carrots. There was no wobble in his steps, and the serious look on his face told her he was stone-cold sober. Was it the thought of her being in trouble or the store being broken into?

She hopped from her seat.

"No, wait here while I go through the building."

"I'm coming with you." She followed him up the steps.

"Man, you are stubborn." Justin cupped her cheek. "I don't want anything to happen to you. I couldn't live with myself if something did."

Shelby couldn't help but lean into him. "And what am I supposed to do if you're injured or worse, and I'm left standing out here when I can help?"

"Grab onto my belt and stay behind me." Justin opened the door, making the bell jingle again.

With only the dock remaining and every row of displays, pieces of decor large enough to hide a person, and her office cleared, he peered behind him. "Do you still want to continue, or do you want to stay in your office?"

"I'm following you." She was proud her voice didn't waver.

"Yes, ma'am." He kissed her forehead and held his lips there for a split second, his hand wrapped around the back of her head, holding her to him.

There was nothing. The hum of the fluorescents charged the room as they flickered on.

"Who keeps getting in and then not taking anything? It doesn't make sense." Shelby sagged in her office chair as Justin took the one closest to the door.

"Not sure. Do you want to call the police on this one?"

"No, I'm not wasting their time, and I'll probably get the same one as last time who still believes I left everything unlocked, and that was how they're getting in." Shelby angled her lips and puffed out air, disturbing the flyaway wisps of hair framed around her face.

"Alright." He stood up and called back to her. "I'll lock up on my way out unless you want me to stay."

"No, that's not necessary. I know no one is in here, so switch on the security system, and I'll put a chair under the knob to the door upstairs."

The beeps told her it was armed, and she double-checked her app to confirm it was indeed set. She still couldn't help walking past the door and the deadbolt. Changing the code might deter who was entering.

Shelby dragged her feet up the steps and swore this would be her last week above the store, even if she had to use an inflatable mattress until the moving truck arrived. Everything wedged in a pod awaited her approval for transport. She didn't want to try to rearrange everything in the cottage immediately, and she wasn't on a concise timetable.

Changing the locks checked off the number one box on her agenda with the missing hide-a-key. She wasn't taking a chance since she couldn't confirm nor deny someone pilfering the small life-changing piece of metal. It amazed her how the thin scrap of nickel silver led to destruction and fear when in the wrong hands. Look at the unwanted visitors at Rupert's Relics. Nope, it was better to take over the cottage early than to always be on the edge of her seat waiting for the person to come back.

The hardware store carried more styles of deadbolts than she knew existed. The owner's son, a friend of her uncle's, handled Rupert's Relics hardware needs. She scribbled a note to remember to stop by, she taped it to the monitor.

She'd identified at least two points of entry to the house where the locks should be replaced and wanted to add an additional bolt to each one to be sure. It wouldn't hurt to include the store, either.

Shelby toed off her shoes past the table as she headed to bed. She looked to be upgrading the security to include cameras in the future. If they caught the person on video, the officers could question him on why he targeted the store—unless she was the mark.

Did she unknowingly do something that followed her from the city?

No.

She thought of the acquaintances from college who would acknowledge her in passing, but again, no one she held a close rapport or kept in touch with even now.

Shelby didn't have any disgruntled exes, and her most recent was years ago; he agreed they weren't right for each other. They had too differing opinions on what they wanted out of life. He wanted the hustle and bustle of big-city life to include a high-rise apartment overlooking the glitter and glam of a metropolis. She tried to walk on the quieter spectrum of life—small-town living where you knew your neighbors and didn't go years trying to meet up with family and friends because life was hectic and stressful.

They had split amicably, and he was seeing someone he worked with within a few weeks of their separation. He wasn't yearning to win her back or sitting forlornly, waiting for her to return.

Shelby brushed her knotted hair as she unbraided it for bed.

Stumped over her predicament, she drifted off, more confused than ever.

Nineteen

Shelby surveyed the empty dining room and parlor, devoid of antiques. The truck left twenty-five minutes ago, and Dean offered to overlook the delivery. He would catalog all the pieces and track coinciding manifests to tie them to a sale.

She took the day off to prepare more of the house for her to live in. Sleeping in the cottage relieved a stress she was ready to eliminate.

The small table and chairs that had been moved from the kitchen eating nook would leave plenty of room around them in the now-vacated dining room. Shelby mopped the hardwoods and let them dry while she prepared the bedroom. She had the bedframe routed on the round trip. The back-ordered mattress was delivered the day before. She snapped the sheets out and tucked the edges into tight corners even the hardest military drill instructor would be impressed with.

A thud froze her in place. When no other noise sounded, she went into the hall and saw a book lying on the floor. Odd. It was impossible for it to fall, with the distance between the spine and the edge of the bookcase.

She looked around but didn't see anything else out of place. The bookcase shifted out of the way as she tugged on the upper right corner. One of the old quilts would look perfect on the bed. She imagined its weight as she snuggled under the fabric.

When she flipped the switch, the light flickered and popped, plunging the room into darkness. She remembered seeing lightbulbs in the mudroom at the back of the house. With the bulb replaced, the light extended farther than the last time.

She snagged the brightest pink-and-yellow quilt. She stood back, admiring the beautiful bed. The goal was to finish cleaning the master bath, but her mind kept wandering, trying to work out what was happening with the treasure trove of wonders.

Shelby stood in the narrow aisle, taking in the view, armed with a pen and paper. Her phone was in her back pocket, ready to document each piece. This was more than she wanted to tackle. When it appeared to be only a few pieces, it didn't seem so daunting, but this was a whole new degree, when the daylight bulb bathed the room like the blinding sun.

Each discovery cemented her suspicions that her uncle was up to something. Off the top of her head, she thought three of them were included by the fed's for verification of ownership. How many more would cement the ruination of Uncle Rupert's reputation? Would Dean or Justin turn her into the feds for withholding this information?

Several of the pieces, no question, were worth thousands, according to their price tags. Shelby could chalk up having one or two pieces around the house he coveted and kept for himself, adding to his personal collection. Except this, no, this was so much worse. Her heart hammered against her ribs. She hadn't even gotten through half the room before her hunger told her her body needed nutrients.

Now, she second-guessed her decision to tell Dean. Refusing to let him see it after her excitement at the discovery only increased the suspiciousness. He took time out of his schedule for her, reneging added undue stress of explaining her reasons for retracting the invitation.

He knew things about her uncle, though.

Her phone beeped. Speak of the devil.

Dean: Have everything documented and logged in. Should I go ahead and post them on the site?

Shelby: Sure, thanx.

Dean: Got it. Did you need help over there? This won't take me long, and I can help with Rupert's mysterious merchandise.

Shelby shook her head. No way after discovering these—the FBI was looking for some of the items. Her gut cramped thinking about the repercussions of not alerting them, but hopefully, she would unearth the truth before they found out.

How was she going to explain her uncle having them? Deep in her soul, she knew Uncle Rupert was innocent, but she had to discover why he moved them here. Not ready to have them declare the case concluded and her uncle a criminal, she had to uninvite Dean to help.

Shelby: Not right now. I just want to clear out enough to live here since the store was broken into again last night.

Dean: What? Why didn't you say something?

Shelby: It's not like the police believed me the first time, so why tell them?

Dean: I would have stayed to make sure you were okay. You can't keep things to yourself. What if they are after something they think you have? You could be in danger.

Shelby: Justin was with me, so he knows. I didn't keep it to myself.

Dean: This doesn't just concern you and Justin. I would appreciate it if you would include me when something like this happens in the future. I have a right to know, especially when it could affect me.

Three dots appeared and then disappeared before she could respond to his irate text. They popped up again, but no message came through. She put her phone down and opened the fridge. A nice ham-and-cheese panini sounded perfect.

Several minutes later, she sat at the small table, which gave the illusion of being the size for a kindergartener in the empty, overly spacious dining room if not for the full-size chairs sitting around it. She took a large gulp of ice water before taking a bite out of her sandwich. "Oh yeah, good stuff right there."

Beep.

She forgot about her phone. She hopped on her left foot to untangle the one still hooked around the leg of the chair to answer her message. Her hand skimmed the black, gray, and white marbled stone countertop where she left it, but it wasn't there. She turned every which direction and intently listened.

The birds sang, chirping in a cacophony of songs intertwined between the different species in the mass of trees overhead while others gave answering tweets.

Beep.

Where did she put her phone? She ducked her head under the ledge to see if it fell. The buzzing dryer told her the towels she put in earlier finally finished. On the dryer sat her phone.

Did she take it with her when she switched the laundry over?

No, definitely not. She left it in the kitchen while giving Dean a chance to calm down.

Beep.

The window was latched tight, so no one could have exited through it.

Or come in.

Beep.

She swiped her hand over the screen, turning on the messages.

Dean: I didn't mean to push.

Dean: Are you mad at me?

Dean: Let me know you aren't under a large table you tried to move on your own, and I need to come rescue you from it.

Dean: I don't care if it makes you mad. I'm on my way.

Shelby: Sorry, I lost my phone for a hot minute. I'm fine.

Maybe Shelby was losing her mind. She had been in and out of several areas of the house today so far. If she indicated she was worried someone moved it, he would come over all huffing and stressing, going all alpha male and flexing his muscles about her staying alone, offering to move into the guest room.

Dean: I don't have to help you go through what is over there. I thought it would be interesting, kind of like exploring an underground tunnel under a moat surrounding a castle. Past a dragon's lair with knights trying to rescue a damsel in distress being held in an evil witch's tower.

Shelby barked out a laugh, the tension easing from her body. She sat and finished the rest of her sandwich, unsure how to respond. His comment made her more comfortable, letting him see what her uncle hid. Who knew Dean was funny?

Shelby: Not today. This afternoon, I'm working on the living areas I'll be using. Then I'll pack what's at the apartment, load it into the beast, and transport it here.

Dean: Beast? Nice. Okay, sounds good. See you at work.

Shelby didn't mention she had already started documenting the mess her uncle left behind. He would never know. Agents Irving and Jackson wanted to know if she ran across anything, even the smallest detail. She didn't know how furnishings in a boarded-up room qualified as substantial when she didn't know when or why her uncle put them there. Right? It didn't matter that they had them listed. They requested the corresponding documents. They didn't mention the antiques themselves. Okay, so she was overreaching and stretching the truth on a technicality.

Shelby cringed and knew that if she told them, a search warrant would be issued, and she'd be out of a place to lay her head and banished to the apartment again.

Wasting their time would only sidetrack them from running down viable leads. Shelby knew she was trying to convince herself to assuage her guilt.

"Come on, Shelby. You have tasks to complete to have a secure place to live." She expected the store to deliver and install the locks at any moment.

She moved anything hindering both entrances. Before she finished her thought, the doorbell croaked out its greeting.

Next was to swap out that horrible thing.

Sam smiled. "Long time no see."

"Come in." Shelby let him pass but left the door open. "It will be this one and the one past the living room. It's a French door, but I don't know if that makes a difference in installation. I should have told you before."

He raised the bag. "I've got you covered. Rupert had the cabinet hardware replaced, so I remembered the side-by-side French doors. I won't need to change them out; simply rekey them. It will save you money in the end since we don't keep those styles on hand. The front door and kitchen will have whole new systems with additional locks per your request because it's so outdated, but the multipoint locks on the back are fine."

"Oh, thank goodness. I'll get out of your way." Shelby crossed into the kitchen and continued organizing the pantry.

"Shelby," Sam called out an hour later.

"Yeah." She dusted off her hands on her jeans.

"I'm done. Come try the locks to make sure they work to your satisfaction." He handed her the keys.

The ease of the metal turning in the well-oiled new hardware was a nice change to the jiggle, then try and turn it at least fifteen times-method she'd employed with the old one. "Perfect! It's smooth like butter."

He shook his head, and with his tools packed, he stopped on the porch. "I was sorry to hear about your uncle. Holler if you need anything else."

"Actually, can you stop by Ruperts on the way and switch everything out?" Why not get it done while she was already at it?

"Did something happen?" Sam put his bag down.

"It's been broken into twice, but I think they have an old set of keys because they aren't damaging anything. It's also the reason I'm shifting everything I own here."

Sam nodded. "Done, I'll just send a bill there so it's on a separate invoice than the house."

"Perfect." Shelby would drop a payment off the next day.

"If there's anything else, just holler." Sam waved and jogged down the stairs.

"I will." Shelby was glad she already paid for everything, so she didn't have to search for her bag in the mess she made removing everything from the pantry.

She shot off a quick text to Justin and Dean to expect Sam and have three sets of keys made. Justin replied with a thumbs-up emoji while Dean confirmed her request. He didn't seem to be the emoji sort of guy.

The pantry's innards dominated every bit of the kitchen countertop's surface.

"Uncle Rupert, your disorganization is going to kill me. I have no clue how you found anything. Nothing is grouped together or even alphabetized." Spices littered over several different spots now clumped together in one slot.

She moved the small appliances from above her head to the lowest corner. Canned food was to the right at eye height while baking and essentials clustered around the spices to the left. Glancing at the clock, she saw she had a few hours before she had to head back.

Her phone rang. Shelby couldn't help but smile. "Hey, Mom, how was the cruise?"

"Oh, it was fantastic. It is so beautiful out here. How is everything going there?"

Shelby sighed, told her mom everything about the hidden room, and asked if Uncle Rupert mentioned anything to her.

"No, honey, but it had been a few months since we spoke. We were both busy. I know that isn't a good excuse, but sometimes life gets in the way." Her mom's regret hung heavily in the air.

There was a tap on a window, which made her wonder who was trying to get her attention. Why not ring the doorbell? She couldn't tell where it came from and stepped out quietly, resting the latch of the door against the jam behind her. "Hey, Mom. I gotta go, okay?"

"Sure, sweetie. I'll talk to you later." Her mom disconnected.

No other car sat in the driveway besides hers. She went to the left. A bird lay on the ground twitching twice before stilling, its neck broken.

"Oh, you poor little guy. At least it was quick." Shelby left it, refusing to touch it without gloves, and figured that with all the wildlife, some animal would enjoy the snack.

The cycle of life and all.

The door wouldn't open. Weird, she didn't fasten it behind her. She plucked the keys from her back pocket, where she stored them so she wouldn't lose them while cleaning. She listened silently, partially standing between the foyer and the great room.

She didn't see or hear anything to warn her of danger, so she started with the bathroom off the master bedroom.

Dusk was fast approaching. Shelby felt safer with the newly rekeyed and installed locks but shivered at the stillness of nature. She did not want to encounter the truck that had stalked past the shop sporadically over the last few weeks. Did the person know she also owned the cottage? If it was the FBI, their background on her uncle included every property he owned.

The evening anchor reported police discovered another death linked to the serial killer. This time, there were two. A couple who had been married for over seventy years. Their paths crossed as children as their parents struggled through the Great Depression, then moved out to Red Peaks when their kids had grown and had families of their own.

Both in their nineties with great-great-grandchildren, the cause of death was the same. Strangulation from an antique braided rope. Their families, in an uproar, demanded justice.

Twenty

Shelby wiped the sweat from her forehead with her right shoulder, her hands full of books to take to the cottage. They thudded against the bottom of the small carton she'd dropped them in. It was the following weekend and Dean and Justin promised to manage Rupert's while she packed.

Shelby's place was a reservoir of riches and memories. More than junk, she staged it with small nick-nacks she collected as a teenager, each a precious memento. Some of the cheap, cheesy ones she tossed in the garbage, but others, like the gifts from her uncle, were too precious to part with. A ceramic Siamese long-necked cat figurine slipped out of her grasp and shattered. She tried not to cry but it was one of the first antiques Uncle Rupert gave her.

She studied the space. Boxes piled two and three high packed under the dining kitchen combo shelf. It would take her a few trips to the cottage. She should have done this when she first moved.

In her defense, she'd planned to linger upstairs for a lengthier time than she had. However, the continued trespassing of a delinquent sped up her timeline. The new locks and alarm code helped alleviate some of the nervous jitters.

A knock on the door interrupted her.

Dean rolled in a two-wheeled cart. "Figured you wouldn't want to traipse up and down more times than necessary. This should save you a few trips."

"I could hug you right now." Shelby kept the smile from creeping up from the corners of her mouth when she saw his discomfort.

She turned her back and rolled it to the first stack by the door.

"Do you need help? I can load up the back of my truck while Justin mans the store."

Shelby was surprised at his offer. She bit the corner of her mouth and surveyed the room. It would be nice to go on one trip instead of four. Justin's advice to learn to ask for help had her speaking out. "You know, that would be a relief. Do we have any shipments this afternoon you need to be back for?"

"Not today." He lingered on the small platform, waiting for her invitation.

"Then I would love your help."

"I'll move my truck around and let Justin know." Dean thumped down the steps.

This would give her time to unpack most of it before returning to work in the morning. If she had anything to say about it, she would never move again.

Justin helped them load up between customers, and they headed out in less than an hour. She told Justin to holler if he needed help before Dean returned. He gave them a thumbs up as a customer drove in. He jogged to the door and held it open for the woman, whose shocking white hair showed off a slight blue tint. Back hunched with age and a pronounced limp slowed her down but didn't affect the smile on her face.

Dean's truck loomed in the rearview mirror, and she twisted her hands up and over the top of the steering wheel.

Was there an ulterior motive for him to offer so he could smooth talk his way into the secret room?

It had been almost two weeks since she told Dean about the closet-slash-cargo area she'd discovered. He wanted to come over yesterday, but she finagled her way out of it.

She hated second-guessing her judgment. Shelby decided if he hounded her while unloading both vehicles, she would tell him she changed her mind, but if he didn't bring it up, then God was telling her to have faith in him.

Her tires bumped over the graveled driveway as she parked at an angle in front of the garage so Dean's truck was closer to the house.

She studied the cottage and took in the intricate details the builder put into the quaint house. Clay planters hung under each window, offering a splash of color from blooms and bright green foliage to enhance the face of the house against the varying shades of the gray stones. Charming shutters, in need of paint, adorned either side of the windows. The curved top of the front door almost made her think it belonged to a hobbit more than a human. It was bigger than she would ever need unless she found the *one* and enlarged her family.

Dean parked behind her and had the dolly out before she got out of her car.

"So I have a question for you."

Shelby tensed, ready to revoke the privilege of unraveling Uncle Rupert's mystery.

"Do you want to go through the front or the garage?" He folded his arms over the push bar of the cart and rested his chin on them.

Shelby smiled. "Guess it doesn't matter."

"It depends on where you want all of this." He waved his arms behind him. The corner of his mouth ticked up on the left side. "Is the destination by the garage or the front door? If we go through the front, do we have to go around any tight corners where we might scuff the walls?"

Shelby smiled. "I was going to put them in the dining room we previously emptied out until I decide where everything goes. It's closer to the garage."

"The garage it is." Dean stacked several boxes while she unlocked the door, darted through the house, and opened the interior garage.

She didn't have the key, but since she lowered the overhead garage doors, she didn't worry about having it replaced.

They put everything in one room, unloading it hastily and effortlessly. Shelby sweated up a storm.

"Did you need help unpacking?" Dean strapped the dolly to the side of the truck's bed so it wouldn't roll around.

"Thank you, but no. I still have a few things to do before I unpack half of those. I'm mainly going with essentials such as clothing, personal items, and kitchen gadgets."

Dean hopped into the cab and rolled down the window, cranking the AC and adjusting the vents to blow directly on him. "Let me know if you need anything."

He swiped a towel over his face. It wouldn't be long before he cooled back down if he drove with the window lowered. The chill in the air was already drying the dots of perspiration on her skin.

"Dean, thank you for saving me three more trips. It was very considerate of you to offer." Shelby smiled shyly.

"Anytime. Do you want me to secure the second floor at Rupert's so no one can get in? Since you're living here and it's pretty much empty, we can use it for the smaller items if we don't have room by the dock." Dean's suggestion was perfect.

"Establishing that as an extra storeroom will accommodate more in the back, making it easier to organize the larger pieces after the smaller ones are moved upstairs."

He gave her a nod and turned the truck around. The roar of the large engine drifted away as he left.

Shelby breathed out a sigh. He didn't bring up the hidey hole, much less try to find it. The stress of his knowing eased. It would be good to share the burden with someone else and get their opinion. The alley incident seemed to be in the past; she hadn't seen that side of him since. If she didn't know any better, she assumed he restrained that part of himself under duress. The meeting with the unidentified stranger didn't seem to affect his temperament while carrying out his duties in his job. He was always the Dean she had grown to know.

Her bruisable skin healed quickly. Shelby admitted if an average person had been manhandled the same way, they wouldn't have had a mark on them.

Her clothes hung in her closet, and her toiletries sat on the vanity and in the shower. Sweat curled the hair at her neck and around her face.

A creak on the floorboards stopped her in her tracks.

She didn't move for at least a minute. Edging herself over, she sharply inhaled. The bookcase sat ajar. A sliver of light filtered through the opening. She lurched forward, propelled the bookcase against the wall, and reinforced the bolt she found the other day.

She plopped down in the middle of the hall in a dining room chair, facing the offending bookshelves. She popped the top on a soda and guzzled half of it before she sat it on the floor. She dialed the emergency police number, ready to push send. She expected someone to pound on the wall to be let out.

Time ticked by.

Nothing.

She was tempted to search for Dean's truck to see if he came back and let himself in but was afraid if she moved, they would sneak past her.

After twenty minutes, she stood. Did she leave the light on the last time she was in there? How did the latch release? It wasn't as if it had a hair trigger.

Shelby banged on the wall. "I'm calling the police. If you are in there, you better call out!"

Nothing.

She switched her phone to her left so she could use her dominant hand to open it. She hid behind the shelving unit as she forced it out of the way. It was eerily silent. After checking all the corners, she huffed and turned her phone off.

She put her fists on her hips and circled. For her sanity, she needed to get a grip and latch the case correctly. She didn't want it to accidentally pop open in front of someone she wasn't ready to know what her uncle had been up to.

She turned the light off and secured the lock. There were no unlatched windows in the room for someone to slip in under the cover of darkness. Shelby was worried she was losing her mind. Maybe she did leave her phone in the laundry room the other day.

A baked macaroni and cheese pasta dish sounded delicious. Her childhood favorite called out to her. She pulled out a small casserole dish. Elbow pasta plinked against the sides of the ceramic. She sprinkled salt and pepper over everything. A stick of butter was sliced over the noodles. Milk poured to within an inch from the top. Cheddar cheese overflowed the pasta, making it ready for the oven.

Her mouth watered at the delicious carbs waiting for her. Cod, bought from a local who only sold freshly caught fish, was seared in a pan to join the concoction in the oven. Forty-five minutes later, she moved the food from the oven to cool on a trivet. She put more on her plate than she'd be able to eat but didn't care.

Shelby rubbed her belly fifteen minutes later and groaned. Overeating was the worst.

The last of the sun's rays filtered through her blinds. She removed the atrocious curtains and threw them into garbage bags. She twisted the flimsy plastic rod on the yellowed, brittle blinds and shut out the world. Replacing them was added to her never-ending list of things to fix.

Her phone chimed.

Dean: Did you get everything done you wanted to today?

Shelby: I did and ate too much and now I can't move. I may have to roll myself into work.

Dean: Ha. Wanted to check in before I head home.

Shelby: Nothing exciting happening over here. See you tomorrow.

Dean: Tomorrow.

Shelby abandoned the phone on the nightstand and rinsed off the day's grime. With a little more work to make it her own, she relished the sanctuary of the cottage. She remembered the first time her uncle said he bought a stone house. She had imagined all types of scary woodland creatures lying in wait, to a fairy tale witch as a neighbor, eating small children.

Now, it was still a huge home for someone but also cozy and picturesque. Most people wouldn't associate those descriptive words with the building around her.

Shelby thumbed to the page in her novel and read about mystery and suspense. Soon, she drifted off. Dreams of Justin riding in to rescue her shifted to Dean lurking in the corners, watching her with red glowing eyes.

He lived in the closed-off bedroom and would sneak out while she slept and watch her. Then, he would eat her leftovers and sit on the end of the bed until the sun rose. She tossed and turned, lightly dozing, never falling into a deep, restful sleep for a productive day.

She threw the covers off as she overheated. Not used to the heavy weight of a handmade quilt, she found herself chilled and once again tugged up the corner to cover herself. At thirty minutes to five, she gave up, shuffled her feet into her slippers, to turn on the coffee. She would need a gallon to make it through. Her thumb hovered over the on button. It was already lit. Heat coming off the pot warmed her palm.

The hair stood on the back of her neck. It was scheduled to turn on in an hour. She put her back to the sink. The pantry door stood wide open. She pushed it and heard the latch click. She yanked back and forth to see if it would pop back open. Her dreams of Dean filtered through her mind, and she double-checked her fridge to confirm nothing was missing.

"Dean did not come in and eat your food." She slapped her palm against her forehead. "You need a grip on reality."

If it wasn't for the coffee missing from the pot, she would have figured she punched in the wrong time. At least two cups of the brown, aromatic liquid were missing from the full pot she always brewed in the morning. She sipped on a cup while getting ready and then filled a travel mug to fuel her through the first hours of the day. She examined the locks, and they were all engaged. She snorted picturing the officer's faces, if she called to report sixteen ounces of coffee missing. To some, it would be a travesty to steal someone's coffee. If she filled it to the wrong line on the pot that could explain the missing beverage.

The rest of the morning went off like clockwork, except she headed to Rupert's two hours early. She had a shipment she wanted to oversee.

Twenty-One

Dean was scheduled to come over after they left the shop for the day. She was nervous about him being in her personal space and sharing something she thought was a tremendous leap of faith in trusting him.

He hadn't mentioned the invitation again since she moved in. There had been no more instances of her phone moving around or strange noises since the coffee incident.

Dean was right. Her uncle delighted in the intrigue of a good mystery. Usually, it was to uncover the history and scoop behind a great dresser, buffet, armoire, or something of that nature. The stories behind the families who cherished each piece. How they passed from one generation to the next. Sometimes, he put his own quirky spin on their lives. He even told her of a knight who rescued a princess in a daring sword fight with a dragon, so the king, expressing his appreciation for saving his daughter, gave him the desk she stood in front of as a child.

But a sealed doorway to a room in the house would have put him over the top. Was it something he added later or part of the house's original design? She found that another door on the wall to the right led to a washroom. Why would a room be made inaccessible if there was a fully functional bathroom?

Shelby shook her head, focusing her wandering mind on the documents she copied for the FBI. Since she arrived and Justin expressed his desire to see where their connection could go, he spoiled her with hot drinks in the morning and a couple of dinners. He was true to his word, and they either split the bill or took turns paying. Would her uncle be disappointed if she opened a part of herself to someone at work?

She started looking forward to those nights when they shared a meal, touching up her makeup before she joined him, and getting giddy when she saw a text from him. Another gift showed up on her desk the day before. A figurine exactly like the first antique Uncle Rupert gifted her that she dropped and broke upstairs.

He loved to make people laugh and always looked out for her. She respected how he naturally got along with everyone. And when she said everyone she meant every single person, and he treated them as his best friends. Perfect for their front sales and acquisitions of new antiques. When she parked farther away from the restaurant than he did, he would walk to her car and escort her inside. He put himself between her and danger, not permitting her to walk on the side closest to the street. It warmed her heart.

Speaking of, Justin's head popped around the doorframe to her office. "Shelby, I'm heading out; wanna meet?"

She looked up from the ancient workstation as the screen pixelated another few inches from the corner that had been giving her a fit already, another thing she wanted to upgrade in this antiquated equipment. Since saving everything digitally rescued her office from being a fire hazard, she deliberated on what else she needed to concentrate on. Justin had been an enormous help, and they'd both stayed over for a couple of hours every night and finished scanning the final pages the night before last.

Shelby slyly checked the names on the pieces the FBI questioned with the purchases on file. The owners' names didn't match. The first victim's name of Edith Johnson didn't appear in any of her files for antiques, but Arley Windham's Auctioneer purchase order overlapped with a buffet sold from the store. Reflecting on Rupert's Relics possibly being in the clear once the forms were submitted, relieved her anxiety. Similar matches were bought at auction with the auctioneer's signature securing the sale.

They had a great time. He flirted, and she sometimes responded with a quip of her own.

"No, sorry, I have plans." She winced, then scolded herself when she realized she was worried about what he would think.

His voice lowered to a chilling intensity. "Are you seeing someone?"

"No, I have plans tonight." Suddenly, she felt the need to keep quiet about Dean's plan to help her wade through the gold mine.

"What kind of plans?" He crossed his arms over his chest and stalked toward her.

Shelby cleared her throat. "I have more rooms to go through, and I want to soak in a nice long bubble bath with a glass of my favorite wine."

Justin's shoulders slumped, and he backed up. A veil of nonchalance dropped over his face. "Oh, have fun."

He turned on his heels and stomped out as if he were a child that didn't get his way. Shelby shook her head and concentrated on the documents in front of her, confused by his reaction.

She couldn't single out why some of the files seemed off to her. What was she missing? They were easier to go through while on her screen instead of chasing loose-leaf pages all over every surface in the already small office. She hoped her uncle would be satisfied with her choice to upgrade to the digital age and the correct century. She couldn't bring herself to destroy the originals, so she stored them in the old stone cellar below the shop. A dehumidifier was vital, or the pages would mold and disintegrate due to the moist air.

Shelby signed off and turned off the light. She would barely get home before Dean got there as it was, and she still hadn't eaten. A plan to stop at a burger joint on the way home had her stomach rumbling.

Clunk.

Shelby looked up at the ceiling.

Clunk. Clunk.

The slow rise to her feet led to more steps being taken above her.

The loft was now relegated to store overstock. No one should be up there. The keys hung on the nail outside the door. She was halfway up when the door opened to a dark figure backing out of the room.

Shelby screamed.

Dean held up his hands.

"You scared me half to death!" Shelby clutched the front of her shirt in a fist. "I thought you went home."

"You asked me to look over the stock and post it online before displaying it."

"I completely forgot." She waited for him at the bottom.

"Didn't mean to give you palpitations." His laugh lines deepened but he didn't quite grin. "You gonna survive?"

"Very funny. I'm thinking about getting a defibrillator for my jumpiness." She gathered her purse and belongings.

"Let's get out of here. See you in a few." He set the security system before he walked her to her car.

"Yep." She waved as she drove out of the lot.

Twenty-Two

Twenty minutes later, she licked the last of the salt from the fries off her fingers and pulled around to the side of the monstrosity her uncle had called home. She didn't normally eat in her new car, but with Dean on the way to meet her, she didn't want to wolf down her meal in front of him.

The doorknob jammed again and she had to jiggle the key for several seconds before it triggered the tumblers and let her into the cottage through the garage. If spray lubricant didn't fix it, she'd budget for Sam to replace that one also. She found the key hanging from a nail in the garage. She mentally berated her uncle for being so careless. She juggled the bag of trash, her drink, and her purse to avoid dropping anything.

When she turned the television on, it blared, causing her to jump. Jamming down on the volume button, she finally got it under control as the broadcast started. How did her TV reset to an ear-splitting degree for a third time, giving her a minor coronary? Her finger drifted over the button to change the channel; there was enough bad in the world she was aware of, and she didn't want to listen to it after work. Still, the newscaster's voice stopped her cold.

"Another elderly widow was found murdered today in an adjoining county. The police are still on the scene, and we'll take you to our onsite reporter. Shawn, what can you tell us? And is this the work of the same serial killer whom authorities are so desperately trying to stop in his grim reaper's spree?"

The anchor droned on as Shelby continued to her bedroom. She shook her head at the news. How many now? When would they catch this person? She had only ever heard about serial killers in other places too distant to be her concern. Sensationalized through movies and books, never one close to home.

She shivered again.

The doorbell rang as she finished straightening the towel when she washed her hands in the no-frills-allowed hall bathroom. Rupert refused any dainty decorating of bathrooms. Perfect timing. A smile curved her lips, and she was excited to finally share the room with Dean. She opened the thick, solid wood door to a beaming Justin holding a pizza from her favorite place in town. Her heart raced. "Justin, what are you doing here?"

"I'm going to help you." He quirked the smile she found most women melted at and invaded her personal space.

It didn't work on her, and Shelby stood her ground, not moving. "I told you I didn't want to tonight."

"No, you said you had plans for a boring night of cleaning and going through antiques. I want to help." He tried to push past her into the house.

"Not tonight. I'm sorry, I had a burger on the way here, so I already ate." Maybe he would take the hint if she was short with him. Unless her uncle told him where the cottage was, she would have to discover how he knew where she lived. Did she let it slip one day? It was a small town with very few similar cottages, so it wouldn't take a genius to know which one was hers.

She never understood people who showed up on someone's doorstep unannounced. It was rude and out of line.

"Oh, okay. I can eat this entire thing myself." His hearty laugh echoed through the foyer as he tried again to edge past her.

"Justin, I didn't ask you over or for you to come in. I'm not comfortable with you being here without being invited. I would like it if you would please leave." Shelby clenched her fists.

"You're kidding, right?" He reached forward to touch her cheek.

She dodged him, giving him the opening he was looking for, as he walked past her to the kitchen. "Justin, leave now. I've told you twice. Now you are bordering on creepy behavior."

He jerked as if she slapped him, almost sliding the pizza off his hand. "Creepy. Seriously, I don't understand what the big deal is. I thought you would see my act as endearing. I want to help. This is too much to go through by yourself. You need help and you don't know when to ask for it. I guarantee Dean wouldn't be caught dead doing a good deed like this." He softened his voice at the end, saying it quietly enough so she couldn't hear, but she did anyway.

"Please leave. If I haven't given someone a direct, concise invitation, which I haven't, then they are unwelcome. I like my privacy and don't like unannounced visitors." Her heart palpitated. Dean should be here any second, and with his comment about him, she was unsure how he would react.

"You're going to kick me out?" He pouted.

"I never invited you, so I'm technically not kicking you out. You can consider it a lesson learned: I do not take well to people showing up without warning. It's rude." She wouldn't hesitate to call the police and have him escorted out. How he reacted would tell her if she was in jeopardy of having to fire her first employee.

His eyes darkened. "Lesson learned?"

"Justin, you need to go." She urged through clenched teeth, her nails biting into her palms as she kept her fists by her sides to keep the shaking at bay. She refused to show any anxiety at his forceful attitude and stood her ground.

"You know, you're right. I'm sorry. I didn't think about it from your perspective. I would be livid if someone barged into my home. Shelby, I'm so sorry. It won't happen again." Justin stalked past her and out into the night, his spine rigid.

An engine revving told her he was leaving. She blew out all the air in her lungs and slumped against the wall. She had just secured the front door when she heard a car approaching.

When the doorbell pealed, rang in a garbled tone, and then in broken static, she yanked open the door and yelled, "I told you to go away!" Her heart stumbled, taking in Dean. Faded jeans with a gray paint-smeared T-shirt were a good look for him. The faintest whiff of his cologne, wearing off from this morning, soothed her nerves. Did Justin pass Dean on the way out?

Twenty-Three

Dean took her in, his hackles up due to her agitated state. He kept his hands in his pockets, not moving an inch. He checked out the vicinity before looking back at her. "You asked me to come."

"I'm sorry. I thought you were someone else." Her tension bled from her.

"Shelby, is someone bothering you?"

"No, I'm fine. Please come in." She opened the door wider and studied the dark as he walked past her.

Dean's hand on her shoulder made her jump. "Shel, what's got you skittish and jumping like a cat being chased by a coyote? And don't you dare tell me you are fine! You're trembling."

She sagged and rested her head on his chest. "A little adrenaline dump."

He knew the instant she put him right back into the employee category and started to pull away. He wanted her to lean on him. There was something so different from her than anyone he met.

"I'm so sorry—" Shelby straightened and said, "I don't know what came over me. Have you eaten?"

"Yeah, scarfed down a burger and fries on the way over."

Shelby chuckled. "Great minds. I did the same, and I never eat in my car."

Dean struggled to keep his attraction in check. The walls he kept up while at the store wanted to slowly crumble being around her like this, and he had only arrived five minutes ago.

"Do you want to tell me what has you so stressed out? I can see your pulse hammering away at your neck like it offended it." He traced his thumb over it.

She covered her throat with her hand. "Justin came over, and I had to practically yell at him to leave. I even informed him I had plans tonight and declined his invitation when he asked to hang out after work. What was he thinking, showing up with a large pizza and forcing his way into my house? I'm so furious!"

Dean angled toward the sidelights, peering through the tiny diamond-patterned shards of glass. At the mention of Justin forcing his way in, he twisted back to her, making him lose his calm at the idea that Justin would do that.

"He forced his way in? Are you hurt?" Dean let his eyes trail up and down, looking for injuries.

"It was more of a dart around the side of me to gain entry. He didn't actually touch me, so no." Heat crept up her cheeks. "I mean, who does that? It's rude. Plus, when I told him to leave, he said no."

"He said no?" Dean clenched his fists.

"Yes...I mean...no...sort of. Ugh, okay, let's start over for tonight. Did you want to see the room?" Shelby flexed her fingers and hands several times at her sides.

Was she hoping to diffuse the intensity rolling off him?

"I don't like the fact he showed up after you said you were busy. Or the fact that he manipulated his way inside. Let's not get me started on him refusing to leave."

The pinched lines in her face eased. Her reaction to his proclamation of frustration on her behalf tore at him, stirring a deep need to protect her. It boosted his confidence he affected her as much as she did him, but didn't change the fact that he hid a horrible secret from her.

"Lead the way. You have to show me this room. I've been dying to see what's in it." His lips thinned in an attempt to hide the smirk he struggled to keep at bay.

"Right this way, sir." She made a grand gesture with her hands to follow. "I haven't gone through all of it since I told you. The store is taking more time than I thought it would."

"You know, all you have to do is ask. And there are people right here for you." Dean's goal tonight would be to show her she didn't have to do anything alone.

Over the past several days, Justin's assistance in clearing up old files and creating new folders on the cloud meant he spent hours with Shelby. Dean didn't care for how close they worked and that they spent time outside of Rupert's.

"Justin's a miracle worker digitizing Uncle Rupert's workplace. I'm hoping with all our records digitalized, it will free up a lot of the time I put in this last week. Now I have to find a new computer. The one I have looks like it's from the dark ages. I'm shocked there isn't a floppy disk drive along with Uncle Rupert's old, antiquated filing." She coughed, getting his attention, and pointed to the doorway standing open at the end of the hallway behind the bookcase.

Dean nodded. "Rupert's filing left much to be desired. He asked me to find a slip one day, and I thought I was never going to leave the room before I turned eighty. I'm glad Justin is organizing the files with you."

The severe turn in his voice told him to rein in his dislike of the man.

"Shelby. You aren't the only one who misses him. It will take a while before it doesn't ache when you think of him. Soon, all the good times will outweigh this moment of hurting in your heart." Dean ducked past her and disappeared into the room.

"Don't you need a flashlight?" She shivered as he passed, and he knew it wasn't from the temperatures in the house.

"Wow, you have a mess in here." Dean didn't look at her as he made his way to the back.

"How am I ever going to get through all of this?" She shook her head in bewilderment.

"We. Shelby, it is *we* will get through this. One section at a time. Don't look at the whole room; it will overwhelm you. Look at one stack at a time. Before you know it, you'll have gone through everything. And you are right, these are absolutely gorgeous. No wonder he kept these here and didn't sell them." Dean fingered the delicate edging on one of the handmade quilts draped over a stand to showcase the intricate craftsmanship. "I thought you found them in a linen closet. Have you been holding out on me?"

"I was worried about what you would think, so I might have fibbed a little about where I found them. But yes, they are amazing. I need to store them properly so moths don't ruin them." She joined him at the rack and ran her hand over them.

Dean moved off to the side and pointed at an armoire. "Looks like it can take you to a magical land."

Shelby snorted at his joke. Dean had a good-humored side he didn't let his targets see.

"After what Justin pulled tonight, is it going to be hard to work with him?" He moved farther down the aisle.

"I hope I don't have to fire him." She startled when his shadow fell over her.

"Give him a chance and see how he acts." Dean turned her with a grip on her elbow. His eyes scrutinized her. He couldn't give her a reason to keep Justin, but he needed to keep his archnemesis close. "Are you worried he will come back?"

"No, he wasn't happy but when I told him the third time to leave, I think he realized I was serious. He even apologized. I was ready to call the police if he didn't take the hint."

"Did you tell him I was coming over?" Dean narrowed his eyes.

"No, it's none of his business who I welcome into my home. I hope you don't mind. I'm not hiding the fact you're here. It put me in a defensive mood; he thought showing up was okay. I had a friend in high school whose boyfriend did that all the time. Showed up out of the blue. I found out later he was abusing her and controlling who she saw and where she went. She hid it from her parents. I can't stand bullies and people who think they are entitled. I like my privacy." Shelby rambled and stared at her feet.

"I'm not offended you didn't tell him. There's nothing going on except one friend being there for another who is going through a tough time. I'll be here as often as you need. And if you don't want your boyfriend to know, I'll honor that and keep it between us because we don't have anything to hide." He held out his hand. "Friends?"

She lifted one corner of her mouth. "Friends, on one condition."

He arched his left eyebrow. "What condition?"

"Don't refer to Justin as my boyfriend. Justin has never been anything more than a friend." Shelby tilted her head to the right. "I'd like to consider you in that category also."

"Duly noted." He extended his hand and held it there until she slapped hers into it and shook it up and down in an animated jerk. "Okay, let's do this. Do you want to tackle the same areas? Or find our own stack of mysteries to uncover?"

Relief flooded him about her declaration of where she and Justin stood.

"Oh, such a dilemma. I say cover the same zones since I don't know what is all here, and you won't know what I want to send to the shop to sell or keep for myself. For some reason, my uncle kept these from everyone. Maybe until we figure out that reason, we can organize everything here and make those decisions later."

"Excellent idea. Should we flip a coin to decide where to start?"

They took in the rows. Almost too much for two people, much less one, to try and tackle what lay before them.

A shudder traveled over her giving away her secret dislike of the dark; as she looked at the other end, and the bleak light which seeped to the farthest side. "Maybe here until we can bring in some more lamps?"

"There are lights up and down the rows. We can begin down there and work our way back here, so once we reach this spot, we know we're near the end." Dean put his hand on her upper back.

"Actually, that's a great idea. Do you think there's more than one way into this room?"

"There's only one way to find out." Dean stepped around her and started for the other side, turning on the overhead bulbs.

Bright lights swung from the ceiling after a click sounded from each switch for the single bulbs dancing above them, creating elongating shadows as they swung back and forth. The coated electrical wire ran along the ceiling to the wall and down to an outlet held in place by cable staples.

Before he knew it, light flooded the room, and all that lay in front of them was excitement and mystery. It was so much larger than he imagined. It stretched approximately twenty feet. Did the dimensions inside correspond to the outside measurements? This place also extended out farther than the room and hallway, possibly taking the entire width of the house. Were these two bedrooms side by side?

Rupert had done this for a reason. He hadn't needed to lure Shelby into solving the riddle with him. The excitement in her eyes said he made the short list of people who knew about it. It looked promising that she didn't intend to shut him out. He now had unfettered consent that benefited him. Shelby didn't realize she had just given him access to a smoking gun. He held the power to affect the outcome of a federal investigation in his favor.

"Come on, lazy, get your butt in gear and get a move on," he called to her.

Shelby smiled. Dean would have to survive the next couple of hours being close to her.

After only a couple of hours, they realized they not only had to log the pieces and discover where they came from, but tucked into drawers, they found several gems. A shoebox filled with coins piqued his curiosity. Vinyl records in protective sleeves ranged from various genres and artists. A pure silver vanity set with brush, comb, and handheld mirror.

"Shelby?"

"Yo." Her head popped up from the following section they would look at next.

"We need a notebook to log everything. Maybe I should get shelving units here for everything in the drawers to catalog properly. There is too much to try and remember." Dean did a slow turn.

He sneezed right behind her and catapulted her feet a few inches off the ground.

Shelby brushed off her jitteriness. "You're right. There is way too much here to keep going back and forth, trying to match everything to the logs. Unless you have an eidetic memory."

"Sorry, the dust is my enemy. And no, to the eidetic memory, although it would make my job easier." Dean got a faraway look as he took in the huge task before them.

"Did you see the P&S stamp on the last side table?" Shelby's comment had him spinning around, his eyes darting to several works of art.

"Show me!" His excitement rose at the question.

Rupert's enthusiasm over antiques had drawn him in. With no previous experience in this field of work, it had been nothing more than old furniture before working with him. He'd padded his resume for the job.

Shelby stood by a desk nestled against the wall. "Check it out, and right there is the five-digit code used to mark certain pieces. What was my uncle doing with a Pottier and Stymus? Why would he do this?" Her fingers trembled as they grazed the marble insert in the top of the exquisite piece.

"I'm not sure, but he had to have a reason to stash away so many." Dean frowned.

"With that in mind, let's call it a night, and I'll grab an empty logbook to itemize everything here." Shelby started back to the door.

"I can help any night you need me to." Dean stopped her with a hand on her shoulder.

"I was thinking. Dean, what if all of the items here are the ones the FBI is looking for? Do you think my uncle—?" Her voice rose in pitch.

Dean pursed his lips and peeked over her shoulder. "No, not at all. Your uncle was one of the most upstanding people I've ever had the privilege of knowing. I can guarantee he was definitely not, so erase the thought from that pretty little head of yours right now." He tilted her head up with a finger hooked under her chin and wiped a smudge of dirt from her cheek. He showed her the smear on his thumb.

"Promise?" Tears threatened to fall.

"I promise, Shel, he was a good man, who I proudly considered a friend." He hugged her briefly before pulling her by her hand. "I'll see you at work."

"Can I ask you not to tell Justin about you being over here? I don't want to give him the wrong idea about us, and I don't like how he reacted tonight. At least until I get feelers out about why he wanted to help me go through everything in my own home when I never hinted at it. I know Uncle Rupert kept a lot of pieces here, but it doesn't make it open season for anyone to come and go on their own whim. I know it's a lot to ask when you don't know me well." She twisted her fingers around.

She wouldn't invite him back if he didn't answer in the affirmative.

"I agree. I swear I won't say a word to Justin about this. You should look at installing a video surveillance program. I can recommend a couple if you want. It takes less than a day to install and is easily accessible on your phone. You can see any of the camera angles and give yourself peace of mind." Dean extracted his phone from his jacket. He needed to make a few calls.

"You know, that wouldn't be a half-bad idea if you can get me those names. I guess I'll see you." Shelby fiddled with the door handle as Dean confirmed he would see her at work the next day.

Dean let himself out, closing the door softly behind him. He had a stop he had to make before going home for the night.

The drive was short as he slipped under the cover of darkness to the last victim's house. Pulling a knife from his back pocket he sliced through the police tape sealing the front door. He pressed the button on his small red flashlight and panned it around the room. The feds had already cleared the scene, but he was looking for evidence that may have been left behind.

Local police put the house on a rotation for extra patrol until the family could secure the residence. The last two nights he memorized their passes through the neighborhood. He had less than twenty minutes to look over the room. Black fingerprint dust coated the surfaces. He freely swept the red beam knowing it wouldn't register if someone drove by.

The room hadn't changed since the first and only time he was in there, except the body being removed and sent to the coroner. It was hard to tell where evidence markers had sat since the police never left them behind. He could picture in his mind the scene as he ran it through his memory, checking the room for any indication that the police might have any leads.

Satisfied there was nothing to find, he slunk out to his truck parked one block over, leaving through the winding back streets and taking the long way home as headlights from the next patrol car made a pass in front of the house.

Twenty-Four

Shelby saw two FBI agents approaching her store. Agents Irving and Jackson strolled in and up to her. She wanted to roll her eyes at their attire. She wasn't sure if they owned anything else in their wardrobe.

"We are observing the inner workings of your store today. Just act like we aren't here. If we have any questions about your operating practices, we'll ask." Agent Irving sipped from his to-go cup.

Justin faced away from the agents and rested against the glass-cased counter. "What are doofus and dorkus doing here?"

"Knock it off," Shelby hissed.

Jackson and Irving whispered while taking pictures with their phones of an item on a shelf.

"Shelby, you keep glaring at them like that, and your face will freeze, and no one will be brave enough to talk to you, darlin', or ask you out on a date." Justin stepped out to help a customer.

She didn't know how to take the fact that hours later, the agents left with barely a few questions answered. Was their lack of queries good or bad?

While the agents were in the store, she breathed a sigh of relief as they offered a buffer between her and Justin. She had gotten through the day without any undue drama. They hadn't talked about the tense encounter they'd had when Justin had shown up at her home uninvited.

A knock interrupted her thoughts. Justin rubbed at his ear and wouldn't look at her.

He partially closed her office door. "Shelby, I need to say something, and I hope you understand how sincere I am. Showing up the other night was the worst mistake I made in our friendship. You are so important to me, and I was blindsided by how quickly my feelings developed. I realize you aren't in the same place I am."

Justin joined her on her side of the desk and kneeled in front of her.

"Justin." Shelby stumbled over what to say.

"No, just listen. I understand if you want to put a little distance between us, but I'm asking you not to. I have never felt the way I do about anyone before. My heart will wither away without you. You are the reason I breathe. This is a lot to take in, but I give you my solemn promise to wait for an offer before barging in again. Can you find it in you to give me another shot?"

She breathed a sigh of relief. She hated confrontations where someone thought she had done something wrong. Justin, being his sweet self, was apologizing profusely and asking for her forgiveness.

"I promise I won't pull anything so pigheaded again." Justin wasn't that much shorter than her, even though he was kneeling.

"I forgive you." She grinned.

"Your Highness, if I may be so bold to request that you not chop off the head of your most loyal liege." Justin bowed.

"I say we start over." She glanced at her watch.

"Let me make it up to you by buying dinner tonight."

"I can't. I'm planning to thwart a coup of my laundry by catching up on some loads that are taking over the floor in my closet." It wasn't a lie.

When living in the apartment, she tried to use every single article of clothing before forcing herself to do a load, and it had gotten out of control. The towels and bedding put a dent in the arduous task, but she still had more.

"Later this week?"

She nodded at his question as she turned off the light in her office.

Justin's turnaround was a relief. It still didn't change her perception of him, but she hoped to work past the uncomfortableness between them.

***

Shelby expected Dean any moment. She texted her mom as she waited. Her mom immediately responded.

Mom: Shelby, sweetheart, how is everything?

Shelby: Good. When are you and Dad coming back?

Mom: Probably in a couple of weeks. It will be after Christmas, so we can spend a month with you. Your dad is leaning over my shoulder yelling that he loves you. Like you can hear him.

She snorted at her father's antics.

Shelby: I love you too, Dad.

Mom: Did you find any hidden pirate treasures in the room?

Shelby: It's been hectic around the store. I haven't had a chance.

Mom: We can come home earlier.

Shelby cringed as she thought about spilling the federal case surrounding her.

Mom: We can be on the first flight home.

Shelby: Mom, no, I'm fine.

Mom: I don't know, honey. Maybe it would be better if we flew out anyway.

Shelby: Just keep your regular plans and give me an exact date once everything is finalized.

She had to keep her parents safe and away from Red Peaks.

Mom: If you need us, just call, and we'll be there.

Shelby: I know. You have always been there for me. I have to go; I'm expecting company.

Shelby opened the washer and gagged. She forgot to put the load in the dryer and now had to run it through a cycle again.

Mom: A guy? Do you have a real date finally?

Shelby: I'm not going there. I'll talk to you later. Bye.

This was the second night Dean came to help her catalog everything. They agreed to keep it from Justin, and true to his word, Dean hadn't mentioned it to him. Justin's joking and flirting hadn't changed, and he never confronted her about Dean being at her house.

Headlights flashed across the windows as Dean pulled to a stop. He hopped out with Chinese takeout and jogged to the front door she had open before he got halfway there.

They'd decided to have him grab dinner on the way so if Justin saw them; they wouldn't leave in the same direction at the same time since Dean lived on the opposite side of town. Shelby hated feeling like she was lying to Justin by suppressing Dean's visit.

The smell of the exquisite food made her mouth water. She pulled down plates and forks because both admitted to being unable to operate those obnoxious chopsticks.

"We can go ahead and verify everything we found and then catalog the next section." She bit off a huge chunk of her favorite eggrolls. She held up the notebook she started before Dean's exposure into all unexplained mysteries of Rupert.

Dean finished chewing. "I think we can easily get through it by the end of the week. Then compare them to the acquisitions."

Shelby bobbed her head as she twirled her fork in the noodles, catching a large amount around the tines before shoving them in her mouth. She was starving and hadn't realized she hadn't eaten all day until she was leaving to meet Dean. The store had been jam-packed, and the FBI's surprise visit to observe her set her on edge. They had stated their surveillance of Rupert's Relics originated at their superior's request. They never bothered the customers, but their glances back and forth convinced her to retreat to her office for the rest of the afternoon while Justin took care of the purchases.

Their stares cracked her armor, and she wanted to tell them about everything she found in the cottage.

They finished their meal and stuffed all the takeout containers into the compactor before trudging down the hall for another go at logging everything.

After catching up with yesterday's finds, they started on a new stack when she thought she heard a noise. She edged around a large dresser and saw Dean taking pictures of one of the older pieces.

"What are you doing?" Shelby tilted her head to the side.

Dean jumped and pocketed his phone. "Figured we could match the photos to what is in the files since every piece is supposed to be photographed to denote damage or flaws in the descriptions. Whether they are listed on the site for the store is another thing. I can validate it later."

"You know, that isn't a bad idea, but we aren't listing these items yet until the FBI is done, and if they are already on there, we should unlist them."

"Let's hold off on doing that. If they are dissecting the site, it may look bad to no longer show them if they aren't sold. Did you tell them what you found while in the store earlier today, asking for a timeframe on the report they need?" Dean moved over to another piece and started pulling dishes from the cupboards onto the tables they had against the back wall.

"No." Shelby turned her back to start on the other end when Dean gently stopped her with a hand on her wrist.

"Shel, I think you need to tell them. What if you're right, and they need to know about some of these." He waved his hand around.

"I know, I know. I...not yet, okay?" She tried to pull her hand free.

Shelby finally finished the fourth row and heard clicking again. What was he taking so many pictures of?

"Dean, let's get this all done. Then we can worry about pictures and matching them up to acquisitions and go from there."

There was no answer. Shelby stood on her tiptoes, trying to see over the obstructions, but didn't see Dean anywhere.

"Dean?" She kept her footfalls as muted as possible and went on the hunt to find him.

Clicking came from about halfway down the stack. Why wasn't he answering her? A shadow fell across the doorway, making her scream and teeter on her heels, almost losing her balance when her socks skidded on the slick floor.

Dean's feet thudded behind her, and he yanked her behind him. "What happened?"

"I...I...heard clicking sounds and thought it was you. When did you leave the room? I thought you were in there. You didn't answer. Then, a shadow moved. It scared me." Shelby gripped the sides of his shirt as she clutched the back of Dean.

"I was getting water. Stay here. If I yell for you to call the police, do it." Dean twisted out of her grip and made a sign for her to shush.

Dean reappeared moments later and glanced behind him. "No one is here."

"But the shadow," Shelby stammered and walked two paces forward.

Dean shuffled over, blocking the room, turning off the light, and shutting and locking the entrance. "I think we are done for the day. We can pick up where we left off some other time."

"Yeah, but..."

"Shelby, everything is secure here. Did you want me to stay?"

"No. If I'm okay, why do I need you here?" Why did he want to head home early when he planned to stay as late as she wanted? They stayed late the night before, but she didn't figure he was tired enough to give up so soon.

"I can crash in my truck if you want." Dean's blue eyes cut her to the quick.

She shook her head. "No, that's not necessary."

The light bulbs blinked out, plunging them into a black abyss. The humming of the refrigerator ceased. An unearthly quiet settled around them. "Dean?"

"Right here." He panned the flashlight on his phone. The round light beam bounced off reflective objects, sending out an array of secondary glimmers.

"Follow me so I can get another light." Shelby had small flashlights in each room of the house for instances like this one.

"Where are your fuses? Maybe it's as simple as a tripped breaker."

"Um, maybe the basement. I've never been down there." Shelby started toward the kitchen.

"Isn't it weird that you've never been down there?" Dean smirked.

"I'm not scared," she blurted.

His chuckle made her smile. "Never said you were, but I find it odd you own a house and have never been down there."

"Uncle Rupert refused to let me because he said he was worried about one of his many, many stacks of junk falling over and hurting me." Shelby stood in front of very gloomy, crooked stone stairs.

"I don't blame you for not wanting to go down there. I think I've seen this troll movie before. Next, we'll hear growling and roars. Did you want me to go first?" Dean stepped in front of her.

"I can cope with basements with or without trolls, and I'll have to go through it sooner or later, so why not see what I'll be getting myself into so I'm prepared." Shelby stopped when he held up his hand.

Something tapped against a pipe somewhere in the far corner.

"If you are not a fan of rats, I'd stay here. With the age of the house and the cellar, it could be infested." His right foot thudded on the first step down.

"I'm coming with you. No rat is going to keep me from a part of my home."

Dean shook his head and grabbed her hand, wrapping it around the side of his shirt. "Don't let go."

Shelby couldn't believe her eyes as they shuffled their way through an almost empty cellar to the electrical panel. She let go while Dean checked how to turn the power back on.

Her brows rose, and she plastered her hand over her mouth. No, this had to be wrong.

"Dean, you know what? I can take care of it. I'm exhausted. I don't need electricity to sleep, so I'll walk you out," she rambled.

"Hold on. All I have to do is flip this little circuit here." A click flooded the room into a glaring brightness. Shelby squinted until she was accustomed to the change.

Dean had switched on the lights when they descended so he'd know if it fixed the problem without running upstairs.

He whistled as he turned to the wall she gaped in front of.

"Dean, I want you to leave." Shelby's voice shook.

"Not getting rid of me that easy, Shel," Dean bit out and held his phone up, sweeping across the wall the light didn't reach.

She tried to push Dean away, but he skated an arm around her waist and held her steady.

"Simmer down, and let me look at what Rupert had going on." Dean released her and stared at evidence hinting that her uncle was in league with a killer.

Tears streamed down Shelby's cheeks. Pictures of every victim were tacked to the wall. Beneath each were details of the crime and printed reports. Their address, the antiques taken, and the date of occurrence, printed in her uncle's block letters, told their story. Neon blue string looped around each pin and ran to a center tack, a black-and-white generic silhouette of a faceless male profile with "unknown" printed underneath.

She heard the tick of a switch being flicked, which led to an additional overhead fluorescent light bathing the expanse in a pristine white glow.

"Did my uncle do this?"

Dean pulled her to him. "No, your uncle is not involved like you think he is."

"How do you explain this?" Shelby swiped her arm at the wall. "Wait, like I think he is? So he was, in some form or another?"

"I can't give you an answer, but I promise you we will get to the bottom of this." Dean rummaged through six boxes sloppily stacked in the corner.

Shelby undid a crate of her own and found files not pertaining to his makeshift crime bulletin board. "They've established fifteen victims with the kills ramping up over the last two weeks, but there are more names here than the ones posted on the wall."

Thirteen faces stared up at her, pleading for help.

"I have eleven over here." Dean lined up his next to hers. "Mine represent Nebraska. What about you?"

"Give me a sec. I've got Idaho."

"See, your uncle was not galivanting all over God's creation on a murder spree."

"There are four more boxes." Shelby choked on a sob. "I hate that I had reservations about my uncle's innocence. I hope he can forgive me."

"Anyone in your shoes who didn't have a little skepticism is a liar. Even a two-second notion is normal. I wonder how he linked these to Red Peaks' deaths. This is detailed like a seasoned spy. Are you sure your uncle wasn't James Bond or something?" His lips twitched.

Shelby couldn't stop the burst of laughter that bubbled up. "Not even in the slightest. Dean, I needed that. How did he make the connections with all of these cases? The FBI didn't mention knowing about these."

"Anytime." Dean stacked his folders and replaced them. "They didn't mention anything outside of the Red Peaks area?"

Shelby started for the wall. "I need to take this down before someone sees it."

"No. It will only make you look bad." Dean stopped her with a hand on her arm, much like he did in the alley, but his grip was so much lighter.

"Who's gonna know? Unless you tell someone, like those agents, I can destroy this before they see it. I refuse to let my uncle's name be dragged through the mud. Even if he is proved innocent, there will always be a lingering doubt." Shelby pulled against his grasp, but he didn't relent and wrapped both his arms around her, locking her arms at her sides.

"Do they have those other names? Could they use this hard work your uncle put in to capture a killer? Could you, in good conscience, destroy something your uncle was passionate about? Shel, think about this. Your uncle created this for a reason, and until we can uncover why, I say keep it the way it is. In honor to the great man he was." Dean pulled her around and cupped her cheeks with his hands, wiping the tears with his thumbs. He brushed his lips against her right cheek, followed by the left, in feathery, light kisses.

Shelby shivered at the gentle caresses. Her synapses were overloaded. She snapped out of it when he stepped back, taking the heat of his touch with him.

"When you put it like that." She would be sleeping above her uncle's tracking of a murderer.

"I'm going to go. Promise me if you have a change of heart, call me first and let me know. I have a place where I can stash everything until we need to reference the collections." Dean lowered the switch, forcing the basement into gloomy, pitch-black oblivion. "I'm going to get you through this."

Dean hopped down the porch stairs as she stood in the doorway. He pulled out of her driveway before she bolted the door. She eased the sage green curtains she hung earlier in the day to the side and watched his phone light up. He held it to his ear before his taillights disappeared.

Twenty-Five

Shelby addressed Justin as she strolled into the warehouse looking for him because he wasn't up front. "There are a couple of customers in the front if you can help them. I have to run a few things by the post office."

Justin fumbled with his phone, sliding it into his back pocket as he schooled his features, easing the lines on his forehead. "Yeah, sure. Want to grab lunch on your way back? You fly, I'll buy."

"Deal. Let me ask Dean and see what he feels like." She sucked in a breath as the chilly breeze from outside knocked the wind from her lungs, as the overhead door rolled down. The harsh winter temperatures would only tumble the further into the season they traveled. The sparse snowfalls they witnessed in the last few weeks would soon become heavier. One of the many blessings of living near mountains was the cooler temps and more frequent snowfall than in the city she grew up in.

She couldn't believe next week would mark the third month since she moved to Red Peaks.

Dean stood next to the dock on his phone. When he saw her, he swiftly slid it into his jacket and lingered for the door to shut before walking her way. "Did you need something?"

"Justin asked me to pick up lunch on the way back from the post office. Did you want me to grab you something, too?" Shelby spent every night the last week going through the endless chamber with Dean and still couldn't comprehend how his personality turned on a dime while in the store. What was it with men being cranky after being on the phone?

When he was here, he converted into a dull, impersonal brick wall but seemed to blossom into a charismatic, caring guy when they dug through the antiques. She was drawn more to him after seeing him outside of his work guise than she was to Justin.

"You'll have no arguments from me. Where are you headed?" Dean pulled bills from his wallet and handed them to her.

"Sal's Sammiches?" Shelby was addicted to their turkey club. The sauce Sal whipped up was addictive, and if given the opportunity, she would drink it.

"Oh yeah, grab me an Italian sub with all the fixin's and a bag of plain chips," Dean ordered.

"Sure thing. Be back soon." Shelby strolled to the front to find Justin finishing up a sale.

"I was thinking sandwiches."

Shelby laughed. "Great minds, I was thinking the same. Dean already put in his order. What did you want?"

Justin handed her two twenties. "Oh, the usual. Chicken salad with salt and vinegar chips."

"You got it. See you in a few." Shelby threw the envelopes on the passenger seat to mail along with the one to drop off at the local police department for the FBI.

She'd copied the purchase orders for the items they informed her were stolen. Dean didn't know about the specifics they wanted. Still, she almost told him last night that several of the items in the envelope matched what they organized late at night. Her hands shook when she realized the majority pinged on the FBI's radar. Conflicting owner information gave her hope Rupert's would be in the clear.

Initially, the signs pointed to Justin. Many of his acquisitions were compatible with missing antiques. But two of the last victims were discovered when he had been with her either at work or out at dinner. It made her breathe easier, knowing she was his alibi. On the flip side, Dean's absence after the news reports left her skeptical.

There had to be a perfectly good explanation for why her uncle created a crime wall and hid antiques. Deep down, he was the best person besides her parents. Her mom knew nothing of the walled-off possessions besides what Shelby told her. They had called with their flight details, arriving three days after the New Year. They planned to stay with her into February. It would be her first Christmas alone since she became a responsible business owner. She didn't mind knowing her mom cherished every holiday with her parents while she still had them.

There was a long line when she drove past Sal's, so she kept going to the police station. She would pick up the sandwiches on the way back. The agents had told her they would work remotely for a few months and to drop off the files there. Her heels clicked against the dingy linoleum floor as she made her way up to the front. The woman behind the reception desk didn't even look up but continued to type with fingernails so long she used only her two index fingers.

"Are you here to bail someone out? If so, you need to go outside around the building to the large, lit "bonding" sign. It's not hard to miss." The woman still hadn't looked at Shelby. Her head was down in concentration, and her hands came up dramatically with every strike of a letter on the keyboard.

"I'm not here to bond someone out..."

"Then fill out the form and wait for an officer to be with you in a minute." Still no eye contact.

"I'm here to talk to..."

A sigh permeated over the desk and echoed off the glass-fronted building behind Shelby. "Please fill out the form."

"I'm not here to file anything." Shelby tapped the corner of the envelope on the desk.

"Step back behind the line. Don't need to be crowdin' my desk, and state your business." Finally, eye contact.

Shelby first wanted to say that someone with a pale complexion shouldn't wear such bright neon colors. They washed out her skin tone. The bright pink eyeshadow and green eyeliner matched her hair, teased to within an inch of its life.

Shelby glanced down and darn if there wasn't a short piece of masking tape on the floor. She automatically backed up, placing her toes behind the offending line. "I'm here to see FBI agents."

"This ain't no FBI office; you need to go to their field office." Her head dropped back down, her pink and green curls bouncing, as she took up her unmatched typing skills.

"I was told to come to the local..."

"I done told you. You don't need no attitude about you not understanding this ain't no FBI office." She pursed her lips and snapped her head to the left and then right. Shelby was ready to snatch her fingernail right off her as she pointed the digit at her.

She took a large breath. "I don't have an attitude, and if you would allow a person to finish their sentence of what they need, maybe you would have better customer service skills. Barring that bit, there are, in fact, not one but two FBI agents who are currently working out of this office. They informed me personally to come directly here and give them the documentation they asked for. Now, if you would mind finding someone who actually wants to earn a paycheck instead of giving people a hard time, then maybe I could get out of your hair so you can get back to working on your preposterous talents with the keyboard." Shelby was done with people being rude.

"Ohhh." The woman stood up. She wasn't much taller than when she had been sitting. Shelby realized the lady had perched on a tall stool. "No one talks to me like that. Guess I'll have to have an officer come in to talk to you about this harassin' problem we gots here."

"Sharnelle!" A loud booming voice from the back hollered, making Shelby flinch.

"Don't you yell at me, Chief!"

A couple of officers watching the entertainment snickered before ducking their heads when a giant mountain of a man walked out of the back. His dark, flawless skin glowed while his chocolate gold-flecked eyes zeroed in on her. He was not the sheriff she recognized from her yearly summers. He'd been the giant that cleared the warehouse during the first break-in. This man was heart-stopping, but he didn't have anything on Dean. Woah, no, no, she cleared those images with a shake of her head.

"Sharnelle, you have been written up numerous times for your lack of, shall I say, customer service skills, as this lady said. You treat the citizens of this town with respect. You are fired and have less than five minutes to pack up your pathetic excuse of a desk and get out before I have *you* arrested for trespassing. Are we clear?" The man's face was a shade of red, matching his burgundy shirt, with a gold star shield pinned on the left side of his shirt.

"Look, I can't lose this job. It pays all my bills!" Sharnelle screeched.

"You should have thought about that after not one but eight write-ups. Simons!" the Chief yelled.

"Yes, sir." One laughing officer joined him, grinding his jaw to keep the smile off his face.

"Escort her out of here." The large man indicated for Shelby to follow him. His southern drawl hinted he wasn't from Red Peaks. "This way, ma'am. They told me to expect someone to come in regardin' the analysis they're headin' up."

"Yes, sir," Shelby said, startled at how he had gone from annoyed at his employee one minute to pleasant and polite with her the next.

"Agents Irving and Jackson have been using our conference room; you will find them in there. Miss Samuel, it was sad to hear about your uncle. He was a good man. It's a shame to have lost him." He waited by the open door next to them and gave her a sad smile. His shockingly white, straight teeth only added to his handsomeness.

"Thanks, Chief." Shelby knocked on the doorframe.

Agent Irving looked up from several slips of paper covering over eighty percent of the tables arranged in rows. "Glad you obtained everything this fast. We figured a couple of months at least."

"The documents you asked for are in there." She deposited the envelope onto one of the few visible bare spots.

As she turned to head out and grab their sandwiches, Agent Jackson stopped her. "Since we last spoke, has anything come to light we need to be aware of?"

Shelby gulped past a lump in her throat and wanted to tell them about the room in the house, but she kept her mouth shut and didn't mention her find in the basement either. Until she proved her uncle had nothing to do with the stolen relics, the murders, or anything else illegal, she was going to keep the little tidbit to herself. She shook her head and turned the doorknob to leave; her sweaty hand slipped on the metal.

"Miss Samuel, are you sure? If you keep anything from us, it will be a tampering with evidence charge. You don't want a felony conviction on your permanent record." Jackson towered over her. "If these files lead to further queries, we can requisition a warrant from a judge to audit all of your files. We can and will shut down your store, which I don't think you want, to nitpick every receipt, paper, and scan."

Shelby twisted her fingers together and opened her mouth to tell them everything. At the last second, she changed her mind and clamped her mouth shut. "I'll let you know if I have anything to help with the case."

By the time she got to the front, all of the gaudy nicknacks that adorned Sharnell's desk had disappeared, and it looked like a professional workstation. She bit her lips to stop the smirk from turning into a full-fledged smile. She would have fired her long before she got to three disciplinary write-ups, much less eight. The officer now stationed there gave her a smile and a head nod.

The drive to Sal's was uneventful; not even her favorite radio station played. She tossed the mail in a drop box by the post office. Her request for her uncle's autopsy report was never received, even though she mailed two requests previously. This time, she dropped it off directly into the outgoing mail terminal at the post office. Her mailbox being compromised didn't sit well with her. All of the utility payments were posted to the appropriate accounts, confirming her mail got through. Her suspicions someone tampered with the envelopes came to light when the coroner's office said they never received her requests. The third time's the charm, as they say.

The line had dwindled to a few people waiting for orders at Sal's. Shelby parked and hopped out, ready for the mouth-watering goodness of his top-secret sauces and delicious kettle chips made from scratch.

When she returned, Dean and Justin loaded an armoire into the bed of a pickup. She waved the bags to them as she paused in the doorway.

She took the bags to her office and waited for the men to join her before she ate.

"Oh yeah." Justin folded into the seat farthest from the door, ripped his bag open, and chomped on the end of his sandwich.

Dean shook his head and dug in only after she unwrapped her own meal.

Justin swallowed the bulging bite seconds before he asked, "So, how did it go with the suits?"

"Nothing to it. Handed off the paperwork, then ran by the post office and Sal's." She crunched on a chip.

Dean didn't look up. "They didn't have any additional demands?"

"No." Shelby peered at her sandwich as if it were the most interesting thing she had seen all day.

"That's a good thing, right? Is it over?" Justin polished off his sandwich.

"I guess. I've never been under a microscope before, so I'm unsure how it all works." Shelby crunched another delectable crispy slice of deep-fried potato and aimed the next chip in Justin's direction. "Did you even chew?"

Dean covered his mouth at her humorous question.

"I don't remember; I was so hungry. This growing boy needs sustenance." Justin glided out the door as the bell rang and called over his shoulder, "Stay and finish eating. I've got it."

Dean stared at her. She shifted in her chair before he lowered his voice. "You sure they didn't ask anything else?"

She lowered her eyes to inspect the half-empty bag of chips. "No. Did you think they should?"

His mouth fell slack and he leaned back before he schooled his emotions. "Naw, surprised they didn't want to know if you found anything else or whatnot."

He stood and wadded up his paper bag before tossing it across the room, where it sank perfectly into the wastebasket behind her.

"Nice shot." Shelby gaped at the flawless shot.

He smirked and left.

Did he know something she didn't? If the FBI got to him with the photos on his phone, would he point the finger at her? The urge to call him back and question him increased her pulse. Instinct told her she may not like the outcome.

Dean skidded a large box across the floor past her office. He'd brought down the Christmas decorations. That afternoon she worked on decking the store in the holiday garb. Justin hung lights in the windows as Dean framed the overhang outside with exterior, simple, large lightbulb strands.

Rupert always went all out for Christmas, decorating the week before Thanksgiving.

Next, they placed a small tabletop tree next to the register. Large red-and-gold bows were clipped to the shelves evenly spaced along the edges.

Shelby stood back while Dean flipped the switch, lighting up the red and green bulbs hanging from the roof. She rubbed a fist against her sternum, missing her uncle even more.

"Wonderful." Justin fist-bumped Dean and slung his arm around Shelby.

Twenty-Six

The driveway to the cemetery was blocked with brightly painted orange-and-white striped barricades. A note on the front stated the driveway and parking lot were in the middle of being repaved and to bear with them while they performed the much-needed maintenance.

Shelby huffed and parked to the side of the road with two of her tires halfway in the grass, pulling off the two-lane road as much as possible. After dropping off the merchandise sheets, her mind whirled with the possibilities of whether the FBI thought she and her uncle were implicit in the crimes revolving around Rupert's Relics. How would she support herself if she didn't have the store anymore? The rumors alone might damage their reputation as a legitimate establishment.

She kneeled in front of her uncle's headstone, which had finally been positioned. "Uncle Rupert, I'm so confused. I don't know what to do. So much is going on. I wish I could talk to you. I need your guidance and opinion. Dean is becoming someone I find myself drawn to, but other days, I wonder who he is. He's probably the least personable person I've ever come across. Then he's at the house, and this other half surfaces, and he's sweet and talkative."

She brushed some grass clippings off the corner of the marble etched with her uncle's name, date of birth, and date of death. There was a small cross and the word brother between the dates and his name. The sun skirted along the horizon. She'd had to wait until the store closed before she came out. It would be dark soon, and the graveyard had no lighting.

She crossed her legs. "Justin is nice; I like him, Uncle. He is so attentive. He practically reads my mind and acts before I can say anything. I only wish Dean wasn't edging his way into my life like he is.

"Why can't you be here to help me? Is it wrong I haven't told the agents about the room? And by the way, how could you keep something so huge from me? Where did you get everything that's in there? Will they issue a search warrant for the cottage? If they do, will they find the room? The basement blows my mind. Were you some secretive CIA covert operative, and did you use the store as a cover? How else do you explain all the proof you collected? And that cellar is not a hazard of burying me alive under stacks of junk. How long have you been tracking this guy?

"I keep praying I'm making the right choices, but I need a sounding board to bounce ideas off of. You never held back and always laid it all out there. Even if I was in denial of the truth. But those hurts didn't outweigh your love and guidance.

"Ugh, I miss you; I want to hear your voice one more time to give me advice so I can process this. I hope you don't mind about everything I sent to the store so I didn't feel so boxed in at the cottage. You know how different our tastes are on antiques." Shelby giggled. She and Uncle Rupert differed from night and day in their styles.

Leaves crunched behind her. She was glad to have the flashlight from the glovebox. She aimed the yellowed beam at the row of trees. A dark shape shifted behind a large trunk.

She'd lost track of time, and the sun's glow dipped lower on the horizon.

Slowly, Shelby untangled her legs and stood, holding the light where it was. Once she was on her feet, the shape moved farther away. She gauged the distance between her and her car. If they wanted to, they could overtake her before she got to the safety of the vehicle.

A branch snapping behind her had her whirling around, splaying the beam of light, searching for what made the sound. Was there more than one person? The shadows didn't help her identify who it was, but the burial plots didn't extend that far on the property.

She didn't wait a second longer and bolted toward the beast of metal to provide a barrier against whoever stalked through the trees.

Shelby wheezed as she skidded on the wet grass down the embankment. The cemetery stood on a hill, making it hazardous to approach the road without a car. She pinwheeled her arms as she lost her balance when she descended.

Shoes squelching through the water-logged soil fast approached her. She fished for her keys in her coat but didn't find them. Oh no. Shelby peered into the window, hoping she had left them in there, but the cupholder she put the fob in while she drove was empty. She scurried around the back bumper, trying to slow her breathing, ducking under the windows.

She frantically patted her other pockets as the person's feet disturbed the gravel, crunching with each heavy footfall. Remembering when she accidentally activated the horn one day, she shuffled to the back passenger door and yanked on the handle. The door opened, making the horn honk and headlights flash.

As the person ran around the side of the car, Shelby dove in and secured herself inside. An imposing figure filled the rear passenger window. She assumed he was male due to his height and build. He had his face masked with a balaclava and the hood up on a dark gray sweatshirt. The string, drawn tight, didn't allow her to glimpse his skin tone. She scrambled away from him. His silhouette slinked away into the darkness as she climbed into the front seat.

Shelby turned on the dome light and moved her hand between the seats, fishing for her key fob to turn off the horn and leave. On her knees, she leaned over from the driver's side and fumbled between the door and the passenger seat when she hit paydirt. It must have fallen when she started to walk away and then opened the passenger door to grab the flashlight. If the fob had fallen out while she ran, the engine should have shut down once she was far enough away not to register its location.

She said a prayer, expressing her gratitude, and cranked over the engine. Not wasting any time, she tore down the road and headed home.

Mr. Stein, the neighbor at the end of the street, was at his mailbox when Shelby arrived home.

"Hello, young lady. How are you?" He shuffled over in his pajama pants, robe tied around him, and slippers scuffing across the rough ground.

"I'm good, Mr. Stein." Shelby gave him a quick hug.

"What have I told you? Call me Eddie." He smiled.

"Have you eaten? I can make us dinner." Shelby didn't mind cooking and sometimes made extra for Mr. Stein.

"Only if you join me watching my nighttime shows."

"Alright. Give me a minute to gather the ingredients, and then I'll come over, and you can keep me company while we cook."

"I'll never say no to a good home-cooked meal." Mr. Stein waved bye.

Shelby didn't mind spending time with her neighbor. He was lonely and she wasn't sure he had any family who visited. She loaded a tote with what she needed for spaghetti and a salad and then trudged through the brush instead of down the driveway and around to his home.

He laughed as they recounted memories of Uncle Rupert.

"That man adored you, young lady. He was so proud of the grown-up woman you grew into. Now what you need is a nice fella to have kids with," Mr. Stein pushed.

"Oh no, you don't. It's bad enough with my parents hinting about that, I don't need you suggesting anything of the sort. First, there has to be a worthy guy that Uncle Rupert wouldn't have chased off." Shelby picked up their plates and slid them into the hot soapy water in the sink.

"He could definitely run off any little hoodlum that thought he had a chance with you. What was that one punk's name? Shawn? Russell? Your uncle did not like him, especially after he asked you out and was caught necking with Sheila the next day. Rupert laid into him—you'd a thought the kid's pants were on fire with how fast he hightailed it out of town." Mr. Stein set the rest of the dishes on the counter while she washed.

"His name was Ryan, and he was positively pleasant."

Mr. Stein's eyebrows hit his hairline.

"Okay, okay, he was that bad. I never had to worry about that with Uncle Rupert around." Shelby swallowed against the lump in her throat.

"Darling, you just bring any suitor by, and I'll pick up where Rupert left off. We'll make a pack and be there for each other."

Shelby held out her soapy hand. Mr. Stein didn't hesitate to take it, sending bubbles floating in the air.

Twenty-Seven

This would be the last day of tagging all the antiques in the room. Dean admitted he would miss working this closely with Shelby, as they had for the past week. Being in their own little world helped him see her as Rupert described her over the past year. She got all of his undivided attention, and the green in her iris called to him, permitting him a glimpse into her soul.

Dean rushed to Shelby's side after walking in from making a phone call he didn't want her to hear when something clattered to the floor.

"What happened?"

Shelby was bent over and rested her hands on her knees, gulping in huge gasps of air. "Where did you go?"

"To use the restroom. We've been here for three hours, and after how much water I drank, it was an inevitable outcome." Dean flattened his hand hesitantly on her back.

"I called your name when I heard a clicking." Shelby straightened.

"Where was the clicking sound? Did it sound the same as before?" Dean thought he had heard the same thing earlier, but it had stopped.

Shelby nodded and led him to a large item obscured with a sheet. He pinched the edge before getting her approval to reveal what lay under it. Fine particles erupted from the fabric he tugged free. He turned his face into his bent elbow and sneezed several times. Dust was not his friend.

"Dean." Shelby's voice wavered.

"No." Dean was shocked, to say the least.

Shelby walked around it several times before the clicking sounded again. "This can't be what I think it is, can it?"

She looked at him as if she wanted him to forget he ever saw it.

"Shelby, you're right. We can't tell the FBI about this room until we know what's going on."

"But is that...those finials, rosettes, and ogee feet are the signature trademark of that maker."

"I agree it's a Chippendale grandfather clock. I think your uncle stumbled onto the killer's stash. Whatever possessed him to store such evidence, I don't know, but now it's fallen on you." Dean started to smile.

Finally. He quickly schooled his features into a scowl. Dean personally knew this was the killer's, and Shelby wouldn't like to find out how he knew.

The FBI would target Shelby as a co-conspirator. The idea that they could keep this from the FBI was ludicrous. Offering his promise of secrecy as a protection for her uncle's involvement may sway her to his side. They would hold her until the case was solved, and he refused to let that happen. Even if he had to stash her away against her will. He wouldn't lose her...at least not yet. And definitely not to the FBI.

"It's one of the items on the purchase orders they wanted a copy of." Shelby took several steps back and started shaking her head. Moisture welled, and she blinked it away.

Dean snapped the sheet out, instantly fluttering it over the clock. "Shelby, have you told anyone else about this room?"

"No."

"Look at me!" Dean turned her toward him with his hands on her shoulders. "Are you sure?"

"Yes, why would I tell you I didn't want anyone to know and then tell someone myself?"

"The clicking means it is operational, and someone has been winding it. The functional clock alone makes it worth well over a hundred thousand dollars. Your uncle never had a piece of that quality and value in the store in all the history of Rupert's Relics, has he?" He gently shook her.

"No, not as far as I can remember. If he legitimately acquired such an expensive piece, he would have called my parents or told me directly. There have been a couple of orders for a few thousand dollars but nothing close to the Pottier and Stymus table, much less that thing!" Shelby started to panic.

"Here's what we're going to do. We tell no one about this. Let me take a few pictures before I leave tonight and then see what I can dig up on the previous owners. There are a few calls I need to make." Dean couldn't seem to keep Shelby's interest.

"You tell no one about this until I can figure out how Rupert ended up with this thing." Dean lifted the sheet enough to snap pictures, then lowered the stiff, flowered cloth. "If you want to clear your uncle's name, we keep this to ourselves. Tracing this back to the original owners may be our only option to prevent Rupert's Relics from closing its doors permanently."

"Do you think the serial killer knows it's here?" Shelby backed up and stood in the doorway.

"Oh, trust me, he does. This was the last item, so we have this room inventoried. You aren't sleeping here tonight, are you?" Dean didn't want to leave her, but this needed an immediate response.

It threw a wrench in his plans.

"I have movers coming to take the final pieces in the front room and bedroom to the store." Shelby thrust the books back in front of the entrance.

"Is there any way you can put it off for a few days?" Dean swiped his keys off the kitchen table.

"I'd rather not. It's not like anyone knows it's here." She swept her hand behind her.

"When's it scheduled?"

"Around nine a.m. or a little after. I'll open the store and then make it out here to unlock the house for the movers." Shelby wrapped the long cardigan around her body.

"Make sure you keep them away from the other side of the house." Dean jogged toward his car.

His mind raced at the implications of what they discovered. This was definitely going the way he planned it to. Now to work a little magic and create a diversion and disappearing act to rival anything he had done in the past. A little-known fact was that he knew Rupert hid everything in that room and why, but he had to put on the best shocked performance of his life.

Shelby would not be happy with him, but he had no choice. After she realized how deep his deception cut her, she would never speak to him again, and the heirlooms in that room would disappear right along with him.

***

Shelby couldn't relax and slipped out of bed. She shuffled her feet into her slippers and started down the hall. She would honor her uncle's legacy and finish what he started with the stone wall downstairs, with or without Dean's permission.

The warped stairs made her hesitate before she sucked in a breath and descended into the abyss of the basement. She stood in front of the wall for Red Peaks, Washington. Shivers violently coursed over her. All fifteen faces pleaded with her to solve the puzzle in front of her. Uncle Rupert died before the last four victims suffered their demise. Who updated the wall?

She dialed Dean before she could stop herself.

"Shelby? What's wrong?" Dean's groggy voice reminded her of the early hour.

The screen blinked. "Dean?"

The call disconnected. Weird. Living on the outskirts offered spotty cell reception, but it hadn't been bad in a while. Her phone rang, making her jump and drop it.

"Dean?" Shelby answered before her voicemail clicked on.

"Talk to me." Dean was not one to stray from a topic, always to the point.

"I forgot how late or, I guess, early it was. I'm so sorry," Shelby stuttered.

"Should I come over?" Dean shuffled around in the background.

"I didn't know who else to call."

"Shel, if you don't give me a hint of what upset you enough to call me before three in the morning, I'm going to press the gas pedal down so far I'll be putting my life on the line coming for you as fast as I can." A horn honked in the background.

"I don't think Uncle Rupert did the final arrangement of this collage of victims." Shelby licked her lips before she continued. "The last four were after he died."

"You mean to tell me they are on that wall?" Dean huffed.

"How many people died so far?"

"Fifteen by last count." A whistle split the air through the speaker. "All fifteen were tacked up when we were down there. I never put two and two together."

"The new security program would indicate if someone was coming and going, but I've not seen any alerts since it was put in." Shelby scrolled through her app.

"Shel, that's because there haven't been any new vics since it was installed," Dean reasoned. "I'll be out front in a second."

"I'll let you in." Shelby jogged up the stairs and had the door open as his headlights swung into her driveway.

Dean's boots plowed into the ground, sending up bursts of earth. His determined, confident steps communicated his ability to take charge of a situation.

"This one is on me. I should have realized the last four were included. Come on." Dean snagged her hand and pulled her along.

Now that she stood with Dean, her worries settled. Shelby grabbed a corner of the first box and pulled it into the open. Dean joined her with his own.

"Let's group everything according to what each box holds." Shelby nodded in agreement to his proposal.

She lay six in a row. Her collection looked off from the last time she perused its contents. She ignored her gut and gripped the next one. The dates on each photo revealed the order.

Each container was emptied onto the floor. They walked back and forth studying each grouping. Neither said a word for over an hour.

"These aren't the same." Shelby's brain finally spit out a memory.

Dean furrowed his brow. "Why do you think that? They are still the same files."

"Yeah, but the pages are too crisp and pristine. That one over there had a coffee cup stain on the upper left corner, curling the paper around the ring slightly. Now, it's a shadowed brown and crisp. And over there, the date on Crystal's photo had a tear partially through it that's now missing." Shelby rolled her neck from side to side.

"Are you saying someone took the originals?" Dean squatted in front of the group by the wall.

"It doesn't make any sense."

"Why not just take them? Why go to the hassle of copying everything and bringing it back? That doubles their chance of being exposed." What Dean said was logical. "Or did someone hack the alarm? Everything has a weakness. It isn't infallible."

"I don't know. How would I find out?" Shelby threw her hands in the air.

"Do you think the FBI has the originals?"

"Do you?" Shelby didn't reckon they did, or she would be cuffed and sequestered in some remote jail somewhere, left to rot for her tampering with evidence charges. What length of sentence did that felony carry?

"I need to get ready for work. We are both going to be zombies today. If there are no shipments, take the day off and rest." Shelby started for the stairs.

"I'm good. I've gone with less." Dean chuckled. "Maybe there's an obscure entrance to an underground tunnel under us."

Shelby almost gave herself whiplash when she faced him. "Oh no, you will ruin any likelihood of me ever staying here again if you keep that up."

"Forget I said anything." Dean yawned as he traipsed out the door.

Shelby shivered and decided to limit herself to one shocking revelation a year involving secret entrances and access points to rooms. She raced down the stairs and ran her hands over the thick stone walls. Unless there was a section of stone that shifted out of the way, the only way into the basement was through the door in the kitchen.

Twenty-Eight

Shelby checked her reflection for the third time in the mirror. Tonight didn't count as a date, date, but with how things were headed, it wouldn't be long before Justin asked again to cross that line and blast past the friends category. He did a one-eighty since intruding in her house and apologizing the next day. He pampered her with respect and let her pace their friendship to her comfort level.

They discussed it but had yet to take that leap. Shelby admitted it wasn't the first thing to cross her mind when she took over for her uncle. When she imagined spending time with someone, Dean popped up.

She shook her head clearing that thought. She was going out with Justin, not Dean.

She liked how the green skirt flowed below her knees. The floral wrap blouse was made of springy material, so if she ate a little too much, it had enough give to not make her utterly miserable before she got home and changed into her pajamas.

A little lip gloss, and she was ready. Shelby stuffed her feet into her small, heeled sandals, which let her pedicured pink toes peek through. She carried her small green clutch, which sported several cute rhinestone flowers.

She pulled into the Italian restaurant Justin wanted to go to as he emerged from his jacked-up truck. A shiver ran down her spine, reminding her of the truck stalking her daily. She shook her head as Justin opened her door and offered to take her hand. Too many people in the area drove dark-colored trucks.

She smiled. He smelled amazing. His low whistle sent a rush of heat through her cheeks.

"Shelby, you look fantastic!" Justin dramatically hooked out his elbow.

She curved her fingers into the crook of his arm and let him lead her to the building. The aroma drifting out made saliva flood her mouth and her stomach rumble. Justin smirked but didn't say anything jokingly like he had in the past. He was very proper, a side of him not normally presented to the public.

"Right this way. Your table is ready." The hostess handed them menus as they sat.

"I've never been here before. Is there anything you suggest?" Shelby browsed the selection of entrees.

Justin chuckled. "I've never been here before."

"Oh, I thought..."

"I said Italian was my favorite, but this isn't a place a person comes to eat alone."

Shelby tittered, taking in the romantic ambiance. Dotted throughout the room were tables for two draped in dark tablecloths, with centerpieces of candles and single rose vases. The dimmed lighting complemented the atmosphere, boasting of a place couples frequented. "No, I guess not."

They decided he would get the lasagna, and she opted for the mushroom carbonara. They'd share the meals. She was nervous because she had never shared a main course with someone other than her family. Was this a date? Did he see this as something more than sharing a meal?

They made small talk, and before long, the waiter presented their entrees on hot, steaming, pristine plates. Not a drop of sauce out of place. Her mouth watered as she awaited taking her first bite.

"Good?" Justin licked the corner of his mouth before wiping it with a napkin.

"So, good." Shelby scraped some of her food to his side. "You have to try this."

Justin stabbed a mushroom and pasta. His eyes rolled back as he hummed his agreement over the flavors. "Try this."

Shelby used a knife to cut a small square off his slab of lasagna. "I don't know what I like better. They are both wonderful."

"I see a lot of pick-up orders in my future. Think they sell stock on their online order form?" Justin smirked.

They ate in a comfortable silence, enjoying the pasta, thick sauces, and freshly baked breadsticks coated in butter and parmesan. After a while, Justin cleared his throat.

"Think the feds will be closing up the case soon? So we can absolve Rupert's name entangled in anything salacious? That man went to church every Sunday and even kept his Bible at work. Come on, it should be in the FBI handbook somewhere on how to not waste people's time."

"Ha, you would think. Spend five minutes with my uncle, and you would immediately know he wouldn't hurt a hair on anyone's head, much less kill someone." Shelby was grateful that Justin seemed to know Rupert. "I can't wait for things to go back to normal."

"You're telling me." Justin pushed his empty plate to the side. "I wanted to ask you something."

"Okay." Shelby stacked hers on Justin's.

"Would you mind if I came to church with you? Rupert invited me, but I didn't feel a calling like I do now. I'm embarrassed to admit I haven't been as strong in my faith as when I was younger. I strayed, but seeing how Rupert and you never let anything sway you in your beliefs, I miss it."

Shelby's heart raced. It was the main reason she held back from spending more time with Justin. A relationship with someone who didn't have the same convictions she had would only end in heartache. "I would love that."

He reached across the table and held her hand. She twined her fingers through his. The waiter approached and tried to talk them into dessert, but they agreed they had no room for another morsel of the scrumptious food. Justin picked up the tab, and Shelby started to reach for her clutch, but he waved her off. "Please, let me."

Shelby had butterflies as he reached for her hand when they walked to their cars.

"I had a great time tonight. I know you have walls up, but I'd like to see where this can go." Justin cupped her face.

"Can you give me some time? I've barely gotten my feet under me and don't want to throw dating in the mix. How about we revisit the topic when the feds move on, and I don't feel like I'm under a microscope." Shelby leaned into his palm.

"Like I said before, I'll wait as long as it takes. You're worth it." Justin kissed her cheek, then jogged to his truck.

Shelby slumped behind the wheel, her knees weak. The man was lethal, with enough charm to make any princess swoon. So why did she picture Dean sitting across from her?

As she turned down the dead-end street where the cottage sat, headlights blinked on behind her. The height of the beams told her it was a large vehicle, but Mr. Stein, her only neighbor, drove a small sedan.

Was the driver lost?

The lights blinded her in the rearview and side mirrors as the vehicle nudged her back bumper. She yelped and cut the wheel to the right, bumping over the ditch and landing in the grass.

The truck peeled down the street toward the cul-de-sac. Gravel spit out from under the tires as they flew past, pinging against the back hatch of her vehicle on their way out. Shelby's hands shook as she fumbled for her phone and called the authorities.

An hour later, she thanked the officers who winched her out of the rut, her tires cut into the soil. The damage was minimal, with the barest of scrapes across the paint. She would still get it repaired since it was a new vehicle.

She sighed. The first part of her night was memorable for entirely different reasons than the second half. She toed her shoes off and padded across the cottage to wash her face and curl up in bed.

Her watch read a little after midnight. She picked up her phone to call Justin but scrolled to Dean's name instead. He had gotten under her skin after they spent time together over the past week cataloging things. Did she bother him at this time of night? He wouldn't hesitate to show up if she needed him with how he'd reacted when she realized someone else had been updating the wall in the basement. What if it was just a coincidence and nothing more than a simple collision?

Shelby shook her head and put her phone down. She didn't believe that any more than Dean would, but she was safe in her home with everything secure. If someone showed up, she would wake him. After calling the police first, of course. She had to get her mind on something else or she would have nightmares and be unable to sleep.

She'd discovered a new mystery series and wanted to read it. Seventeen books had been penned so far, and she couldn't understand how she'd missed them. She loved a good mystery.

She tucked her legs under her, pulled the comforter around her, and turned the first page.

Twenty-Nine

Undercover

The undercover agent pulled out his phone for his weekly check-in.

Undercover: Have time for an update?

Rana Samuel: How is she?

Undercover: She is safe and I will keep her that way until this is over.

Rana Samuel: That doesn't answer my question.

Undercover: She misses her uncle and her parents.

Rana Samuel: Are you telling us it's time to be with our daughter?

Undercover: No, I'm honestly expressing what I see when I spend time with her. She is holding her own; she is a strong woman. You should be proud of the child you raised to be such a force of nature.

He updated them on the case and where they stood on putting the killer away. One of their stipulations for staying away was a weekly update from the agent assigned to the store. So, every week as he sat outside in his truck as Shelby's guardian, he would update her parents on what he was permitted to release.

Rana Samuel: You call if at any time the status changes, and we can come to be with our little girl.

Undercover: You got it.

Next, he called Agent Winters. It had been several days since he had been able to make a call and had sensed someone following the night before.

Shelby was a confusing woman. She was a beautiful spitfire and turned heads when she walked into a room, but she seemed oblivious to men's reactions to her. He wanted to know her personally, but it wasn't in the cards with the FBI breathing down their necks at the store. The undercover had to ride this out and convince her to take a chance on him. He was drawn to her like he had never been with any other female. It would take time, but he would wait for her as long as she needed to see he was sincere in his quest for her to see him as more than what he put out there.

Getting chummy with her before nailing down and finalizing the investigation could harm the case. He wouldn't jeopardize the conviction even if Shelby was incriminated. In his heart, he didn't believe she was, but he was good at his job, which was why his superiors put him in the position he was in. He had the highest conviction rate in his department and was proud of his accomplishments.

The undercover still didn't have any proof of his suspicions, but her employee was a killer. He had to irrefutably prove it. He would have to decipher the specifics before she was brought down with him. Not only did the team have no proof to back their hunch, but without that, it was possible their superiors would think Shelby was involved in the murders. He heard about her perilous brush with a truck running her down, which didn't sit well with him. The officers circulated the story the next day after typing up the report. Even if he hadn't heard them, the police notified them of any contact with the subjects in their fact-finding mission, whether as the victim or defendant.

He was tasked with her safety while on the job, but when they decided to replace Rupert's files in the basement, no usable fingerprints were found when they processed the scene. That was a common occurrence when processing paper. They photographed everything before removing it.

Once the copies were ready, they snuck back in and put everything in its place. They hadn't planned on her having an eye for detail spotting the copied documents. He didn't stalk her those nights. Tonight, he presented to the agents in town updates on the situation. Otherwise, his nightly surveillance would have thwarted her attack.

He made it a habit to keep his distance but guaranteed she would make it home. The only account was a nondescript truck that matched half the town's vehicles.

So far, they had fifteen widows and widowers murdered, strangled with a rope not made in over fifty years. The tiny fibers in the wounds on the neck told them the age of the offending braided weapon, but they had yet to find it at any of the crime scenes. On the last three, they pulled DNA from the ligature marks around the neck and found three previous victims' DNA. There was no camera footage to match features or characteristics. This man was an enigma. There were no hits or clues to the one doing this; his team suggested shutting down the store.

With the six other states on their radar, thanks to Rupert, they scrambled to requisition those police records and autopsies, hoping for confirmation to snatch a killer off the streets, hoping he slipped up in the first crime scenes.

The undercover still argued that if they shut down Rupert's, the killer would either bolt or wait until it reopened to continue killing. As an agent paid to protect the citizens, he didn't want to wait and worry the killer would start again at a different location. He wanted to stay undercover as long as possible. Close to Shelby, to keep her out of harm's way. Yeah, he needed to keep telling himself that. He was drawn to her. His first obligations were to the job and his assignment. Yet he found it harder and harder to keep his secret. Yes, he knew the ins and outs of police work. Leaking any part would cost him more than his job. He would lose all of his friends' respect and perhaps be served with a jail sentence. That was all more important to him than anything.

He wanted to keep her unscathed by the evil surrounding her. If the suspect was discovered, especially by her, it might produce a fatal outcome. Her store was used to move the merchandise through and made Rupert a pretty penny, but not all the items were priced correctly. His FBI superiors suggested she was implicit in the crimes, working behind her uncle's back until the first documented murder put her still in high school.

A load was lifted, proving her innocence. He told his direct superior of his assumptions, but he didn't want to hear it. His superior wanted proof, contrary to what he felt. Once that was accomplished, it was another checkmark in the done column. They couldn't present gut instincts before a judge, or they would have arrested his co-worker months ago.

He cracked his neck one way, then the other, stretching his muscles. It was after two in the morning, and he was still moving copies of the purchasing records on the stolen items to his flash drive.

The filing organization was orderly but left much to be desired to a federal agent. She listed the items under the year obtained, then by maker's design labels, not the owners of the antiques. Trying to go through the files for specific items by the designer was slowing him down. A perusal of the victims would have been faster if it was by name. Although he had only connected eight of the items so far, he was talking about thirty-three more objects. The names didn't match their files. That meant he needed to do an intensive search to track down the surnames on the forms. The temptation to copy everything over and read the reports later disintegrated when the download status bar informed him it would be over six hours before it finished.

They hadn't been able to hack into the online files, and if she had only written down the password somewhere, he could have bypassed all of the after-hours research since a copy was saved on the computer's hard drive.

The front door opened, with the bell jingling, alerting him someone had entered the shop. He dashed his flashlight, plunging him into darkness. His fingers flew over the keys, ejecting the memory stick before he turned off the monitor. He silently edged to the office door. Who would be here in the middle of the night? Well, besides him?

Light footsteps announced someone at the door. "Ouch." Shelby's voice called out as she ran into the front counter.

He started to dodge around the door but didn't get a chance before she was on him. He hid behind it and grasped the handle, pulling back the slab of wood to cover his presence.

Another muttered word in frustration told him Shelby ran into something else. He hung his head as he thought about how betrayed she'd feel when she found out about him. There was no going back, and he hoped she wouldn't hate him after he explained everything. He would do anything to protect her like the night she spent time in the cemetery by herself. The killer following her would have taken her if she hadn't activated the horn. He made the mistake of being too far away to be of any help when he made his move. Again, he couldn't positively identify the killer with the hood drawn over his head. He never got a look at his face from a distance.

As an agent, he shouldn't care about that with someone he was investigating, but he couldn't help it. Shelby was different than any other woman he'd ever met. He barely contained his attraction to her when they toiled side by side. She was the source of his biggest struggle; he'd never had problems focusing on other jobs, but Shelby drew him to her. Her love of antiques reminded him of her uncle. He knew where she got the love of the solid wood exquisite pieces they dealt in.

The light from her office flicked on, seeping under the door, exposing the scratched and nicked linoleum he stood on. He inhaled, sucking in his stomach, not that he had much to worry about, and pressed himself into the wall behind him. Pages slid across her desk as she skimmed through them to grab an envelope. Shelby tugged the doorknob behind her as she stepped from the room. He let go before his grip gave resistance to her pull.

Darkness blinded him as the light was extinguished. "Hello." Shelby's voice wobbled where she stood when there was a clatter by the register.

He held his breath. He prayed it wasn't anything serious since he couldn't jump out and save her without outing himself. She paced toward the other end of the hallway and called out again, the fear evident in her voice. She put on a brave front, but her wavering words told him there was a fragile side to her no one ever saw. Tapping out a message on his phone, he sent off a text and waited for a distraction.

Technically, he didn't trespass being in the store after hours. However, the uncertainties it cultivated were more than he wanted to explain right now since he couldn't give anyone answers, or at least answers they wanted to hear.

Something scraped across the floor around the front.

"Who's there?" Shelby turned the office light back on.

Something was knocked over like it came from the same corner, causing her to yelp. The agent wanted to let her know it was okay. Her palpable fear broke his heart.

"I'm calling 911!" Shelby broke on the last word.

He couldn't have her call the police; they would find him during their search. How could he escape? Protecting the innocent was his life. It was why he did the job and went undercover every opportunity he got. He couldn't reveal his identity too soon, but Shelby wormed her way under his skin, and the temptation to expose his hiding place was great.

Thirty

She wasn't alone in the store. The front doorbell jangled while she stood at the end of the hall. Her finger hovered above the send button on her phone, ready to complete the call to the authorities. The police station was on the other side of town, but would they have someone patrolling? She dialed, waiting for the dispatcher to answer.

"Cascade County 911, what is the address of your emergency?" the calm voice on the other end of the phone asked.

"I'm at Rupert's Relics on Pine Street in Red Peaks." Shelby's voice steadied as she asked for the police to be dispatched.

"We have a deputy down the street from you. What is going on, ma'am?"

"I think someone was in my store. The door was opened and closed in a short time span since I arrived and was in my office."

"How do you know the door was opened? Or can you see it from the office?"

"I can't see it. There's a bell above the entry to announce customers when the door disturbs it." Shelby rubbed at her temple.

"Okay, that makes sense. Do you hear anything now?"

"No," Shelby made her way to the counter, her eyes adjusting to the dark corners of the showroom.

An umbrella stand skittered over, and she yelped.

"Ma'am, I need you to tell me exactly what's going on?" The calm of the dispatcher's voice reminded her of the fact she had the phone still up to her ear.

"An umbrella stand tottered back and forth. I think there's more than one person here." Shelby bypassed the front door used by the intruder and backed up as headlights splashed across the front of the store, wringing a gasp from her lips.

"The deputy is here." His strobing blue-and-red light bar sent ribbons of colored beams dancing across the front windows.

"Okay, go talk to Deputy Reyes. He knows you're coming out to talk to him," the dispatcher instructed her.

"Thank you so much." Shelby breathed.

"It's what we're here for. Don't ever hesitate to call on something like this." Her calm words helped to slow Shelby's racing heart.

Her feet took her to the door, bringing the deputy into view as he exited his vehicle, his hand migrating to his holster. She wanted to run to him, for him to guarantee her safety, and that everything was all right. The front door was open a crack, and she jumped with the tinkling of the bell over her head.

"Ma'am, step over to me, please." The Deputy's voice broke through her fog of fear.

"Thank you. I'm with the deputy." Shelby disconnected before the dispatcher replied.

A second cruiser pulled in, facing the opposite way as she made it around the front door of the patrol car.

"Can you tell me what's going on?" His eyes cut into her.

"Someone was in the store." Shelby swept her hand toward the front door as she explained what had happened.

"Stay here. We'll go in and see if there is anyone still in there." He stared at the other officer as they approached the front of the store, guns drawn.

The first officer on the scene had his gun in his hand and a flashlight attached to the top, its beam cutting through the darkness.

"Police department! We are about to enter; if you come out now, you won't get bit. If you don't come out, we are sending in the dog!" the second one to arrive yelled about deploying the K-9.

Shelby glanced around, but neither of the police vehicles had warnings about a police dog. If they had a dog in the back, they required cages.

Fierce barking sounded, causing her to spin back to the front door. To her shock, the second deputy was the source of the frantic dog sounds. She practically shoved her fist into the front of her mouth to keep the hysterical giggle from erupting from her. They disappeared a few seconds later. She scanned the trees, sweeping from left to right around the building, feeling eyes on her. After several seconds, she wanted to scream and demand to stay with the deputies. She felt exposed and a target.

Flashlights swept the front of the windows and then bounced along the floor as the deputies emerged from the building mere seconds later.

"We found your burglar. Do you wish to identify him?" They holstered their weapons.

The second officer snickered all the way to his patrol car.

"He's still in there?" A bubble of panic built. "Why did you leave him in there? Why isn't he in cuffs?"

He held up his hand, silencing her. "It's not our area of expertise, but I can help you remove him if you want."

"Uh, yes, please." Shelby's hands shook. Why wouldn't she want him removed?

"Can I ask what prompted you to be here at this time of night? I take it you aren't open twenty-four hours a day?" He nodded at the door, which didn't latch when they walked in.

"I forgot to grab the overnight purchase order to be mailed off on my way to work in the morning. I woke from a dead sleep, remembering it was still sitting on my desk." She shrugged as if waking up thinking about something she forgot to grab was normal.

"You don't email those?"

"Normally I would, but a lot of the purchases are from the elderly who hardly ever use computers or don't know how. They are old-fashioned and prefer paper copies. I'll do whatever makes the customer more comfortable. So, if I have to put an invoice in an envelope and affix a stamp to it then so be it. It's a small price to pay for helping someone." Her shoulders drooped. It was a relief she didn't see anything missing, but it made her curious why someone would come to the store after hours to do what? Nothing.

"Okay, if you will follow me." He pointed behind the register. "Check it out."

Shelby screeched at the beady eyes staring back at her, and the deputy snatched up the broom leaning against the wall. "Where did you come from, and how did you get in here?"

The deputy propelled her behind him and raised the broom. "Open the front door wide. I believe this guy may be aggressive. Since your front door doesn't close all the way I would say he was casing the joint waiting for his opening when you gave it to him tonight."

Shelby pulled a chair, wedged the door open, and hopped out of the way. She did not want to be a raccoon's obstacle between it and its freedom. "Very funny."

"I can clear the rest of the building after we get this guy out if it will help ease your concerns."

"I was in my office, and no one was in there, so I think this guy is the issue."

The deputy swept out, causing the raccoon to dart around the other side and down an aisle. Its claws scratched against the floor as it bolted.

"Oh, come on. We don't have time to chase you all over creation, and this kind officer has other things to do. You will set off the motion detectors if you stay. And there is no telling how many of my nicknacks and china sets you would break."

She jogged over a row, swept her arms back and forth, and chased the critter toward the deputy. It hissed, making her squeal and jump before he skirted out the door.

She shook and snatched up the obstructing seat. She found her keys at the bottom of her purse and set the alarm quickly before closing the door and securing it.

"That won't happen again. Thank you for coming out. I appreciate it." Embarrassed, she set herself up to be a victim.

"No problem. Will you be fine getting home by yourself? I can follow you." He stood half in half out of his car, waiting for her answer. He was the officer who responded to her crash.

"I'm fine, don't worry." She turned and shuffled over to her car. Coming down from an adrenaline dump, she wrested a yawn from her as her limbs became heavy.

She hoped to make the twenty-minute drive home without falling asleep. Her hand trembled as she held down the ignition button. Her throat constricted. Nope, it wasn't going to happen; she had never had a panic attack before but had a roommate in college who suffered through them and had explained how it felt when they came on. She drew a deep breath, held it, and let it out slowly. Thankfully, her friend also told her how to calm her brain and heart rate to keep them at bay. Another deep breath held in, then slowly released, drove the shakes in her hands away. After several more slow breaths, she almost felt normal. At least enough to start her car and go home, where she planned to crawl into bed.

Justin was due back in a couple of days, and he said he had a tip on a possible large estate sale over the border in the adjoining state. He left a few days after their dinner. She couldn't wait to see what he found; the excitement alone was enough to feel like Christmas. The anticipation was almost as exhilarating to her as it was to a small child.

Shelby would scramble down the stairs in the morning and look out the window, hoping for snow, but then sit in front of the decorated tree with twinkling lights reflecting off the glass ornaments, counting the presents. She tried to guess from the shapes and sizes what was under the colorful

Christmas-colored papers and ribbons beautifully adorning each one.

Dean reverted to his former glory of not talking when Justin was in the vicinity. It was like he was a different person when Justin was gone. He was still polite and great to talk to when they cataloged her house, but she couldn't break through the ice and get him to spill about what he was hiding. Her heart pounded at the thought he might be immersed in the unthinkable. Two of the last four murders occurred during the day. Justin helped customers both days while Dean disappeared on personal days he requested off with little to no notice. He was somber the following day.

She still hadn't told anyone about the small file she kept to herself that added up to being part of the FBI file. She hadn't told Dean after they found that whopper the other night that culminated the balance of what they were searching for. She wouldn't be able to keep it to herself. The guilt of keeping quiet about someone she knew participating in the acts of ending a life was taking a toll. She lost sleep, and the dark circles under her eyes weren't completely camouflaged, no matter how meticulously she honed her makeup skills.

She decided not to tell Dean or Justin about the truck, either. They epitomized alpha males, protective of her, and she didn't want the stress of them hounding her to put in security cameras and a better software product with ease of access monitoring.

After a trip past the mailbox, she pulled into her garage and clicked the remote for the door. For the first time in a couple of weeks, she thought about resting. Tomorrow being

Sunday, napping all day if she wanted after church service right into nighttime sounded perfect.

Her uncle never opened the store on Sundays. It was a day of worship, and no matter how much it upset someone, he said it wasn't worth upsetting his Lord and Savior. Since it was normal for it to be closed, she never thought differently about opening it now. It gave her, Justin, and Dean a day off.

They usually chose a day during the week to have their second day off since they both came in on Saturdays, which worked out great.

***

Undercover

The undercover agent watched the camera feed as they shooed the critter outside. What were the odds a better distraction than he planned fell in his lap? He quickly typed out a text calling off his backup.

He chuckled and shook his head. How a raccoon got in and created the perfect distraction was anyone's guess, but God put the creature there for him, without a doubt. He sent up a silent prayer of thanks. He couldn't wait to start attending Sunday services again once his assignment was over.

Small local police departments apparently didn't have protocols of assuming no one else was in a structure if they located a raccoon, which saved him from being discovered.

Shelby laughed after setting the alarm. Her lyrical voice filtered through the speakers. He scanned the exterior cameras and only moved after she left. He turned on the monitor and continued to collect mandatory corroboration to prove his gut instincts.

He pulled the records out, determined to finish what he started.

Thirty-One

Shelby's parents' flight home for January was finally booked and she had a flight number and arrival time. She updated them on the case, which wasn't much, since handing in the list.

She told them the bare minimum about some deaths and the FBI investigation of some of the pieces she sold regarding those deaths. They had everything under control. It was less than what the broadcasts reported, so if they wanted more specifics, all they had to do was an online search for Red Peaks. Since they were halfway across the globe, she would fill them in on more details when they finally arrived back in the States.

She loved them, but they taught her to be self-sufficient and reliant. How to use common sense and think outside the box. Visiting them in Egypt would be fun, with them having their own home now. She couldn't wait to see it in person. She straightened her spine, shoring up her defenses, charging herself with the fact that she was an entirely competent woman who didn't need her parents to fix everything for her anymore.

Who was she kidding? She was freaking out alone at night, even when she kept the bedroom door locked to block out the ghostly pieces in the house. She added one of those simple fasteners and hook latches on the basement door. If there was an entrance down there, even though she hadn't found one yet, they would have to make a lot of noise to enter the upstairs. As long as the serial killer never knew about the antiques in her secret room, she'd be OK. She wasn't a target; they only targeted the elderly who were alone. Okay, well, maybe the last couple had scared her because they brazenly killed two at the same time. And she technically landed in the same classification of living alone with antiques in her home.

At least, she told herself, she was okay, until she noticed a package on the front porch when she checked her mailbox. A shiver quivered down her spine. There were no deliveries due.

Shelby huffed when she read the label and couldn't believe this was the third time in a week the delivery driver left another of her neighbor's parcels. She saw a truck driving away. She bolted down the front stairs in her socks, soaking them through as her feet slapped against the concrete covered in snow. She frantically waved her arms over her head back and forth in huge arcs, to attract the driver's attention for him to do his job and take it next door to Mr. Stein's house. Typically, deliveries arrived early in the afternoon, but not today. The first misdelivered package she dealt with was the one after a wild, crazy raccoon broke into the store while she went to grab the invoice she had to mail out.

The sun, low on the horizon, peeking its last rays over the mountains, created the famous blood-red drips down the side of the distinctive clay, causing it to appear as if the peaks bled. Sometimes she still had a hard time not getting creeped out from the view.

How lazy for someone not to go the few yards separating hers from the next? So, what if it was a dead-end street and their truck couldn't turn on a dime? It wasn't her fault. She would call the company and file a complaint. This was ridiculous.

Tromping up her front steps that were in dire need of sanding and staining, she jammed her soggy sock feet into her snow boots, not even taking the time to lace them, and threw on a light jacket to take Mr. Stein his order yet again.

The tops of the trees swayed as she wound her way toward his driveway, and the loose tendrils of her hair blew around her face. Goosebumps jumped out on her skin. Perhaps she should have gone for the heavier down-filled coat.

The doorbell pealed through the house, eager for him to answer. Glancing in the sidelights on either side of the ornate front door, she saw no movement and pressed the round plastic buzzer again. The melodious chimes announced her being out front, but there was still no movement. Trying the door, she found it unlocked. Knowing he wouldn't mind if she left it inside, she edged the door open with the toe of her shoe as she picked the box back up and made her way inside.

"Mr. Stein?" Cold seeped through her at the eerie silence.

Stomping her feet on the front rug, she removed as much snow from her boots as possible, yet still left small tracks in the shape and molded pattern of her rubber soles. The edges immediately started to melt and pool around each pattern. Her neighbor's delivery joined the package from over two days ago on the foyer table. A thump had her spinning left toward the parlor where Mr. Stein's feet twitched on the area rug. It was the only part of him she saw before someone dragged them around the embellished molding on the half wall separating the two rooms.

She lunged around the corner to find a man holding a rope wrapped around Mr. Stein's neck. His angry eyes squinted, glaring at her through the black knit mask hiding his features. Screaming, she took off. Her heel skated in the snow and missed two of the three front steps, making her land on her side. Discomfort shot through her hip and bit into her lower back.

Heavy boots thudded on the wood-planked foyer.

Shelby's feet finally found traction under her, and she darted around the house toward the trees lining the property. She left tracks in the snow for any imbecile to track, but if she got to the trees where the snow had yet to drift through, it would be easier to escape the madman. Running down the middle of the street made it easier for someone to be run down by a car. And she refused to be that too-stupid-to-live woman in scary movies who didn't have a lick of sense.

Her breath sawed out of her lungs as she forced herself to go faster when she heard unmistakable footfalls, crunching through the upper layer of melted, refrozen snow, sounding closer and closer with every plodding step. The first evergreen she ran past gave her a sense she might be able to gain some ground as she zig-zagged around the next one, taking a left and putting another stumbling block between them. Five acres separated hers and Stein's property on this side; since her property was more of a pie shape than a rectangle, it flared drastically toward the back of her acreage.

A broken branch on the next cedar she skirted around gouged her cheek. Her hand flew to her face, and warm, thick liquid seeped between her fingers. She didn't dare stop and inspect the damage.

An arm wrapped around her waist from behind the next tree as her foot skimmed on the slush, now starting to accumulate on the frozen, uneven ground. A squeak didn't escape when a hand clamped over her mouth, silencing her as she was yanked against a hard-muscled brick wall, knocking the air from her lungs. She clawed frantically at the leather-gloved hands holding her.

She swung her elbow back, cracking the man in the ribs. His hold loosened for a split second, allowing her to drop her weight and slip out of his arms. She pushed from the ground, her boots finding purchase against the muddied surface, to sprint forward as mud squished between her fingers before she was upright again. She only made it a few feet when she was tackled from behind. As she collided with the ground, air whooshed out of her, disturbing the leaves in the immediate vicinity of her mouth, fluttering them away from her.

Strong hands grasped her biceps, pulling back before forcing her wrists around her back as a knee pressed between her shoulder blades, preventing her from pushing up from the soggy earth. A second pair of boots appeared as she turned her head to the side so she didn't suffocate and inhale the moist soil under her face, keeping her gash away from the dirt and grime.

"Stop fighting; I won't hurt you," a gruff whisper instructed above her head. Recognition flared in her at his deep tone, and it was on the tip of her tongue, but panic surging through her veins wouldn't give in to its familiarity.

She struggled to kick back and twist her torso around.

"Stop it," he hissed.

"Get off me!" Her voice whispered when he pressed his knee further down, knocking the air out of her lungs.

A second shadowy figure kneeled beside her. "I'll take her."

"Keep her quiet, or he'll hear her."

She continued to fight and drew in a large breath to scream. A hand clamped over her mouth, squeezing against her scratch; mud squished past her lips, making her gag. A fresh trickle of blood oozed around his fingers.

Heavy footfalls sounded to the left. Both men stopped and became as still as the trees surrounding them. Who was the bigger threat, a killer or the two masked men?

The second one's towering shadow practically blotted out all other light as he straightened, gun in his hand. Both wore nondescript black clothing. Ball caps hid their features in the shadows of the bill.

Shelby's heart beat a staccato rhythm and had her screaming before thinking it wasn't her best decision.

"Knock her out. We need her out of here before he hears and she gives away our position. I'll go after him while you take her into custody."

Custody? Shelby's mind tried to grasp that one word to understand what he meant.

A third man stretched out his hand and yanked her to her feet, wearing a gaiter that covered the lower half of his face, hiding his identity.

She put everything she had behind her scream; it was muffled by a hand reclaiming her mouth from behind like a vice. Not enough sound penetrated the fierce hold he had on her. Both wrists ached, manacled in his one beefy hand. She maneuvered one free and tried to claw at the man in front of her. "Would you stop screaming!"

The third stranger restrained her hand, easily subduing it, and forced it back with the other. Soon, something bit into the delicate skin around her wrists.

The two voices murmured back and forth as they shuffled backward, slipping between branches to where they hid before grabbing her.

Heavy footfalls sounded to the south, tromping through the underbrush. Would they be her rescuer or the one to seal her fate? Could they take out the two men who held her? She started to hyperventilate with short pants of air not filling her lungs to capacity.

Her arms became useless. Her traitorous eyelids closed against her will as black dots danced in her vision. She had to slow her breathing, or she wouldn't escape. She didn't get a good look at who held her. Yet something was comfortable in the tone of the first man to tackle her.

They shifted her around before she was hoisted over someone's shoulder. She tried to keep from passing out. She didn't stand a chance of getting away if she was unconscious. She made her body limp to give them a false sense of security they had the upper hand.

They lay her in the back seat of a car. A hand brushed against her forehead in a kind gesture. Her body shook with tremors she had no control over. A blanket was draped over her. She pulled her feet to her and thrust out as fast as possible and connected with a rigid body.

Their oomph told her she hit her mark, but was it enough? She sat up and opened her eyes, seeing a male on the ground. She shimmied to the other door since she couldn't leap over the guy and get away. Her fingers, restrained behind her back, fumbled over the hard plastic until they found the lever. She yanked and toppled out. She got her feet under her and took off.

Their yells behind her only spurned her on. Her feet found purchase on the asphalt, and she stumbled into the trees. She lost her footing in the ditch, unable to prevent the impact with her hands restrained behind her. She rolled several times, stopping just before plummeting over the ravine on the other side.

She sat on her hands and inched them under her until she tucked her legs through and maneuvered the cuffs to the front. Getting her legs under her, she was captured from behind and felt a pinch in her neck.

Thirty-Two

Undercover

"You're all right; let it take you." The undercover agent breathed a whisper against her ear. They didn't like to sedate people they took into custody. The extenuating circumstances and her fighting them made the decision easier. It was to keep her from not only hurting herself but also them. He practically smelled her fear and hated himself for it.

Being part of a classified branch, they had a little more leeway. Their protocols allowed them to detain people for days if they were suspected of participating in high-priority cases.

Her slurred response leaked out as a low moan. He watched Shelby fight the inky blackness that lurked on the edge of her consciousness. As she was able to move her right hand an inch, he wrapped his fingers around her, pressing on her pulse point in her wrist, and resecured them at her back. Her heart rate slowed under the pads of his index and middle fingers. The drug was finally taking effect.

"I'll give her more."

"No, give her a minute. Shelby, relax." He couldn't believe she still struggled against the sedative. No one had been able to resist its effects this long. She was a fighter, but this was beyond anything he imagined.

She'd run out of the house they staked out, due to being tipped off it might be the next target. It held countless heirlooms; the other agents put her in league with their prime target. Especially when his team informed them of the victim who lay inside, barely breathing. They hadn't had time for surveillance when she burst out the door, spurring them into action. It didn't make sense why she ran from the scene.

Her uncle bragged nonstop about Shelby. He felt he knew her, the little girl who grew into the beautiful woman he held. And if he was truthful with himself, a part of him fell in love with the woman from the stories well before he ever laid eyes on her.

Rupert spoke of their time together during summers, of his love of that little girl as if she were his own. He built his life around her and what he would leave her in his legacy once he was gone. The young girl the agent heard about was not someone who would partake in the death surrounding Red Peaks. Her green eyes held so much life and innocence. She didn't know the true harsh cruelties of the world. He hadn't seen someone so innocent in a long time. He may need a break from his job after this gig. A respite in the small town of Red Peaks pulled at him.

He rubbed at the ache in his chest at the impending interrogation she would endure. She was at the house where the last victim was found. Actually, she'd been running from the scene through the trees toward her house. They had more proof against her than the killer at this point. The killer was a male, but was she part of it? Did she know the antiques *sold* online were from fatal interactions with a sadistic madman? The two people in the store weren't aware the feds used bogus contracts for the stolen antiques. They held them in a warehouse for the families to pick up after everything was settled.

The undercover jumped into the passenger seat. His coworkers advised they exaggerated the outcome of the attempted murder of Mr. Stein, freeing him to ride with Shelby to their interrogation room. They pulled a trump card to lure out their target. The killer wouldn't know Mr. Stein survived. They would splash his death all over the newspapers and local stations, claiming him as the latest victim.

Shelby wouldn't be happy when she roused and woke handcuffed to a table facing a two-way mirror. He would be on the other side, so she wouldn't see him. He huffed out a breath as Agent Winters steered the SUV over the rugged terrain, and they headed toward their warehouse in the next county. He wouldn't be the one to interrogate Shelby and perform the necessary tasks he normally did since he was still undercover.

"She may be the break we've been looking for." Andy Winters didn't look at him as he drove. "Just because she was in school during the first killings doesn't mean she didn't join up with the killer later on."

He grumbled under his breath. Winters had a point. They were partners for the last decade or so. Something about the close-knit cases they ran together made them as close as brothers—dealing with the grueling details most people couldn't come to grips with hearing. He was closer to him than his real brother. They became each other's sounding boards and prayer warriors when an assignment was particularly nasty.

"Guess we'll find out." He had to keep his suspicions neutral, or Andy would unearth that he may be compromised. He hadn't crossed a line, but Andy wouldn't hesitate to alert their superior and let him know he may be prejudiced and unable to keep a clear head where Shelby was concerned.

As they pulled into a warehouse's parking lot, they proceeded around back, where they'd amassed the antiques. They each held an arm and hauled her through the aisles, getting questioning looks from their coworkers. The toes of her rubber-soled snow boots skidded and jumped along the floor as they hefted her into an interview room.

He watched Andy secure Shelby's wrists to the table in front of her with handcuffs looped through the ring bolted into the middle of the cold metal desk. Her head lolled to the side. The abandoned warehouse, where most of the stolen merchandise was coincidentally stored, behind a false panel, would have to be where they kept her until they heard differently.

"I'll let the boss know we have her here and see if he wants to interrogate her or if he wants us to do it." He left, closing the door quietly behind him.

He heard the snick before Shelby groaned. His heart told him she was who she presented to the world and didn't participate in the crimes involving her uncle's store. Rupert had made him promise he would look out for her until this was over. He never thought it would take as long as it had, or for him to develop feelings for her. Yeah, he prayed she wasn't tangled up in this fiasco.

Her fingers twitched. He wasn't ready for her to see him. Especially if he stayed under, a decree sanctioned by his boss's authorization. Stepping from the room before she regained consciousness, he nodded to Andy and disappeared around the next corner. He would let Andy get answers. And keep her out of the way while he investigated more. Could he spin it with her traveling out of town, leaving them in charge while she checked out an estate?

What if they released her and she arrived at work? How did he keep her from leaking their location? This might crash down around him. He committed to putting in more hours than he wanted, to see this through to the end.

"Boss wants you to confiscate the items in her house. Warrant is being emailed to you as we speak," Andy groused before joining Shelby.

He shook his head as he jogged out the door after nodding at Andy and headed to the cabin. This could get sketchy if he didn't play his cards right.

If he was honest with himself, the length of time he'd been under was nothing compared to two assignments ago when it was for more than two years. He didn't dwell on that time. He had barely made it out alive. This assignment was easy in comparison. They didn't know this one would last more than a couple of months, but then, with Rupert out of the picture, it extended the ruse. Adding Shelby to the mix threw a wrench into everything.

He punched in the code and let the other agents into the cottage. "This way."

Agents Glass and Sanders followed him down the hall.

The shelves pulled away from the wall and he stormed back out of the room. Everything was gone.

"Where is all the evidence?" Glass tapped the top of the opening with his flashlight.

"It was here the other day." The undercover agent didn't know what to think.

"So, who did she have to move it?" Sanders motioned them to hit the basement, the second part of their search warrant.

If the files were gone, he would have no choice but to have her arrested as a co-conspirator. The light reflected off the pages still tacked to the wall. He was dreading the weekly check-in with Shelby's parents and informing them they had Shelby detained so she would be out of contact.

"Guess I'll be shredding all afternoon since we already have the originals." Glass stacked two boxes in his arms.

Sanders grabbed three while he cleared off the wall and snagged the last few.

Glass stood at the back of the vehicle, informing Winters of the snag in their investigation.

Thirty-Three

Shelby sat at a silver metal table in a small room with a mirror on a wall facing her, her hands cuffed to a metal ring bolted into the surface. Oh, come on. She wasn't dumb enough not to know a camera perched on the other side of the reflective glass.

Agent Jackson entered the room in his usual attire, and she almost wondered if he only had one suit since it looked like the exact one he wore the last two times she'd seen him. He handed her an open water bottle. She took a drink, swishing it around in her mouth and spitting it into a trashcan he held to rinse the dirt out.

Next, he set a first aid kit on the table. "May I?"

She nodded, not ready to say anything.

He moved his chair around and popped the lid up on the kit. He snapped on a pair of gloves. She winced when the wet antiseptic pad pressed on the gash on her cheek.

"Sorry."

He diligently cleaned and sterilized the wound before pulling out steri strips, tacking the sticky sides to her skin, and pinching together her cheek as he applied them. Her eyelids flickered as her cheek started to throb at the pressure. Her eyes watered without her permission.

After finishing, he retrieved the trash and kit and joined another man at the door.

"My name is Agent Winters," the other man said. "We have a few questions. But first, you have the right to remain silent." He read her her rights and asked if she understood them.

"Yes."

"Do you wish to speak with us without your attorney present?" He stared, his features devoid of any emotions, making him appear inhuman.

"No." She didn't have an attorney, but weren't they supposed to provide one?

"Okay, no problem. I'm going to lay a few things on the table for you to consider before we allow you to call for representation. First, you ran from a murder scene. Second, your store is the epicenter of a serial killer probe. Third, your refusing to speak with us only points to your guilt. I would think someone who is innocent would be rushing to clear their name. But hey, that's me. Nothing to hide; don't need a lawyer." Agent Winters sat back and crossed his ankle so it rested on the knee of his other leg, inching the fabric up so a small line of leg was revealed between his sock and the bottom of his pants. Spending time in the sun wouldn't be the worst decision he made to add a little color to his pasty pale skin.

Shelby didn't say a word but only studied the table and the small ring she was tethered to in the cold, unforgiving cuffs.

"Nothing?" He looked at the mirror behind him. "Fine, but it's your funeral. I'd make sure you have your heart right before you meet your Maker."

"If I'm in custody, shouldn't I be at the police station?" Shelby didn't like this one bit and yanked on her hands.

"Not gonna happen," a another agent called out from the door she didn't hear open again after Jackson left.

"Please let me go. I didn't do anything," Shelby pleaded.

"Rich coming from someone who ran from a murder scene." Agent Winters scoffed.

"Mr. Stein is dead?" She stifled a sob.

The agent at the door didn't budge or nod. She realized she probably witnessed his last few seconds on this earth.

"God, please help me out of this." Shelby lowered her head as she mouthed her prayer.

The shuffle of a chair scraping against the floor as someone stood wasn't enough to raise her eyes.

The click of the latch sliding home echoed in the room as he left.

She got to have one phone call. Why weren't they taking her to the hospital for her injury? The bigger question. Were they even legit federal agents? Her head pounded from her sprint through the cold, windy air and the smack to her face by a limb, along with the stress of the situation.

She dropped her head into her hands. She was scared and she didn't care who saw her at her weakest. Her eyes drifted shut, and she soon fell asleep.

***

Shelby groaned when the brightness in the room hindered her from opening her eyes fully. A door clicked somewhere, and there was a thunk in front of her. She tried to rub the drowsiness from her eyes, but her hands wouldn't budge. Her forehead rested on a hard surface.

"Miss Samuel? A situation has developed." She bolted upright at the man's voice and practically pulled the table she was secured to, back with her. "We only have your best interests at heart."

Instinctively, she pulled her hands harder against the shackles. No one wanted to be restrained without a way to elude their enemies. Her breathing hitched. She didn't remember how she got here. Did they arrest her? Why couldn't she remember? Why would they bring her in like this?

"I want my lawyer." She gulped down air, trying to keep herself from vomiting. Where were Agents Irving and Jackson? Then everything clicked. The killer, her neighbor, and a man in a ski mask. Her trying to run away. Someone injecting her with something.

"We can discuss that, but since we are part of a clandestine department of the FBI, we can detain you for an indefinite number of days. We would prefer not to and want you back home as soon as possible." Agent Winters plopped down in a chair across from her and slid a glass of water to her. It held a straw, so she didn't need to use her hands.

She wanted to refuse any act of kindness when she didn't know why they held her. She'd provided them with all the purchase orders they requested from her, and they hadn't contacted her since.

Her parched throat cried out for the ice-cold liquid in the glass sitting in front of her. She closed her eyes as the water soothed her.

"We need to discuss your involvement in your neighbor's murder."

She gasped. “Mr. Stein?”

“Yes. You ran from the house as agents converged on the site.” He tapped a couple of photos printed on matte photo paper. Shelby captured mid-stride, darting around from the front of the house.

“Miss Samuel, may I call you Shelby?”

She jerked as his hand covered hers. Tears crested her lower lashes. “I didn’t kill him.”

“When you ran, we followed you since we were already in the area. We received a tip Mr. Stein was in the market to sell several items. He listed them online. We flagged the post and set up an alert. Someone on your store’s business line contacted him.” Agent Winters tapped on the next piece of paper he thrust her way.

The words and numbers blurred as she tried to read it through unfallen drops of moisture collecting in her lashes. “I don’t know anything about this. If he wanted to sell anything, he would have contacted me directly. He and my uncle were friends for years. I would visit with him a couple of days throughout my summers with Uncle Rupert. He wouldn’t go to anyone but me.”

“We’ll look at the post and see if we can confirm our suspicions he didn’t post it. Is there anyone you can think of out of your employees, delivery drivers, or maintenance staff who may have done this and drew in you or your uncle?” Agent Winters pulled the pages back and tapped them together before sliding them into a folder.

“Wait. Do you have my phone tapped? Don’t you need a warrant or something?” Shelby’s head spun.

"We don't have to have a warrant for phone numbers dialed from a specific phone. Only if we are listening in on conversations." He tapped his fingernail on the page with the records. "Now, can you tell me about your employees and other staff and if they might be a person we need to look into more closely?"

"No. I want my lawyer." The store was everything to her uncle and now her. She relished coming to visit every summer. He opened his house and store to her. She always knew she would end up in Red Peaks to take over for him, but she thought it would be years from now. This was too soon. She didn't plan on being here right now. So, she couldn't think of anyone who would do this to her uncle or her and use the store for their own gain. Shelby's mind raced through everything since she came back.

Justin was such a people person. He lured anyone into buying anything they hesitated over. He didn't need to kill them to wrestle their heirlooms from them. All he had to do was sweet talk them. He pointed out facts and design features customers wouldn't think of. Did he use those people skills to finagle people out of their heirlooms? She couldn't see him killing anyone. He was too kind. Would someone who killed elderly people act so genuinely sweet over a fallen ice cream cone like he had the first day she'd worked with him?

Dean was standoffish and had the strength to commit so many killings. She still couldn't get the thoughts of him out of her mind of the day the ancient oak tree fell on her car and how caring and gentle he was with her until she was taken to the hospital. The numerous nights he spent going through the house with her.

She didn't know the delivery drivers and other contractors well enough to point any fingers.

The fact her uncle trusted Dean also cemented her decision he couldn't be guilty. Her uncle was the best judge of character. He had an insane ability to see people in their truest form. She remembered the boyfriends he ran off, promising her they weren't good enough for her after meeting them one time.

He had been right in every instance. After a talk with Shelby's uncle, they moved on too easily, which proved to be precisely how Rupert predicted they were.

"Agent Winters, I don't know either one of my employees, Justin and Dean, well enough to give any insight on the subject."

"What can you tell me about the two men you mentioned?" After starting a recording app on the fanciest device she had ever seen in cellular stores, he sat back. It was probably the highest classified spy phone ever made with all the bells and whistles.

"I believe I've already asked for a lawyer. If you think you can out stubborn me, you're wrong." Shelby once gave her mom the silent treatment as a teenager because she wouldn't let her go out with friends who ran with a rough crowd. At the time, she didn't see what her mother recognized in their actions and the trouble they got into when Shelby stayed home. Her parents got a glimpse of her tenacity when she believed in something.

If they wanted to know about her employees then they could bring them in and question them themselves.

Shelby cleared her voice after several minutes passed. "You questioning them yourself will give you a bigger picture of who they are and what they are capable of. A few months of supervising them doesn't give me an inside look at their personal lives or how they spend their spare time."

Agent Winters interrupted her. "You seemed pretty cozy with Justin on several occasions. Has he asked you out in a personal capacity? Are you and he in an intimate relationship?"

Shelby sat unspeaking.

"Is that a yes or no, Miss Samuel?" Agent Winters raised his eyebrow.

She couldn't meet his eye. Would Justin answer that question and contradict her answer?

She'd pictured what dating Justin would be like, but she hadn't acted on anything because she was still settling in. Honestly, Dean crept into her thoughts, shoving Justin to the side as soon as she spent time with him. It wasn't any of their business if she entertained the idea; it had no bearing on the current situation.

"You aren't convincing me you want to help us out. What about the other night when you had a romantic-style dinner at the Italian place?"

"Are you following me?" Shelby didn't remember anyone standing out.

"Locating all parties in an ongoing fact-finding mission is what we do. What about spending time with Dean outside of work? Has he been to your house?"

"You're following me. Shouldn't you know the answers to your own question?"

"He has been seen coming over at all hours of the night."

"We are friends and coworkers, nothing more." She shook her head and bent forward to take a drink from the straw again. "Can I go now?"

"I'm sorry but we need to keep you here. I have a few queries involving what stock Dean assisted you with." His eyes narrowed.

Was there anything they didn't know?

He sighed as if he didn't want to be there any more than she did.

"He's in charge of an accurate account of the store's supply and demand." So, what if more than a few were at her house? Her palms began to sweat, and all she thought about was wiping them off on her jeans.

"We need you to be specific. Where is it? What type? You know, things of that nature." He sat back as if he was having a Sunday afternoon conversation. "Because to be honest with you, I believe you are withholding information, making it a chargeable offense for tampering with evidence, as we advised earlier. There's more than what is in the building you operate out of." Agent Winters glanced at a message on his phone and glared at her. "Where is the stock from the house? An agent went to confiscate certain items, and when they arrived, it was emptied out."

"Don't you need a warrant?"

He swiped over the screen to reveal a document with the word warrant in bold letters. "Got one. Now, where is everything you neglected to inform us you discovered? And we haven't even gotten to the incriminating files in the basement with your prints all over them."

The rapid beat of her heart pulsed in her ears. They knew? How did they know what was in her house? Dean agreed with her to keep it from the FBI so they didn't hear it from him. Dean was the wild card. Did that mean Dean was the killer? Did he move the inventory before they could serve the warrant? They must be following him. Who was chasing her from Mr. Stein's house? She couldn't breathe past the tight band at his betrayal. Dean looked guiltier the longer she sat there. Her vision blurred. She thought he was such a nice guy. How did they know it was her prints? She never had them taken.

Dean, a killer, was in her house with her!

For over a week!

Shelby's vision blurred. Woozy from her short rapid pants she felt like she might tumble out of the chair.

"Miss Samuel? Ma'am, can you hear me?" A door opened, and someone yelled. Then, someone loosened the cuff on her right wrist.

Dean was the only one aware of all the speculative commodities in the house. Did her uncle tell the FBI about it before he died? Did they use the cottage to store the pieces? Did they set her up to be a scapegoat for a serial killer?

A cool, wet towel swathed the back of her neck, jolting her. A hand guided her head down between her knees. "Miss Samuel, I need you to calm down, okay?"

"What did you say to her to upset her like this?" The voice sounded familiar. "Miss Samuel, Shelby, it's Agent Irving. It's going to be okay; take a few slow, deep breaths."

Agent Irving was here? Why wasn't he doing the interrogation?

Her vision cleared, and she was able to breathe again.

"Can you tell me what scared you so bad you had a panic attack?" Irving removed the cloth from her neck and let her sit up.

Her eyes darted from one man to the next, trying to focus.

Agent Winters said, "There are some things we are working on, potentially dangerous to your well-being. I wanted to tell you after this initial talk I've had with you. I don't believe you have anything to do with the murders. Unless you were hunting down and killing people in your junior year of high school, you aren't entangled in this disaster. The timeline doesn't fit, and it would have been too cumbersome unless you were nearby.

"We finally got your itinerary from the antique expo you attended, showing you, in fact, held a busy schedule during several deaths in Red Peaks. I hoped if you found anything incriminating, like a walled-off room with all the missing antiques we need, your first instinct would be to call the authorities, but you didn't. If you witness any suspicious activity on either of your employees, you need to let me know immediately." Agent Winters was agitated. "Charges will be determined at the conclusion of this case and how much the withheld information was detrimental to our catching a killer. Don't leave town."

"Is that room empty?" Shelby assumed Dean removed everything.

It was the only explanation. Meaning that he didn't work for the FBI, or they wouldn't be so mad.

"It is, but we hit paydirt in the basement. Those cases weren't triggered in our VICAP inquest for similar MOs because not a single county had duplicate deaths. They weren't entered into the database because they thought they were a one-and-done. Some even made arrests of relatives who they alleged were linked to the kill. They're growing bolder.

"I'll leave my number with you. When we allow you to leave, I expect a call as soon as anything comes your way to help solve this," Agent Winters continued and pulled out a key.

After unshackling her second wrist and pocketing the cuffs, he beckoned with his hand for her to proceed out the door.

"You mean I can go?" Shelby rubbed her wrists, where she tried to tug her hands from the table.

"We got our answer from your reaction. We're on top of this. Here's my number if you want to add anything or if you have any problems after you get home." Agent Winters didn't meet her eyes but looked at the two-way mirror on the other wall.

He placed his hand on the small of her back. "We need you to stay out of sight for a couple of days. Can you help us? Stay in your house and don't answer any calls or invite anyone over. We have someone in a position who can cover and say you're out of town at an estate auction so we can have our guy get chummy on the inside."

"Someone inside? You have an agent in my store?"

"Miss Samuel, don't put words in my mouth."

"No! You have someone lying to me and in my business snooping around?" Her breath sawed out of her. "I am not going to stay away from my store and not talk to people who call me because you're in the middle of your job. I won't say anything to anyone, but I have to be reachable."

"I'll tell you what I can, but you said you wanted to help bring this guy in. I could be disciplined for letting you know we have someone on the inside who visits the store often so we can keep an eye on the people who work for you. How about if you let us keep you company for a few days, and then we can revisit if it would put you in danger to have you go back? Do you have confidence in both of the men who work for you to keep the store open and running?" He stopped her with a hand anchored around her elbow.

"Well, yes, but you implying you have an agent in the store to keep an eye on my employees means you think the other one is the killer. So, I technically don't have any employees if what you insinuated is true. And what do you mean to keep me company and *let* me go back? This is too much. I want to go home."

"Correction, I said someone on the inside was *close* to the killer, which could include a delivery person working with an employee. Or even not related to the store but selling the stolen items after killing them, and the employee is an innocent caught in the web without their knowledge. We are after the person responsible and want to exonerate any innocents of wrongdoing, including you. We want to keep you under wraps while our undercover goes into the store and sees what he can dig up without your employees being alerted." Agent Winters pointed at another agent and turned her around, taking her past where they held her.

Shelby was completely confused. Here, she thought her employees not only included a murderer but also an FBI agent. How he worded things blurred the lines. Or were other people drawing them in, and they had no clue someone they communicated with was the person responsible? She had the urge to defend her employees if they were innocent. Her head throbbed, and she wanted to close her eyes; her bed was calling her name. She nodded and was instructed to go through another door.

She stopped short when she saw it was a small concrete room. A bed sat with the headboard against the side wall. No windows existed, and a complete wire cage-type ceiling protected the light fixtures. A tiny, flowered, opaque shower curtain on a metal ring pulled around a small toilet next to the most undersized stand-up shower she had ever seen, so small it couldn't cover both at the same time. A metal sink bolted into the concrete blocks snugged tight in the other corner across from the bed.

She pivoted on her heels. "No, wait!"

Before she offered a protest, they shut her in. She tried the doorknob, but it wouldn't budge. "Agent Winters!"

It was quiet on the other side. Was he even a badge-carrying agent, or was she held by a criminal? What federal agency puts innocent people in windowless rooms and locks them in for an indeterminable amount of time?

Yet Agent Irving had been in the police department. If Winters worked with him, that made him an agent.

Shelby pounded on the door until her fists were bruised. What would happen next?

Thirty-Four

Shelby scooted back on the bed and pulled her legs up. She laid her head on her knees and wrapped her arms around her shins. The room was beyond chilly, and her skin pebbled as the vent over her head blasted more arctic air into the small cell.

The air-conditioning detonated chilly air on six separate occasions in short intervals, leaving her shivering. The thin blanket on the bed held no heat. The doorknob rattled as it was opened. Agent Winters placed a tray on the table across from the door and turned to leave.

"Wait!" Shelby stumbled to her feet. "I want to go home!"

"I'm sorry, Miss Samuel, that isn't an option right now. Our agent and your employee are handling all the accounts. We informed them you traveled out of town for the foreseeable future. I would settle in and enjoy a nice little vacation courtesy of your tax-paying dollars."

"There you said it again."

He clenched his jaw. "What?"

"You said an agent and my employee. That means someone within my store works for you. You can't hold me without letting me talk to my attorney." She tried to keep her teeth from chattering. That was how cold she was.

"I can neither confirm nor deny your allegations." He turned toward the door.

"We will get to that later."

"It's freezing in here. I'll end up with hypothermia if you don't adjust the temperature. Can I have a change of clothes? I can't stay here indefinitely without some of my things." Her teeth chattered.

He nodded and then secured her inside. The vent spewed its arctic front, and she shuffled to the food, hoping for a hot meal. Instead, she was given a turkey sandwich, ice-cold soda, and a small cup of chocolate chip ice cream. "Are you kidding me?"

Shelby stomped to the bed, shoving it away from the wall. It took her several minutes to push it to the other side of the room so it didn't receive a direct gust of air.

Agent Winters came back and took in her remodeling. He said nothing but dumped a bag she was familiar with and a heavy blanket at her feet. Once alone, she opened her emergency bag from the back of her car. Everything was out of order and unfolded. She blushed at the thought that they saw her underwear.

She had two pairs of leggings, a sweatshirt, a T-shirt, a pair of shorts, a fleece blanket, several undergarments, tennis shoes, hiking boots, and numerous socks. Clothing-wise, she was in pretty good shape, depending on how long her so-called vacation lasted.

Bar soap, deodorant, dry shampoo, lip balm, and a toothbrush and toothpaste were added to the pile. Other essentials like a small first aid kit, not even containing a pair of scissors, which she hoped she didn't need, rounded out the contents.

Shelby hammered her fist against the door, refusing to be treated like a criminal. "I want my lawyer! You can't keep me here!"

She pulled the plastic curtain around the shower to change out of her work clothes, which had pine needles and mud caked around the knees where she fell. Her snow boots normally made her feet sweat, but they were still soppy from running through the snow to try and stop the delivery vehicle, making her colder in her igloo. The shower curtain gave her a false sense of privacy. She wondered if they would take it away to punish her if she disobeyed some convoluted rule she had no clue existed.

She put the dirty laundry into a bag she extricated from a pouch of her go-bag. She threw the snow boots on the floor by the door. The thin blanket covering her thick fleece leopard print throw kept her warmer, holding in the heat. She snaked her arm out from under the covers when she shuffled over to the food. She didn't risk lowering her body temperature if she ate the sandwich, but the ice cream? Yeah, not happening.

The condensation on the paper cup screamed at her bladder, informing her she would need to go sooner rather than later, completing her humiliation.

She hammered on the door again, trying to get someone to notice. She gave up and used the facilities since going home was out of the question.

A full tummy relaxed her enough that she dozed for several hours. When she woke next, the tray had been removed, and more bedding had been provided.

She hadn't heard anyone in her room, which worried her. Did they drug her food?

When they next delivered the trays, the agent didn't talk to her or ask if she needed anything. Had her friends tried to call her? What about Justin or Dean? Were they told where she was? Or just told to handle things?

She wrote a complaint in her head so many times she almost had it memorized. Agent Winters would find she was not some wallflower who would let them get away with how they treated her. She counted the days by the types of meals they fed her. Breakfast was a lukewarm bowl of oatmeal, so thick it stuck to the spoon, which she diluted with water so she could swallow it. Lunch was a typical sandwich, but after the first day, they never served any more ice cream. Dinners, unhealthy fast food. The choice depended on who delivered them.

Winters was a burger kind of guy; another tall but reed-thin carbon copy preferred one of those popular lean rice and veggie bowls weighing at least five pounds, while a third guy favored pizza. They were slick by removing the establishment's logos and names from the meals. The burgers were set out on a plate, and fries emptied from their portable containers next to the burger. Pizza deftly had the top of the box cut off. There was nothing to give her a clue as to her proximity to civilization.

Four days passed, and Agent Irving arrived to drive Shelby home. It was dark outside when they loaded her in the car. The blindfold had her hands sweating, and with the twists and turns he took, it confused her where they started from. He didn't say much, directing her to remain quiet and not speak about anything ongoing with the case. Her dead phone and purse lay on the table by the front door. She promised herself to add a few more conveniences to her bag, including a Bible and maybe a riveting paperback.

Shelby soaked in a scalding bath to erase the humiliating situation she faced. Her muscles knotted from the stress of no private showers or bathroom facilities. Plastic silverware had been accounted for after every meal. Did they think she would fashion one into a shiv?

Who could she go to for her mistreatment? If what they said was correct and they were part of a special task force in the bureau, then she had no recourse. It would be her word against theirs with no corroboration.

They wouldn't even let her have a Bible while she was there. How hard was it to pick one up?

The nights in her cell, absent of any sounds, were the hardest. She was used to the nightly song of the wildlife in the forest behind her quaint cottage lulling her to sleep, as her body relaxed with the symphony they performed.

Shelby crawled beneath the quilt and decided to never complain about being hot again. Her phone beeped as it finally had enough charge to load her messages. Justin texted twenty times, while only a few came from Dean. She started a group text informing them she was back in town and would be back at work after catching a breather.

Her phone pinged about seven times with their concerns and requests to come see her. She shut them down and said in no uncertain terms she would discuss it the next day. She tugged the pillow to her and burrowed under her fresh bedding.

The creaking of a floorboard as if someone walked around woke her. She gripped the baseball bat beside the bed and tucked her phone in her robe's pocket.

Realizing it was only in her dream, she lay back down. The doorbell rang, making her jump. A glance at the clock indicated it was four in the morning. Who in their right mind goes to someone's house at this awful hour? She was ready to give someone a piece of attitude they wouldn't forget any time soon.

Shelby stormed to the front door and yanked it open, hefting the bat above her head, ready to take a swing.

"Whoa, Shel, it's me!" Dean screamed as she swung the bat down.

It was already too late to stop her as the momentum took her forward when he wrenched the bat from her grip, pinwheeling her into him. One arm slithered around her waist, holding her upright so she wouldn't face plant. The heat from his chest against her spine heated her more than her soak in the tub did, giving her pause, feeling safe for the first time in months. She shook herself from her confusion about what it meant to trust Dean and to want a connection on a personal level.

"What on earth are you doing here?" Shelby took back control of her weapon and blocked him from coming into the house. "By my last calculations, you are numero uno on my killer checklist."

He crowded her in the doorway. "If I wanted to take you out, don't you think I had more than ample opportunities to do just that over the last couple of weeks?"

Neither one said anything but stared the other down. Okay, so maybe he had a point.

She huffed and stomped to the kitchen, laying down the pine tar bat. "What do you want?"

"You didn't answer any of my texts after you told us you would be at work in the morning. I wanted to know what's going on. There was no antique show three counties over." Dean ground his teeth together and put his hands on his hips.

"How do you know?"

"Because your car never left your garage." Dean pursed his lips.

"Were you watching me?" A spine-chilling shudder rushed over her.

"I came because I didn't think it was like you to shirk your responsibilities at a time when everything is under scrutiny by the feds."

"I can't talk about it." Shelby turned on the faucet and filled a glass.

"I may have found info regarding the antiques behind the wall. Some of the items were acquired but never sold. I looked up the orders you requested, and every single antique in that room was unaccounted for once purchased. There are no sales showing once they were added to Rupert's Relics inventory." Dean threw his hands in the air.

Shelby choked on the next gulp of water and had to spit it out in the sink.

Dean patted her on the back until she got herself under control.

Shelby didn't hurry to the room.

When Dean turned on the light, Shelby's gasps drowned out his.

"What did you do with everything?" Shelby shuffled away from him. "They said everything was gone."

"Me? What happened in the last four days? Is that what you were doing? Getting rid of the proof of Rupert's involvement? And what do you mean they? Who is they?" Dean walked the length of the empty room.

"You were the only person in this room with me. I trusted you, Dean." Shelby had nothing to back up her claims she didn't remove anything. If she came forward with paperwork, it would look like she was covering up for her uncle after everything conveniently went missing. "I was held in a windowless cage for the last four days."

Dean stalked toward her, making her retreat until her back was against the wall. "I don't have a way in this house without you. You and I aren't the only two who know about this room. Rupert had it built. Who else did he tell? Did he do the work himself or hire a contractor? And who held you?"

Shelby shook her head. "Uncle Rupert didn't have anything to do with those deaths."

"I'm not saying that, but someone else had to know about what was in here. Who did your uncle trust?" Dean twirled a strand of hair between his fingers as he inched closer.

"He had friends, but I don't know who he would confide in. Had there been anyone frequenting the store lately who stood out?" Was it one of the delivery people Agent Winters hinted at?

"I'm not sure. I mean, he would go into his office and close the door, but I didn't pay any attention. I was hired for digital marketing and shipping. I did what Rupert paid me to do. Someone we don't know definitely made sure any and all evidence disappeared. If it wasn't you and it wasn't me, who was it?" Dean motioned for her to head into the house.

"I changed the locks when I moved in. I couldn't find the hide-a-key in the rock out front, so I had new deadbolts installed. I'm the only one with access." Shelby shivered, thinking about being put back in the windowless room.

How long would they hold her this time?

"Hey." Dean rubbed his hands up and down her arms. "We'll figure this out. Okay? What if we went over the files in the basement?"

"The FBI has them." Shelby couldn't bear to see his anger, so she ducked her head.

Dean growled, "When did that happen?"

"During the last four days. They served a search warrant on the house to retrieve the antiques but said they were missing and mentioned the incriminating boxes in the basement." His sucked-in breath caused her hurried statement. "Their words, not mine."

Dean pulled her into a hug. Shelby tensed, waiting for him to push her away when he realized what he had done. His arms only tightened. "We'll get through this, I promise."

For the first time since stepping foot in Red Peaks, she felt cherished and somewhat precious, something she hadn't experienced with Justin.

Dean's taillights grew faint as he drove away. She glanced at the clock. It was three in the afternoon in Egypt. She put her phone on speaker and dialed her mom. After a couple of rings, she picked up.

"Shelby dear, why are you up this early?" No matter when she called, her mom could convert the hours in seconds.

"I haven't been to bed yet," Shelby confessed.

"Uh, talk to me hon." No one knew her better than her mom.

Shelby spilled everything that had happened over the last four days and the ordeal of the agents holding her. Her mom gasped, at the appropriate moments mad for what her little girl was going through. Hearing the anger in her mother healed her own.

"I know a few lawyers I'll speak with and see who they suggest to take your case. You can't talk to them without representation. Maybe it's time to close Rupert's."

Her mom had a point but she didn't want to let her uncle down. "Uncle Rupert would stand up against being bullied into doing something he didn't believe in. I found his laptop and stowed it on the top of the bookcase. I can't bring myself to look in it. What if he has information on there I have no right to intrude on? Why haven't the feds asked for access to the computers?"

"Don't worry about that. When we come to town, I'll handle his personal items. Just collect them and leave them to me. I'm ashamed to say I don't know if Rupert even kept a journal or anything like that. I felt we were close, but now I'm not so sure..." Her mom's voice faded.

"Mom, you cut out."

"Actually, there's another sandstorm that's supposed to blow through in the next hour." It was one of the hazards of living in a desert.

"What do I do, Mom?" Shelby put her forehead against the cold table next to her phone and watched her breath fog up the slick surface of the varnished wood with each exhale.

"You get a supervisor's name. Stand up for yourself like the strong woman I know and love. Remember God saying that there will always be trials and tribulations, but He will never leave you through them? Go to Him. Let Him lead your heart where He wants you to go. Pray, baby girl, never stop praying. Your father and I pray every day for you." Her mom always knew what to say to make her feel better.

"Thanks, Mom. I needed to hear that."

"We can change our reservations and fly in early."

"No, Mom. I don't want you to lose money on the change. You are right. I'm capable of standing up for myself."

"Oh honey, if you're sure. Your dad says we have to leave for a tour we signed up for. I'll talk to you later, okay?"

"No problem. Love you, Mom." Shelby was glad she had her mom to talk to.

"Love you too. If you need us we will be on the next plane." Her mom disconnected.

Thirty-Five

The next day at Rupert's Relics felt as if she hadn't been away. Shelby went through the opening procedures while Dean worked on a large order loaded on an outbound shipment.

While they were quietly working, five FBI agents stormed in through the front door, guns drawn and aimed in front of them; Shelby yelped as she scurried away. She trembled when one swung in her direction and told her to sit down. They all wore masks, concealing their identities. The only clue they were FBI were the initials of their agency in blinding white letters on the back of their bulletproof vests.

Not again! Were they detaining her? For the first time ever, she debated whether resisting them and running would be worth the effort.

Shelby didn't say a word; she did what the man told her to do as the other four moved as a single, well-choreographed unit to the warehouse. "Can I ask what's going on?"

"Someone will talk to you as soon as we have the suspect in custody." The man was no-nonsense but had at least lowered the weapon so it wasn't aimed at her anymore.

"Suspect?" Shelby's head flinched back slightly.

They filed out with Dean in handcuffs. He struggled to wrench his arms free of the agents, who marched him through the front door and into one of the waiting SUVs. He muttered about it being against his constitutional rights, and he hadn't done anything. The agent in front of her joined his colleagues before nodding in her direction in the macho way men do at the man he spoke with. She expected them to grunt over power tools next.

"Wait, what's going on? You said someone would talk to me."

Soon, Justin came in through the back, put his arm around her, and gave her a squeeze before sidestepping when the agent approached.

"We're sorry for interrupting your business, but we had a break in the case and have a few inquiries for your employee." He turned to leave.

"The other guy said he was a—"

"He misspoke; more accurately, he's a person of interest. We think he may have witnessed something he isn't aware he saw so we need to question him about it." The agent was out the door before she could ask follow-up questions.

The vehicles left a dust cloud as they almost peeled out of the parking lot, kicking up dirt every which way.

"Mr. Goodie Goodie, arrested?" The corners of Justin's mouth curved, but he never took his eyes off the door.

Shelby rolled her eyes. "They said person of interest."

"Earth to Shelby. That's cop-speak for numero uno on their most wanted. They don't take people to help them on a case out in handcuffs, princess."

"He doesn't seem like the type of person who would be a serial killer, does he?" Shelby's intestines twisted.

Images sparked of Dean being in her house and his featherlight kisses. Was she so incapable of reading someone she couldn't recognize a man who kills people with no remorse standing right in front of her?

"How many serial killers out there are the friendly guy next door? All their neighbors say, oh, he was the nicest guy. They never believed him capable. Then, in the next sentence. He always kept to himself. He never talked much but he was always watching everything around him. He was a loner." Justin's voice increased in octave as he batted his eyelashes.

Shelby slapped his arm. "I'm serious. He's been in my house."

"When was he in your house?" Justin grumbled.

"Oh." Shelby swallowed. She couldn't believe she let it slip when they had done so well in maintaining the confidentiality he was helping her. "The day you stayed at the store when we took my belongings in one trip using his truck."

"You would tell me if there was something between you two, wouldn't you?" Justin stood beside her. "He clearly has a questionable background. You're not a blip on the feds' radar if you're innocent. He must be dangerous if they think he's shady."

"There's nothing between us."

"Because you know I like you. I've tried to keep us in a professional-based relationship, but Shelby, I want to see where this can go between us. I don't think it's one-sided, is it? Not with how much I care about you. I want to keep you safe." Justin crowded her.

"Justin, I'm your boss." Shelby avoided admitting her initial attraction shifted away from being interested in seeing where things could go between them.

She wanted the case finalized and the killer brought to justice. Sitting in a room for four days with nothing else to do but pray and put every aspect of her life under a microscope changed her views of how her life brought her to the here and now. She didn't trust her own intuition. She had Dean in her house, and he was the feds' leading guy. The hug the other night more than swung her view of him to the other side—one she hoped to expand on. That was, if he wasn't the reason for the manhunt.

"What if I was a contract employee? I'll be a supplier or distributor, whichever word works for you. Since I won't be your employee anymore, there won't be a line you have to cross." Justin cradled her face in his hands, and she had to admit it made her feel wanted. "You will need to replace Dean."

"Why?"

"Wake up, sugar. The feds hauled him out in cuffs. You aren't safe around him."

Shelby shook her head and cleared the fog. "I need someone who takes care of the customers with another in the warehouse for shipments of our sold stock. I can't afford to hire someone to fill retail and keep you on a contract employee basis."

"Look me in the eye and tell me you don't feel something." Justin looked like he wanted to cry.

Shelby's heart clenched. "I do, but only as a friend."

"I can work with that because you would have said you only see us as friends instead of saying you feel something too before tacking on the friend part at the end like an afterthought." Justin grinned wide and went back to the warehouse when a truck pulled around the building.

Shelby groaned at the pending flirting she saw in her future. He held back since his apology. She didn't want to hurt him but would need to put her foot down until the case was solved. She did a good job lately, making sure he didn't get the wrong idea. Now, she blew that out of the water.

The more significant issue immersed Dean in the pool of suspects. How did her life get so out of control? Were she and Justin in danger if they released Dean?

The bell over the door announced a customer. Shelby plastered a fake smile and asked if they were browsing or interested in something specific.

The next few hours blurred by. The majority of the business dealings involved the gossip mongers hunting for details about Dean being led out in cuffs. They begged to know if he was someone they should be worried about living around their children.

Was there a toll-free hotline if they had tips about suspicious activity they witnessed? If it led to him being charged was there a reward? Not wanting to alienate potential future auctions and acquisitions, her themed comments only mentioned they thought he might be a witness and had nothing further because the feds hadn't released any information. She felt terrible, but she then referred them to the local police department, suggesting if anyone had the details about what was going on, it would be the authorities.

Word must have spread after she repeated it enough. The looky-loos found entertainment somewhere else. She giggled, imagining Sharlene trying to deal with the calls if she still worked for the police department.

Shelby glared at the clock, urging it to speed up. When the second hand reached six o'clock, the sign scraped back and forth on the hook as she flipped it.

"You weren't ready for the day to be over, were you?" Justin joked as he pulled the cash drawer to count down for the day.

"Don't start. We have a large shipment booked, and I'm not sure where Dean keeps all the packing slips. Want to help me look?"

Justin smacked the money in his hand back and forth, making the bills slap against each other before stuffing them in a bank bag and filling out a deposit slip for the night drop. He returned and tagged her hand, pulling her along to the warehouse. She had to take two steps for every one of his.

Shelby snatched her hand back.

Justin sat and propped his feet on the desk. "Relax, Shelby, I helped Dean with more shipments than I care to admit. He keeps the labels here. The next order is always on the front of his clipboard. Dean is a perplexing human being in his ability to have the most organized desk of anyone on the planet. I swear he dreams about organizational charts."

Shelby sighed. "Oh, thank goodness."

They thumbed through the stack, and she agreed everything was in order. All they had to do was attain the driver's signature and load the truck. The antiques sat beside the dock on pallets, wrapped in moving blankets with foam taped to the corners. She was impressed. No wonder the website was as well maintained as it was. He was a stickler for any and all aspects of warehouse shipping etiquette.

Justin bid her goodnight as he left.

Her phone beeped and she laughed when she saw Skye's text.

Skye: Help! This child is going to be the death of me. What was I thinking getting pregnant again? JK lol

Shelby: What is he doing now?

Skye: He wanted red hair so he got into the pantry and got into the food coloring. I think you can fill in the blanks of what he looks like.

Shelby: Oh, my gosh. I just spit out my drink!!!!!

Shelby coughed as she tried to get herself under control.

Skye: He looks like a tomato!

Shelby: Please tell me you have pictures!

Skye: Sending your way, I gotta go and see if I can use some baking soda and lemon juice to dull down his stained skin.

Shelby's phone beeped several times in a row. Tears tracked down her cheeks as she cracked up.

Skye: We leave next week for the holidays and won't be back until after the first of the year.

Shelby: Have a great time and we'll have lunch when you get back.

Thirty-Six

Shelby narrowed her eyes as headlights swept over the front of the store. Justin had gone home hours ago, and she perused the files to print off hard copies of the gems stolen from her house. Everything was accounted for except the last three she was looking for. She clicked on the next file and sent it to the printer. Could she link Dean to the crimes? Justin had unfettered access to the purchases. The owner's names didn't coincide with the victims the news and FBI had announced. What was she missing?

The front bell jingled.

Justin was in charge of closing up. She started to dial the police when she heard beeps from the buttons pressed on the panel, disarming the system.

She peeked her head out her door and sighed, seeing it was Dean. He looked worn out. Was it the accusations of such horrendous acts weighing on him? "Dean?"

"Shelby, what are you doing here so late?" He didn't move from where he stood.

"I was looking at the requisitions for those pieces." Would he understand what she was saying?

Dean nodded. "Good idea. Did you unearth anything?"

"What did the feds want?" Might as well ask about the elephant in the room.

"Some questions. No biggie." Dean glanced over his shoulder when a car passed.

"In handcuffs?" There was a tug in her heart, but he looked more guilty the longer he was in her space.

"Procedure." Dean moved slowly as if approaching a skittish animal. "Shelby, it's all right. I know this is a scary time for you, but you can have faith in me. I will never do anything to put you in danger."

Who said things like that? If she called Irving or Jackson, would they tell her what they found out when they grilled Dean? Would they've released him if they thought he was a danger to society?

"Did you tell them about the evidence?" Was he let go because he propelled the blame onto someone else?

"I didn't have to; someone beat me to it. They aren't happy everything is missing." Dean sat across from her desk. "I'm not comfortable talking about this here. Can I follow you home?"

Shelby's stomach lurched. "Do you think they hid listening devices?"

"Anything is possible."

Shelby nodded as Dean secured her in her car, his head on a swivel. If he wanted to kill her, he would have done it one of the nights they scoured the antiques. His headlights in her rearview mirror brought up memories of a similar situation when she was forced off the road in front of her house. He parked and hopped out of his truck, darting around to her.

"Did you want anything to drink?" Shelby needed something to do.

"Water would be great."

She handed him a glass, and he motioned for her to sit on her couch.

"Are they going to charge you with anything?" She looked at his fingers to see if black ink stained his skin from having his fingerprints taken.

"There is nothing to charge me with. They don't have anything concrete pointing to me being the killer." He seemed nervous as he sat on the coffee table facing her.

Shelby folded her hands together. "Dean, I need to hear it for myself. Please don't get mad."

"Shelby, I'm not a killer. No hard feelings. I'd ask the same thing if I were in your shoes. You have to protect yourself and the store. I would never put you at risk of losing your uncle's legacy." Dean inched forward and studied her. His knees bracketed hers.

She felt the lure of him, the truth. Did that mean Justin was the agent since Dean's arrest took the spotlight off him? The FBI wouldn't detain one of their own. Well, he wasn't arrested per se.

How Justin cozied up to her right from the beginning meant he was doing his job. He didn't see her as anything more than an asset. She wasn't sure what bothered her more, Dean being her only employee or Justin using her to further his job. Granted, catching a serial killer took precedence.

"Then Justin is FBI." Shelby slapped her hand over her mouth with a resounding pop, realizing she said it out loud.

"He's what?" Dean glowered at her.

"I'm praying you aren't the killer they are looking for. Please don't be the killer because I don't think my heart can take much more of this. I heard there was an undercover agent in the store." Shelby slouched on the sofa. "One of the agents let it slip."

Dean supported his arms on his knees. "There is no one else you can depend on more than me. I think we need to talk about everything you know and compare notes."

"I'm scared."

"Don't be scared of me," Dean snapped.

"What if you are an expert liar and are using me? I'm so confused. First, they inferred a killer and agent hijacked my store. They switched the wording around, so I thought they monitored the store. Then they mentioned the agent inside again. I don't know what to think. I've had a headache for almost a week since they held me in a concrete room, and I don't know who to believe. The customers are only there for gossip about Mr. Stein's death. I want to yell at them to leave, but I don't want to show them they are getting to me." Shelby was close to crying.

"You upchucked so much stuff; we'll need a mop and bucket to clean this mess. Start at the beginning. We finished going through the room and logged the last item, the Chippendale grandfather clock. I left, and about a week passed when you disappeared." Dean dipped his chin for her to continue.

Shelby told him about the package for Mr. Stein and the subsequent murder she witnessed. The online news only mentioned his death was an open case at this time with no suspects identified. She talked about her abduction in the woods between their property lines, waking up confused in a room with a mirror, an interrogation, and having a panic attack. Her stay at the concrete vacation cell and then being released.

She shook with anger by the time she spilled everything. "I want to sue them but they said they operated by a different set of rules because of their stupid cloak-and-dagger man's club only the cool guys get to play in."

Dean gripped her knee. "I can't tell you how sad I am for what you had to go through. I don't know about all the covert ops teams out there and their accountability to the citizens in this country, but at least you are back home."

Shelby nodded.

"We can put our heads together and solve some of this puzzle. Rupert had to tell someone else. Are there any password-protected files on his desktop at work? Anything look fishy?" Dean didn't push her past what was comfortable for her.

"I didn't think to pry through everything here. It felt like I was a voyeur peeking into someone's life without their permission. I didn't have any business doing that to my uncle. I went through everything at work, and nothing stood out. The only personal files I found are pictures of us he affixed as wallpaper or background." Shelby noticed Dean slouch. "But..."

His head snapped up. "Go on."

"I couldn't bring myself to cross the line and look at the laptop here. I figured his work was at the store, and the laptop here would be personal. I didn't have a right to go exploring. My mom said she would handle it when she got back and to not stress about anything of Rupert's that was personal like his computer or journals if he had something like that."

"Where is it?" Excitement sparkled in Dean's eyes.

Shelby had relocated it to the bookcase next to the fireplace in the great room. She found it the other day when she was adding her books to her uncle's.

Dean scrambled to the device and sat next to her on the couch, pulling the coffee table to them. Her shoulder rubbed against his upper arm. The hard drive whirred as it booted up. A password request popped open.

He turned to her.

"I don't know it."

"It has to be something simple. You know Rupert couldn't handle complex issues." Dean drummed his fingers along the edge.

Shelby heated as her face flushed. "What about the one for work?"

The keys were whisper soft. Incorrect password.

"I have no clue." Shelby ran her hands over her face.

"Yes, you do. You knew him better than anyone. It would be something simple he didn't give any thought to type in. Is there a phrase he liked to say?" Dean urged her brain to work.

It clicked. Shelby inched closer. "Iwillfearnoevil. It was his favorite saying when it felt like the world spun out of control."

Small crosses floated all over the screen, bouncing off the sides. Dean smiled and bumped into her, almost making her fall over.

"Okay, let's see what we have." Dean was a guru with electronics. Not just competent but a genuine genius, the way his fingers flew over the keys.

He opened files, read them, and closed them again before Shelby had a chance to read over his shoulder. She was in awe of his ability to skim over so many documents in such a short span.

Shelby poked him in the arm, pushing against his muscles. He didn't budge.

He stopped and frowned at her. "What are you doing?"

"Checking to see if you're real. No one can peruse all you did and be human. Nobody's brain works that fast." She poked him again, earning a hearty chuckle.

He plugged a USB into a port and transferred a slew of files before palming the device. "I have to go. Don't let anyone in. Not even the agents. I'll be back when I have more."

Shelby stood, mouth gaping as he left. She looked down at the screen and the computer showed thirty percent out of one hundred erased. "No!"

She slammed her hands down on the buttons, trying to stop it, but the screen turned blue and blinked out. What happened? Did he destroy it? Was there some program on the flash drive that he downloaded to wipe all the files from the device? The fans under the device whooshed air as a welcome screen appeared, asking her to select her language to set up the computer.

Shelby slumped, sliding onto the floor, her heart hammering against her sternum.

Thirty-Seven

Shelby's heels tapped against the floor as she made her way across to the loading dock. Justin's mutterings caused her to slow her steps.

"Where is it? It should be here." Anger poured out in Justin's words with a vicious bite.

Shelby stopped in the shadows. Who was he talking to?

She had to discuss what she found, but could it wait?

Justin's voice roared, and a loud thud followed. She had never seen this side of him. First, his refusal to leave her house after showing up unannounced, and now this.

She backed up and tiptoed to the door, making sure her heels produced enough noise for Justin to hear her clomping her way over to him. His head popped up from behind a crate, and he smiled at her.

"I'm heading out. I wanted to know if you needed something before I go." Shelby smiled, but it faltered.

Her stomach was a mess of knots.

"Nah, I'm leaving also. I'll walk you out." Justin cupped her elbow as he steered her toward the front door.

"I do need to talk to you about some things not matching up on the forms you submitted on a few acquisitions." She fastened the deadbolt and then yanked on the door to double-check it.

Justin crossed his arms over his chest, taking up a defensive stance. "You can ask now."

"I'm tired, so we can go over it tomorrow." Shelby stalked to her car.

"Or you can ask now and put it out of your mind. It will bother you all night if I know you, and you will lose sleep over it. Then those cute little furrows wrinkle your forehead the next day because you're already thinking about it before work." Justin hurried to her as she reached her car.

He bobbed his eyebrows up and down, making her laugh.

"Fine. The Orville piece with the latticework in the screen panels of the room divider."

"Yeah, what about it?" Justin's brows narrowed as if thinking about the specific piece she was questioning him about.

"Where did you get it from?" Shelby met his eyes but hated the confrontation.

"Orville. You said it was the Orville piece."

"No, I know who the owner was; I'm talking about where you found the screens." Shelby wondered if his aloofness was an act.

A smile spread wide on his face. "A facility where she moved it to clear out some space in her house."

"The form you completed says you found it in a barn." Her abdomen twisted at his admission that he had written the forms incorrectly.

"Latticework wouldn't have lasted a year, much less fifteen, stored in the oppressive heat and humidity of extreme weather."

"Hence the concern." Shelby tossed her bag over into the passenger seat.

"A momentary lapse on my part. I logged several pieces at the same time and probably mixed up when I filled it out."

He shrugged and amped up his swagger as he strolled to his car.

Shelby waved at him as she slid behind the wheel. She didn't like his easy answers when she noticed what she believed was a blatant lie on the location field. Auditing the accounts pointed to a lot of finds in dilapidated structures or auctions. It was an odd, frequent happenstance on all the acquisitions involving Justin. Did the federal agents notice the oddity also? But if he was undercover, they wouldn't care about that. Or were the forms filed out for the sake of the agents to draw out the killer? Was Justin with them and dangling fresh antiques to bait a trap?

The trip to the cottage was short, which she had to admit was perfect for her. She was glad her uncle bought it when he did instead of living the rest of his life in the small nook above the store. Her stomach growled loud enough; she wondered if it would eat itself to satisfy its craving for food.

She removed the mail from the box at the end of her driveway. Mr. Stein's eerie, forlorn house sat empty and dark. When would his family arrive to handle his affairs?

She climbed the three small cobble steps and let herself in. She adored this house. It was home to her. She had finally gotten the majority of items moved to the warehouse and rearranged several others with Dean's help over the last few weeks while he came out and helped go through the antiques. She removed her shoes at the front door and went in search of something to eat.

Her living room now sported the new leather sectional she splurged on before her uncle's passing. Yes, she cherished her antiques, but there were only so many pieces she wanted to have before it looked like her cottage resembled a museum. Her couch was her sanctuary to unwind after a long day at work, with her bed being a close second. The headboard and dresser were joined by an armoire closely matching their style. It finally felt like home, decorated the way she wanted. And since the agents didn't include it so far, she considered it rightfully hers.

Shelby couldn't wait for Skye to come back from the holidays so she could update her on what she missed so far. She wasn't one for interrupting her holiday and didn't think she needed the stress with her pregnancy when she couldn't do anything about it.

She'd packed the last of her uncle's belongings, donated some, and hauled away what she couldn't. Dean had sweetly offered to cart them off when she got emotional. Her goal was to have some peace and quiet over the next couple of months after working at the store and unpacking when she moved to Red Peaks. She hadn't heard from Dean since he wiped the hard drive without her permission a couple of days ago. Another killing flooded the airwaves making the total now sixteen.

After watching mindless television for background noise, she headed to bed, knowing she would have to speak with Justin about his misfiled forms. How could he be so nonchalant during federal scrutiny? Accurate info improved the prospect of catching a killer. Where were all the antiques stolen from her home? Dean convinced her not to file a police report because it would make her look bad, and since it was the feds' jurisdiction. She didn't technically withhold information since they already knew about their theft.

Would she tell Justin? Maybe he would know what to do if he was the agent she thought he was. It would explain his nonchalance about the incorrect data. The pages were forged for the investigation's purposes. So she had to look beyond the forms and the misinformation on them.

Shelby tossed and turned most of the night before the alarm on her phone woke her the following day. She groaned as she rolled out of bed and cringed when she saw the dark bags under her eyes. Concealer only obscured so much, but it was all she had to work with for now. She was able to put a liquid bandage over her cheek to keep her makeup out of the still-healing wound. She shrugged and found her way to work, not remembering much of the drive.

She was the first to arrive, unlock the store, and reach her office. The night before, when she spoke to Justin as they left, she already printed off everything she questioned.

The bell over the door announced someone's arrival. She rolled back from her desk. Her chair's wheels loudly squeaked, disgusted at moving in the early morning. If there was a break in business transactions, she would have one of the guys oil it later today.

"I have donuts!" Justin's voice boomed.

"I could so hug you right about now." Shelby couldn't pass up a good Boston cream pie.

"I wish I'd known sooner. I'd bring donuts every day." As she picked up a napkin, Justin toasted her choice by lifting his red velvet cake.

"You got a minute?" Shelby started to her office, not waiting for him to answer.

"Sure, boss lady. What did you need?"

"To continue our conversation from last night." She skated the paperwork over to him, as he sat across from her, to see what she found.

"I already said I labeled it wrong. Won't happen again." Justin started to stand.

"Wait."

He slumped into the chair across from her.

"Justin, I need you to go back over and make sure these are correct. We can't have the wrong paperwork on our acquisitions. It can get us into legal trouble. Uncle Rupert put this procedure in place for a reason. Even you said it helped us with the FBI wanting to audit our files." Shelby hoped he understood where she was coming from.

"Shelby, I know, but I'll go back through them and make any necessary corrections. If you give me privileges to the online files, I'll update those also." Justin swiped the pages from her desk.

"Don't worry about the digital files. Handle the paper copies, and I'll update the electronic site." Shelby hadn't allowed anyone access to the scanned records. Neither of her employees understood she was a little old school. She also saved the files to a nice solid-state drive, only hackable if she had it plugged in. If Justin was an agent, it explained why he wanted her online password, allowing him to log in from anywhere and compare the files. She would demand a warrant before permitting them access.

"A password, and I'll be done before I head out for a new client, who I have a meeting with this afternoon." Justin towered over her desk.

"What new client?" She didn't remember seeing anything on the schedule.

"Last minute; haven't even updated the calendar." Justin's nature and magnetism suddenly made her office seem tiny.

"I'll come with you. If Dean shows up, he can oversee the fort since no shipments are going out today." Shelby stood.

Justin didn't say anything. His eyes became icy cold, void of his jovial self. "Don't you have to meet those agents or something?"

Shelby smiled; apparently, Justin didn't want her tagging along on his little trip. "No."

Justin muttered. "All right, but you will be bored. Don't say I didn't warn you.."

He didn't mention requesting the password for any more files, so Shelby let it go.

Dean crept in through the dock without announcing his arrival. He agreed to cover the store after Shelby explained overseeing the trip with Justin. She would confront him about deleting the files a couple of days ago when they got back. She didn't want to say anything and have him bail before she returned.

Justin didn't speak on the way out of town. "Gotta stop by my house for some water. Did you want one?"

"Please. I didn't think of that when we left. How far is it?" Shelby felt like a horrible boss and friend. She didn't know where her employee lived. Of course, she had the address but never looked at how far outside Red Peaks it was.

"Oh, it's not far." True to his word, he turned off the highway after a couple of miles.

The tires bit into a gravel driveway, disappearing into the hills.

"I've never been out here. It's so peaceful and beautiful." Shelby took in the wilderness and smiled as several deer darted through the trees.

They stopped in front of a small cabin she wasn't sure was inhabitable. "Be right back."

The agent's warning of someone undercover trickled through her thoughts once more. Justin made so much sense as an undercover spy. He was charming. His protectiveness made sense when he rushed to her side when the store was broken into and said he didn't want anything to happen to her. Imagining him darting around with a gun in hand saving damsels in distress had her chuckling as he jogged back out to the truck.

He twisted the cap off one water bottle and handed it to her as he uncapped his own. The cool liquid soothed her parched throat.

"That tastes so good." Shelby drank more. "Didn't realize how thirsty I was."

Justin stared at her.

"Are we leaving?" Shelby shifted uncomfortably in her seat.

"Sure. We'll be on the road for an hour until we hit our destination." He checked his watch.

Shelby angled to face him.

"There's something we need to discuss first. I have a confession to make." He twisted in his seat and ran his thumb over her cheek and down her jaw. "You are so beautiful, and I know what I have to say will ruin any likelihood of an us. You'll never know how sorry I am for the lies I had to tell while I was here. I didn't plan on the impact you would have on me.

"My feelings for you are real; I want you to know that upfront. I will never forget my time here, and I want to thank you. You showed me there is so much more in life than just surviving day to day."

This was it. Justin would disclose his covert assignment and ask for help. Maybe set the scene to allow her to confess her knowledge about the room. To ask for his advice on her chances about the FBI charging her with withholding material, that was now lost and taken by the killer. She intended to forgive him for his subterfuge. It must be hard to be undercover, unsure who to entrust his life to.

"You're the undercover agent, aren't you?" Shelby took another sip. "I understand why you had to lie, and I forgive anything you had to do while investigating."

Justin cackled as he threw his head back. "Oh honey, you have no idea how hilarious that is."

Shelby's eyelids started to droop.

"You going to fall asleep on me and deny me company, sweetheart?" Justin sneered as he pulled out onto the road.

"Sorry, I'm so tired all of a sudden." Shelby rubbed her palms over her eyes.

She dropped the water bottle. The water glugged out of the top as it lay on its side.

"Yeah, kinda happens when you're dosed with ketamine."

"Ketamine?" Shelby's head fell forward. "What?"

"Oh, sweetie, I'm sorry it has to be this way. You got too close. If only convincing you to join me was enough." Justin tipped her head back and brushed the hair away from her face. "I'm not a federal agent; I'm something a little more sinister."

"No." Shelby frowned as she caught sight of her home.

"No one will think to look for us here. I'll stow my truck in the garage, and when the calvary starts looking for you, we'll be snug in the comforts of your mansion." Justin triggered the button on the visor above his head and snarled when she gasped. "I've had this programmed for months. Before Rupert died and you moved to town. Your little buddy at the hardware store may have helped you change out the locks on the exterior, but you didn't take into consideration the garage door. It's okay; most people don't, because who has an opener to access the interior?"

How many times had he been in there, and she hadn't known? All the thumps in the middle of the night? The scraping of things being moved around. Her body shuddered as it grew dark. She felt the door give way next to her but couldn't stop herself from being lifted from the seat and carried inside.

"I wish it could have been different, sweetheart. I was falling for you." Justin kissed the top of her head before she sunk into oblivion.

Thirty-Eight

Blackness danced around the edges of her vision. Cold seeped through her neck and started down her spine as her legs went numb. Did she ingest a fatal amount of ketamine? Her legs dipped down as someone sat on the edge of her bed.

"Wake up, princess." Her eyes connected with Justin's, and it clicked. He killed all those innocent people for their antiques. He was no agent trying to stop the bad guys but the one they hunted. Then, who was the agent? Had they followed them? Would there be a rescue?

Shelby groaned as the light in the room pierced through to her brain. The pulsing pressure was worse than any previous headache.

"I've got to move you. They're getting too close to searching the house. Once I have you in the basement, I'll move my truck and have it go over the ridge and crash at the bottom. I love that truck, but it will lead them away from my trail long enough for me to finish with you here and get out of town. I found the room where good ole Rupert hid my cache. I was going to fund my next adventure with that. The old goat pulled one over on me and had all the antiques I pilfered from my victims stored here. I won in the end. While the feds had you all tucked out of harm's way, I waltzed right in and pinched my own stash right out from under their noses." Justin threw her over his shoulder.

Her head swam, and she blacked out again, but not before she heard his boots tromping down the crumbling stairs.

Shelby woke to a hood over her head, and panic set in as she tried to remember how she got to wherever she was. She held her breath, listening to her surroundings. Was anyone with her? She kept her movements to a minimum until she determined if Justin left.

The distinctive scraping of chair legs across the floor reverberated off walls. Heavy booted footfalls drew near.

"Someone is awake." Flashes flooded her mind.

Justin hoisted her under her arms, slamming her into a chair. He guided her restrained arms, secured behind her back, over the back rail before attaching them to the slats. Her breaths sawed in and out, her head dizzy at the fast movement.

He wrenched the hood off her head, taking some of her hair with it. She gasped as the roots tore free from her scalp. She blinked several times to adjust her eyes to the blinding sun coming through the dilapidated slats of a barn. Mildewed hay choked the air, causing her eyes to water.

Justin stood before her arms crossed after tossing the hood on the floor. The anger on his face turned him into the monster lurking under his charming demeanor. Who was this man who stood before her?

"Justin, what's going on?" She couldn't keep her voice steady.

He backhanded her across her cheek. Stars burst in her eyes as she cried out.

"What did you tell them?" Anger seethed out with his words.

"About what?" She didn't know what he was asking.

Why did he move her if he was going to kill her?

He grabbed her by the neck, practically pulling her off the chair with his one hand, making her back bow. Gasping, she tried to draw in air, but the room blurred. Black dots danced on the edge of her vision. She kicked out with her legs, making contact with his shin. He cursed and slammed her down before hitting her again.

"Tell me, what do they have on me? I wanted to finish this at your house, but they moved in too fast. I had to relocate you. They had you in their custody for four days. Did you spill everything you know about me? Did you give them a catalog of what I stole back from your pesky uncle?"

This was not the man who worked for her over the past six months! The one who flirted and made her think he wanted more. This was a monster who stood in front of her. Not the man who charmed anyone into buying anything he wanted them to. How could he be two completely different people?

"I didn't tell them anything. I don't know anything!" She spit out the words. "As of my last conscious conversation with you, I thought you might be an agent."

She schooled her features, trying to present only shock and confusion, even as the details started to click into place. Justin collected the antiques they sold. Who better than him to kill the person who got in his way? Yet why withhold the expensive pieces? Why not collect his commission and pad his accounts? The victims' names didn't match his paperwork. He was in the clear.

When he pulled a rope from behind his back, her eyes widened. It was the same rope she saw in the person's hands who strangled Mr. Stein, her neighbor. Oh my gosh, he also killed him. Her brain played catch-up to what she already observed. He was the one in Mr. Stein's house. Nothing covered her face when she was in Mr. Stein's house so he would know it was she who saw him that day. The light pale blue eyes, the only feature visible on his veiled face as he took a life, snuffing it out as if Mr. Stein didn't matter.

She swallowed against the impending nausea that roiled through her, building to dangerous levels toward expulsion. What could she have done to stop this from happening? Everything pointed to Dean. The FBI took him into custody and questioned him. He reformatted the laptop, erasing all data. The room she only told Dean about was emptied out and not by the FBI. If she judged Justin's character wrong, what did that say about her impressions of Dean? Was he even worse? He was distant, keeping to himself. Any time there were any problems, he was right there, helping her figure it out, including the day at Uncle Rupert's gravesite and her accident. He was so gentle and didn't leave her side until she told him to. He was the first to come to her when she was held for days. The agents informed her of the undercover agent working in her store.

Did Dean go from being the primary lead to an agent hiding in plain sight? Four days was more than enough time to verify every file and piece in the store.

Justin moved behind her. Her heart stuttered. Was he going to kill her? His hand, so tender on her head, made her jump. "I liked you, Shelby. I wish this had a different ending. But you turned me down. I really wanted to change...for you. I tried, but the pull was too strong. The adrenaline of watching life slip through your fingers as the spark dimed in your victim's eyes. It is so satisfying. I wish I could have been whole for you, but it wasn't in the cards.

"Maybe watching your light darken and fade away will cure me. I can move on and let you go since you refused to give us a chance. Tell me I'm not losing my mind, and it isn't all one-sided. Tell me I haven't lost you. Just a small nod to erase all the angst between us."

Shelby's eyes grew wide. A serial killer wanted to date her? She was dreaming. That had to be it. She would wake up any moment to the smell of coffee brewing in the kitchen.

"Ah well, can't say I didn't try. I arranged to implicate you. The government would assume you were complicit so you couldn't leave me. Keep you with me, but you ruined it, and you have no one to blame but yourself. The grandfather clock tipped off the FBI, didn't it? If only I hadn't taken it, I might have been absolved, but it was my Achilles heel.

"I would have been clear to skip town until your nosey uncle tripped me up. I was ready to put a fake order in and have the recognizable antiques shipped to a climate-controlled facility. Imagine my surprise when I walked in, and everything was gone. Gone! I had to start over. I had specific buyers who didn't care where the exquisite pieces to decorate their snobby penthouses or mansions came from. This would have set me up in a nice little villa on some island. White sandy beaches while watching sunsets and sunrises in a hammock, letting the ocean breezes rock me to sleep. You can't get much better than that. I wanted to take you with me. We could have been happy together. You would look amazing walking on the beach, all tanned to a beautiful golden bronze."

He kissed her head before looping the rope over and around her neck.

"A psychopath is incapable of feeling anything toward others. Otherwise, you wouldn't have been able to murder all of those innocent people!" There was no way she would get out of this alive. Hopefully, she made him mad enough that it would be quick.

Did the FBI even know she was taken? Dean expected them to be gone all afternoon and was prepared to close the shop alone.

"Oh, my dear Shelby, there has never been a woman like you. I think I may have developed a real attachment to you. Or at least what other people refer to as feelings. I wanted to at least try and see what all the fuss was about." Justin kissed her on the back of the head.

Her scream cut out, and she thrashed her head from side to side as he tightened the soft braided material. She kicked, trying to find purchase on something, anything to give her leverage to move up and relieve the pressure around her windpipe. The conundrum of how something so deadly felt soft against her skin as she struggled to pull air into her lungs flitted through her head. Her mouth opened in a silent scream. The bindings around her hands slithered to the floor under her torment. Her fingernails gouged her skin as she clawed at the offending braid.

His lips held to her temple were the last thing she sensed before the blackness took over, and her vision failed as the room grew cold and dark.

"Get off my niece!" the familiar voice bellowed.

"Uncle Rupert?" Her voice was a scratchy whisper.

Rupert stood with a baseball bat in his hands, his old eyes full of life and anger. He was the most beautiful sight she had ever seen.

***

"Get off my niece!" Rupert yelled again.

A soft thump sounded as Shelby tumbled from the chair. The tension around her neck eased as Justin let her go. Shelby gulped in life-saving air. Color returned to her pale face. Rupert had to show himself or lose his niece.

"You old man?" Justin's voice boomed.

Justin circled the chair and yanked Shelby to her feet, spinning her so her back was to his chest.

Rupert had never felt such vengeance rolling off a person.

Tears streamed from Shelby's wide shocked eyes as she took in Rupert. It would take time for her to forgive him for the anguish he caused. But did he damage their relationship beyond repair? Four months believing the worst.

"You're supposed to be dead." Justin twisted the cord around her, then punched her in the side, wind whooshing from her lungs.

"Touch her again, and it will be you with the broken ribs." Rupert's love for Shelby commanded a menacing side he never knew existed.

"You think you can take me, old man?" Justin punched her again.

"Uncle," Shelby cried out when Justin tossed her aside and ran at Rupert.

Rupert hated seeing his niece introduced into this harrowing world of murderers. The FBI had already staged his demise to save his life, putting his niece in danger. Not his first choice in handling this, but he was in a coma for the first two months she was here.

Justin was livid and confronted him when he saw the pieces gone later that day. Rupert tagged the false shipping request while Dean and Justin handled a delivery across town. Rupert planned to share it with Dean but couldn't call and tip off Justin of Dean's identity if they were still together.

Taking the case into his own hands, Rupert moved them to the hidden room and sealed it up with the intention of seeing Dean at his apartment to apprise him of the situation. A shot rang out, hitting him square in the chest, red blooming wide on his light blue shirt. The agents surveilling his business rushed in and saved his life but twisted the ending so it looked like a massive coronary was his downfall. No one could place Justin at the scene. All they saw was someone running from the back of the docks, and they lost him in the countryside.

By the time he woke up from surgery and had them contact Dean, a couple of months had passed, and Shelby had confided in Dean about the room.

The bullet had done significant damage, and they had to induce a coma to provide his body with time to heal and give him a chance at life.

Rupert swung the bat, connecting with Justin's shoulder. He howled and stumbled back to Shelby.

"Thought I shot you." Justin connected with her ribs once more for good measure.

"Young man, I will not hesitate to take you out if you touch her again." Rupert couldn't even tell if she was breathing.

"Give it your best shot. Speaking of shot, answer me, old man, did I miss?" Justin asked.

"No. I almost died, but you didn't know that, so they played it off as a heart attack. Sorry to disappoint you, but my ticker's back to full health. Confused you about where all those antiques disappeared to, didn't it?" Rupert taunted Justin, hoping to stall and draw him over since he messaged Dean before he followed Justin and Shelby inside.

Justin roared and charged. Rupert squared his form and balanced on the balls of his feet before he swung. Justin twisted to the side and only received a glancing blow. He tucked his shoulders in and came up into Rupert's ribs, tackling him.

Rupert's hand fell open, the bat rolling away as he tried to breathe through his shocked diaphragm, his body not back to one hundred percent.

"You are no match for me, old-timer. This time I'll finish what I started. I think it will be sensational for me to take you out the way I did all those others." Justin twisted the cord around his hands, shortening the length that drooped between the two ends.

Sirens in the distance stopped Justin.

Rupert coughed as his lungs started functioning again. "Here comes the calvary."

"You stupid old coot!" Justin ran to Shelby, allowing Rupert to roll on his side and reach for his weapon.

He was still in the game, not giving Justin a clue; the full force of his swing smashed him square in the back of his left knee.

Justin went down howling and rolled several times, gripping his knee. "You're a dead man."

"So you say. I have yet to see it happen." Rupert smirked as he stood over him.

Justin pulled a gun. Rupert was already diving to the side as shots peppered the dirt around him. He kept rolling until he settled at the side of the barn in a dark corner.

Rupert came up on his knees as Shelby roused and sat up trying to suck in oxygen, alerting Justin. Instead of going to her, Justin lobbed the bat at him. He tried to duck out of the way, but pain lanced across the back of his head as it made contact. Shelby screamed as tires on the gravel propelled Justin to the back door, limping and trying to support the side of his knee as he ran.

A bright, blinding flash and loud noise saturated the barn. Rupert prayed it affected Justin as much as it did him. Men yelled as Justin darted through the smoke. Rupert held the back of his head; sticky wetness coated his hair.

Thirty-Nine

Thirty minutes before

Dean paced back and forth. Justin took Shelby an hour ago, and they were no closer to finding her than when they first saw the video, from one of Rupert's cameras, of her unconscious body being stuffed into the back of Justin's truck.

He was the prime suspect, but it wasn't until Dean saw the video with his own eyes they finally had the proof. The countless hours of surveillance didn't yield any clues. During two of the kills, he had the most trustworthy alibi, Shelby. The tingling down his neck told Dean Justin wasn't working alone unless he was able to stage the scenes to bypass normal discoveries surrounding a death. The man was meticulous in his crimes and coverups, such as tampering with the temperature to offset decomp speed.

He never left fingerprints, hair, or anything at the scene; no records or clues led back to his guilt. The only DNA they collected was from previous targets. He reused the same corded rope every time, layering skin cells through the fibers with every death.

This was the unfortunate, frustrating part of undercover work. The blast of adrenaline of finally reeling in a suspect was a rush like nothing else and made it worth it. You know in your gut who it is, but until you get hard proof, you can't do anything about it. If they put him on a forty-eight-hour hold waiting for a warrant to come through, no judge in their right mind would sign off on with the lack of corroborating evidence; he would be in the wind off to his next destination.

The first glitch in his killing spree was the grandfather clock. It was such a defining piece, and there was no way to offload it without someone noticing. Rupert must have been suspicious enough to tuck it away with so many other stolen pieces.

Dean was upset Rupert hadn't been able to confide in him what he discovered. The freak timing of the flu that knocked Dean out for two days gave Justin the advantage he needed. Rupert's fake death upset Dean. He never got close to people when he was undercover. Rupert was so happy to help solve some of his friend's murders that he gave Dean free rein to do whatever he needed to. He never had such easy ingress to files, computers, and suspects. Shelby's grief was almost his undoing. By the time Rupert woke from his medically induced coma, Shelby had already shared the secret stock.

Two months later, Rupert refused to stand on the sidelines and had exterior cameras mounted at the cottage, in the garage, and in the room by a company outside of Red Peaks. They were so high-tech even his coworkers didn't discover them when they attempted to reclaim Justin's ill-gotten gains.

Now, they had to face the fact Justin kidnapped Shelby, and she wouldn't be alive for very long. Racing against a countdown, only Justin controlled when the clock ran out. Agent Andy Winters pushed to have Shelby labeled as hostile because of her private dinners with Justin Dean documented in his surveillance videos. The only positive to come of her abduction would be proving she was not complicit in his crimes.

She was a loose end. Justin's mask may have disguised his identity, making it impossible for a jury to place him at the scene. Yet if Dean swooped in and saved Shelby, her testimony would garner a guilty verdict, capping off the end of a very wearisome case.

Justin was obligated to get rid of her as soon as possible. They had finally pulled a print from the last serving dishes he brought in to sell before he wiped them down and removed the previous owner's, proving he forged the ownership. Along with Shelby's testimony, it made a slam-dunk case.

His name wasn't Justin; at least it wasn't the name on his birth certificate. They were hunting one of the more prolific serial killers of their time. He was the highest ranked of their most wanted, with well over seventy kills across the continental United States. With numerous name and location changes, he was one of the most complicated people Dean had ever had to track. Justin was known to be able to change his appearance as he did to fool facial rec scanners, a slight change in the shape of his cheeks to a dimple in his chin no longer being there.

Jake Travers was Justin's real name. He started several states away and ended up in Red Peaks after the local police department turned up the heat. He was almost captured in the act of getting rid of one of his victims, staging them in barns. Winter temps distracted them from the timeline of the attack. The story was the same in every place he targeted: He sought out the elderly. His knowledge of antiques, relics, collectibles, heirlooms, whatever someone wanted to label them, opened the door for him.

"We need to find out where he took her!" Dean couldn't believe this happened. Everything was falling apart at crunch time.

Rupert had one request: to stay on and keep an eye on his niece. First, Dean detained her, and his partner interrogated her, thinking she was involved somehow. They had held her in a cell for four days. Now, she'd been kidnapped by the real killer, and Dean had no clue where to look.

He needed to save her and then walk away if he could force himself to. His attraction for her had only grown over the last few months since she took over Rupert's business. Watching her with Justin flirting the way he did made him want to do bodily harm. He couldn't do or say anything to break his cover. He couldn't approach her and say, "You know, the other guy working with us is a murderer, and Justin isn't his real name. I thought it would be bad form not to give you a heads-up. You might want to tone down the friendship and not hang out so much."

He intended to be under the radar, assuring all shipments went out. The legitimate commissions were conducted professionally, with the customers promptly receiving their goods. An entire warehouse was stored full of antiques to be reunited with their rightful owners—the ones stolen after he extinguished their lives before their time for those treasures.

The finale included Dean walking away. He had the job; she had her life. And those two didn't mix. He would ignore his fascination with her and let her move on from this to find someone to fill her life with. That is, if they could find her before Justin, Jake, whoever he was, killed her.

"We've got something; aerial footage shows his car parked at one of his victim's barns. They are twenty minutes away. Local SWAT is mobilizing. They will meet us there." Andy slung his tac vest over his head, tightening the Velcro strips on the side.

Dean's phone pinged with a message from Rupert. He turned the screen for Andy to see. "Same location. It's hot. Let's roll."

Dean's energy amped up. A nervous force flowed through him. He slid across the hood of the government-issued sedan with Andy behind the wheel since he knew which direction to head. Several of his team followed in identical vehicles. At least he wasn't going in alone; he had his entire team at his back. Eight more agents, all equally trained like him. The only thing fighting against them to keep them from winning was time. And no one could turn that back except God himself. He trusted the men with him; they had joined forces years ago, taking down the lowest of the low. He fiercely prayed she wouldn't become a casualty in this war.

Justin had Shelby for far too long. What had he done in those precious hours he had unfettered contact with her? She was no match for the size difference. She was tiny, and he cringed at what she was going through. Rupert's message only gave a location, no additional details. If his niece was in trouble, Dean had no doubt the cantankerous man wouldn't hesitate to jump in and get himself killed, for a second time, in the process.

How was Shelby going to take seeing her uncle again? They had presented their findings to her parents, asking them to play along. Since they weren't in the country, it had been easy to have them read the prearranged script over the phone. They'd demanded weekly check-ups threatening to bust their case wide open if they didn't get them.

Andy took the next corner practically on two wheels before killing his lights and cutting off the road into a patch of trees. He shut off the engine before turning to Dean. "You grab Miss Samuel; we'll take out Justin. But your goal is Shelby."

Dean appreciated what Andy was doing. She had a magnetism that drew her to him as if she were his true north. They talked late into the night when they had their meetings about pulling him from the op. Replacing him with another agent would take too long to vet and, in addition, would appear suspicious.

How would she react to his subterfuge? What would she say about her uncle helping him establish his cover? Families of the victims conveyed their suspicions to the agency before the deaths became a blip on the FBI's radar. Family heirlooms were stolen from elderly members, only to be sold on a site advertising those same cherished items.

Andy clasped him on the shoulder before hauling himself out of the driver's seat. "God's in charge. He's got this."

Dean appreciated his friend's words.

County SWAT rounded the street coming from the opposite direction. Ten officers in full riot gear unloaded from the back of their BearCat, one of the necessities for having your own designated tactical unit.

County advised Dean and Andy that they only functioned as the entry team and support, but the case was theirs. The FBI was to take the credit and file the charges. Dean didn't want to talk; he only wanted to breach the building and get Shelby. Dean couldn't think straight, and he hated that. This was why he needed to leave as soon as they got in there to rescue her.

She muddied his thinking, and he couldn't keep his head on straight when she was around. She had his attention from technically the second time meeting her. Yet if he was honest with himself, she burrowed herself into his every waking thought before moving to town with her uncle's stories about the woman she grew into from the scrawny kid with scraped knees running around his store during her summer visits.

He shook his head, cleared his mind, and returned to the present and the entry team gathering at the tree line, ready to charge across the overgrown grass to the barn where they'd heard a female's voice cry out seconds before. His heart hammered, knowing she was at least still alive.

The wailing of the wind blowing past the collapsing side of the weather-worn structure muffled their heel-to-toe steps as they trudged their way across the thigh-high dormant grass, bending in the breeze. The entry team threw a flash-bang through each door at the front and back of the building before charging in. Justin skirted through the back, and several agents took off after him. Dean couldn't think about them. He followed his team in and stopped at the sight of two officers cutting the rope from Shelby's throat and laying her flat on the floor to perform compressions. At the same time, another had two fingers on the pulse point in her neck.

His knees hit the ground beside her, replacing the officer's fingers on her delicate but bruised skin, tilting her chin up to open her airway. No, they weren't going to lose her. She'd screamed minutes before they breached. There was no way they weren't going to rescue her. She had her whole life ahead of her. This beautiful woman who stole his heart. This woman whom Dean fell for though he tried to keep a lid on his attraction.

"Where's the ambulance?" Dean refused to give up.

Agent Winters stood with his phone to his ear. "One's already been ordered and is on the way; only three minutes out."

Two officers helped Rupert to his feet. Blood dripped from his head.

"Rupert, you good?" Dean raised an eyebrow at the Louisville slugger next to him.

"Nothing that won't heal on its own." Rupert rubbed the back of his head. "He was choking the life out of her. I couldn't remain quiet and stay out of sight, so they wouldn't know I was alive. I had to save her. She's my world."

"I would have done the same." Dean didn't blame the guy when he failed to keep her unharmed.

"Be careful of her ribs," Rupert advised.

Dean and Shelby had never had a date, yet he loved her with a furious vengeance. If she didn't make it...he couldn't even go there. The officers' counts on every downward compression kept in beat with the famous song "Staying Alive."

"Wait...wait." He repositioned his fingers, sure he felt something.

"No pulse, keep going." He prayed God wouldn't take her.

There again, he felt a faint thrum under his fingers. "Stop," he whispered.

Father, don't take her, he fervently prayed.

He tilted his head to the right as if listening for life's rhythmic beat. Yes. "She has a pulse."

The smallest hiss of air passed through her lips as their medic checked her airway. Dean didn't acknowledge the tear slipping down his cheek until it dripped from his jaw onto the hard-packed dirt floor where he knelt.

An ambulance backed up, and paramedics jumped out, grabbing their bags before unloading the gurney.

Dean moved down as the medic kneeled on the other side. "She was strangled but has a strong pulse."

Paramedics flipped open their bags and tilted Shelby's head back, monitoring her breathing. "Throat's swollen. We need to establish an airway to make sure it doesn't swell shut again."

The second medic squeezed and shook an ice pack before placing it on her neck.

Andy whistled for him before motioning with his head.

Looking around, he frowned. "Where's Justin?"

"He got away." Andy didn't look him in the eye.

"He what!?" Dean's voice rose two octaves.

"I know. He had another vehicle waiting over the edge of the cliff on the other side. He had a rope tied off and scaled the side before we could apprehend him. He pulled the rope up with him as he ascended. We never scanned for more than one vehicle when we found his from the drone footage; we concentrated on guarding this site. Good news is, Rupert did some damage. He had a very pronounced limp."

"She's a target. He'll try to finish her off." Dean kicked at the dirt.

"Yes, he will. And with no knowledge of where he may head, she and her uncle are in danger. He won't walk away from paying them back per the profiler. He's not someone who likes to be made a fool of." Andy updated their superior before he turned his back and walked away.

Dean gritted his teeth, aware of the damage to his molars from the pressure he applied. Shelby would only be safe once Justin was dealt with. He wouldn't let her out of his sight until that happened, whether she liked it or not. This was one fight this stubborn female would definitely lose. He would suggest putting her in protective custody with him as her roommate before letting her walk away.

Andy cocked his head to the side, and he took it for what it was worth and hopped into the back of the ambulance and rode to the hospital forty minutes away. The wail of the sirens reminded him how close he came to losing the one woman who managed to capture his heart.

Shelby's hand was cold. He rubbed it between his, hoping the friction would warm her up. The paramedic added a second blanket. Her hand twitched. Her long eyelashes fanned across her cheek and fluttered.

The rig slowed down as they approached the ambulance bay. Doctors and nurses rushed past the automatic doors, waiting for them to unload.

Shelby didn't respond to the jostling as they transferred her to the hospital's gurney and hurried inside for the doctors to perform their life-saving efforts.

Rupert held an ice pack to the back of his head and followed at a slower pace. Dean would need to insist he was attended to, or he would wait for word on his niece before his treatment.

Dean rested his hand on his weapon. He stood between Justin and Shelby. He would die before he let Justin get his hands on her again.

His saving grace was God helping to keep him on task to take a prolific killer off the streets.

Forty

Shelby's throat was sore. She didn't remember ever feeling this bad. She wanted to chug down a cup of water even though it would be unladylike.

She tried to open her eyes, but the bright light made her wince. Her chest ached so badly; something else was wrong. She noticed the beeping, and it all came back to her.

Justin was a killer! She jolted upright and yelped at the sharp pains coursing through her.

"Easy, Shel, your ribs are broken." Dean leaned over from her right and twined his fingers through hers as a nurse entered from her left.

"Good to see you awake, Miss Samuel. Agent Wolfe has guarded you the entire time and never went home." The nurse's perky voice grated on Shelby's nerves.

Dean sighed and hung his head.

"Agent?" Justin was a killer, and the nurse confirmed Dean was the agent the FBI informed her was working at Rupert's Relics. She tried to free her fingers, but he held her hand hostage.

"I wanted to tell you when you woke up." Dean scowled at the nurse, who made a hasty retreat. He stood and turned his back to her, staring out the window.

"You lied to me?" Shelby pulled the blanket up higher.

Why did it hurt worse that Dean lied as opposed to Justin?

"I never technically lied because you never outright asked if I worked for the FBI. My superiors denied my request to let me and my team bring you into the loop. It was out of my hands; I couldn't go against a direct order," Dean explained. "They would have pulled me and put someone else in my place. I didn't trust anyone else with your life."

"Between you and Justin, you put my store in jeopardy, and now I have no employees." Shelby scrunched her eyes shut. Could the day get any worse?

"We didn't have enough on Justin to bring him in. He would skip town if he thought we were onto him, changing his name and disappearing to start over somewhere else, putting us that much farther from getting the evidence we needed to arrest him. Rupert kept meticulous records, and with you scanning them all to an online account, I perused them one night and found vital data. But it was too late, and he already took you. When I saw him drop you into the trunk on the cameras Rupert installed, my heart almost stopped." Dean gripped her hand, and she was surprised by how much it shook.

"Why weren't you following him?"

"We were, but he slipped by my fellow agents several times. We don't know how he did it. They would track him, keeping their distance only to have him disappear into thin air as they rounded a corner. We have never been so frustrated. We are an elite group, but we aren't perfect. He's been doing this for a long time so he's honed his skills."

She thought agents had it all together, intensely trained to deal with dramatic and scary situations without batting an eye. They ran into the fray ready to jump between danger and citizens. "Oh my gosh! Uncle Rupert is alive! Did my uncle know about you?"

"I'm sorry, your parents and uncle, along with the FBI, believed you were safer if you didn't know we staged his death. And yes, when we came to him with the allegations by family members of the victims, he jumped at the chance of bringing down a killer. Rupert promised he would help us get what we needed. Then Justin got suspicious, we had to fake his funeral, and you moved to town. I hoped you'd keep me on to protect my cover."

"But Uncle Rupert wrote a letter." Tears trekked down her cheeks.

"Yes, he did." Dean slid his chair closer.

A sharp pain tore through her, winding her.

"Lay back; ribs hurt like crazy until they fully heal. I've been there and done that; I didn't get the shirt, though. You have a long road ahead of you. When the officers did compressions, they broke a couple more, so it will be several weeks before you won't have a twinge when you inhale." Dean asked for permission to lower the bed.

Suddenly tired, Shelby's head drooped forward. Both Dean and Justin had lied. They kept so much from her. Her parents had lied. Uncle Rupert had lied. Granted, she knew a cold-blooded killer wouldn't come out and ask, "Can I stay on? I have a ton of people I can kill for their antiques," but her family's lies cut through her.

"What happens now?" Did Justin know she made it?

"You disappear until we hunt him down. We were getting ready to move in the next day or two but waited for the judge's orders and warrants to come through when he took you, giving us more charges." He paced back and forth at the end of her bed. "He finally made his first mistake and left a smudged fingerprint belonging to one of his victims, which is what the judge needed to sign the appropriate paperwork. But that was before his second mistake."

"What was that?"

"He took you and you lived."

"Won't he run away since he knows you're after him?"

"No, our profiler believes he considers you unfinished business. He won't stop. It's how his mind works. He manipulated at least six different aliases over the last decade. He even gets plastic surgery to change his features enough so facial recognition software can't pick him out of a crowd. Shelby, I'll keep you safe and sound. I promise." His eyes were full of emotions she had never seen in him before. Vulnerability.

"You told the FBI about the pieces in the hidden room, didn't you? After you told me not to tell them, you ran and told them anyway." She wasn't sure what the problem was with her telling them or him, but she was upset he didn't have enough conviction in her to confide in her.

She didn't care if he said his boss told him he couldn't, but they read in her uncle; why couldn't they treat her the same?

"I want to be alone." Shelby turned her head.

"Your uncle wants to see you." Dean touched her leg through the blanket.

"I can't. I missed him so much, but everyone lied to me. You had me locked in a cement room!"

"We needed you out of the way while we cleared out the evidence in your house. I couldn't tell you I was undercover, and if we'd shown up with a search warrant, it could have given me away. You could have tipped our hand letting it slip to Justin I worked with the feds. When I got there, the room was empty, so we took everything from the basement since that was covered under the search parameters." Dean squeezed just a fraction so she felt the shift of his grip through the blankets.

"Please leave." Shelby choked out a sob when she heard the door close.

An undercover agent was one thing because they must obey orders, but her family? Would she have to move again? Did it mean she was homeless and jobless? Would her uncle be mad she tossed or donated all of his belongings? He didn't even own a pair of socks anymore. Blackness pulled her under as a nurse fiddled with her IV, sending pain meds to do their job.

Forty-One

Shelby moaned as she rolled wrong and twinged her ribs. She was nervous about seeing her uncle today. She slept all night between the raging pain in her head and ribs combined with the delightfully helpful pain meds administered through an IV pump.

A soft knock tapped on the door.

"Come in." Shelby cleared her throat and repeated it when her voice cracked and cut out the first time.

Uncle Rupert walked in. He sported a bandage on his left temple and had a black eye. His usual cardigan sweater over a button-up shirt warmed her soul. She never saw him in anything else. She joked he had an obsession with sweaters and shirts like women do with shoes.

She couldn't stop the grief. "You made me think..."

"Oh, my sweet little Shelby. I am so sorry. It was a way to draw Justin out. I wanted to tell you, but I was unconscious for the first two months you were here. By then the FBI *leaked* my death in a ruse to keep the store open until they gathered enough proof of his guilt." He sat on the bed next to her hip and patted her hand.

"What's buried in your casket?" Shelby clasped her hand over his, sandwiching them between hers.

"Didn't think about it. Dean contacted my sister and brother-in-law when Justin shot me," Shelby gasped. "And they made the decision to keep you out of the loop. They threatened to sue and expose their sector if you were hurt. It would be the last act of the FBI. When Dean told me, I almost choked on my drink. They weren't prepared for your dad's protectiveness. They asked if I wanted him arrested for my attempted murder."

"Why didn't you?" Anger simmered under the surface of her emotions.

Rupert sighed. "Because the families who lost loved ones deserved closure. I did it for them. Me, I lived. I get to enjoy the rest of my life, but to never know where the man who snuffed out their family's lives was, I couldn't live with that weighing me down. I agreed to play dead to keep the case open and fight for those whose voices vanished, unable to tell their stories. Attempted murder doesn't carry as long of a sentence in this state."

"But he could have been stopped." Shelby grabbed her uncle's hand.

"And with a good lawyer only served a couple of years. We wanted to stop him for good. Let the families of his victims get their day in court and put him away for life or even a conviction with the death penalty. If I had gone ahead with the charges for his crime against me, it would have let him out to do this all over again. Could you look at me the same if I let a serial killer free to torment and stalk victims who can't fight back?" Rupert squeezed her hand before pacing from the bed to glance out the window.

"I suppose you have a point." Shelby winced as her head started pounding again.

"This way, he didn't leave, so the agents assigned to the case could take him down before too many people got ensnared in his web. Your reactions to the investigation had to be real." Rupert's shoes squeaked against the linoleum floor with every step.

Shelby couldn't help but laugh. "Didn't work out too well for me. I still became his target when I discovered your hoard of all things stolen by a serial killer."

"I never will forgive myself." His drawn features told her how much he suffered for not being able to be there for her.

"I gave up my studio. I moved across the country. And now I have no home, no job." Shelby let the tears fall. "I guess I'll move. I'm sure my old job will take me back. I heard they haven't filled my position yet."

"You aren't going anywhere." Dean's voice jolted her.

"I can't stay here." Shelby couldn't complain; she had her uncle back. How many people got a second chance?

"Justin will come after you." Dean pulled up a chair on the other side of the bed.

Shelby jerked. "You mean he's still out there? What about Uncle Rupert?"

"You are both going into protective custody." Dean gazed at the doorway.

As if on cue, three agents entered and stood to guard her room.

"No, I don't think so. I'm leaving. Justin won't know where to find me. Then, when Uncle Rupert is ready for me to take over, I'll move back to Red Peaks." Shelby scooted up so she sat higher.

Dean shook his head. "Rupert, you need to talk sense into your girl."

"No can do. She has been independent since she was a toddler, running around Rupert's Relics in the summers."

Rupert held up his finger when Dean went to interrupt. "But I'll go with you if she does."

Shelby's mouth hung open. "Wait, you mean to tell me you think a serial killer with how many agents, police, and the like are after him would stick around to take out me and my uncle?"

"That is the likely scenario. We have a place we will take you, and you will have a guard every hour of the day."

"And the store stays closed? No. What about above the store? We can stay there. Can't you guys do your hero ninja stuff and secure it so we can work during the day and stay there at night? That way we can keep the store open. We are together in an easily defendable place and not lose our minds," Shelby suggested.

One of the agents by the door smirked but nodded.

"Might work. Let me get a team to sweep the building and egress points to decide if it is doable. I'll be back."

Dean put his hand on her shoulder, sending goosebumps down her arms. "I'm glad you're okay."

She had never heard him talk so much. He was in his element, confident and in charge, a true alpha who was secure in himself and who he was. Seeing this side of him finally showed her his true self. And if she was honest, she had already forgiven him for lying to her and stashing her uncle.

"You like him." Uncle Rupert's eyes glittered with mischief.

"Oh no, don't even." Shelby laughed, then groaned and held her ribs. "I don't even know his real name. It's probably something ridiculous like Clarence Leroy Bartholomew Stackhouse the Fourth or something equally horrendous."

Shelby started to nod off as her uncle patted her leg.

Voices yelling woke her. A glance around the room told her Uncle Rupert wasn't there.

"I don't care. I need to see her!" Who was so angry?

"We have not been informed of a different doctor assigned to this case. I'm sorry, but if you have your chief of staff call us, then we can settle this. However, until Agent Winters gives us the go-ahead, our orders are not to allow anyone in."

Shelby tucked the nurse's call button under the edge of her leg.

Where were Dean and her uncle? She sucked in air, realizing she wanted Dean to be there. She felt safe with him. Even when he was angry in the alley or bossy trying to control her safety. One thing she knew for sure: he would protect her.

A popping sound echoed, followed by a thud and a yell. Another pop silenced the hallway. The door to Shelby's room rocked violently against the hinge that autoclosed to stop it from slamming into the wall behind it. Justin dragged in two men in suits who safeguarded her door and dumped them at the bottom of her bed. She pressed the nurse button several times before Justin walked over and yanked it away.

"So much less dramatic than I wanted my entrance to be." Justin clapped his hands together. "Hello, sweetheart, did you miss me?" Justin yanked down the blankets. "Let's get you up, my dear."

The cool air made her skin pebble. She opened her mouth to scream when a barrel was pressed to her temple. She winced as the hot metal burned her.

"Ah ah ah. Don't get the pretty nurse who is on duty for your room tonight killed. Wouldn't you feel so guilty?" Justin read her easily. "Thought so."

He tugged her from the bed, ripping out her IV port, sending blood splattering onto the cold, dingy tiles. He opened the door a crack and then dodged through, towing Shelby behind him, unaware of her inability to keep up. Her ribs ached; she couldn't take a deep breath.

Where would she end up?

Where were Dean and her uncle?

Did he kill the men he shot? Would doctors find them in time if not?

"Where are you taking me?"

"Somewhere, no one will ever find us. I've made a decision. You will make a worthy wife. Together, we will be unstoppable. I've tried to kill you twice and haven't been successful. A divine intervention; you are meant to be mine." Justin squeezed her hand.

"I'll never be yours." Shelby stopped walking and yanked.

"Oh, my dearest, you are wrong. I'll enjoy breaking you and then rebuilding you into the best subservient wife. I can start right now if you don't come quietly. I'll shoot every person between us and the car until you behave yourself." She could tell Justin meant every word.

She shivered as a nurse passed them and smiled.

"Good girl. See, this is going to be so much fun. I have a nest egg to support us until you can help me rebuild what I had to walk away from when your uncle stole from me. If I didn't have to repossess them, so to speak, then I would have already delivered them to their rightful owners, only those who can pay an exorbitant amount for the bragging rights of those overpriced antiques on the black market. Instead, they are sitting in a facility I can't access. I guess you'd say you're going to pay off his debts. Sins of the father or uncle, as they say." Justin pulled her to him, tucking her into his side.

She was as good as dead if she couldn't make someone aware of her predicament.

"Don't think about it. I can see your mind working out a solution. You're wrong. You can't get away. I will only kill whomever you try to have help you." Justin exaggeratedly smacked his lips against her temple.

The humid night air made the thin hospital gown stick to her skin. Thank goodness she wore scrub pants beneath it.

"Do you smell that?"

When she didn't answer, he pinched her arm. "Ow."

"Next time you answer when I ask you a question."

"Smell what?" Shelby gritted her teeth.

"Freedom." Justin cackled as if he were telling a joke.

Her heart plummeted. There was no one to rescue her this time. No uncle back from the dead or federal agent hiding in the wings, ready to intercede, wearing a cape to save the day. She couldn't count on anyone but herself. As he tossed her into the cab of a truck from the passenger side, he nudged her over to slide behind the wheel. He climbed in after her, never letting the gun waver from her head.

Shelby glanced over her shoulder to see Dean dart out of the back door as she reversed out of the parking spot.

"I will pull the trigger." Justin had the gun aimed through the open window behind her.

She slammed down on the gas and peeled out of the lot. Dean ran after her with his phone up to his ear. At least he knew what vehicle to look for. She made sure her antics were detected.

"You brat." Justin punched her in the side.

She wheezed as she squeezed her eyes shut. Justin steered until she lifted her head.

"Don't draw attention to us. Now, I have to dump this truck sooner than I wanted. No biggie; it's stolen anyway." Justin scanned the road, looking for witnesses to their erratic driving who would call the police.

Forty-Two

Dean jammed his phone into his pocket. Andy had taken the car to pick up food, so he couldn't follow Shelby. He had two dead agents and a BOLO out for the truck, and he wasn't confident it wouldn't be found abandoned down the road.

"He took her, didn't he?" Rupert stood outside Shelby's room.

"I'm sorry, Rupert. I didn't think he would come here in the middle of the day to a hospital crawling with law enforcement and abduct her. It's my fault." Dean scratched his head, his throat closing as he swallowed.

"Good thing I'm one ahead of you." Rupert smiled and held up a tracker.

"You didn't." Dean pulled up the app on his phone.

They secured several trackers on the furniture they sold, unsure if the pieces would lead to another dead body. Rupert must have swiped some.

"The nurse who gave her scrub pants was kind enough to let me sew one into the hem of one of the legs."

Dean accessed the tracker's ID and watched a dot move. "You gave us the best hope of saving your niece's life."

He ran through the corridors and to the entry as Andy Winters pulled up.

Dean didn't give him time to slam the Explorer into park before he jumped in the passenger seat. "Go, go, go."

"What's going on?" Agent Winters threw it in gear and jumped a curb headed for the exit.

"Rupert tagged his niece. We have a route." Dean tapped his phone and told Winters to turn right.

"Crazy old coot. If only all our points of contact were as sly as he is."

Dean flattened his fingers, gestured to the windshield to stay straight, and held his left hand out for Winters' phone. He unlocked it for Dean, who then called the rest of their team and advised them of the situation. Soon, they dispatched a second and third team.

"Hold on, Shelby. I'm coming for you." Dean took in Andy. "We need to activate our Specter protocol."

Winters tilted his head but didn't disagree.

Would he have to fight for the upgraded level to take Justin out permanently? It wasn't a decision they made lightly on their team, but sometimes it had to be done. For the safety of the world, some of those they hunted couldn't be allowed the risk of a mistrial and be released.

The Specter initiative was created for those who prey on innocent lives with no remorse for their actions. They were incapable of rehabilitation, which proved everyone was at risk of falling prey to these monsters.

"Are you sure it's the only outcome?" Winters took the next corner wide since no cars dominated the oncoming lanes.

Dean braced his hand against the dashboard. "You know the toll it takes when one of us makes that decision. The target is unredeemable."

"Do it." Winters punched the sync on the steering wheel. "Call Lincoln."

It rang three times. Dean held his breath, ready for it to go to voicemail.

"Lincoln."

"Agent Winters here, requesting the Specter protocol be initiated."

"No other option?"

"Agent Wolfe here, no sir, I requested the upgrade. He took another hostage and killed two of our best agents. He needs to be stopped permanently." Dean's voice was steady. It would be another life that ended on his command, and he didn't take it lightly.

"Advanced protocol approved, code alpha priority. Document everything we need to cover ourselves with this." Lincoln disconnected before either acknowledged the action.

"Okay, let's go find your girl." Andy smirked.

"Deal." Dean wouldn't deny what his heart and mind already told him. She was it for him. He struggled the last few months working side by side and not being able to tell her his identity.

The tracker stopped. "Up ahead, there's a pull-off on the right. It doesn't look like it goes anywhere."

"Tell me when we are close and where to turn." Winters gunned the engine.

Less than two miles later, he saw the spray of gravel from a car taking the turn faster than it should. "Up there."

"I see it." Winters took the curve.

Dean almost kissed the dashboard with how fast Andy slammed on the brakes. The truck he saw them leave in sat at an odd angle beside a small white sedan. Both doors to the truck stood open. Dean didn't have a good feeling about this.

"Shelby, if you stop now, there won't be a punishment!" Justin's voice yelled through the thicket.

Winters was already on the phone, calling in their GPS coordinates, while Dean checked his phone. The app pinged Shelby about a mile into the woods. Dean stuffed the phone deep into his front pocket to avoid it falling out and grabbed extra clips from the back of their vehicle.

Andy held up his fist for him to bump. "Specter is the only way to go. You're right, and I back you one hundred percent. Don't let this decision weigh you down. Come on."

This was one of the many reasons he valued the classified group he belonged to. No one let you flounder; someone always had your back.

A shot rang out.

They both sprinted for the trees to escape into the darkness, eclipsing the horizon as dusk settled in before they prowled forward, hunting their prey.

A lumbering shadow emerged as the barrel of a gun glinted in the moonlight.

"Freeze, Justin. It's over." Dean and Andy targeted their suspect.

He curled his lip and started to raise his weapon.

"Justin, don't do it. You won't win this," Andy yelled next to him.

Justin's shoulders slumped in defeat.

Dean let out a breath.

The next second Justin raised his gun and Dean and Andy pulled the trigger simultaneously. Justin's gun went off as he fell back.

Andy shook his head. "You hit?"

"No, you?" Dean holstered his weapon.

"I'm good. Go get your girl." Andy waved as backing officers and agents pulled in.

Dean took off at a jog.

Forty-Three

Fifteen minutes before.

Shelby skirted around a large fallen log, not stopping to hide behind it, which would be a mistake. It would be the first place Justin looked.

She got the idea to run when she pulled into the cutout and spotted the white sedan. No one knew about the car switch. Once Justin had her away from everyone she relied on, her life would be over. She jammed on the brakes, stunning Justin long enough for her to hop out and put some distance between them. The truck rolled forward, almost clipping her in the hip before Justin could chase after her. With no possible victims of his violent nature in the vicinity, she chose the trees as her shelter.

"Shelby, do I have to punish you?"

Oh no, not going to happen. She wasn't a child. If he thought punching her in her broken ribs was a little tap, what would he believe a punishment was equal to? Cutting off her fingers?

She tripped over her feet as the incline increased. She was too small to keep the distance between them for long. His strides ate up the gap. She had to find a hiding place he wouldn't think of. A prickly bush tugged at the thin fabric, not shielding her from the thorns tearing at her skin. She held her side with one arm wrapped around, holding her ribs.

She backed up and felt the needles of a pine at her back. With the branches starting at ankle height, she took a guess he wouldn't think of finding her in a tree. She wiggled through until she was at the trunk. Justin tore past, yelling her name.

When she no longer heard him, she shimmied up the first several feet until she felt the trunk swaying in the stiff winds. She controlled her breathing with each inhale that twinged her ribs. She wasn't a fan of heights. Snapping twigs to her left made her stop.

"Shelby, stop playing games. You don't want to see what I do when I'm pushed." Air sawed in and out of his lungs.

She wanted to laugh at how out of breath he was.

"Shelby!" He raised the barrel and discharged a round.

She held as still as possible, hugging the trunk. Her ears ringing, she took in his retreating form. Her mind shattered from fear, and she had to bite her lip to stop the insane laugh bubbling up when she asked herself if this made her a tree hugger. She was shocked at her erratic thoughts.

"If you disclose your location right now, I'll go easy on you, but if you don't, you will see what I'm capable of." Justin wasn't revealing anything new.

She already saw what he was capable of. He tried to kill her twice.

He started cursing about waiting for dawn and then he would find her, as he stomped to the vehicles.

Shelby shimmied a few more feet until she felt too shaky to climb higher. She sat on a limb, her back against the scratchy trunk. Brightness disappeared on the horizon, and she shivered. Hopefully, the sun setting wouldn't make the temperatures dip too low.

She heard yelling in the distance, which meant they were no longer alone. Shelby clung to the branch as she crept to the side and almost fell. She tried to lift her leg, but her arms gave under the weight, and she dangled, digging her fingers into the rough branch. Giving herself a second to collect her nerves, she tried again to swing her leg up but only managed to ease over a bit; she still couldn't even reach the trunk.

Maybe if she shifted down since she couldn't go up? Her feet searched the air for the next branch below her. There was nothing directly under her, but she did spy a branch behind her that she might reach if she stretched far enough. It would have her body in a precarious position to hang on with her hands, so she would have to let go and hope she didn't plummet to the ground.

Shelby swung her legs back as shots pierced nature's sounds, startling her enough to lose her grip. She screamed as she fell several feet, but a branch hooked her in the middle of her belly, folding her in half and letting her hang, held up by her midsection. Pain lanced through her core muscles, sending ripples along her sides and ribcage, knocking the wind from her.

Someone hollered her name.

She ignored them until she embraced the limb and was able to swing a leg over, so she straddled it and shifted to the trunk.

"Shelby!"

"Dean!" She didn't know the miracle that led him to find her, but she thanked God for sending her help.

"Shelby, my app shows you are around here somewhere. Call out so I can get to you." Dean's head popped up at the bottom limbs of her pine.

"Look up." Her smile was huge.

"What on earth? Do you need help?" He put his phone away.

"Maybe?" Now that it was over, she couldn't stop the trembling.

Dean slapped the boughs out of his way and climbed up so his legs braced on the two lower branches below her. "Ready to go home?"

"Yes." Shelby almost sobbed.

"Come on, Shel. I'll get you down. I won't let go." Dean turned her to face the trunk and guided her with each step.

They were on the ground faster than she thought it would take them.

Shelby squealed when he swept her into his arms and trudged through the brush.

As they cleared the tree line, red and blue orbs flickered on the tops of several vehicles, and a yellow tarp covered a body.

"Is he...?" Shelby buried her head into Dean's neck.

"Don't look. He will never bother you again."

The stress of being retaken overwhelmed her, and her sobs muffled against the man's skin who had saved her in more ways than one over the last several months.

***

Winters joined Dean as he sat in the back of their car. Shelby clung to him as if she would never let him go. He was okay with that.

"You good?"

Dean looked up at his best friend. "Yeah."

"We're losing you, aren't we?" Winters crossed his arms.

"I won't go under again. I belong here. If Lincoln can work something out so I can be tactical assist, then we can talk. Otherwise, yes, you lost me. She's more important."

"Thought so, I already talked to him. He wasn't happy to lose his best operative, but he understood when I explained the outcome." Winters nodded to Shelby, who had quieted in his arms.

"We'll set you up with everything you need to begin operational oversight while agents are in the field. You won't be boots on the ground on those ops, but the go-to for resources." Winters clapped him on the shoulder. "Happy for you, man. Does she know?"

"Not yet." Dean couldn't keep the smile from his face.

"How do you think she's going to take it?"

"Take what?" Dean didn't know what he was referring to.

Winters laughed. "That you kept a pretty big lie from her. And don't spout nonsense. Lying by omission is still a lie."

"Right now, I'm more worried a serial killer had her in his sights and the trauma she will have to face to heal not only physically but also mentally. I'll tackle the rest now that I know she's secure." Dean rubbed his knuckles against his sternum.

Shelby's breaths evened out, and her arms fell limp at her sides. He pulled her to him and held her tight as Winters left the scene to the sheriff and drove back to the hospital.

Rupert lingered as Dean strolled through when his movements initiated the sensors at the entrance, allowing him to proceed unimpeded.

"How bad is she?" Rupert brushed the hair away from her face when Dean arranged her on a gurney.

"She climbed a pine to get away from him. We reached her before he did any more damage." Dean summoned the nurse who was on duty to let her know they returned.

"I'll grab the doctor for you if you want to take her to room 10, next to where she was before. The deputies cordoned it off as a crime scene." The nurse pointed to where she wanted Dean to go.

He scooped Shelby into his arms, and she moaned. "Shh, I've got you."

"Dean?"

He put her head on the pillow and positioned a basin to clean her feet. "I'm right here, Shel. It's over; rest while I take care of your feet."

She murmured something unintelligible, and Dean only chuckled as Rupert opened the door for the doctor.

Dean learned Shelby was a tad ticklish when he ran the cleansing cloth over her arches and she tried to pull out of his grasp.

"She seems fine, exhausted, but no further injuries besides small scrapes. She'll be checked in until I can see how much further damage she might have done to her ribs. Other than that, you have permission to stay in the room with her."

The doctor made a few notes on a tablet and then nodded to him before he quietly left.

"You can go home. I'll stay." Rupert pulled up a chair so it touched the side of the bed.

"Not leaving my girl, Rupert." Dean bit the inside of his cheek.

Rupert smirked. "That's how it is?"

"Yes, if she'll have me." Dean tucked the blanket around her.

"Good to know. Are we going to see you Sunday at church service?"

"Yes. It will be nice to be there in person and not have to watch the video on the internet." Dean wanted to be there but had to operate in the shadows, one of the downfalls of his job.

Now, he didn't have to worry about missing sermons about his love for his Savior. He would be there every Sunday until the Lord took him home.

"People will be talking," Rupert kicked back, resting his feet on the side table.

"No more than what they will be saying about you. It's not every day someone comes back from the grave." Dean chuckled when Rupert's smirk disappeared. "They'll probably want to have a parade."

"I hadn't thought of that."

Forty-Four

The window was on the wrong side of her bed. Shelby was ready to leave the hospital. The doctor hinted he wanted her to stay another night, but she threatened to sign herself out if he didn't get her discharge papers to her today.

Rupert came in with a large cup of coffee, and she almost clapped when he held it out for her.

"Uncle, you are the best!" She sipped the hot drink carefully, trying not to gulp down the delicious nectar.

Rupert nervously bounced his leg. "Listen, Shelby, I'm sorry you had to go through the grief of losing me. I never imagined a scenario where you lost me."

"What did happen, if you can tell me?" Shelby wondered if she would finally get the whole truth.

"Dean came to me about a year and a half ago. They were working an angle about antique thefts in the surrounding counties. He wanted to use Rupert's Relics as a base to build a background of him working in the field of antiques in hopes of luring out the killer. They had a line on him but nothing else. A man filled out an application months before, and I had told him I would be in touch. I provided Dean with the resume, and it piqued his interest. Their background check showed mismatched information on the resume. They had me hire him as an acquisitions clerk, hoping he would slip up and give himself away. I called Justin the next day and told him he was exactly who I was looking for.

"Over the next few months, he would bring in purchases, and I recognized several pieces. We stored them in the back of the warehouse but were unsure if he took them from people whom he murdered because he forged the owner's provenances. He had highly respectable fake paperwork even I couldn't spot as counterfeits.

"God put it in my heart to disguise a door to a room no one knew existed. Dean and Justin were out on a delivery when the clock showed up on a shipment from an auction. I took it upon myself to hide them in the cottage since I didn't want Justin to overhear me talking to Dean since he was with him. When the truck dropped off the pieces, I returned to the store to close up for the day. Justin ranted and raved in the warehouse, asking where his stock was. I told him it sold and the truck left several hours earlier. I didn't know Justin watched me fill out the fake purchase order.

"He demanded them back and said he had clients expecting to take delivery. He pulled a gun and shot me. He didn't wait around and tore out of the parking lot, thinking he left me for dead. Dean lived down the street. I called him before passing out. He saved my life. I didn't know they came up with a plan to play up my death when the doctors put me in a medically induced coma because of the damage to my aorta. They said I shouldn't have survived otherwise. Another couple of minutes, and I wouldn't have.

"I woke two months later and you already occupied my job and told Dean about what you found. I told him to bring you to me, but he said you believing I was still dead was for your safety. I went along because he promised to keep an eye on you. Sweet little Shelby, my heart hurts with the knowledge my actions made you think you lost me. Your parents were freaked, to say the least, and they didn't want you anywhere near the store, but Agent Winters convinced them they would always have a man on you."

"The letter?" Shelby picked at a cuticle, making it bleed.

"Dean and I came up with that one night when we initially discussed the possibility of me being caught in the crosshairs of a madman at the beginning of the case. The very real truth was that he could have killed all of us. I couldn't in good conscious miss the chance to say goodbye."

"The black truck?"

"Dean never let you out of his sight when you ate with Justin. Dean's truck matched half the population's choice of vehicle so he could blend in and not stick out by having an easily identifiable truck," Rupert told Shelby.

"What about the person walking around the cottage?" Shelby was glad an agent was close by. The fact it was Dean who warmed her soul.

"Guilty as charged. I needed a place to bunk while I healed and rejected hunkering down in some hotel room. Plus, you outcook me any day of the week."

Shelby smacked his hands. "I thought I had some weird creeper eating my food!"

"I only ate a few meals and only when you weren't there." Rupert winked at her.

"I'm glad you're still here." Shelby swiped at her face, collecting the moisture that leaked from her eyes.

"I think we need to talk about where to go from here." Rupert sat forward after sleeping in the chair last night.

"No biggie. I'll move back when you are ready to turn the store over to me." Shelby felt awful because she got rid of all of his stuff. "You don't have any clothes left. Anything sentimental I couldn't part with is stored in the third stall in the garage."

He stopped her with a hand on her arm. "That's not what I meant. I want you to stay, and both of us run the store together."

"Really?" It was more than she ever fathomed.

Rupert nodded. "Yes, my dream was to share the store with you."

"Well, we'll have to empty out the apartment again so I can get out of your hair at the cottage. I'll rent a unit and stow what won't fit upstairs in there; you can get your house back." Shelby would be cramped, but it would be better than moving three states away.

She'd fallen in love with running Rupert's Relics. She couldn't imagine struggling through any other job until Uncle Rupert handed her the reins for good.

"I was thinking, I want to travel. Dean hijacked my clothes you asked him to donate, so I'm not starting out from scratch. It only makes sense for me to move, and you keep the cottage. It's all going to be yours one day anyway. I kind of like how you decorated it. You always had an eye for the details."

Shelby was already shaking her head. "That isn't right."

"If you move out, then it will make me have to move a bunch of heavy furniture again, and the house is too big for one person. It is perfect for a family, though. Have little kids running around for Uncle Rupert to come visit." He lifted his chin to the door.

Dean stood with his fists in the pockets of his jeans, head up ready to face whatever Shelby hit him with. She had never seen this side of him. The confident agent and take-charge attitude was a good look on him. It let her finally see who he truly was as a man comfortable in his own skin.

"Family?" Shelby leaned toward Rupert. "He doesn't even like me."

"I wouldn't say that." Dean's voice on the other side of the bed had her jumping.

"But the case is solved. You will move on to your next assignment." Shelby popped her knuckles, picturing Dean helping another woman who needed a hero. She gulped, not liking the jealousy that burned under her skin.

Dean stopped her with his strong, warm hand over hers. "I think we need to talk."

"Good, it's settled then. You stay in the—what did you call it once—monstrosity? I'm comfortable being above the store, and it's a lot less for me to keep up with and clean." Rupert cackled as he left the room.

"I don't know what to do with him." Shelby fiddled with the edge of the blanket.

"Shel."

She didn't raise her head.

A finger hooked under her chin had her meeting his brilliant blue eyes. This man could be lethal in so many different ways.

"I can never apologize enough for lying to you. I was afraid if I'd told you, you would give away the investigation."

"I would never." Shelby forced his hand away.

"Not intentionally. You wear your heart on your sleeve, sweetheart. It's not a bad thing, but Justin started worming his way into your life because of it. He is a master manipulator. I was afraid he would earn your confidence, and you would unknowingly let something leak we couldn't allow him to know." Dean pursed his lips.

He had a point. Shelby never played poker with her college friends. They said she had the worst tells whenever she had a good or bad hand. "I understand. My conscience is my worst enemy."

Dean threw his head back, and she couldn't breathe. He was breathtaking when he smiled, but when he laughed, he knocked her for a loop.

"You look good when you laugh." Shelby bit the inside of her cheek.

"Well, you're beautiful no matter what you do. Shelby, I have to tell you, I fell for you when you visited last summer for a few days. Then, your uncle's stories only cemented my fondness for you. But when you took over, and I saw how generous your heart was, you became my reason for living. I want to see if there is anything between us because I believe in giving us a chance to let something amazing develop." Dean blushed.

"I thought you couldn't stand me." Shelby suffered from whiplash from his back-and-forth interactions. They should definitely give him a raise or promotion with how well he did his job.

"I have been told I make a halfway decent covert operative. This was the hardest op I've ever conducted.

Keeping my feelings under wraps, not touching you, it about broke me." Dean wrapped his large fingers around her wrist.

"What now?" Shelby twisted her wrist around to link her hand with his.

"One day at a time."

"No, I mean, do you still work for me? Are you still an agent? Where will you live?" There was so much more she didn't get to ask about before he cut her off.

"Yes, yes, and here." He kissed the back of her hand.

"Uh, I have more questions."

His dimples surfaced again. "I will never go under again. My occupation is a newly created position, sort of an overwatch. I'll be technical support for the guys who are out there risking their lives. I have a house I rent I'll live in for the time being. And if you'll have me, I can still manage the docks.

"Shelby, I don't think you understand. I offered to walk away from my job for you. They are adding a position because I'm one of the best profilers and instinctive agents they have. I can read a room better than anyone else on my team, so they don't want to lose me. I think I'll be better at overseeing cases instead of down in the muck. Besides, I want to be here with you. If you can find it in you to forgive my deception, I'd like to see where we can go." Dean's gaze bore into her as if he glimpsed her soul.

"I'm scared."

"Of me? Oh honey, I'd never deliberately hurt you." Dean ran his thumb over the back of her hand.

"Not you, well, maybe, sort of. I don't think I could survive if you walked away after I opened myself up to you."

Shelby's head was a swirl of emotions. "I've only glimpsed the regular side of you a few times. Mr. Secret Agent, who has nothing invested."

It felt fast, but seeing this side of Dean produced emotions she never felt in all the times she and Justin ate together. Butterflies swarmed around in her, violently wreaking havoc on her nerves.

"All I ask is for a chance. I plan on staying in Red Peaks. Take you out, show you I have a soul who cares deeply for you. Attend church with you." Dean's thumb moved faster as he waited for her answer.

"Okay." Shelby nodded.

"If at any time you are done, I'll leave. Quietly, no regrets for the time I was blessed to spend with you."

"I can't believe I was dumb enough not to see Justin for who he was. Uncle Rupert said he shot him. How did he look me in the eye every day? Who does something like that?" Her emotions got the better of her.

"Shel, I got to him in time. The decision to keep the op going came from my superiors. We gave your parents a stipend to stay so they weren't underfoot. It kept them out of the spotlight."

"Can you tell me about the case and everything you found since Justin is—"

Dean nodded. "What did you want to know?"

"The stuff Rupert stashed, will it be returned to the families?"

"We don't have it. Do you know where it is?" Dean hopped off the bed.

"Justin mentioned a location he couldn't get to to fill orders where clients expected to take delivery. Individuals will pay high dollar for black market antiques. I think he has a whole network and clientele list. They put in an order and he targeted people posting on social media." Shelby wanted families to have closure and their heirlooms returned.

"Did he say where it was?" He dialed his phone before she answered.

She shook her head.

"Andy, he stashed them in storage." Dean walked the length of the room. "If we can find the location, it will give us a lead into how he operated, and there may be more proof to give the case a final resolution with no loose ends."

The doctor came in with Uncle Rupert and went over her orders after she left their care, and she signed where she needed to.

Dean bent over the bed and kissed her forehead. "Sweetheart, you helped us out tremendously. I have to go but I'll check in later. Will you be at the cabin?"

"Yes. I'm planning on a big feast. Come on by after you wrap this up and bring your friends." Uncle Rupert's cooking was always a good thing.

It would be good to sit down with everyone on Dean's team and clear the air, including the arctic realm they held her in.

Forty-Five

Uncle Rupert's whistling made Shelby want to cry. He was here with her, and nothing made her happier. She spoke with her parents earlier, and they apologized profusely and all three cried on the phone.

She understood after they told her about Agent Winters and Dean's call asking for their assistance. To be honest, she wasn't sure she wouldn't have done the same thing if the roles were reversed.

The scents coming from the kitchen made her mouth water. Rupert made his famous stuffed peppers and had three trays cooling on racks as he pulled a cheesy corn dish from the oven. The sauce bubbled against the glass sides as he pulled foil from the top, releasing wisps of steam.

Dean called, saying they were on their way and hoped they had plenty of food. Agents Winters, Irving, Jackson, and three others would be attending. Shelby was nervous to see Dean again.

Her heart tugged at her to give him a shot. He saved her uncle's life; there were no words to express her gratitude. Uncle Rupert did nothing but sing his praises as he prepared the feast. He refused to let Shelby help, so she was positioned on a dining room chair with her feet propped on another one. She zoned out, mesmerized by the twinkling lights on the Christmas tree she decorated by herself one night when she was feeling melancholy.

She was shocked when she'd walked in, spotting a large dining set she recognized from her parent's house. They already had it shipped before she was discharged. It was their housewarming gift to her, telling her it would cost too much to ship it to Egypt.

Sauteed green beans simmered in the corner crock pot with bacon bits, garlic, and almond slivers. The doorbell croaked its pathetic greeting.

Shelby held up her hand. "Uncle, you cooked. I am well enough to answer the bell."

His laughter rumbled from deep within him.

Dean's wet hair clung to his scalp as if he had taken a shower not long ago.

"Are you supposed to be walking around?" Dean stepped around her when she let him and his colleagues in.

"Not you too. I'm fine. My legs work like always." Shelby showed the men where to hang their coats.

"We found it all." Dean beamed.

She couldn't stop her huge smile. "I'm so glad."

"We have you to thank for finally closing this out. The families will pick up the pieces at the end of the week, and we'll ship the rest to those who don't have the means to collect them themselves." She had never seen Dean so antsy.

"What else did you find? I have never known you to not be stoic and composed." Shelby sat in the chair she vacated earlier.

"Dinner is served!" Rupert arranged the scalding hot platters on trivets in the middle of the table. Steam rolled off the food, sending the delicious aromas through the air.

Dean scooted her chair in when she turned to face the table. Rupert bowed his head to say grace and to thank their Heavenly Father for the men who put their lives on the line in the job they did, for the killer being stopped, and for Red Peaks being a safe place once again. Everyone said amen and then dished out large helpings on their plates.

Agent Winters nodded to the three men across from him. "Shelby, I know you were introduced to Jackson, myself, and Irving, but the other three men who are a part of our team are Steve Blackmore, Daniel Glass, and Mark Sanders."

"Nice to meet you, gentlemen." Shelby gave a small wave, then flattened her hand across her stomach to keep the nausea down. It was weird inviting these men into her home after her stay at the concrete cell hotel.

"When does Mr. Stein get out of the hospital?" Agent Winters asked Rupert.

Shelby gasped. "He didn't..."

Dean enclosed his arms around her. "Oh, sweetheart, we hadn't told you yet; he made it. You interrupting Justin saved his life."

Large tears blurred her vision. "I can't believe it."

Conversation saturated the room. There was laughter and jokes as they told Shelby some of the funnier, non-confidential cases. These men appeared so normal, but they had one of the most dangerous jobs out there. Everyday heroes lounged in her house, partaking in dinner with her and her uncle.

She caught Dean's eye, and he winked at her. She felt herself blush, and he smiled.

"What were you going to tell me earlier?"

Dean looked at Shelby and then at Agent Winters, who nodded. "Justin kept trophies of his kills; if we'd realized earlier that he rented the container, we'd have taken him down months ago. You would have never had to go through the grief you did."

She placed her hand on his. "It isn't your fault."

"If only."

"No. You can't go there with the what-ifs. It will only make you second-guess yourself. You can't let it get to you." Shelby knew Dean didn't believe her. "Was it registered under his name?"

"No."

"Under another name, one he may have let slip?" Shelby heard the agents talking about Justin having aliases while protecting her in the hospital.

"No."

"Then how were you supposed to know? It's not like there are actual crystal balls you can use. What happened, happened. You can't beat yourself up. Do you blame any of the other men sitting here?" Shelby saw his eyes light up.

Agent Jackson chuckled. "She's got you there."

"Yeah, yeah." Dean hooked his arm around her neck and kissed her cheek.

Agent Winters pushed his plate away. "Justin kept a ledger of antiques sold on the black market. We plan to take some downtime until we catch our next case, so we can retrieve them and return them to their rightful owners."

Headlights flooded the room as someone drove up so close she thought they'd crash through the front window.

Dean and his team jumped up and pulled firearms she didn't know they had with them. The door slammed open, and Justin stood silhouetted against the night, holding an assault rifle. His black-ringed eyes, were a sharp contrast against his skin, and his nose was crooked. He didn't look like that when he took her from the hospital. He favored one leg, hopping to steady his stance.

"Honey, I'm home. And you killed my brother!"

Shelby screamed as Dean threw himself over her, and shots filled the air. Her ribs yelled at her as he pressed her lower against the hardwoods. His arms propped next to her head as he braced himself above her. He grunted seconds before silence deafened the room, his body a dead weight.

The coppery scent of blood floated in the air, along with gunpowder. Shelby shook and couldn't budge Dean's weight to roll him off her. Warm liquid dripped onto her back. "Dean?"

"Get me an ambulance now!" Agent Winters yelled.

Shelby almost sprung up once someone rolled Dean off her. Another agent was gasping for breath while Glass pressed napkins against his wound. She couldn't tell who else was injured. Dean blinked, and Agent Irving pressed a stack of napkins into his own shoulder to staunch the bleeding as he leaned against a wall.

Jackson pulled her away as Winters started working on Dean. He tilted his head back to open his airways and pressed his fingers to his neck. Shelby tried to lunge at Dean, but Jackson held tight. "Let him do his job."

Shelby sobbed, praying God didn't take him away before she ever got better acquainted with him.

Agent Blackmore booted the gun away from Justin and shook his head; he had no pulse. He marched outside, gun drawn.

"Does nobody stay dead in this town?" Shelby choked out.

"I don't know what's going on, but if he's Justin, then who did we kill in the backwoods when he took you the second time." Jackson relaxed.

It clicked for Shelby. "He told me he had a brother, but I didn't know he was a twin. Uncle Rupert hit him in the face, so this is Justin, but whoever picked me up in the hospital didn't have any bruising or a broken nose."

"Our background never exposed any living relatives. We believe he killed his parents at a young age and then jumped around the foster program before an aunt took him in."

Uncle Rupert joined her when the paramedics took over life-saving measures for the injured agents.

Agent Blackmore came back in on the phone as deputies flooded the scene. The firearms were rendered harmless, with their clips removed, then collected and bagged for evidence. Yellow numbered markers, steepled on the floor, denoted every bullet strike and spent shell casing.

With a dreaded sense of déjà vu, she saw a plastic sheet draped over a body.

Agent Jackson never left her side as she gave her statement and drove her to the hospital. Uncle Rupert stayed behind to coordinate between the different agencies who combed the area.

"I'm sure he's going to pull through and be up and around in no time flat." Jackson smiled but his eyes didn't crinkle like they did all night while they reminisced about old ops.

Shelby stuttered in a breath as they pulled up to the entrance. He let her out while he parked the car. With so many agents injured, law enforcement from all over flooded the hospital to show their support. Agent Irving's arm was in a sling as he sauntered over and guided her into a chair away from the action.

"Have you heard anything?" She looked but didn't see Winters.

"There's no information yet on their conditions. Sanders was shot square in the chest. Dean took one off to the side, but it didn't go all the way through. They think it was a ricochet." Agent Irving shook hands with Jackson when he jogged through the swishing automatic doors.

Low conversations as people passed lulled her to doze with her head on Irving's good shoulder.

"Family for Dean Wolfe?" A strong voice snapped her awake.

"He's my partner." Agent Winters assisted Shelby in standing with him.

"He is stable and made it through surgery like a champ. The biggest threat was it nicked the left pulmonary vein. The bullet actually saved his life when it lodged in the vessel, plugging the hole, and didn't continue further, so there was very little blood loss. The shock to the body caused a vasovagal syncope. It drops the body's heart rate and blood pressure. In layman's terms, he fainted from his body's reaction to the pain he experienced. You can see him once we have him settled in the suite he will be occupying with your other agent, who I heard made it through surgery." The doctor turned on his heel and was off to his next patient.

"He had a basil bagel? What?" Agent Irving's comments elicited a roar of relieved laughter to sweep through the emergency department, relieving the tension that everyone survived tonight's attack.

The nervousness physically left her body as she sank into the chair behind her.

Forty-Six

Dean listened to the voices in his room. As he woke, he recognized several, but not the one he wanted to hear. The pain lancing through his back and into his chest was like nothing he'd experienced before.

"If I'm supposed to be resting, why are there so many knuckleheads in my room bothering me?" Dean smiled when everyone shut up.

"Brother, don't ever scare me like that again." Andy clapped him on the shoulder.

"Sanders? I heard a doctor talking." Dean knew several of them had been hit. His only concern at the time was to shield Shelby. She had been through enough.

Dean sat up and glanced around. "Justin was alive?"

"Excuse me." There was the voice he wanted to hear.

Shelby sat in the chair by the side of his bed, toting a cup full of ice chips. She made sure he had a good grip and held up a spoon.

"Perfect." The first couple of chunks acted like a balm. "Thanks, sweetheart."

The medical equipment was the only sound he heard as he nodded off. He woke with a jolt. Shelby's hand covered his, and her head rested on the side of the mattress.

"She refuses to leave," Winters informed him.

Dean selfishly didn't want her to. "Sanders?"

"Is your roommate." Winters pointed to the other bed.

Dean nodded, glad they hadn't lost anyone else. "How was Justin alive?"

Shelby twitched, and he ran his hand over her head until she settled back down. "He had a twin." She raised her head and smiled.

Dean looked at Andy. "How did we miss that?"

"The aunt hid him when their parents died. No one thought to match birth records. Justin or Jake never divulged it to any of the social workers assigned to him. So when his aunt got custody of Jake, he was reunited with his twin Jack. To divert suspicion away from Jake, Jack would kill one of the victims when Jake was in a prominently populated club or restaurant, giving him an alibi. Then they would move on." Irving shifted in his chair, rearranging the sling for his arm.

"The background should have pointed to a sibling." Dean couldn't believe what he was hearing.

"Never registered with the Department of Motor Vehicles or License Bureau. We think they used the same identification. In every state they hunted in, two months after updating to their current license, Justin would request a duplicate card, saying his wallet was stolen. No one questioned it since it's such a common occurrence."

"In all my years, I've never seen such a clever ruse." Dean squeezed Shelby's arm.

"I'm glad it's finally over." Shelby darted a look at Winters. "Please tell me he doesn't have a triplet out there somewhere."

Dean groaned after his laughter died down. "Don't jinx us."

Sanders's laughter turned into a coughing fit.

"Good to see you awake." Dean was relieved he didn't lose any more friends.

Irving bumped his feet on the floor. "I'm going to go home and sleep for a week."

Dean gave him a chin lift. "Shel, go home."

"I'm not leaving...I can't."

"What do you mean?" Was there another threat?

"I thought I lost the opportunity to see where things between us can go. I was so scared. I refused to admit the way you wormed your way into my days. I have never felt fear on that level when you collapsed and I could feel blood running over me." Shelby sniffled.

"Sweetheart, look, I'm all good. Couldn't get rid of me even if you wanted. You heard what the doctor said. I'll be released with limited restrictions. I'll be fully healed in a month. So I get a nice little vacation to sit back, kick my feet up, be lazy, and be pampered. You get to serve me ice chips." Dean cupped her cheek, trying to lighten the mood.

"I want what you said." Shelby gulped down a sob.

"To be pampered and lazy. Oh, hon, that's my plan."

Shelby snorted. "No, to see where this goes between us. I want to give us a shot. You put my life ahead of yours. Literally took a bullet for me. Don't ever do that again. I don't think I'm ready to lose you when I just found you."

Dean sighed. "It's who I am. It's an instinct to protect someone I'm falling for. You've only known me for a few months, but I've known you for over a year working on this assignment. From the five minutes Rupert introduced you on your last visit, you made an impact. I know so much about you from Rupert, it's as if I've known you for years. I can't imagine a day without you in it. If that makes me some creepy sicko, so be it, but I won't deny myself or you what God has planned. No matter how I tried to rationalize the need to keep my distance, God always threw a wrench in my way, guiding me back to you. So no more tears unless they are happy ones. This is happening."

Epilogue

"Uncle Rupert, we're going to be late." Shelby stepped up on the shelf by the door and rang the bell back and forth, making it clang annoyingly.

"Young lady, knock that off right now." He stood at the bottom of the stairs, rolling his luggage behind him.

"And what are you going to do about it besides missing your plane? Mom will kick my butt if you don't make your flight. It's been a year since they moved to Egypt. It's about time you went and visited her." Shelby was so happy everything had settled into a droll, boring life. If she never went through the drama surrounding her when she first moved to Red Peaks again, it would be all too soon.

Dean held the hatch open for Uncle Rupert's suitcase. He put his hand on the small of her back as she opened the passenger door. His lips grazed her cheek before he jogged around to the driver's side.

They made it to the drop-off point and saw Uncle Rupert off on his first vacation in decades. Shelby wrung her hands together. Uncle Rupert had told her she didn't have to accompany him to the airport, but she'd refused to take no for an answer.

"Sweetheart, he will be fine." Dean pried her fingers apart before she twisted her skin from her bones.

"I know. It's odd none of my family are in the same country. Is that weird?" Shelby curved her hands into his chest as if trying to pull him to her.

"No, babe, it's not at all. Come on before we get stuck in traffic on the way home."

The scenery passed in a blur as they chatted about options for the store before her uncle returned. Dean was true to his word and spoiled her on every occasion he got. The town was in awe of Uncle Rupert rising from the dead and the covert agents roaming through their quaint suburb.

Dean still rented the house on the opposite side of Red Peaks from Shelby's cottage. Uncle Rupert outdid himself expanding the apartment so it included the space over the warehouse. It was over fifteen hundred square feet. He still tended toward the overly ornate antiques but kept it to a minimum.

Dean pulled off into Rupert's Relics' parking lot and turned off the engine.

"What are we doing here? We won't reopen until Monday." Shelby didn't get an answer because he jumped out and rounded the hood to open her door.

"Dean?"

Still nothing.

He unlocked the front and turned off the alarm. Shelby gasped as she took in all the candles lit on every shelf in the showroom.

She circled. When she got back around to Dean, he was on one knee holding an open ring box with a quite large, round, cushion-cut diamond.

"Shel, before I knew what happened, you stole my heart. You are the reason I breathe; without you, I would be lost. God put you in my life when I never planned on having a wife. Now, I can't imagine life without you. Before you, I was a shell of the person I am today. You are everything I ever imagined I wanted in a woman. You walked through the door and blew away all of my preconceived ideas. You are so much more than I ever dreamed of asking for. I love you. So I'm asking you to make the rest of my life better with you in it and accept my proposal. Please, Shelby, my heart and soul, will you marry me and agree to be my wife?" Dean's eyes shimmered.

"Yes." Shelby jumped as several people materialized from the back, cheering.

Dean chuckled as he slid the ring on and pulled her in for a quick hug and kiss.

"My baby girl is getting married!" Shelby's mom and dad stepped out of the office.

Shelby squealed and threw herself into her parents' arms. Uncle Rupert wiped at his eyes.

"I thought you were on your way to visit them!"

"Dean wanted to propose with us here. You were so stubborn about seeing him off at the airport. We scrambled to grab him as you drove off and raced back here to set everything up." Her mom beamed.

"Dean, it's nice to finally meet you in person." Shelby's dad gave him a firm handshake and then pulled him in for a manly hug and hard clap on the back.

Dean had been out of the state wrapping up all the reports and submitting all their discoveries from Justin's reign of terror, so this was the first time he met her parents.

"Nice to meet you both."

"Welcome to the family." His mom gave him a hearty hug.

Shelby wrapped her arms around Dean's waist, finally finding her place to create a family.

Dean kissed her. "I love you."

"Love you too."

Don't miss out!

Visit the website below and you can sign up to receive emails whenever K. A. Moore publishes a new book. There's no charge and no obligation.

https://books2read.com/r/B-A-MAMI-YJIDF

About the Author

K.A. Moore, born and raised in Kansas, is a retired 911 police dispatcher with over thirteen years of service and will be the first to tell you dispatchers are a special breed all their own. Her real passion is writing and putting her imagination into works of fiction. Faith-based Christian suspense is her preferred writing theme, with wild, crazy dreams as the backdrop to many scenes that seem to come alive in her writing. As she writes, her Chihuahua scampers for the coveted position of curling up in her lap while creating her stories.

www.ingramcontent.com/pod-product-compliance
Lightning Source LLC
LaVergne TN
LVHW050918080826
845145LV00001B/124